DANCERS

OF THE

DAWN

ROCK THE BOAT

ZULEKHÁ A. AFZAL

A Rock the Boat Book

First published in the United Kingdom, United States of America,
Republic of Ireland and Australia by Rock the Boat,
an imprint of Oneworld Publications, 2024

ISBN 978-0-86154-507-0 (hardback)
ISBN 978-0-86154-829-3 (trade paperback)
eISBN 978-0-86154-508-7

Typeset by Geethik Technologies
Printed and bound in Great Britain by Clays Ltd, Elcograf S.p.A.

Oneworld Publications
10 Bloomsbury Street
London WC1B 3SR
England

Stay up to date with the latest books,
special offers, and exclusive content from
Rock the Boat with our newsletter

Sign up on our website
rocktheboatbooks.com

MIX
Paper | Supporting
responsible forestry
FSC® C018072

For my family, thank you for encouraging me to dream.

I hereby swear to uphold the light in service to our queen and will honour Amaar as a protector of our land, only unleashing my magic in the face of the enemy and in the name of peace and unity. With every sunrise, until my final day, I pledge my life as a warrior and a dancer of the dawn.

Dancers of the Dawn Oath

ONE

S he glares at us. Always watching. Never blinking. Never wavering.

The red sun.

Citrus skies bloom overhead, but the moon lingers, not yet ready to fade like the stars that succumb to the dawn. I feel the sun's pull as her light dances over the cinnamon-coloured sand and the village we seek comes into view behind the low dunes.

People already dot the village. Some emerge from their homes to collect the day's water from the river that meanders out of sight from the Hamaaj mountains that rise up in the distance, while others begin making breakfast from what they can and milking the cows gathered beneath the dying trees. We haven't seen rainfall in the desert for so long, we've lost count of the days. But at least the river still flows, a constant just like the sun's heat.

Some stop what they're doing as they see us approach: a band of twelve, seven on foot and five on horseback. Kaleb, the leader at the Leharanji where we train, swerves his horse to the right. He's clean-shaven and wears just the right amount of oud, the scent of rose and musk lingering around him. His grey hair is slicked back, while his white kurta is stark against his black mare and marks him out from the four guards who surround us – still astride their horses – in Amaar's armour of white, gold and emerald. The guards follow Kaleb's lead, breaking away to let us dancers and musicians through while they wait at the edge of the village, just inside the boundary wall. The bells round our ankles sing with each step and I see the recognition on the faces of the villagers toiling at the fringes.

A man calls out and immediately some of them disperse back into the confines of their homes. But, before the signal can spread throughout the village, Kaleb nods and soft notes swirl round us as Saara plays her wooden flute. Nadia joins in after a few bars with a low thrum on her dhol, but it's not until Amina hums that the power of the trio takes hold.

Entranced by the music, the villagers spill out of the shadows until every adult and child watches us in a daze. But there's only one person we're here to perform for; we just need to find them. The musicians hang back as Sahi leads us dancers through the crowd and our performance begins.

The four of us dance the choreography we've rehearsed over and over with Mistress Zaina back at the Leharanji, leaning away from each other with gentle hand movements before twirling in a pattern that resembles a flower opening, its petals peeling apart one by one. I sweep my arms above my head like the wings of a bird and the air around me shifts as the others do the same. When we come together again, we face each other with one leg extended behind, our mehndi-adorned hands almost touching. Slowly, we rise, then swiftly fall out of the position and turn in time with the flute.

As the music caresses the air at our backs and it builds, so does our dance. With every spin, our ivory skirts glimmer as the glass beading that decorates them reflects the morning sun. Some of the villagers shield their eyes from the glittering light and we almost lose them from the musicians' enchantment, but Meera is quick to react as we move into the most technical phase of the choreography.

A nightshade, her hands shimmer and tendrils of dark blue dust pour from the star symbols that decorate her palms, weaving round our audience. One by one, they fall into a slumber, rooted to the spot as they surrender themselves to the nightmares Meera spins for them. She stops dancing, black hair bobbing at her shoulders as concentration commands her whole body. Her magic flows from her hands, her eyes like pools of midnight rather than their usual honey-brown. There must be at least thirty people here, more than she has ever had to hold within her terrifying dreamscape at one time.

Sahi's magic follows. Her hands glow from the crescent-moon symbols on her palms and threads of iridescent white dust intertwine with Meera's dark blue strands. I see the tension in Meera's fingers as they pluck at the nightmares she's created, while Sahi walks between the villagers, searching their minds for the person we're here for.

I glance back at where Kaleb watches intently with the guards. He catches my eye, the gold ring on his little finger glinting as he gives his signal to Dana and me. We continue to dance through the village towards Sahi, who pauses when she reaches a small outbuilding draped in the smell of liquor that's smuggled from overseas. Sahi's long plait swishes at her back as she turns to the rest of us, her amber eyes glossed a milky white, and gestures to Meera to release her magic from the man frozen in the doorway. Meera does so slowly, one hand calling back her nightmare to reawaken him, the other still holding the rest of the villagers in her terrible dreams.

The man blinks, bemused, as the trance he was under slips away. 'Who are you?' he says groggily.

'I think you already know,' Sahi replies. 'In fact, I know you do.'

He looks unsure, but sweat beads along his balding head and drips down his cheeks into his greying moustache. Realisation dawns. He turns on his heel, but Dana has already broken from our duet and her hands shimmer with a green dust. The sand beneath her feet gathers round her and comes to life in small whirring balls, which mould into the shape of snakes and slither towards the man. He falls forward as Dana's sand serpents grasp his ankles and drag him into the village square, beneath the gaze of the rising sun.

'Get them off me!' he screams as the serpents writhe over his body and pin him to the ground. 'Help!'

But no one does. Not the villagers, still under Meera's influence. Not the musicians, whose song beats to a familiar rhythm. No one.

'Why don't you stop them?' the man shouts at Kaleb as he emerges from between the buildings along with two of his guards, while the other two watch over the horses on the outskirts of the village. Sajid, the Leharanji's head guard and Kaleb's shadow, draws his sword, but Kaleb holds up his hand. They're not here to intervene. They're here to witness the finale of our performance.

'Whatever you think I've done, it's not true,' the man pleads as Sahi kneels beside him, her magic still playing round her hands and within her eyes.

'We will soon find out,' she says. 'Stand up.'

Dana manifests more sand snakes that wind round his squirming body and pull him to his feet. It's only then I stop dancing. I have to hear what he has to say.

'I've done nothing wrong. You must believe me!'

He says it over and over until his voice is swallowed by Sahi's magic. Two white orbs melt together as they leave her hands and blossom over his head like a cloud that's burst, casting him in a pearly glow. He's hers now.

'What is your name?' she asks, calm and measured.

He struggles to keep back the truth, but she's already in his mind, already sees everything he wants to hide. 'Hassan,' he says eventually, voice distant as though it doesn't belong to him.

'How long have you been a citizen of Amaar?'

'All my life. I was born here.'

'And you have been treated well by your country.' She can't bring herself to pose it as a question.

'Of course,' he admits.

'And yet you betray us.'

His eyes shift while his body is held firm by the snakes wrapped round him.

'How long have you been working with our enemies in Mezeer?' Sahi asks.

Heat prickles at my back as we wait for him to reply.

'I…' But he can only hesitate for so long before Sahi's magic reveals his truth. He strains as it's drawn out against his will. 'Three years.'

'Traitor,' the younger guard spits and she's met by a jagged glare from Sajid. But Sajid thinks the same. We all do.

Energy pulses beneath my skin as my body anticipates what will come next.

'Three years,' Sahi repeats. 'And for what purpose?'

The words come easily now as the glow of Sahi's magic wrenches at him further. 'To acquire information about how Queen Sana wields her magic in Amaar. And takes what rightfully belongs to Mezeer.'

Kaleb steps forward then, curiosity in his frown. He's always been close to Queen Sana, once a lieutenant general in our army and a trusted adviser of her mother, the late queen.

'What sort of information?' Sahi says, voice taut.

'Ever since she came to power, Mezeer's rivers have dried up while Amaar's still flow. The people there are dying, unable to grow crops or find water to drink unless they risk their lives and trek to the Imdaal river that our army holds. And it's all of Queen Sana's doing.' Hassan's voice is urgent. 'She has cut off Mezeer's water supplies with her ability as a water-weaver, and even lets her own people suffer a drought she could remedy with her magic if she truly cared for her country.'

'Old lies,' Sajid mutters under his breath and Kaleb shakes his head.

They are old lies, but as I look around at the villagers who are still within Meera's grip, their features gaunt and their crops drenched with only sunlight, I can't help but wonder why Queen Sana doesn't end the drought.

'King Faisal will stand for it no longer,' Hassan says. 'War will be brought to Amaar.'

The musicians stop suddenly, their final notes mingling awkwardly with his words.

'Queen Sana has no heir. Amaar and Mezeer were once one country and will be again under King Faisal's rule. Mezeeri power will rise.' A smile spreads across Hassan's face, belief in his every word.

'Is that so?' Kaleb replies.

Sajid laughs in disbelief. 'Mezeer has brought war to our land before. They've never won.'

He would know. As would I.

Kaleb walks up to Hassan. Sahi keeps him within her charm, as does Dana, whose snakes continue to wind round his body.

'Mezeer's king can spread his lies about our queen to turn his people against us. He can start another war like he's done in the past, but Amaar will survive as she always has.' Kaleb nods to Sahi and her glow dissipates round the prisoner. 'You may take that final thought to your resting place,' he whispers just loudly enough for those closest to hear. He gestures at me to come forward.

The stage is mine.

Hassan snaps out of Sahi's hold and fights against the sand serpents.

'You can't do this,' he whimpers, the sweat on his face turning to tears. 'Help me!'

But the only people who can are still held within Meera's trance, swaying on their feet like river weed in a current.

'Please,' Hassan begs.

You've revealed too much, I want to tell him, but the words don't reach my lips. Hassan may be from Amaar, but he's an enemy, in service to the king who will bring another war to our country. Like the war when I was a child. The war that took my mother.

'Aasira...' says Kaleb.

I step in time to Nadia's drumbeats, twirling once then twice. Fire surges through me, a tingle that starts deep within and branches through my body as my magic takes hold. I look to the peach-painted sky as I spin in front of Hassan, his shouts bouncing off me as balls of shimmering gold dust form in my hands.

'Caliaan hereesi.' For honour and the dawn. My words are a whisper beneath Hassan's cries.

I release my magic, and golden sparks burst across Hassan's chest, piercing his skin like tiny blades before erupting into flames. Dana's snakes disappear into the sand and Hassan slumps forward. He rolls desperately in the desert he's tainted with his deceit, but my flames only burn brighter. They lick his body until he has no screams left.

I catch Kaleb's nod as my fire begins to fade, satisfaction in his eyes. 'You dancers did well today,' he says, gazing at the four of us.

Dancer...you should call me by my true name.

I'm an executioner.

TWO

'Release them.'

Meera does as Kaleb orders and whispers under her breath as her fingers strum the air. Slowly, the nightmares she wove for the villagers unravel from their minds and they wake, catching themselves unawares. Dazed. But fear reawakens among them when they see Kaleb standing over what remains of Hassan's body, my flames now a memory as smoke curls in their wake. Sajid and the guards – Haniya, Ejaz and Camil – are quick to show themselves as Kaleb calls for silence.

'You are all spared interrogation,' Kaleb announces, but it does little to quell their panic, which rises with the sun. 'She has already seen your truth…' He gestures towards Sahi. 'Your innocence has saved you where this man's disloyalty sealed his fate.'

The villagers stare at the charred body at his feet, a reminder of the destiny of those who dare to betray our queen and country. I glimpse a child outside the home closest to the outbuilding, arms hooked round his mother's legs, tears bubbling and lip trembling. He has the same furrowed brow as the man I just killed. I swallow back the lump in my throat, the boy's stare too intense for me to bear any longer.

'We will know if treachery takes hold of this village again,' Kaleb says and looks towards the woman and child. The woman's face is hard, whether to hold back her grief or disgust at her husband's lies, I can't be sure. 'But no further blood will be shed today in the name of Queen Sana.'

Kaleb nods to us and we get back into formation, Sahi and I paired at the front, then Dana and Meera followed by the musicians. The guards mount their horses and encircle us.

'Go about your day,' Kaleb tells the villagers as he mounts his own horse. 'May peace rise with every dawn.'

'And endure with every dusk,' they reply in unison, voices hushed.

We're silent as Kaleb leads us out of the village and across the dunes, interrupted only by the soft tap of the chooriyan at our wrists and the bells that jangle on our paayal with each step. The heat beats at our backs, the sun unrelenting as she continues to rise. Hot sweat sticks my loose hair to my neck so I wrap my dupatta over my head to stay a little cooler.

Thankfully, we don't have far to travel back to the Leharanji, or the sanctuary as Kaleb has fondly named it: a reminder of the school's once peaceful history. Some say it's as old as the desert itself, built in the days when Amaar and Mezeer were one country: Larijaah. The Leharanji was an oasis deep in the desert, a place of study and understanding between cultures and beliefs, a space to learn of our land and those beyond our borders. But for the last century borders are all we have and we're lucky the sanctuary falls on our side of the Imdaal river. Though the scripts that filled its library are now long gone – burned or moved to the palace – it's still a place of education, just of a different kind.

The sanctuary comes into view, rippling in the heat: a collage of white marble minarets interlaced with gold. Our home. One of Amaar's schools for the army, it's now the sole place that trains those with magical abilities, among them dancers of the dawn like me. So few of us are left – the number of people with magic having dwindled to the point where only some girls are born with such powers – that no other schools like this are needed. The rest are now home to those without magic who are trained to join Amaar's army, and who we'll one day fight alongside.

I glance behind me. The village is now out of sight, but the image of Hassan is lodged in my mind along with the others who've come before him: traitors I've executed over the last year. All were believers of the lies. My mother's lies. The lies that she spun to protect herself and that fuelled the war even more.

I breathe deeply to cool the heat that smoulders inside me and, as I do, I see Hassan's son, eyes wide and staring not at the body but at me, the one who stole his father's final breath.

Despite the heat, I shudder as I recall Hassan's words. We've all been affected by the war in some way – a war started a century ago that has echoed through the decades in ebbs and flows – but we wear our scars differently. It's been eight years since the last conflict, but the tension that simmers beneath the desert now bubbles up again with renewed urgency. And that's why we must protect our country from those who seek to threaten the peace Queen Sana has fought for.

The sand thins beneath our feet until we walk on warm stone. I squint as light bounces off the mirrored mosaic wall that encircles the sanctuary and its grounds. The two guards at the large ornate gates nod to Kaleb and swing them open for us. They're from Mareen in the north and built like the mountains that adorn most of the region's landscape. It's as though they were made for the role of 'guard' with their broad shoulders and towering height.

Kaleb leads the way and the guards give a slight nod to us as we pass, a quiet thanks in recognition for what we've just done for our people. It's not until we're through the gates, which rattle behind us as they're closed, that the guards who accompanied us to the village break ranks from around us dancers and musicians. Sajid spares a glance at Kaleb, who gestures that he can leave, then rides down the pink stone path towards the stables with his guards in tow. When an attendant appears, Kaleb dismounts his horse and the young man quickly leads her away.

Kaleb finds shelter in the shade of one of the large white mulberry trees before addressing us.

'You all performed dutifully today as warriors of Amaar. The voices of those who spread false information about our queen must be silenced.' He clasps his palms together.

'Amaar's survival depends on your skills and you have honoured our queen by protecting her country, *our* country, from an enemy within our borders. Thank you,' he finishes solemnly. 'Now go and eat. Classes begin shortly. There are only three weeks until the loornas and you still have much to learn.'

We all bow our heads as Kaleb leaves. I smother a sigh at his reminder that there are just three weeks until we face our last test before graduating from the sanctuary.

'Finally,' Nadia says. With Amina's help, she unhooks the strap round her body that her dhol is attached to and places it on the ground.

Overhead, a bell trills followed by three sharp drumbeats, our signal that classes are about to begin.

'I didn't want breakfast anyway,' Meera says dryly, arms crossed.

As if on cue, Nadia's stomach groans. 'I need to eat something. Anyone else?' she says as she picks up her dhol.

Saara nods. 'That's if there's anything left.'

'We'll see you in rehearsal.' Amina waves as the three of them disappear in the same direction as Kaleb, down the winding path through the gardens and across the neatly manicured lawn to the school's entrance.

It's another moment before anyone else speaks, the morning's assignment a drain on our bodies.

'We should try and get something to eat quickly too,' Sahi says eventually, a natural leader among us dancers.

But the smell of Hassan's burning body still lingers. 'I'm not sure I'm hungry.'

Dana laughs. 'You say that now, but—'

'Are we going to pretend that man didn't just threaten us with a new war?' Meera interrupts, her head cocked to one side and eyebrows raised as she turns to me. 'Because of *your* mother's lies?'

Sahi steps in. 'Meera, don't.'

'No, don't patronise me, *Sahi*,' Meera replies fiercely. 'You heard what he had to say. King Faisal will bring war to our country, which means more death and more suffering because of *her* mother's treachery.'

And she's not wrong. But what would Meera have me do? I atone for my mother's fateful betrayal every day. I play the part of the executioner, killing those tainted by the lies she told about Queen Sana: lies that still plague our desert today.

'How does it feel knowing more people will die because of what your mother did?' Meera challenges me.

'The man we killed today died because of the choices *he* made to spy for Mezeer,' I say.

'I'm not talking about him,' she fires back. 'Your bloodline is corrupt. We're all fools to trust you won't betray us the way your mother did her comrades and country.'

I bite back my words as I remember Meera's desperate cries for her family when she was first brought here from her village, one of the only survivors after a raid by Mezeeri soldiers.

She shakes her head disapprovingly at my lack of a response, then turns swiftly and storms through the gardens.

Both Dana and Sahi watch me closely, their eyes full of apology. But I know Meera isn't the only one who doesn't trust me. I see the same caution in some of the other dancers and in the guards, wary I'll turn on them the way my mother did when she used her magic against her own soldiers, killing them. Sajid likes to remind me of that day seventeen years ago, the year before I was born. He fought alongside my mother and witnessed her fall from army general to traitor when her power destroyed her and she lied about our queen to cover her mistakes. He was even there when she was executed for her crimes.

But that's not my path. I know which side I fight on. I know how to control the power within me.

Sahi rests a hand on my arm. 'Don't listen to Meera,' she says as she tries to console me, but it doesn't dampen the blaze of Meera's words.

'Is what he said true?' I ask her. 'Is war coming?'

Sahi looks hesitant. 'I only saw his truth, and that's what he believed, yes.'

I nod, resolute. 'Then we'd better be ready to fight.'

THREE

'One, two, three. Two, two, three. Three, two, three…'
    Mistress Zaina's counts are like a melody in my head. As the Head Dance Mistress at the sanctuary, she only teaches dancers in their final two years of study. Once a formidable warrior herself, her role is to help us learn how to better amplify our magic through dance, transforming us from dancers into soldiers.

But not everyone's magic can be weaponised for war. There are those with abilities that can help our country flourish in their own way, like the musicians who perform with us and the thread-weavers who, depending on their speciality, create everything from costumes to armour. Others can conjure up a banquet from only a few humble ingredients and keep a bowl fresh with dates using just a few words.

Then there are the girls who were brought here when they were eight years old like me, but never developed any magic, despite all their training. Those who excel in combat are moved to different schools while others choose to return to their villages or stay at the sanctuary and become attendants.

'Listen to the musicians,' Mistress calls out over the crescendo of the violin and flute. 'Dance *through* the music, not against it. Softer arms.'

Dappled multicoloured light streams into the main studio and paints the ground as the sun blazes through the mosaic glass-domed roof. It highlights the gold embroidery down the front of Mistress's black kurta, the embellishment a symbol of her status among the mistresses, and turns her mehndi-dyed hair, styled in a lavish bun, an even brighter shade of orange.

All twenty final-year dancers rehearse together now, an invisible tether between us as we run through the opening performance for the upcoming loornas. Our chooriyan and paayal jingle softly with a music all of their own, adding a subtle flavour to the layers the musicians create. Energy pulses through the studio as, after months of practice, we're confident in our steps and positions. Although Mistress has taught us how to wield our magic against the enemy, it's a relief that here, in this studio and in our performances for the loornas, we can dance not as warriors, but simply as dancers.

Mistress Zaina's chest contracts, her arms moving with ours as she marks the dance with us. She must be nearly seventy now, but that doesn't stop the young performer within her from escaping. 'Suspend...and run.'

We move as one until the moment when Sahi, our lead soloist, breaks away. The rest of us whirlpool round her, Sahi at the heart of our dance as she spins on one leg in the centre.

'Not like you're running through the desert,' Mistress chides. 'Elegantly and on the balls of your feet. The audience should barely see you bob up and down.'

I know what's coming next as I pass Mistress and catch the twitch of her hand, revealing the spiral symbol on her palm.

The studio floor slips away from beneath us. I hesitate as the floor ripples like water and try not to lose my balance as my body tells me I should be falling into the waves Mistress creates with her magic. I close my eyes briefly to escape her illusion, a test of our ability to work as a group and keep our focus as we dance. When I open them again, our perfect circle is distorted.

'You are elite dancers,' Mistress calls out. 'A sudden change in your environment should not distract from what you're doing. When you are in the desert fighting an unknown army with unknown magic, there is no telling what challenges you will have to overcome.' Her illusion ebbs.

Our routine now behind the music, we miss out steps to try to catch up and move into the next formation. My heart is a drum in my chest as Sahi spins and jumps between us, undeterred by what's happening around her, and ends with a triple turn at the front of our would-be stage.

'Remember to breathe, to elevate your body as you jump!' Mistress almost sings in tune with the music. 'And hold…'

Her hand hovers in the air as we all stand on the balls of our feet, arms above our heads before we sweep them down in canon.

'Too fast. All of you but Sahi are ahead of the music. You must follow her lead.' Mistress shakes her head. 'Stop there.'

The musicians' last notes linger in the studio, like the final haze after a sandstorm, while Mistress walks towards us dancers with a stern look on her face.

'When we dance, we're telling a story,' she reminds us as she weaves through the group. 'This dance is a story about... Well, what do you think it's about?'

We're all silent, out of breath.

'Anyone?'

'A new day,' Jamila says from behind me.

'What makes you say that?'

'The dance...' Jamila pauses as if choosing her words carefully. 'It begins slowly, and quietly builds until it becomes more energetic. Night turning into day.'

Mistress stops in the middle of us all. 'That's exactly what the dance does. It is about the waking of the day, a new dawn. The choreography may begin softly and with subtle movements, but that doesn't mean you should dance lazily. You should evoke the mystery of nightfall in your dance, not dance as if you're half asleep. Light and shade.' She taps her right fist against her left palm for emphasis. 'How many times must I tell you that every dance must have light and shade in order to excite and engage your audience?'

Mistress claps her hands and walks to the front of the studio. 'Again. From the beginning.'

Once we're back in our starting positions, faint notes whisper through the heat in the studio until music fills the room once more. When the melody swells, so do our breaths and we dance as if no effort goes into each movement. My body moves on instinct, the choreography so engrained in my muscles, I don't have to think as I change from one position to the next. I wonder how many more times we'll rehearse this dance, one of three ensemble pieces, before we finally perform it at our graduation in front of the palace officials who will attend on Queen Sana's behalf.

It's one of the last times we'll all dance together. Before this month is over, we'll be sent to various camps around the country to train with the soldiers without magic, who have also graduated from their schools, before joining the ranks that already defend our eastern border from Mezeer's threats. All but Sahi, who was selected as our lead soloist by Kaleb last year and has since been primed for the coveted position of Queen's Guard. Soon she will join Queen Sana at the heart of justice in Amaar, the palace in Naru, where her rare magic as a truth-seeker is the perfect asset for court.

I glance over at Sahi as she breaks from the ensemble and begins her solo. With the loornas fast approaching, all I can think about is how we'll soon be apart. She was the first person I met when Kaleb brought me here eight years ago and, despite seeing the truth of my mother's betrayal, she never judged me for it. Because within that truth she saw my innocence, and that, along with Kaleb's generosity when he found me, saved my life.

The door to the studio opens and one of the attendants, Arif, appears. Wary of interrupting our class, he pauses in the doorway and cool air hits us, a welcome relief as we reach the climax of our dance. Only once we've finished our curtsies to our imagined audience does Mistress acknowledge him.

'Yes?' she says and Arif looks a little flustered, a blush rising in his cheeks.

'My apologies for disturbing you, Mistress Zaina. Kaleb has requested that Aasira come to his office once your class is over.'

Eyes dart in my direction, but I feel Meera's glare the most. She's always complained about Kaleb favouring me and has never understood why he would, given my background.

Mistress nods. 'Very well. We've just about finished.'

Arif bows and backs out of the room, closing the door quietly behind him.

'We'll pick this dance up again in tomorrow's class. It's coming along nicely, but we must focus on your other two ensemble pieces as well,' Mistress says. 'As you know, we only have three weeks and many dances to rehearse, including your duets and solos.'

I look at Sahi and she smiles. The choreography for our duet is complete; now all we have to do is rehearse the dance until we can perform it with our eyes closed.

'A new schedule will be shared in the morning so please ensure you check for any changes to your usual rehearsal times,' Mistress adds.

'Yes, Mistress,' we reply.

'You may now warm down,' she says and we all begin our stretches while the musicians pack up their instruments.

Sahi joins me as we run through our usual warm-down routine.

'What do you think Kaleb wants to speak to me about?' I ask.

'I don't know. Maybe about this morning?'

I flinch as I see him again...Hassan's son. The way his eyes accused me.

'Maybe,' I murmur, although I don't know what more Kaleb might have to say about the morning's assignment. 'I'd better go.'

'I'll save you something to eat.' Sahi smiles and my nerves dissolve momentarily.

'As long as it's not more saag.'

'You love saag,' she says playfully as I stand.

'Not with every meal.'

Sahi laughs. 'You'll get what you're given. Now go.'

'Yes, Mistress,' I whisper and she laughs again.

The corridors are quiet as I head for Kaleb's quarters in the west wing. It won't be long until the halls are bustling with students as they spill out from their various classes for their afternoon meal, but for now my only companions are the soldiers on guard. A few eye me curiously as I pass. Most are young and freshly trained, eager to join the frontline but stationed at the sanctuary until they're called up. They wear their armour with pride, the queen's signature colour of emerald gleaming where her wave symbol decorates the breastplate. It won't be long until I stand alongside these men and women in the same armour, our skills united in our fight to protect Amaar from Mezeer's threats and my mother's lies.

It's strange to think she once walked these same corridors. What was she like then, as a student, before her magic and mind were corrupted? Did she notice the details in the intricate alcoves and archways the way I do? How the colourful mosaics depict the sprawling desert and trees with roots that stretch beneath the ocean waves?

Sunlight streams into the final corridor and I squint as I step out into the courtyard, crossing the orange-pink tiles to

Kaleb's office. Two guards are stationed outside. The younger one doesn't move an inch, even when a fly buzzes about her, but the older guard tilts his head towards me.

'Aasira, how are we this fine day?' Tahir asks as he always does, wearing a smile beneath his moustache.

'Very well, and you?'

'Never better.' He knocks on the door and there's a muffled response on the other side before Kaleb opens it.

'Aasira, come in,' he says, holding the door wide for me to enter. 'Chai?' He gestures for me to sit on one of the chairs piled with cushions and goes over to his desk.

'Yes, please,' I reply, and Kaleb moves an old map to the side, folding it in half to make space as he pours two cups from an embossed bronze teapot. The steam warms my already flushed face from rehearsal as he passes one to me.

'I won't keep you long,' he says and takes a seat of his own. 'But there is something I wanted to speak to you about.' He pauses but I don't fill the silence. 'It's about the future, more specifically *your* future, as you near the end of your training here.'

Butterflies flutter within my stomach as I anticipate his next words. 'Are you about to tell me I can no longer graduate into the army?'

He takes a long drink of his chai. 'No, of course not. But there are those in higher places,' he says with raised eyebrows as though to exaggerate the point, 'who question such a decision.'

'Because of who my mother is…was,' I correct myself, wanting him to get to the point.

He nods. 'I took a risk the day I brought you here. A risk you have proven to me while on your assignments this year is not one to regret. The queen realises now what an asset you could be to our country.'

Mention of the queen makes the butterflies inside me scatter and I have to clasp my hands tighter round my cup, to hide my nerves. Kaleb has always been honest about Queen Sana's distrust of me, and I can understand her not wanting a traitor's daughter within her ranks, especially when my mother was once a soldier and later a general in her army. 'But...?'

'But...there are some who cannot forgive the decisions your mother made. You heard the traitor this morning. There are people who would spread her lies, seventeen years on. We still deal with the repercussions of her betrayal every day.'

I breathe in deeply to quell my frustration, the scent of the sweet spices calming. I'll never understand my mother's actions. How she could turn her magic against members of our army, then try to cover up their deaths by spreading lies about the queen using her magic to drain Mezeer's rivers.

'What must I do to prove I'm *not* her? That I won't be warped by my power and turn it on our own soldiers?'

Kaleb smiles warmly and sets his almost empty cup of chai aside. 'Protect us, your country's people, as you have been protected. All everyone wants is to feel safe. Show them, as you have shown us during your studies here, that you're a worthy warrior of Amaar. That although you're Lina's daughter, you're not her.'

I shift uncomfortably at the sound of my mother's name. It's easier to remember her without it. To disassociate the army general who turned traitor from the mother who raised me for the first eight years of my life.

'You have done well here, Aasira,' Kaleb says. 'Your mother may have abandoned Amaar, but she would be proud of the warrior you've become.'

Somehow I doubt that. If she were here and could see the person I am now, we'd be enemies on opposing sides of the river that divides Amaar and Mezeer. An emerald tide against one of the king's crimson flowers.

FOUR

A navy sky weighs heavy outside, lit up with pinpricks of stars that fade behind wispy clouds drifting across the surface. My body is tired, but my mind is awake. I know the sun is waking too and that tendrils of her light will soon bring the desert to life. The dormitory is quiet but for heavy breathing as the other elite dancers sleep.

My paayal tinkle softly as I get out of bed and, like most mornings, quickly change and pad to the door on the balls of my feet, slipping out into the corridor. I learned my lesson years ago when I sprang out of bed and woke the rest of the girls – never again. Rahim, the guard stationed on our corridor between the elite dancers' dormitory and the lead soloist's room, where Sahi sleeps, nods awake.

'I wasn't asleep,' he says, wiping away the crust nestled at the corners of his eyes.

'I didn't think you were.' I smile and he smiles back gratefully.

Silence hums in that way it does before the world fully awakes and is pierced by the everyday backdrop of voices, music and commands. Attendants wash the floors and I'm careful not to step where they've just cleaned. I spy a few other elite students in the rehearsal rooms, getting in as much practice as they can before they too must exhibit their talents at the loornas.

The air is cool as I step outside and follow the winding path that flows through the lawns like a stream, the soft scent of the roses and jasmine flowers fragrant, towards a secluded part of the gardens. Out here, the silence is already easing. Birds summon each other with their morning song beneath a transforming sky streaked with lavender highlights as dawn approaches.

The sun calls to me as she ascends, the fire that turns her red on the hottest of days drawing me to her. In the mornings when I miss her greeting, my body too tired to leave my bed, I feel off balance, as though my mind and body aren't engaged and working together. Something that always leads to mistakes. I open the gate to the walled garden, overgrown with wild flowers and climbing vines that scale the walls. A sunburst mosaic decorates the ground, the perfect place to feel the sun as her light radiates at the start of a new day.

With a deep breath, I roll my neck forward, then to the left and right, before looking up at the layers of lavender, pink and gold that paint the sky. Slowly, I raise my arms above my head, then gently stretch to both sides, easing out the ache across my shoulders. Lunging backwards, I stretch one leg then the other, eyes closed as I focus on each breath. The hum of insects, the breeze through the leaves and song of the birds create a melody my body can't help but fall in time with as I smoothly move from one pose into the next. The sun's energy entwines with my own as she rises, rejuvenating my aching muscles before another day of training. She warms my brown skin, lighter than some of the other girls', but a mirror of my mother's colouring.

My mother swims into my vision. She was the one who taught me how to move gracefully between each position and how to control my breathing and core. No matter where we were as we constantly moved from village to town, we would always wake early together. The desert was our stage and the sun our audience as we performed these stretches before she'd teach me the dances passed on to her. The woman I grew up with wasn't the woman I hear of now: a liar, a traitor.

An ache tugs inside me as I close my eyes and the sun's rays dance across my eyelids, an orange and red light flickering behind them. My mother's smile wavers in my mind, then disappears.

'I thought you might be here.'

My eyes flicker open as Sahi enters the walled garden.

'Can I join you?'

'Always.' I pull out of one pose and move into another, leaning forward into a stretch as Sahi begins her own routine.

'How are you feeling after your conversation with Kaleb yesterday?' she asks. I spoke about it briefly to Sahi and Dana during our evening meal, out of earshot of Meera and the other dancers.

I shrug. 'I've always known things might not be straightforward when I leave here. It's hard to prove yourself as loyal when people have already decided you never will be because of your bloodline. Kaleb practically confirmed that in our meeting.'

She tries to disguise her frown, but sympathy furrows her brow. 'Things are about to get a little less straightforward at the sanctuary as well,' she says in a low voice.

'What do you mean?'

'Kaleb came to speak to me after my solo rehearsal last night. You'd already gone to the dormitory so I didn't have a chance to tell you until now.'

'Tell me what?'

She breathes deeply. 'Queen Sana will be attending the loornas.'

'What?' I say a little too loudly and she hushes me. 'Why?'

But Sahi doesn't need to say it.

'Because of me?'

'Kaleb didn't say that explicitly.'

'But you saw that was the truth behind his meaning.'

'You know I can't see his truth.'

'Won't…not can't,' I correct her. 'You choose not to.'

'Because I took an oath, as did you, to "only unleash my magic in the face of the enemy". Not to use it on our comrades.' She reaches out and clasps my hand. 'Or our friends…our sisters.'

I smile and squeeze back.

Her gaze wanders and she shakes her head in thought. 'What that man said yesterday, his truth, it keeps playing on my mind. I think it's because for the first time the threat feels like it's edging closer. I believe that's why Queen Sana wishes to attend the graduation this year, to see for herself the warriors who will fight to protect her land in the inevitable conflict that's coming.'

The weight of it settles and I'm reminded of what Kaleb said, about how we still deal with the repercussions of my mother's betrayal.

'Also,' Sahi says with a grin, 'I wouldn't want you getting a big head and thinking the queen is only coming to see you.'

We both laugh. 'No,' I say. 'If anything, she's here to inspect the newest member of her Queen's Guard.'

Sahi blushes. 'That role isn't a certainty.'

'Maybe not, but you are our lead soloist. Who else would it go to?'

She smiles gratefully. 'Kaleb will announce the news in the next couple of days so keep it to yourself until then. I wanted you to know though.'

'Thank you.'

I wonder why Kaleb didn't tell me himself when he summoned me to his office; he must have known. But then his relationship with Sahi is different to the one with me. Of course he would tell his rising star before the rest of us, his gift to the queen with her rare ability to see the truth in a world full of lies.

Amina's voice rings out over the grounds, projected by her ability to sound like a choir as she calls to everyone to wake.

'We'd better get ready,' Sahi says.

'Ah yes, I can't wait for a morning of combat training with Sajid,' I reply.

'At least you'll have me as a partner.'

'I promise to go easy on you,' I joke and Sahi shoves me aside.

'How dare you,' she says, laughing. 'I taught you all your best moves.'

'I think you're remembering things the wrong way round.'

'Is that right?' she scoffs. 'Well, I've been saving some skills all for myself so you just wait.'

'With bated breath…'

She laughs again and links her arm through mine as we leave the seclusion of the walled garden.

FIVE

'Walk like that on the front line and we won't have an army left!' Sajid's voice vibrates in the air, sharpening our senses like the assortment of blades waiting for us. 'Line up.'

We hurry into the groups of four we've been put in ahead of our graduation. I take my place at the front on Sahi's left, while Meera and Dana position themselves on Sahi's right, and the rest of the ensemble form their rows behind us. Unlike our dance classes, Sajid prefers to conduct our combat training outside to replicate the conditions we will one day fight in, often reminding us that the sun is also our enemy as her heat will tire us as much as the physical fight we're engaged in.

He strolls into position. Tahir joins him, along with the guards who accompanied us to the village yesterday morning: Haniya, Ejaz and Camil.

Sajid's face is stern as he steps forward, light stubble shadowing his jawline. 'Today you will work in pairs and demonstrate what you have learned over the last year. I have chosen a new opponent for each of you,' he says and his eyes narrow at me. 'Aasira and Meera, you'll go first. Don't kill each other.' He waves his hand, indicating for the two of us to collect our swords.

Meera smiles smugly as she runs her finger along the curved silver blade. Gone are the days when we would practise with wooden weapons where a few bruises were the only threat. Tahir gives me a knowing look as I take my place inside the large circle the rest of the dancers have formed. While they sit on the grass, Meera and I face Sajid, who stands outside the circle. Our swords are positioned on the right-hand side of our bodies and pointing down, our shoulders back and eyes and chin up.

This training is about precision, much like in a dance rehearsal, except here the wrong step could mean lasting injury. I reflexively touch my left side where a scar still sits, a reminder of when I was new to the sanctuary and stumbled across the combat equipment. I'd seen the older girls practising, but when I tried to replicate their moves I quickly regretted it. Combat is the one part of our training where magic is prohibited. Instead, we're trained the way soldiers without magic are; the way Sajid and Tahir were when they joined the army.

Sajid calls out a string of commands and Meera and I respond with a bow to him, then each other, before performing the sanctuary's customary sequence. In unison, we cut the air with our blades and swing them down to our left side, back up to the right and round in a circle, finishing with the tips pointed at each other.

'Begin,' Sajid says as coolly as the light breeze that whispers through the gardens.

Meera doesn't hesitate. Her blade slashes upwards and mine meets hers in an X. When she lunges forward, I react, stepping back but with my weight forward on the attack. I have to give Meera credit: she's always been strong with a blade. But there's a new menace in her today as her lips curl into a snarl. Sajid instructs us over the harsh ring of metal and the bells jangling at our feet. I swerve away from another of Meera's swings, catching her blade as she almost nicks my plait. I carve my blade upwards, forcing her into a back bend, and our blades meet again.

'Attention!'

We stop abruptly and turn to face Sajid, both of us trying to disguise our efforts with controlled breaths. Sweat gathers along my hairline and my kurta clings damply to my back. I realise then how quiet the gardens are as the guards stationed throughout them look our way.

'If any of you have any hopes of becoming a warrior in Amaar's army, then you need to start fighting like you actually want to save your skin.' Sajid steps into the circle, his fists tense. 'You're fighting as if you know you're going to walk out of this class alive. Like your magic can save you.'

He glowers at me and I hear the words behind his stare: *Your mother's magic destroyed her and will do the same to you.*

'What if you come across a silencer, someone who can stamp out your magic with one word? What will save you then?'

A silencer? Surely that magic doesn't exist and he's just saying it to unsettle us. The same thought rolls over the rest of the dancers, but he quietens their murmurs.

'You should come to these sessions as though you've been stripped of your magic. As though all you have to protect yourself is a blade and your instinct. When you're in the midst of battle, you don't get to stop fighting because someone tells you it's time to break. When you go out there and fight –' he points past the wall that encloses us – 'you don't know if those breaths you're taking are going to be your last. You have to fight like your life depends on it. You must keep fighting because the moment you let your guard down, you're dead.'

As though to emphasise his words, the breeze picks up and sand rolls in from the desert, performing an unusual swirl through the gardens and around us. Sajid is momentarily distracted and, when he looks back at us, something like confusion, mixed with apprehension, clouds his features.

'It's not just the Mezeeri soldiers you need to be afraid of,' he says, voice sombre. He clears his throat and his furrowed brow is quickly replaced with what we're more used to: irritation. 'You may have trained together since childhood, but Amaar's army has harboured traitors in the past. Don't be fooled; the magic you fight could belong to someone you thought was one of your own.'

He steps back out of the circle, but when he faces us again his stare is for me alone. 'Sometimes betrayal runs in the blood.'

Meera mumbles inaudibly under her breath and I notice Dana and a couple of the other dancers shift uncomfortably where they sit. But I won't be intimidated. I hold his stare until eventually he breaks it.

'You may think your magic is enough to protect Amaar,' Sajid says, 'but you must find a union with your blade as well if you are to survive. Battles aren't choreographed. Dancing will only get you so far in war.' He lets his words sink in. 'You two will fight again, but this time like you're fighting to survive. For your right to live.'

I face Meera. If I thought there was a fierceness in her before, there's something new in her now. Ever ambitious, I know she won't disappoint in giving Sajid what he's asked for. We go through the usual formalities at Sajid's command. My hand is clammy as I grip the hilt of my blade and every ridge is imprinted into my palm.

'Fight.'

Meera twists her blade through the air with renewed energy and I'm immediately on the back foot. I catch her attack with my own blade and respond with the moves of a dancer, despite Sajid's instructions. I crouch beneath her blows, then jump when she swipes low and turn swiftly out of her way as she aims for my body. The gardens are silent but for the sound of our swords clashing against each other, punctuated by our panting as we draw on more strength and push against the tiredness in our muscles.

Our minds are in control of our bodies – that's what Mistress Zaina always tells us. If we allowed ourselves to stop dancing every time our body told us it hurt and needed a break, we'd never make it through a whole routine. Both Meera and I breathe Mistress's words now, her eyes as piercing as her blade.

I clasp my hilt with both hands as her blows hit harder. Our blades crash and scrape against each other, an awful sound that rings in my ears. My heartbeat becomes my song, fast and thudding in my chest. I move in time with it. I arc my blade up as Meera pulls hers away. She shields herself, bringing her blade to her right in anticipation of my next jab. But I surprise her, spinning my blade in one hand and aiming for her left side.

I catch her forearm and Meera recoils. She hisses through her teeth in pain, dropping her blade to clasp her hand over the wound as it starts to bleed. 'I can't believe you did that!'

In truth, neither can I.

Sajid grunts. 'None of the theatrics; it's only a flesh wound. Ejaz, take Meera to see the healers. You —' he points at me — 'sit down.'

I pick up Meera's blade and return both to Camil. Meera glances back over her shoulder as Ejaz guides her inside the school through one of the side entrances. I try to make out what she says, but can't read her lips. Something complimentary, I'm sure.

'Farah and Yasmin, you're next,' Sajid commands.

I take Farah's place in the circle and sit next to Dana, who nudges my arm and smiles encouragingly. We sit like that for the next hour, the wait as gruelling as our training in the heat of the mid-morning sun, as we watch each pair fight under Sajid's instruction. Inevitably, more of the girls get injured with scrapes to hands, arms and legs, but nothing that can't be treated by the sanctuary's healers.

Agitation flickers across Sajid's face when the call for the end of class comes at last. 'Clean yourselves up. I'll see you again tomorrow where you will fight with only your body,' he says, dismissing us.

Last to have been partnered up, Dana now hovers by Haniya as she returns her sword to the rack and I notice the way their hands brush against each other as she passes it to the guard. When she joins Sahi and me, her face is flushed but not from the class.

'Subtle,' I whisper.

Dana flutters her eyelashes, all innocence. 'Haniya's going to see if she can get an early transfer into the army when us lot graduate,' she says with a lilt of giddiness and I can't help but smile. 'I know it's unlikely and even more so that we'll be sent to the same base, but it's worth a try, isn't it?'

'Of course,' Sahi says, then checks that none of the other girls are listening. 'Just don't ruin it for yourselves by getting caught.'

Dana rolls her eyes, but excitement still plays over her face. 'I know the rules. No relationships between students, students and guards, students and teachers –' she reels them off – 'and strictly no relationships within the army.'

The back of my neck prickles at that one, the hairs on my arms rising. Yet another reason my mother was deemed a traitor: because she had a relationship while she was an army general and I was the result.

'Basically—'

'No relationships,' Sahi and I say in unison.

'But where's the fun in that?' Dana says and we all laugh. 'And where's the fun in not using swords during combat training?'

'At least we won't have to worry about the possibility of losing an ear tomorrow,' Sahi says as we make our way inside and are welcomed by a cool embrace.

An image of Meera baring her teeth flashes through my mind. 'I wouldn't speak too soon,' I say and touch my right ear, shivering at the sensation of an imaginary bite.

SIX

I imagine myself in the desert, the sun my audience as I dance. She breathes through me along with the music that flows round the main studio, guiding our ensemble through what will be our final performance at the loornas. We've rehearsed this dance so many times over the last few months, but especially in the last couple of days, along with our other group pieces. I know exactly where the other dancers are as we seamlessly weave between one another, celebrating our country's landscape through our movements.

'Think about what this will look like to the audience,' Mistress Zaina says over the steady beat of the dhol. 'They will see a swirling pattern like a whirlpool, gathering pace and moving as one. Until…'

We break into our smaller groups, each quartet adopting our own pattern for several bars before we become an ensemble once again. The trick is to not get distracted by what the other groups are doing and to trust in our muscle memory.

'Very good,' Mistress commends us. 'We'll leave it there for today. Kaleb has requested that everyone go to the theatre for an announcement this evening.'

We all clap and curtsy, first to Mistress then the musicians, to signal the end of the class. When I glance at Sahi, she nods and joins me for our warm-down. Kaleb must be about to announce that Queen Sana will attend the loornas.

Sahi's breathing is measured, but in that way where she's focusing on each inhale and exhale.

'You seem nervous,' I say.

'Aren't you?'

A laugh escapes me. 'Of course I am. In a few weeks, I'm going to come face to face with the woman my mother betrayed. The woman who ordered my mother's execution... and was close to ordering mine too.'

'Don't say that.'

'Why not? It's true.'

Sahi smiles sympathetically. 'You're not her.'

'The queen doesn't know that.'

'You wouldn't still be here if she thought you were a threat.'

I glance at Meera, her forearm now perfectly healed, talking excitedly about what Kaleb's announcement might be with a group of five others. 'Maybe. Or perhaps this is some sort of test to see if I really can be trusted as a warrior.'

Sahi's silence tells me I might be right.

Hushed murmurs float through the corridors as the guards usher everyone towards the theatre. We funnel through the gold doors and enter the large space where we will soon perform for our graduation. The sunset casts a crimson glow through the windows, which is joined by the subtle light of the lanterns dotted along the walls. Everyone finds their seats, from the youngest year group at the front through to the elite students who sit at the back. Ten long rows are left empty behind us, as well as plenty of seats to our left and right, a reminder of how few of us are born with magic now compared to the past, when this theatre would have been full.

Mistress Zaina and Sajid emerge from stage left and wait by the draped curtains, along with the head mistresses who lead in the other branches of magic. Groups of guards station themselves round the stage and the theatre's various entrances, while the other mistresses sit with their year groups. It's not until Kaleb steps onto the stage that the whispers finally dissipate. We stand and wait as Kaleb takes his place centre stage, before indicating that we should sit.

'Thank you for gathering here this evening. As you know, our final-year students will graduate from the sanctuary in just under three weeks,' he says and a few of the mistresses in the audience clap, encouraging a round of applause from everyone and a few turned heads in our direction.

Kaleb smiles, wider than usual. 'Yes, I'm sure we are all very proud of their achievements over the last eight years of their training and wish them well as they take up their positions within society.'

Further applause follows and Kaleb joins in. This moment isn't just for the elites; it's for him and our mistresses too, for all the work they've put into preparing us for our futures. When he waves his hands, everyone falls quiet again and he continues.

'The reason I have called this assembly is to announce some news about this year's ceremony. Not only will we have the privilege of watching the elites perform, along with the palace officials who will join us, but Her Majesty herself, Queen Sana, will also grace us with her presence.'

Anticipation ripples through the theatre as a chorus of gasps and chatter wells up. The elites are no different as a hum of delirium spreads down our row. For us dancers, this is a chance to show Queen Sana how we can defend her country. A chance for *me* to show I can be trusted. Dana nudges my arm, grinning widely. But I feel on edge with so much to prove, as though I'm within a bubble and the slightest movement will pop its fragile structure.

'It has been ten years since our queen last honoured us with her presence at the sanctuary,' Kaleb says. 'You are symbols of Amaar's bright future, each and every one of you, and I'm sure you will join me in welcoming Queen Sana as we present our final-year students for their graduation at the loornas.'

Cheers erupt. Sensing my apprehension, Sahi takes my hand and squeezes it.

'And that is not all. There is some special news for our elite dancers,' Kaleb says. 'This year, Queen Sana wishes to select her newest member of the Queen's Guard through a series of auditions that will be held at the palace. So perform well, and you may be afforded a position of the highest regard in Amaar.'

Sahi's hand falls slack round mine. She never mentioned that when we spoke the other morning. It's the role she's always dreamed of, the role Kaleb had as good as promised to her when he promoted her to lead soloist last year. Almost every elite student looks at her, but Sahi's gaze is firmly on the stage: on Kaleb.

Whispers hiss down the line until they reach Dana, who leans across me. 'Did you know?' she asks on behalf of us all.

I see the tension in Sahi's jawline. She had no idea.

I catch sight of Sahi as she disappears outside while everyone else filters into the dining hall for their delayed evening meal. She moved so swiftly through the throngs of students as we left the theatre that I couldn't keep up, but I can guess where she's heading and slip out into the gardens where she paces beneath a flowering tree. I give her a moment and follow her eyeline up to the stars that are scattered across the velvet sky. She murmurs something to herself, the breeze her only listener.

'He didn't tell you,' I say as I approach.

Her eyes glisten in the half-moon's glow.

'This doesn't mean the position isn't still yours.'

'Doesn't it?' she says, voice breaking.

'Of course it doesn't. No one's better prepared for the role than you and no one here has an ability that could even compete with what you can offer the queen.'

But Sahi doesn't look convinced. 'Why this year? Why change the way things are done *this* year?'

'I don't know,' I admit.

'It's tradition for the lead soloist to be chosen as the newest member of the Queen's Guard at their graduation,' she says, desperation creeping in. 'That's how the lead soloist *becomes* the lead soloist, because conversations have already been had between the sanctuary and the palace about the upcoming year group and their talents. It's an unspoken rule, but everyone knows it.'

'Which is why you don't need to worry that things will be any different this year.'

'But they already are, aren't they?'

She wipes the tears from her cheeks and there's something new in her I don't recognise. She's usually so self-assured, but in a quietly confident way; it's why the rest of the elites respect her so much. I try to think of a way to reassure her, but what she says next takes me aback.

'I'm not built to fight in a war, Aasira. I'm not like you,' she almost whispers.

'What do you mean?'

She swallows hard and I finally see it: fear. 'My power won't help on the front line. I can't produce flames, conjure up snakes or maim with nightmares. All I have to rely on in combat is what Sajid's taught us with a blade. I can't save lives in battle like I could in the queen's court. If they take this position away from me—'

'No one is taking it from you, Sahi. No one.' I gently hold both her arms to stop her from pacing so frantically. 'I don't know why Queen Sana has chosen to come here this year or to upset tradition, but you will be going to the palace and you will be made a member of the Queen's Guard, I promise.'

'You can't promise that.'

'Maybe not,' I say and swallow back the lump in my throat. 'But how many times have you promised me something you couldn't, just to comfort me?'

The hint of a smile tugs at the corner of her mouth. *Thank you*, she mouths.

I hug her, our roles reversed for the briefest moment as I hold my own nerves at bay and hope I've found the right words to rid Sahi of hers. At least for now...

SEVEN

Sahi's words from the night before play over in my head as I finish my morning stretches in the walled garden. I've always known our abilities are different – hers of the mind while mine manifest physically – but somehow I'd never realised it left her so fearful of being on the battlefield. That her desire to become a member of the Queen's Guard was more than a want but a need.

Sajid always reminds us we can't rely on our powers as our only weapon and should become one with the blade. I see now that for Sahi and some of the other dancers, the blade is their only physical weapon in combat. And, if what Sajid said about people with the ability to silence magic is true, all of us really must learn to fight well without our powers.

I leave the sunrise behind and go to the main studio for my solo rehearsal with Mistress Zaina. So far we've practised a series of steps to best show off my ability to the audience, but they're yet to be strung together as we're still without a piece of music. Perhaps I should be worried when everyone else has already selected their music and we have less than three weeks to polish my solo, but I know under Mistress's guidance it will come together.

'Your mind is already distracted and yet the day has only just dawned,' Mistress comments as I enter the studio.

I curtsy, not expecting to see her here already. 'Apologies for being late.'

'You're not late. I am early as I was finalising your choreography.'

'You've chosen a piece of music?' I ask eagerly.

'It kept coming back to me as the best fit for you, so yes, I have finally settled on a piece.'

I smile and begin my warm-up at the barre as the musicians arrive. I note their instruments: Saara on the flute, Neesha on the violin and Nadia on the dhol, while Amina will add her voice.

'There will be a larger ensemble,' Mistress says when she sees me watching the quartet set up in the corner. 'But I thought we would start with these instruments and build once you have the dance within your body.'

I nod and Mistress examines my stature as I roll through the balls of my feet, rotate my ankles and warm up each muscle while we wait for the musicians to finish tuning their instruments. The moment they're ready, Mistress lifts a hand and they play the tune that starts every class.

My body reacts to the music and goes through the motions of flexing and pointing my feet, arms and legs working together, head emphasising each move with a look towards the barre, then away from it and to my imaginary audience. Everything connected. There's no time to think about anything else as my mind and body work in harmony with each other.

Mistress walks up to me and with each flick of her hand I know what she's instructing me to do: turn out, straighten, use your core, point further, look up, look out, show off your feet. After eight exercises, Mistress signals we're finished by lifting her hand again.

'Into the centre,' she says. 'I think you will like the piece I've chosen for you. It's slower than you might expect, less spritely than what I had originally planned for you, but it exudes a warmth that is perfect for showing off your skills as a dancer and a warrior.' She beckons for me to sit and stretch. 'We will listen to it first so you can get a feel for its musicality, then learn the final choreography.'

Excitement flickers inside me as the musicians take up their instruments again. Neesha begins, her bow lightly touching the strings of her violin and caressing only a few notes. I imagine the quiet, still audience in the theatre as the music sets the atmosphere for the dance. Saara accompanies on her flute and Amina joins in with lyrics from a language we only ever hear in song. It's beautiful listening to their magic unfold between them. The way they can play or sing a few notes and create an invisible loop, then begin a new melody and add layer upon layer to their quartet until they sound like a full orchestra. The tempo rises as Nadia beats her dhol and I watch Mistress mark through the dance as the tune drifts through the studio.

The musicians are lost in the music, eyes closed and bodies swaying with the beat. I close my eyes too and listen to each note roll over the next. As the song crescendoes, it tugs at me with a quiet familiarity, like a dream that slips away as you wake. In my mind, I see the desert, its edges blurred where golden dunes meet a topaz sky. Something moves in the distance, but the harder I focus on it, the more it pulls away…until I see *her*. Her long dark hair flies round her as she spins on the balls of her feet and sand kicks up about her legs. I smile and when I open my eyes Mistress is watching me.

'You recognise the music,' she says. It's not a question.

The musicians continue to play and the weight of their melancholy notes settles round me. 'My mother used to hum something similar.' I can almost hear her now, humming as she plaited my hair.

'It's an old song, one I remember my grandmother singing to me and my sister,' Mistress reminisces. 'And it's the music your mother and I chose for her solo when she graduated from the Leharanji.'

The sun's warmth prickles along my skin as she casts her light through the glass roof. 'She danced to this?'

Mistress nods. 'Beautifully, too.'

'And now you'd like me to perform the same dance.' I want to ask if that's wise given the way people liken me to her, but I hold my tongue.

'Not the same dance,' Mistress clarifies. 'But the same piece of music. It's the only one that feels right and whose melody can complement your magic.'

Something swells inside me and it takes me a moment to recognise what it is. Connection. Like I feel when I run through my stretches each morning, the very movements my mother once taught me. I don't remember much; the stories I've heard of her betrayal are more real to me than the memories of my mother herself. But sometimes I'm greeted by the briefest feeling that we're not so dissimilar, despite how much I've tried to prove I will not turn into the person she became. How I will not be overpowered by my magic. Will not be turned by our enemies to join their side and betray those I train with and fight for.

'I don't think I can dance to this,' I say finally.

The music ends and I await Mistress's disappointment, but instead she says, 'Why don't you try? And if you still don't feel it suits you, then we'll move on to something else.'

'Is there time for that?'

She smiles. 'There is always time. Come, let's get started.'

I join Mistress as she walks to the back corner of the studio and imagine myself on the theatre stage.

'You will start behind the curtain,' she says.

I repeat the movements behind Mistress as she dances the first eight bars of my solo with an admirable energy.

'Do you have it?' she asks and I nod. 'Mark it through with the music.'

I go back to the corner and the musicians play. Mistress counts me in and I get a feel for the timing, practising the steps she just showed me but in a pared back way, without dancing them fully.

'Again, but full-out this time,' Mistress instructs.

The musicians play the same bars and I dance as though I'm performing this time, the first sequence already in my muscles.

'Very good,' says Mistress, then turns to the musicians. 'And played with perfect precision.'

We continue in this way with each new sequence until we're already a quarter of the way through my solo and the story begins to take shape.

'Let's run through what we have so far,' Mistress says. 'And, Aasira, this time I would like you to call on your magic. Only the gold dust, not your flames. We'll build to those.'

I breathe deeply and take my position. Gentle notes breach the stillness and the ability rooted within me kindles. I hear Mistress's whispered counts from the front of the room and my cue to begin. While my body focuses on the movements, my mind calls on my ability. It hums beneath my skin and slowly my palms shimmer until tendrils of golden dust branch over me as I dance through the sun-soaked studio. My skirt flares out as I spin and my magic expands with the music like a halo. I'm at ease, the choreography coming naturally as my dance and magic work in tandem. Is this how my mother felt when she danced to this piece?

It's all too abrupt when the musicians stop, my body lost to the music and eager to continue. Mistress was right. This song is perfect for me.

'Queen Sana will be impressed,' Mistress says, satisfied. 'With all of you,' she finishes and gestures to the musicians.

'Thank you,' I say, curtsying to the quartet.

'The lyrics speak of your ability, Aasira,' Amina tells me. '*Teleraahn con saanaveer eh milraey.* With nature's magic, we sustain life.'

Sustain life...I end life.

'We had better finish there,' Mistress says, smiling.

As the musicians gather their instruments and I warm down at the barre, I mull over Amina's words. I don't understand the old language of her song, a language spoken centuries ago before Amaar and Mezeer became separate countries. We've never been taught it, the texts our ancestors once studied when they were here long gone, though I do recognise its alphabet in some of the inscriptions around the sanctuary.

'What do you think?' Mistress asks when it's only us left in the studio.

'Will Queen Sana know that my mother once danced to this music?'

'They studied here together. I believe she will recognise it, yes.'

I want to dance to the piece, but I can't ignore the voice in my head.

'Is it not dangerous to perform to a piece of music she once danced to, especially in front of the queen?'

Mistress considers this a moment. 'You already walk the halls your mother once did. But that doesn't mean you're on the same path.'

I try to look convinced but, sensing my uncertainty, Mistress adds, 'We all have the ability to do wrong in this world, but it's easier to place blame and distort the truth than admit to our own mistakes.'

'There's no distorting what my mother did though, is there? The lies she spread about Queen Sana to cover up her actions are still believed.' I sigh, shaking my head. 'The traitor I executed the other day… He said war is coming. Her lies are the reason we still train to fight Mezeer.'

Mistress's smile wavers and I'm surprised when she places a hand on my shoulder. 'There is peace to be found in our past, Aasira. We only have to look for it.'

EIGHT

My mind whirrs after class. I have a short break before another ensemble rehearsal and am on my way to the gardens for some fresh air when I hear my name.

'Aasira.' I turn to face Kaleb, who is standing by an alcove at the end of the corridor. 'Do you have a moment?' he asks, beckoning me over.

I join him by the alcove, which is decorated with a mosaic of a leafless tree that branches out over the horizon.

'How are you?'

'Good, thank you.' But our classes have intensified over the last few days and I hear the weariness in my voice. 'I just had a solo rehearsal with Mistress Zaina.'

'And your dance is coming along well?'

'It's coming along.'

He nods and a pause expands between us before he says, 'I heard there was an incident with Meera during your combat class the other day.'

Of course Sajid told Kaleb. 'Accident, not incident,' I correct him.

Kaleb raises an eyebrow in slight amusement. 'Nonetheless, try not to antagonise your peers.'

'Antagonise?' I say, a little sharper than intended.

'You know what I mean.'

'I didn't antagonise Meera. We were partnered together and I fought the way Sajid instructed us to, just as she did. And she wasn't the only one who walked away with a scrape.'

'No,' Kaleb says. 'But under your circumstances it would be wise not to make enemies of those who fight on your side.'

My temples throb and the flames inside me blink awake. I don't usually have to defend myself to Kaleb, but the words tumble out before I can stop myself. 'Meera's always disliked me. I've tried to be her friend in the past, but she doesn't see me; she sees my mother and her betrayal and the Mezeeri soldiers who ordered everyone in her village to be killed. I can't change that.'

'I'm not reprimanding you and I'm not saying it's fair.' Kaleb tries to pacify me, but his words fall flat. 'All I'm saying is try to get along. One day you might need each other. And with Queen Sana joining us I would hate for any concerns from other students to arise, as I'm sure you would too.'

I purse my lips. 'Of course not.'

'Good.' He watches me with an expression that unnerves me for the briefest moment, his dark eyes intense as if he can see my thoughts. But then it softens, creases forming at the corner of his eyes as he smiles.

'Is that all?' I ask. I know he's looking out for me, but I'm tired of the distrust others show me. I don't want to add Kaleb to the list.

'Yes.' He nods and allows me to leave first.

His gaze burrows into me as I bow my head and swiftly walk back down the corridor and out into the gardens. It takes everything in me to keep my step light and not show my frustration. The air is stifling once I'm outside. The sun casts a crimson haze over the sanctuary, coating the grounds in a dusky peach hue. A prickling sensation traces its way across my skin, restless and relentless.

I head for the seclusion of the walled garden and sit on the shaded bench, sweat already glistening on my bare arms. My palms tingle as I stare at the gold sun emblems that decorate them. I was six years old when they emerged, the first hint of the power that was concealed within me. I was scared of them at first. Even Kaleb and Mistress Zaina watched me with caution the first time they saw the untethered fire ripple across my body.

It took about a year for me to understand how to anchor my ability to my dancing and another two to feel like I was in control of my magic as I danced. I would grow frustrated, desperate for people to trust me, but rigid in class because I didn't want the fire in me to explode and scare the other students; or harm them. Now I understand their nature. I've learned through my training how to call on my dust and flames at will and shown time and again that I will only ever use them in combat. In the face of danger to protect our country. But there's only one person who's always known that...

'What you can do is dazzling.'

The flame in my hand sputtered in the breeze as the girl entered the walled garden: Sahi. We'd already met when I first arrived at the sanctuary a week before and she'd worn the same warm smile then. Kaleb had asked her to look after me and she took the role very seriously.

'It is?' I asked.

'Mm-hm.' She nodded enthusiastically and joined me on the bench. She sat so close to me, I clasped my hands together to extinguish the flame and shifted away a little.

'You're not scared?' Of me, I wanted to add.

'Why would I be scared?'

I chuckled in disbelief, the first time I'd laughed since I'd lost my mother. 'Because it's fire and it could hurt you.'

She looked at me curiously. 'Are you planning to hurt me?'

'No.'

'I didn't think so,' she said, pleased. 'That's why I'm not scared.'

I flinched when Sahi took my hand then held up her own palms, the silver markings of a crescent moon visible on each.

'The sun and moon…' she said wistfully. 'Does it hurt when your flames appear?'

I shook my head.

'And you don't feel hot all the time?'

I laughed again. 'Doesn't everyone feel hot all the time in the desert?'

She laughed too. 'Good point.'

'What's it like seeing other people's thoughts?' I asked tentatively.

'What I can do is a bit different from seeing someone's thoughts. I see the truth in people, but it takes a lot of energy and I only see it if someone's hiding something.'

A tingle ran up the back of my neck. 'That must be strange.'

'A little.'

'Can anyone else here do the same as you?'

'Not that I know of. Mistress Salma has said my power is quite rare. All magic is now though.'

I didn't know at the time how magic had dwindled. All I knew was that I had an ability and my mother had wanted me to keep it hidden.

'*Yours is too,*' Sahi told me. '*Not many people can create an element of nature.*'

'*Really?*'

She nodded. 'I've only ever read about flame-wielders.'

I'd felt special in that moment, blissfully unaware of the responsibility that would come from such a power.

'Flame-wielder...' I say to myself. *It sounds better than executioner.*

NINE

The next week and a half passes in a blur of rehearsals, training and costume fittings. Now, with only one week left until the loornas, and the arrival of Queen Sana and her royal courtiers nigh, everyone has exhausted themselves in their attempts to perfect their routines. Mealtimes are quiet as we seek out whatever energy we can get into our bodies before the next class and sleep comes fast when it's finally lights out.

I follow the rest of the elite dancers outside for an afternoon of combat training with Sajid followed by archery with Tahir. The same dusky hue paints the sky as it has done for over a week, but today it's more intense. The sun is a faded blemish behind the gauze of sand and there's a shift in the air, a cool breeze swelling through the gardens.

I've never known a dust storm to last longer than a few hours, let alone a week or more, and it has others' attention too. Some of the guards stare beyond the gates, pointing in the direction the storm comes from. Tahir is with them and, when three horses are brought out by an attendant, he commands two of the guards to join him. The gates swing open and they gallop towards the horizon.

'What do you think that's about?' I ask Sahi.

'I don't know.'

We're all absorbed by the guards as more collect by the gates, but our view is soon obstructed as Sajid gestures for us to take our positions for class.

'Today we will begin by running through your drills,' he commands and a hush falls over us. 'These are the drills you will perform for Her Majesty at your graduation. You must execute them in unison and show you are a uniform faction of Amaar's army. Understood?'

'Yes, sir.'

'Collect your blades.'

We do as instructed, then quickly re-form our usual lines. Everyone bows to Sajid as one and I'm grateful to be partnered with Sahi today as I turn to her and bow again.

'Begin.'

Sajid holds back from calling out the different moves, their timings now ingrained in our bodies as we sweep our blades up and around, away from our opponent, then towards them in a choreographed sequence not too dissimilar from a dance.

Ever since Kaleb made his announcement that Queen Sana will hold auditions for the role of Queen's Guard, I've seen a fierce determination in Sahi. She's always been focused on the end goal and not easily distracted, but there's a new concentration in her features that I haven't seen before. I feel the force behind her blade as it meets mine, not to harm me, but to prove to herself that she can protect herself if the position she's trained for is taken away and she ends up on the front line.

I see the same commitment in all the dancers as the pressure of having Queen Sana in our audience pushes everyone to their limits. We may perform as an ensemble most of the time, but now everyone wants to shine as the soloist. Even me. Not so I can be chosen as a candidate for the Queen's Guard, but to prove to our queen that I'm not a threat. That I am worthy of her army. That the fire within me will protect her country, not destroy it.

The breeze picks up and the bells on my paayal respond as it brushes my legs. I glance at Sajid who's turned towards the gates while we continue the sequence, his hand poised on the hilt of the blade that's strung on his belt. The leaves on the trees whisper to each other with a low rustle, and the birds signal as they erupt from the branches and disappear behind the west side of the sanctuary.

One of the mistresses ushers her young students inside as the wind weaves sand through the grounds in intricate loops like it's riding a current. It almost looks unnatural. The sun's light is suddenly obscured and sand whips at our bare skin, ending our drills.

Sahi grabs my hand as the gates reopen and more guards ride out. Disorientated, their horses buck and try to turn back, but their riders push them on reluctantly. I clutch my blade, tempering my flames as we all move forward and try to see what's happening. But the wind is restless and works against us. Strands of my hair are pulled loose and I have to shield my face against the tiny grains that obscure my eyes, as it swirls into view.

The dust cloud.

It spins on the skyline, a mass of sand lifted up from the dunes and turning over itself.

Sahi's grip tightens.

'Inside. Now!' Sajid shouts.

We're all slow to follow his orders as we try to understand what's going on. We've weathered dust storms before, but even I can feel the unpredictable energy of this one.

'I said now!' Sajid booms and we don't hesitate any longer, all dropping our blades and running back towards the school.

'Do you think we're under attack?' Dana asks me.

'No.'

'What makes you so sure?'

When we reach the steps, I look back over my shoulder to where the dust cloud spins on the spot, as though caught in a web. 'If we were, they wouldn't be keeping us in here. They'd be sending us out there to fight.'

'Then why has a dust cloud alarmed them all?' Dana asks as a group of ten guards rush past us and spread throughout the gardens.

I turn to Sahi for the answer, but she has none.

'All students make their way to the dining hall!' a guard calls out.

Sahi pulls us through the crush of armour as more guards rally past. We have to force our way up the steps and panic rises in me as I'm pushed back to back with Dana and struggle to see beyond Sahi's hand in my own. Finally, we make it through the doors and into the main entrance, where a group of other dancers huddle to one side.

I spot Kaleb in the gardens just as the large double doors are closed and he disappears with the last slither of light. We're ushered into the dining hall where sand sticks to the large windows, casting the room in an apricot glow. Attendants light the lanterns, but they do little to mimic the usual mid-afternoon sunlight.

'Someone needs to tell us what's going on,' Dana says as we find a seat at the elites' table, a cacophony of confusion around us.

'It's just a sandstorm,' Duaa says. 'I don't understand why we've all been made to come in here rather than finish our class in one of the studios.'

The same question circles my mind when I notice even some of the mistresses look bemused as they ferry the younger students to their tables.

I place a hand on Sahi's when I see her picking at the already raw skin round her left thumbnail. 'I'm sure they'll give us some information soon.'

She exhales and nods, but her eyes dart to the guards who station themselves round the room.

'This is what happened in Ramuul before our village was attacked,' I hear Meera say to Farah and Jasmine, who are sitting beside her further down the table. 'The sky turned red in the middle of the day as though warning us of the blood that was about to be shed, and then they came…the Mezeeri soldiers… They killed everyone.'

She has our attention and an eerie silence descends over the rest of the elites as she speaks the words that most think and fear.

'The Mezeeris are here again – they must be.' Her voice shakes, but anger thrives in her piercing gaze. She turns to me and I sense the accusation before it hits. 'The war isn't coming. It's already here.'

TEN

Remnants of the sandstorm whisper on the horizon. For the last two days, all students have been instructed to stay inside the sanctuary, but my body yearns for the sun. I have to settle for doing my morning stretches in whatever pockets of sunlight I can find indoors as it rises, though the sun stays securely behind the veil of sand that coats the landscape and the sky is reluctant to shed its peach hue.

Kaleb called everyone to the theatre the night the dust cloud revealed itself and reassured us there was no threat from Mezeer, despite him sending Tahir and a band of guards to patrol the perimeter. Although Meera's words that war is already here still echo in my mind, most of the elites are now more concerned about whether Queen Sana will still be able to travel for the loornas as planned. We've continued to train as though she will and now, with only four days to go, the veil finally starts to lift and we're greeted by blue skies by mid-afternoon.

'There we are…' Mistress Zaina smiles up at the glass roof of the main studio as the sun reveals herself.

All the elite dancers have been gathered for a dress fitting with the elite seamstresses. The costumes for our ensemble dances and duets sit neatly on racks at the back of the studio, while our solo costumes are still to be finished. Intricately woven fabrics float round us as the seamstresses use their abilities to check the measurements of the patterns they've created and finalise the designs with Mistress, before our dress rehearsal in three days.

'Can you twirl for me?' Maya asks after adding a final pin to the hem of my dress.

The scarlet fabric she plans to use is lightweight and the skirt ripples as I turn.

'Perfect,' she says, pleased. 'I've already spoken to Mistress Zaina and we've settled on the details of your design.'

'Anything you can share with me now?' I ask eagerly.

Maya gives nothing away. 'You'll have to wait and see.'

'Thank you,' I say as she unpins my dress and collects up the fabric she's been sampling.

I look around at the mirage of colours the other dancers wear and how different the designs already are, a depiction of our unique powers. Each of our solos is a representation of our individuality, while our group performances showcase how our abilities work together. Our ensemble costumes glitter in the sunlight. We're all wearing the same design of ivory and gold, except for Sahi whose dress includes subtle swirling embellishments through the skirt and beading across the neckline, to mark her out as the lead soloist.

Sahi's been distant over the last two days, her conversation sparse between classes. I've put it down to our graduation as everyone's attention is solely on the ceremony. But I know

Sahi. She's always had an intense focus, but as the leader of our ensemble she would never normally separate herself from the group the way she has been doing. She's distracted by something.

As the seamstresses pack away, Sajid enters and speaks to Mistress Zaina. I can't hear their whispers, but I'm unsurprised when Mistress Zaina calls out Sahi's name.

'Kaleb would like to see you,' Mistress tells her.

This is their third meeting since the storm began, which isn't unusual as she is our lead and no doubt Kaleb is preparing her for the queen's imminent arrival. But it's the way Sahi comes back from each meeting looking more drained than she does when we finish a day's training that unsettles me.

'The rest of you, I encourage you to go outside and enjoy the fresh air before your next class, now the storm has passed,' Mistress tells us as Sahi follows Sajid out of the studio.

My body itches for the gardens, but I detour when I catch sight of Sahi and Sajid. While everyone else runs out through the main entrance, they head in the opposite direction towards Kaleb's quarters. Keeping my distance, I follow, shame creeping up the back of my neck for spying on my best friend. But she's acted so strangely since the sandstorm. So have Kaleb and Sajid, always keeping a watchful eye on the horizon. They might tell us there's no threat, but then why was Tahir sent out with a group of guards to patrol the sanctuary's perimeter? What if Meera was right? The war that's threatened is no longer a concept we train for. It's ready and waiting.

Voices drift down the corridor as Sahi and Sajid round the corner that leads to Kaleb's courtyard. I hold back behind a pillar for a few moments, then peer out when I hear them greet someone. Sunlight tickles the darkness at the end of the passage and I see Kaleb, his face grave as he talks to Sahi. She nods at whatever he says, but her posture is slumped, despite the years of training to stand straight with our shoulders back. Kaleb gestures to something I can't see and Tahir appears, his armour dulled by the desert's dust and his hair dishevelled.

Their voices are muffled and I desperately try to tune out all other noises to better hear them without creeping closer.

'It's what you thought?' I hear Sahi ask.

Kaleb nods.

Tahir glares at Kaleb and Sajid in a way I've never seen before, anger distorting his features. 'All this time... And you've even involved a student.' His hands turn to fists at his sides.

Reaching for his blade, Sajid steps towards him.

'Now, now.' Kaleb puts a hand between them and both men halt, locked in a battle of fierce glares.

Kaleb's reaction unsettles me when he smirks, as though enjoying the tension that simmers between his most senior guards. He places a hand on Tahir's shoulder, squeezing it.

Tahir shrugs him off. 'Who else knows about this?' he growls.

'This is between us,' Kaleb says calmly, a smile still playing at the corners of his mouth.

'Wrong. This is between you three.' Tahir points at them. 'I want no part in this.'

I back away into the darkness of an alcove as Tahir's footsteps head towards me and he marches past. I stay there, my heart thrumming in my chest. What did he find in the desert? I want to call after him, but my throat closes up when the heavy beat of Sajid's tread approaches and he too vanishes back down the passageway, his strides long to catch up with Tahir.

'Now is more important than ever before.'

I jump as Kaleb's voice rises, his tone darkening with each syllable.

'Don't let her out of your sight. Don't slip up,' he adds.

I realise then that I'm shaking, despite the heat and sweat that trickles beneath my kurta. Sahi doesn't respond but the bells on her paayal give her away as she approaches and walks past my hiding spot.

'Sahi,' Kaleb says sharply, the calmness he displayed before Sajid and Tahir frayed. 'Watch her.'

She stops suddenly. My breath falters as I press my back into the wall; if she were to turn round, there's no doubt she would see me. But Sahi doesn't look back.

'Haven't I always?'

ELEVEN

The main studio is empty but for the full moon's glow. It invites me in. The floor is cool underfoot and the soft light leaves the corners of the room in shadow. I seek out what the shadows hide and light every other lantern, each dotting the wall with a single flame.

I'm alone.

I should be with the others enjoying an evening meal, but my body and mind are too restless to sit and eat after the conversation I overheard this afternoon. The hum of the sanctuary filters through the open door as I walk the length of the studio: a chorus of attendants cleaning, mistresses calling the younger students to their dormitories, and guards handing over for the night shift. I step in time to the landscape of background noise, my body loosening with each step.

Without a thought, I sweep my arms up and spin, first to the right then the left. The dances we've rehearsed for our graduation are ingrained in me, but I push them to the back of my muscle memory and alleviate my body of the pressure that comes with a choreographed routine. There's no music, no counts in my head, no forethought about what comes next. I dance on instinct. Lost in the freedom of it, the tension in me is shed with each jump, kick and turn. Life at the sanctuary is all about precision and it feels good to abandon it for a moment.

But the tension quickly returns when I hear Kaleb's voice in my head. *'Watch her.'* Immediately, I knew who he meant. He didn't have to say my name. Why would Sahi need to watch me though? Have I fooled myself into thinking Sahi and Kaleb trust me in a way most others don't? Her response replays in my mind too. *'Haven't I always?'*

My movements grow more restless as I try to forget about the loornas at the end of this week. About who I'll meet. Our country lives with the repercussions of my mother's choices every day, but I can't keep trying to prove myself to everyone like I have been. The only person who needs to trust me is Queen Sana. I'll show her I'm not a threat, that I can protect her country as I've been trained to and won't be corrupted by the fire that breathes through me.

I stop abruptly mid-spin when a silhouette appears in the doorway.

'Sorry, I didn't mean to interrupt,' Sahi says. 'You missed your evening meal so I wanted to find you and check nothing was wrong.'

Check up on me, you mean. 'I'm not hungry, that's all,' I reply.

'Heard it was saag again?' she jokes as she enters. But it's forced, the strain she's carried since we found out there will be auditions to join the Queen's Guard still there. 'I've lost my appetite too.'

We're both quiet as shadows shift across the floor.

'You would tell me if there was something about the queen's visit and the sandstorm I should know, wouldn't you?'

She looks momentarily taken aback, then says, 'What do you mean?'

But I back out of the challenge. 'I don't know. Things feel a little unsettled at the moment, I guess.'

Her shoulders relax. 'I thought it was only me who felt like that. There's been so much excitement surrounding the queen's visit, and nerves, but I've realised that's not all that's making me anxious.' Her eyes glisten in the flicker of the lanterns. 'It's because I'm not ready.'

'You are ready,' I say. 'You've rehearsed more than anyone, and we've all rehearsed a lot—'

'No, you misunderstand me.' She joins me in the middle of the studio. 'I'm not ready for us all to go our separate ways and the possibility that *we* might not be together any more. Even if we're both conscripted into the army, we could end up at different camps.'

'You know you won't be joining the army.'

'Do I?'

I shrug. 'It won't happen, but if it ever did, tell Kaleb we come as a duo and we have to stay together.'

She laughs. 'You think I have that kind of sway with him?'

After today...maybe. 'If any of the dancers do, it's you. You're the lead soloist.'

'Lead soloist.' Sahi sighs and gazes up at the glass roof and the sky beyond. 'What does that even mean?'

'It means people look up to you.'

She shakes her head in disbelief.

'It's true! Even when we were the youngest students here, you were the one who encouraged us and comforted us when we missed our families. You helped us when the days were long and hard and our magic wouldn't manifest in the way the mistresses and Kaleb hoped.' Sahi blinks back her tears and something catches in my throat. '*I* look up to you. I always have.'

Her lower lip quivers. 'I don't think you realise how much you've helped *me* over the years.'

'That's what sisters do, isn't it? They protect each other.'

Sahi nods and wipes the tears from her cheeks. 'Look at us,' she says, laughing awkwardly.

I realise my cheeks are damp too and brush my own tears away.

'I don't suppose you'd like to rehearse our duet, seeing as we're here?' she asks.

'I'd love to.'

We both take our positions centre stage and, when Sahi counts us in like Mistress Zaina would, the music begins in my head. I turn to my left, then extend my right leg behind me, a mirror of Sahi as she does the same on my right. We're the sun and moon at twilight, greeting each other in that brief moment when the two stand guard over the world together.

But our spacing is wrong as we turn on one leg and inch round on the balls of our feet to face each other. Our fingers almost touch, a distance between us that neither of us can close. Sahi continues to count as we swap places, still mirroring one another as we move across the floor. When we come back together, we make sure our spacing is correct this time as

I leap and Sahi catches me: the sun dissolving into the moon. I bounce from her arms and the two of us perform the same sequence, finally in harmony again, before we find our final pose, bodies tilted away from each other.

'I think this is my favourite duet we've ever performed,' Sahi says as we catch our breath.

'Mine too.' Though something ebbs between us, as the ribbon that's bound us to each other since my first day here slackens.

'Hopefully, it won't be our last,' she says.

'Hopefully.'

We both know it will be though. We're on the cusp of everything we've trained for and, as our lives are about to change, I realise we've changed too, in our own ways. The sun and the moon, always a duet, but drifting further apart.

TWELVE

The glittering lights behind my closed lids disappear as I open my eyes. My dream drifts out of sight, the evening still ripe and the air cool in our dormitory. The sound of footsteps along with muffled voices outside the door draw me back into the waking world, but I can't make out what they're saying. The door opens, sending a shard of light creeping across the floor and up the wall.

The footsteps don't belong to a dancer. My heart beats fast when they stop beside my bed. Unable to see who stands over me as I'm lying with my face to the wall, the flames in me stir. It's like I can feel the air around the figure move as they lean towards me. I turn over, magic poised.

'Sajid.'

He doesn't flinch at how bright the sun emblems on my palms are. They dim slowly as the fire in me recedes.

'Kaleb has requested that you join him on an excursion,' he says in a low voice.

'Where?' I whisper.

'Meet us downstairs in the entrance hall,' he replies, ignoring my question.

As soon as he's gone, I quickly slip into the lightweight lehenga we wear when summoned for our desert assignments, unsure of what else to put on. In the darkness, I pull my hair back into a low bun and slick back the stray strands, before placing my dupatta over one shoulder. The rest of the elites, including Dana and Meera, are still sound asleep as I pass their beds and close the door quietly behind me. I resist the urge to knock on Sahi's door to see if she's also been summoned. I'll soon find out. Careful not to skid on the newly polished floors, I tiptoe down the stairs and along the corridors. Every surface gleams where the moonlight touches it after hours of the attendants' careful work in preparation for Queen Sana's arrival in two days.

'Dressed for the occasion,' Kaleb says when I reach the entrance hall.

A shiver runs up my spine, my instinct right. 'Is that why you've asked for me? For an assignment.'

'Come.' He gestures for me to follow him outside, but I don't move.

'What about the others?'

Irritation dances across Sajid's face, but Kaleb only smiles.

'What others?' Kaleb asks.

'Sahi, Dana, Meera…' I reply as though it's obvious. I've only ever been sent out on assignment as part of a group before.

'Only your ability is required at dawn.' He doesn't give me a chance to respond, disappearing down the steps where his horse awaits.

For once, I look to Sajid for an answer, but he only shakes his head in disapproval. Whether he objects to my question or Kaleb's decision to choose me for whatever task waits beyond these walls, I'm not sure.

'You will ride with Haniya,' Kaleb instructs.

I stare at the chestnut horse as the young guard leads it over. I've never ridden before. We dancers and musicians only ever walk when we venture into the desert.

'Hurry, we don't have long,' Kaleb says in a vexed tone I'm not used to.

I watch Ejaz, Camil and another guard, Fasha, as they swing up onto their horses' backs. Haniya helps me do the same, but I'm unsteady as her horse shifts beneath me.

'Her name is Nada,' Haniya says as she too mounts her and sits in front of me.

'Nada,' I repeat.

'I'll have control of the reins. All you have to do is hold on to me.'

I nod, but nerves pinch inside me at the thought of why I've been summoned for a solo assignment as Kaleb and Sajid ride down the path towards the gates, along with the other three guards. My grip tightens round Haniya as she nudges Nada with her heel. The horse obeys and stays close to the group as they gain speed and gallop out of the gates and into the desert. She's faster than I expected on the sand and I'm grateful for Haniya as she steers her over the dunes towards where the sun winks awake below the horizon.

The sky turns violet with a wreath of pink along the skyline. Eventually, small shapes break up the landscape in the distance as a village rises up out of the sand.

'Where are we?' I say just loud enough for Haniya to hear.

'Nazeem.'

Nazeem… Pinpricks chase each other across my skin.

'Where did you call home?' Sahi asked the first day we met at the sanctuary.

'The desert,' I replied shyly. 'We never stayed long in one village.'

'Well, now you can call the Leharanji your home.'

I see it now: the familiar silhouette of the last place my mother and I were together. So close to the sanctuary, yet when I was a child and Kaleb swept me away from here it had felt like days to reach my new home.

'Why are we here?' I ask, but I'm met by fierce silence.

The horses slow to a trot as three figures come into view at the edge of the village. Sajid puts up a hand and he and the guards stop while Kaleb rides on ahead to greet the trio: two women and a man. They're all dressed in plain black kurtas, but it's the tallest figure who catches my attention, her head and face mostly covered so only her eyes are visible.

Kaleb dismounts and bows to the group. I haven't thought about Nazeem since I left. It looks as I remember yet there's a stark difference: it's a ghost of itself, silent but for Kaleb's hushed voice. I don't need to walk into the village and peer inside the homes to know they're empty. The trees that used to be a vibrant green have lost all their leaves and the scent of spices simmering over a fire is a distant memory, replaced by something that turns my mouth sour.

'Aasira.'

Everyone looks at me when Kaleb says my name. I hesitate, but Haniya is quick to dismount Nada and helps me down. It takes a moment for me to feel grounded as my feet touch the sand, but I see the intensity in Kaleb's gaze as he waits for me. There's a rigidity to him that I'm not used to as I greet the group with a curtsy and search the little I can see of their expressions for any hint of who they are and why I've been brought here.

Their black kurtas and robes are plain, but from their posture I hazard they've journeyed from the palace ahead of Queen Sana to ensure all the necessary preparations are made before her arrival. Why they're here in Nazeem – why *I'm* back here – I can't fathom though. They don't introduce themselves and they already know my name from when Kaleb called me over, so I don't either. The way they watch me keenly, I'm almost certain they know who I am. Who my mother was.

'Follow me,' Kaleb says, but I hold back behind the group, only moving when Sajid prods me forward, both him and the guards close on my heels.

Iyad... Zora... Yara...

Their names drift back into my consciousness after all these years as we pass their deserted homes. We retrace the same steps my mother and I took when we first arrived in Nazeem. The eerie silence that's descended over the once bustling community echoes in my ears. Where is everyone?

Kaleb comes to an abrupt halt at the front and there are gasps from the trio. I step out of line to see what has them turning away in disgust and it's like someone has struck me in the stomach. A stuttered breath catches in my throat and I fight back the nausea. I hear their screams, their panic as they fled their homes, searching for their loved ones, looking for an escape. An escape they weren't granted.

Contorted bodies have been heaped in the centre of the village square. Their blood stains the ground, telling the story of what happened here. Throats cut, bones broken, skulls cracked. They're unrecognisable, their skin blood-sodden and chapped from the heat, grazed with sand where the desert has wrapped them in her embrace. I once knew all these people.

Tears sting my eyes and my voice is thick when I speak. 'Who did this?'

But I already know. Meera *was* right. The war is here.

'History is repeating itself throughout Amaar,' Kaleb says, echoing my thoughts, and the mood of our audience shifts to fear. 'Mezeeri soldiers have rampaged through this village, just as they have with others before now. But this time they chose to spare someone.'

There's a struggle behind us and I turn to see Sajid and Fasha drag a man by each arm. The man digs his heels into the sand, resisting their pull, but he's frail and fresh bruises bloom on his cheeks. Sajid and Fasha throw him down on to the ground in front of me. His face buried in the dirt, he coughs and tries to dislodge the damp grey hair that falls into his eyes. We watch him as he struggles and finally kneels up, his wrists tied with rope behind him.

'Aasira?' he croaks.

I step back, brows knitted together.

'Aasira.' A crooked smile spreads across his face, revealing a cut on his upper lip. 'You're alive.' He laughs but the sound is punched away by Sajid's fist.

The man spits blood at Sajid's feet and he's about to have another bruise added to the collection when Kaleb says, 'He is not your assignment, Sajid.'

So that's why I'm here. To kill this man. A man spared by the Mezeeri soldiers when they killed everyone else who called Nazeem home. The trio eye me as curiously as I watch the man.

'What is your name?' I ask the question Sahi always starts with, impatient to know who gave him *my* name.

Blood dribbles down his chin into his beard as his smile falters. 'Y-you…you know who I am.'

I shake my head. He isn't someone I met in the few weeks we stayed here before my mother was found. I would remember, like I remembered the others as we passed their homes.

'It's me,' he says and laughs again, but this time with disbelief. 'Omar.'

Omar… His name sticks in my mouth as I stare at him. 'I don't know you.'

'Of course you do—'

I stumble back as Ejaz and Camil run at Omar and pin him to the ground, smothering his words as they push his face into the sand.

'What is this?' I say to Kaleb. 'Why does he think I know him?'

Kaleb straightens under the gaze of the taller woman in our audience, who looks as interested as me in his answer. 'You don't know him,' he replies calmly. 'He was an acquaintance of your mother and knows of *you* by name only—'

'Why is he shocked I'm alive?' I cut in, mind racing. Every time I think of his name, a veil clouds my thoughts.

'After your mother's execution, those who knew her and knew that she had a daughter believed that daughter had been disposed of too.'

Disposed of… My flames flicker beneath my skin and I clench my fists to tame them, nails digging into the symbols that burn on my palms.

'This man is a traitor.' Kaleb projects his voice for us all to hear over Omar's muffled cries. He gestures over to the bodies.

'I've tried to protect you from your mother's legacy, Aasira, but in mere days you'll leave the shelter of the sanctuary and the time has come where I can no longer shield you from the truth or the consequences of Lina's lies.'

Sajid paces over to Omar. 'If you're accepted into the army, this is the scum you'll have to deal with. He's the reason these people are dead,' he says sharply. Ejaz and Camil release the traitor as Sajid grabs a fistful of Omar's hair, yanking him upright so he kneels again, his throat exposed as though awaiting the edge of a blade. 'He's been working for Mezeer, one of the spies your mother collected like fake gold in a souk, ferrying lies across our border and helping Mezeeri soldiers cross into our country where they've pillaged our villages.'

My body turns cold.

'But they were after something much greater this time,' Kaleb says. 'Had Tahir and our guards not stopped them...'

The sanctuary.

'Kill the students before they become soldiers,' Sajid finishes.

'Is that the story you've been spinning?' Omar says, voice quiet, but we all hear him. 'Don't listen to these men, Aasira. Your mother never wanted this.'

'Yet here we are, standing over dead bodies once again,' Kaleb replies coolly and a crease appears between his brows.

There's movement within the trio on our right as the shorter of the women steps forward, her pose like that of someone ready to intervene. I glance at her hands for any sign of a symbol on her palms or a shimmer of magic.

'Lina knew what she was doing,' Kaleb says and turns to me. 'Even after her death, her orchestra still plays. Your mother was and always will be an enemy of the state.'

'No,' Omar says, drawing my gaze back to him.

Kaleb ignores him. 'But you're not your mother, Aasira. You can right her wrongs and the wrongs of all those who followed her.'

Omar shakes his head. 'Don't listen to him.'

'You know what you must do, Aasira.'

'You don't have to do anything he tells you.'

'We have protected you and now you can protect us, your country and your queen, by ridding Amaar of this traitor,' Kaleb tells me.

'Please. You mustn't listen to what he says,' Omar pleads.

My heart beats like a dhol in my ears. Breathing shallow. Fire surging.

'Aasira—' But Omar is cut off, this time by Sajid's fist.

'You're a warrior of Amaar. That's how you want people to see you, isn't it, Aasira?' Kaleb's tone is so level, it's almost unnerving as tension crackles round us. 'Show us you're a warrior and not a traitor like this man.'

The four guards pull back on my left and I see the horror that creeps across Haniya's face as Sajid deals another blow.

Omar doesn't give in. 'I'm not a traitor, Aasira, and neither—'

Another punch.

'What are you waiting for?' Kaleb says, leaning closer to me.

'Killing me won't change anything!' Omar shouts.

Another punch.

I try to see clearly, but my mind is drowning as my eyes roam and I glimpse the bodies piled in the square.

Omar's focus is on me, his face already swollen when Sajid moves aside, blood staining his knuckles. 'I'm not what they say I am.'

A traitor. An enemy.

Neither am I.

Gold dust shimmers and flames flare round me before I even think of dancing. I can't contain them. Can't control everything that coils within me.

I see Sajid's sword glint as it reflects my flames. But this isn't his assignment.

Omar's gaze doesn't break from mine. He nods. Acceptance. *'Caliaan hereesi.'*

My magic sings through me and bursts across Omar's body. It's so quick, his yell swallowed by the flames that sweep over him. But they don't look like my flames. They're white. Pure white.

I stagger back, shaking as I stare at my hands. My flames retreat into my body while my golden shimmer fades into my palms, until all remnants of my magic have faded.

Stunned silence grips us all as the fire before us dissolves into the sand. It leaves no trace of the man it engulfed only moments ago. Not even a thread of smoke whispers in its place. Sajid still clutches his sword and, for the first time, he shows a glimmer of fear. Was his blade meant for me?

The only person who doesn't look like they've been caught in a trance is the taller woman in our audience. As she steps forward, the man she's with puts a hand out, but she disregards his caution and walks over to me. Slowly, she unravels the dupatta that covers her hair and face to reveal long dark curls underneath. The air between us tremors and I sink into a deep curtsy.

'So you are Lina's daughter. The one I am told is not a threat to my country.'

THIRTEEN

Sea green eyes unlike any I've ever seen before lock me in their gaze. Queen Sana. I should have realised that was why her face was covered, a disguise rather than an act of modesty. In her long black kurta, she could easily be mistaken for a woman from any of the villages or towns in Amaar, but her smooth brown features give her away as someone who's never experienced hard labour beneath the unforgiving desert sun.

'Your Majesty,' I manage to say.

But she's not interested in my deference. She looks from me to the spot where my flames consumed Omar's body. I'm surprised when she joins me and kneels where he knelt, then runs her hand over the sand, taking a handful before letting the grains fall through her fingers.

'You left no mark,' she says as the rising sun creeps through the pomegranate sky, illuminating the village square and the bodies heaped in its centre.

I don't know how to respond. This has never happened before. Usually, I would have to dance to create anything close to the flames that killed Omar. But they always gleam gold, not white, and, while they dissolve into the ground once they've done my bidding, they still leave behind a mark: remnants of the body, the ground singed, smoke…something.

'This is new,' Queen Sana says as she stands, reading the shock on my face. 'You do not know the extent of your own ability yet.'

She directs her stern gaze towards Kaleb as he joins us.

There's a wariness in his stance and I can't help but notice how he stands a few paces away. 'Aasira has been trained by Mistress Zaina—'

'It is not Mistress Zaina's training I doubt,' Queen Sana interjects.

Kaleb doesn't respond, the heat of his focus on me for choosing this moment to showcase the wild temperament of my magic.

For the last eight years I've studied how to control my magic and prove myself as a worthy warrior and protector of Amaar. But now, in front of the queen, I've displayed everything I've fought against: the threat that I could one day be overpowered by my ability. I don't understand how it happened, but for the briefest moment I lost my grip on the flames that live inside me. When they burst from my body, they were unrecognisable, like they were fuelled by a new force.

'Something has unlocked itself within you, Aasira, and you must learn to control it before it takes charge of you,' Queen Sana says seriously, as though reading my mind, and I catch a glimpse of the silver waves that decorate her palms. 'Elemental magic is of the rarest form. We must not take for granted its power.'

In the hazy light, her eyes shift from green to blue. She flicks her fingers, as though plucking the strings of a sitar, and an iridescent blue shimmer emerges across her hands. The sand at our feet darkens as water rises from deep beneath and, like veins, tiny streams split off from the pool she creates. They encircle us in their grasp, dark rivulets in the ground that spread throughout the village. All of us watch in awe and I'm reminded of the last traitor I executed – Hassan – and his criticism that the queen hasn't used her power as a water-weaver to relieve the desert of the drought. Perhaps now, after seeing for herself how the trees wither over the bodies of the dead, she will.

Kaleb and Sajid move aside as Queen Sana passes them, re-covering her head with her dupatta as she approaches the bodies. I daren't look at their faces in case I recognise them beneath the bloodstains: the villagers who took us in before the truth of my mother's crimes was revealed and everything fell apart.

Queen Sana wanders between them and stops at the body of a child. I watch as she presses a hand to the small head, eyes closed as she murmurs something under her breath. When she stands, she holds out her palms to the unseeing crowd and speaks in a language I don't recognise. Though I understand the meaning in her gesture: it's a blessing of safe passage.

'Kaleb, your guards will honour these people with the burial they deserve,' Queen Sana commands softly. 'Peace is the least we can offer.'

Kaleb nods and Sajid instructs the four guards, who begin their work without delay.

Queen Sana joins the pair who accompanied her and shakes her head in disagreement at whatever they say. They make no show of hiding what they're discussing, both staring at me. No doubt their task is to ensure the queen's safe journey to the sanctuary, yet here I am, a threat. An image flashes into my mind of Queen Sana's rivers drowning my flames, drowning me...

'What was that?' Kaleb says in a low voice behind me. 'Is this what you've been rehearsing with Mistress Zaina?'

'No,' I whisper. His eyes are wide when I turn to him and he pulls back. 'I don't know where those white flames came from.'

'They came from you,' he rebukes. 'If you display anything like that at the loornas... I won't be able to protect you again.'

I bite the inside of my cheeks to stop the tears that prick at the corners of my eyes. Kaleb's right. My flames just overpowered me in front of the very audience who will decide my future. Who will decide if a future is what I even deserve. But Omar's look of acceptance before I killed him is the thing that haunts me. Like a sacrifice, not an execution. And his words...I can't unhear them.

'Is that the story you've been spinning?'

I'm numb to the sun's warmth as I journey back to the sanctuary with Kaleb and Haniya, the queen in tow. I hold on to Haniya's sides as we canter over the sand, steadily growing more used to Nada's rhythm. Sajid stayed in Nazeem with Ejaz, Camil and Fasha to bury the villagers. The smell of death clings to my hair and clothes, a constant reminder I can't escape.

As the minarets come into view, a mirage in the glistening light, I see a string of people waiting for us among the dunes. When we reach Queen Sana's party, they bow their heads to their queen as she takes her place at the front of the group. There are eight guards dressed in different colours depending on their rank, and the man riding beside Queen Sana joins them. Two attendants follow behind, while the woman who stays close to the queen must be an advisor. Usually, several courtiers would attend the loornas, but I suppose they're not needed this year when the queen herself will be choosing her newest recruit. I recognise the three women who are quick to flank Queen Sana – Imani, Maryam and Fatima – all of them recent graduates from the sanctuary who are now members of her guard.

We don't linger. Kaleb gestures to Haniya to follow him and we gallop back to the sanctuary ahead of the queen and her cohort. Although I cling even tighter to Haniya, my body lurches wildly and I'm grateful when the gates open and we're within the confines of the gardens again. I dismount Nada and am on my way indoors when Kaleb stops me.

'Where are you going?' His critical tone bites at me.

'I thought I should change,' I say weakly, my heart pounding inside my chest.

'There isn't time.'

His eyes narrow towards the school's main entrance where a chorus of excited laughter pours down the steps. Students file outside and the mistresses gather everyone along the path that runs through the garden, from the school to the gates.

'It won't happen again, Kaleb,' I say as he turns to join the mistresses. 'I'm sorry.'

He pauses, slow to turn to me. When he does, there's a flicker of the Kaleb I recognise in the tilt of his smile, but then his jaw tenses. 'No, it won't.'

Disapproval settles in the creases in his forehead. Another apology rises in me, but it's lost as more students flock along the path and Kaleb greets them, making his way towards where Mistress Zaina stands, at the bottom of the steps.

'There you are!' Dana takes my arm, pulling me in the same direction as Kaleb to where the elite students are gathered. 'You weren't in bed when we were all woken. Where have you been?' she says excitedly. 'Queen Sana's on her way. She'll be here at any moment.'

'I know.'

But Dana doesn't hear me as she finally notices. 'Wait, why are you dressed in that lehenga?'

I don't have a chance to respond as we're ushered into line among the rest of the elite dancers. Meera shoots me a glare and I hear the surge of whispers as I take my place beside Sahi. My head aches as images of Omar and the bodies of the villagers churn over and over in my mind. I take a deep breath to calm the furnace within me.

I flinch when someone grabs my hand. Sahi. She doesn't have to use her ability to see that something is wrong or to work out I've been on an assignment. The guards and attendants take their positions behind the students, the youngest at the furthest end by the gates, while the mistresses are laced between each year group. A hush falls over the garden as our visitors approach.

Queen Sana leads the procession, now dressed in a shimmering emerald lehenga. Flecks of gold embellish the floral-embroidered skirt and bodice and, no longer wearing her dupatta, her hair cascades in waves down to her waist with an elegance uncommon for someone who's travelled through the desert for several days.

There's a ripple of curtsies and bows as Queen Sana passes her audience. It's easy to see the dancer in her posture, with her long neck and straight back, her hands clasped in front of her. She smiles at the students as she passes and there's a hint of humour in her eyes when the youngest whisper and giggle among themselves, only to be hushed swiftly by the mistresses. I lower into a curtsy alongside the rest of the elites when she reaches us.

'Mistress Zaina,' she says and they clasp each other's hands.

'Your Majesty,' Mistress replies fondly. 'How lovely it is to see you in these grounds again.'

'It's been too long.' Queen Sana's gaze swerves to me and I dip my eyeline. 'We have lots to discuss.'

I only look up again once I hear her walk up the steps, the train of her skirt trailing behind like a waterfall over the white marble.

'May peace rise with every dawn,' she says, turning to face us.

There's a further series of bows and curtsies before we reply, 'And endure with every dusk.'

'I'm so pleased to be here for the loornas. A new era lies ahead for Amaar and you will all play a part in shaping its future,' she says, commanding everyone's attention with a magic of her own.

'We may be faced with ghosts from our past, but together we can stand united against our enemy and bring new life to our land. Whether you join our army or help Amaar flourish with your unique abilities, let the upcoming days be a reminder of our strength when we work together.'

There's silence as we drink in her words, until it's broken by a single clap. Others join in and applause erupts through the grounds. Queen Sana smiles again and I'm briefly comforted by her words.

'Perform and demonstrate your skills with passion,' Queen Sana says directly to us elites. 'Honour your country. Honour your queen.'

Kaleb leads the final round of applause as Queen Sana bows her head to us and glides inside, followed by her party. He leans towards Mistress Zaina, continuing to clap as they speak, and she glances briefly at me. I try to read Mistress's expression as he tells her about Nazeem, but Sahi claims my attention.

'Do you want to talk about what happened?'

'I…' But something about the way she posed the question stops me. 'Not right now.'

She smiles to disguise her fleeting frown. 'I'm here if you change your mind.'

I nod and attempt a smile too.

Fatigue weighs heavy on me and settles deep in my muscles. I don't have the words for what happened this morning. The villagers died because of my mother's lies, lies that still drive King Faisal's intent to bring down our queen and take our country for himself. And had Tahir and our guards not stopped them, the Mezeeri soldiers who raided Nazeem would have gone on to attack us at the sanctuary. Is that why everyone was on edge about the sandstorm? Was it Mezeer?

'Is that the story you've been spinning?'

Omar's protests of innocence were so convincing, for a moment I believed we had known each other once. I can't escape his words or the image of him nodding before all trace of him was erased in a way I didn't know was possible. The energy that wove through me was unlike anything I've ever experienced. Is that what my mother felt before her power consumed her and she turned it against her own people?

'Something has unlocked itself within you, Aasira.'

Queen Sana was right. It's as if I can feel beyond the boundary of my body and the world around me is crisp and glows in colours I hadn't noticed until now. Like a part of me that's lain dormant has been awoken.

FOURTEEN

The breeze plays with my loose hair as I walk through the gardens. I'm grateful to wear it down after it was scraped back into a low bun for our ensemble performance this evening, which marked the beginning of the loornas. It's to be followed by a formal dinner that most of the other students are still getting ready for.

I couldn't stay in the dormitory any longer, the air close and stifling. Everyone's turned giddy after performing our first piece while some claim they've forgotten their solo or the order of the programme, but we all know it's just last-minute nerves. Our dance was a success, as were the ensemble performances from the other final-year students, including the musicians, who showcased their talents while performing with us.

Other than in our final rehearsals and training, I've kept mostly to myself since returning from Nazeem with the queen two days ago. Kaleb has been busy entertaining our guests, but Queen Sana has made her presence known, along with the members of her guard. While the queen has scrutinised our training, her advisor who joined us in Nazeem – Heba – has examined our theory by joining our classes and questioning us about the meaning behind each dance we perform.

Sahi has asked me several times since the other morning if I want to talk to her about what happened, but instinct tells me she knows all the details from Dana, who heard everything from Haniya. Ever since I overheard Kaleb tell her to watch me, I've felt Sahi's presence like a shadow, never straying far. I even caught her peeking through the door to the main studio when I was rehearsing my solo with Mistress Zaina. I keep replaying our conversation as I try to piece together what Mistress told me…and everything Sahi might have overheard.

'Kaleb told me about what happened in Nazeem,' Mistress Zaina had said after dismissing the musicians.

I hadn't wanted to bring it up although I knew Kaleb had spoken to her after we returned. 'He's angry with me.'

'Concerned, not angry.'

'That doesn't make it any better,' I said and Mistress smiled. I hesitated, unsure of whether to say anything else. 'I've never felt like that before,' I finally admitted. 'I didn't have to dance to strengthen my flames and yet they felt more powerful than anything I've ever experienced before.'

Mistress nodded slowly.

'It was like…the more confused I was, the more that ignited my flames. I wasn't focused like I am when I dance. I *couldn't* focus with Omar trying to convince me of his innocence. Even though I knew what I had to do, I also knew I had to hear what he said. Omar…he needed me to hear him.'

I couldn't read her expression. Eventually, Mistress said, 'But in the end you fulfilled your duty.'

'Yes. But what if people have been right all this time and there's a part of me I can't control? A part that makes me a threat.'

'Do you believe that could be true?' Mistress asked, eyebrows raised.

I shrugged. 'It happened to my mother.'

A frown creased her face. 'You control your flames, Aasira. They've been with you your whole life, but that doesn't mean you know the full extent of their capability just yet. What you experienced in Nazeem wasn't something I could ever have taught you in your short time here. It was a part of your power buried deeper than I can help any student access. Indeed, it was a part most will never discover within themselves, for it's rooted in a deeper layer of our consciousness. A part that is in tune with your emotions and chose to emerge in that moment of confusion. But *you* –' she pointed at me to emphasise the word – 'are still the conductor in this relationship.'

And that's when I saw Sahi as she swiftly turned and disappeared from sight. Had she heard the whole conversation?

But, between the times she's followed me over the last two days, she's taken any opportunity she can to rehearse her own dances and combat drills, just like the other elites. When the loornas end in two days, we'll no longer be students of the Leharanji. Some of us will be sent to the palace or the homes of prestigious citizens where we can provide an abundance of clothes or music or food for their galas and feasts. Most of us dancers will be moved to one of the training camps across the country, while a select few will have the opportunity to audition for the role Sahi has always dreamed of. A role she will no doubt still be awarded.

As I skirt round the edges of the gardens, I spot Queen Sana by the fountain in the centre of the main lawn, cast in moonlight. Unusually, she's on her own. Her Queen's Guard are in conversation with the sanctuary guards, who all stand to attention. But I see from the way their eyes shift in the queen's direction that they're as taken by her elegance as I am.

She wears a contemplative look and her gold chooriyan trill as she walks round the white marble structure, her sapphire skirt trailing on the ground behind her. Her hair is pulled back into an intricate low bun where jewels glitter, and the sleeves of her lehenga billow like a wave. She pauses, fingers dancing at her side, and I stop still as the free-flowing water in the fountain is cast under her spell too.

The water in the basin defies gravity and rises like reverse rainfall to create a curtain round the fountain, collecting with it the water that trickled down the stone into the basin moments ago. I watch in awe as, with a simple hand movement, Queen Sana weaves the water into a single stream that tumbles through the air, brushing the seat round the fountain before arcing up and over the spout where she releases it. The water cascades down with a whoosh and flows again with a new vigour, energised by her power.

The sanctuary guards who stand nearest the queen dip their heads with respect and clap softly, at which Queen Sana smiles. But her performance wasn't for them.

Our eyes lock and I see the meaning behind her display: my flames are no match for a water-weaver of her ability. I'm first to break eye contact, unsettled by the warning that emanates from her like a current. But I can't help admiring the way she controlled the fountain as she leaves the gardens and enters the school. The queen's power has opportunities to bring new life, to heal the drought, where mine ends it. Omar... Hassan... The enemies who came before them over the last year...they're all still with me. Ghosts of the desert.

The sound of low voices breaks into my thoughts and I follow them towards a secluded corner of the gardens.

'I can't stop thinking about it.'

'About what?'

'What he said.'

I stop in my tracks and realise it's Camil and Ejaz, two of the guards who were with me in Nazeem. Ejaz leans against the wall that surrounds the sanctuary and picks the petals from a large red rose. They float to the ground, a scattered crimson carpet, where they're crushed by Camil as he paces back and forth. I tuck myself in behind the flowering bush Ejaz must have picked it from, careful of the thorns along the rose stems.

'Do you think he was telling the truth and Aasira's mother wasn't actually a traitor?' Camil says. He stops in front of Ejaz, demanding his full attention.

'I don't know. Aasira still killed him,' Ejaz says almost flippantly.

And I did, despite the way Omar defended my mother. But that's what traitors do, so caught up in their own version of what's right that they don't see the hurt they've caused.

'On Kaleb's orders,' Camil scoffs. 'I wouldn't have known what to do if that were me.'

'Sajid said that man was the reason all the villagers were dead.' Ejaz shudders. 'He was a traitor and worked with Aasira's mother. He had to die for his crimes, just like she did.'

A renewed restlessness grasps Camil and he paces again. 'But that's my point. The man said Lina *wasn't* a traitor. What if we've got it all wrong and Queen Sana really did interfere with Mezeer's waterways?'

'You don't believe that.' Ejaz discards the stem of his beheaded rose. 'Not after hearing *one* person come to that traitor's defence?'

Camil sighs. 'I don't know what to believe.'

'But surely you do to make such accusations,' a voice drawls. 'Do enlighten us.'

Both men jump to attention and I bury myself deeper among the brambles as, out of the darkness, a woman appears. I recognise her immediately. Imani: one of the Queen's Guard. It was her role of executioner that I took over when she graduated from the sanctuary last year.

'I can't hear you,' she taunts, her features fierce as she closes in on the two guards.

They pull back, but have nowhere to go with the wall behind them.

'I w-wasn't accusing a-anyone,' Camil stammers.

'That's not what it sounded like,' Imani says as she stops in front of them. 'It sounded like you were questioning your queen.'

'No! Of course I wasn't. Was I, Ejaz?' Camil says desperately.

'He really wasn't questioning—'

'How lovely of you to come to his defence,' says Imani mockingly. 'But I know what I heard.'

'Please, Imani,' Camil begs, 'I meant no harm by it.'

'How am I to be sure of that?' The raw playfulness in her tone sends a shiver through me. 'And *don't* use my name as though we're friends.'

'Please, I didn't mean—'

Camil's words trail off into a slow gurgle. I clamp my hand over my mouth to stop the cry that threatens to escape me as, without so much as touching him, Imani's hands shimmer black as she crushes his throat with her mind. His whole body stiffens and blood trickles from his nose and ears until, finally, he collapses to the ground, his stare blank and mouth frozen in a grimace.

My body is tense as I try not to let the jingle of my jewellery give me away.

'Do you have anything to add?' Imani turns to Ejaz, who's completely rigid as he stares down at his dead friend.

'N-no,' he barely whispers.

Imani steps back from her kill. 'Sahi!' she calls out.

My stomach flips. She must have seen me and mistaken me for Sahi. I'm about to step out of my hiding place and plead innocence when Sahi appears out of the shadows.

'Do what you have to,' Imani commands.

'Please, don't,' Ejaz implores. 'I don't even know what Camil was talking about.'

'Sahi,' Imani says again.

Hesitation in each step, Sahi walks over to Ejaz. 'I'm not going to hurt you.'

Of course, he doesn't believe her and turns to run.

'Stop, unless you want to meet the same fate as your friend.' Imani threatens him through gritted teeth.

Ejaz does as he's told, his tears the only thing that can escape.

Sahi stands in front of him and places her right hand on the back of his neck. It looks so intimate that if anyone were to see them they would be scolded for inappropriate behaviour. I can't make out the words she mutters under her breath, but Ejaz's shoulders relax and his eyes glaze over with the milky tint of her magic. She stays like that for a few heartbeats, repeating the same phrase over and over. When she finally releases her hand from his neck, Ejaz blinks as though he's just woken up.

'What is your name?' she asks him.

'Ejaz.'

'And who is this man?' Sahi gestures to Camil.

'He's…' Ejaz's brows knit together as he stares at the lifeless body of his friend. 'I don't know,' he says eventually.

How? How can you not know? I want to shout.

Imani smiles. 'You found him like this,' she says. 'An intruder wearing our armour. Dispose of him and make sure no one sees you. Understood?'

Ejaz senses the threat even though he doesn't remember what just happened. But how can he not remember? What did Sahi do to him? He manoeuvres Camil over his shoulder and Camil's limbs dangle like broken branches on a tree. How could Sahi have let that happen? How could *I* have let that happen?

'I'm impressed,' Imani says once Ejaz is out of earshot. 'Your magic has come on a long way.'

'You didn't have to kill him,' Sahi says, her voice a monotone.

'And what would you have had me do instead?' Imani challenges.

'You didn't have to do anything. I could have—'

'You need to save your energy, Sahi. From what I hear, you're engaged in a far more important task.'

'Isn't that the sort of gossip that just got Camil killed?'

Imani laughs. 'And you're more feisty now too.' At that, she strides off in the same direction as Ejaz.

Sahi stares at the ground where Camil was just slumped. He was one of our guards. Not a traitor like the people I'm assigned to kill, nor an intruder. And yet he's dead, assassinated by one of the Queen's Guards: a student we all used to look up to. His execution hadn't been ordered, so why did Imani take it into her hands to mete out justice?

In my mind, I run at Sahi and scream. Scream at her to explain what just happened. She may not have killed Camil, but I need to know what she did to Ejaz to make him forget his friend. Anger and confusion swell inside me like a wildfire. I have to fight every tingling nerve in my body to tame it, for fear the white flames will overcome me again. My hands tremor and my chooriyan clink together. Sahi looks directly at my hiding place, eyes wide.

I hold my breath, hoping my jewellery doesn't glimmer in the moonlight and give me away. We stay like that for a long moment and I'm sure she must see me among the shadows of the rose bush. But finally she looks away and puts a hand to her chest, as though the reality of what happened has only just dawned on her.

I watch as she leaves with one final glance at where Camil lay. But I can't move, not yet, as the fire in me smoulders.

FIFTEEN

The stage is set and the theatre cast in darkness as we take our places and wait for the first chords to breach the silence. Mirrors of each other, Sahi and I begin our duet. We face the back of the stage and, as the music ebbs, we pivot on one leg towards our audience then each other. The dimmed stage lights slowly brighten and the mauve powder that covers the stage swirls round us as we dance, mimicking a twilit sky.

Dancing with Sahi always used to feel so natural. We could close our eyes and each still know exactly where the other was. While offstage I can feel an ever greater distance growing between us, the choreography demands we stay together. But my mind whirrs back to what I saw last night, pulling my focus away from our dance, and I have to concentrate to stay on the beat. We break from our mirror image. I scoop down to pick up a long scarf, the colour of saffron, trailing it behind me as I leap and depict the rising sun. Sahi's movements sink lower to the ground where the mauve powder that coats the stage streaks her pearlescent dress: a daughter of the moon.

The music swells and we dance across the stage in unison again, criss-crossing in front of each other before Sahi catches me in her arms, the sun and moon dancing as one. I jump from her arms and we spin away from each other, fast at first then slower until we take up our last pose on either end of the stage. The final notes of the violin linger and the theatre falls silent, before thunderous applause erupts.

We both stand to take our bows, curtsying first to our audience then Queen Sana, who sits in the royal box with Heba at her side, followed by Mistress Zaina and Kaleb. We finish by thanking our orchestra, clapping them before curtsying once more. The applause follows us as we run gracefully into the wings.

'I can't believe we won't dance that duet again,' Sahi says as she catches her breath. A smile lights up her face. 'After all the rehearsals, it goes far too quickly once you're up onstage.'

I nod, but can't smile as she does. How can she speak so lightly after what she did? For me, there's none of the adrenaline I usually feel after a performance.

'What's wrong?' Sahi asks when I don't say anything.

My heart races, faster even than when we were dancing. 'I saw you last night…with Imani.' I keep my voice low as the stage lights dim and Zahra takes her place for the first of the solos. 'I saw her kill Camil… What you did to Ejaz. How you made him forget the murder he'd just witnessed. How you made him forget his friend.'

'That wasn't what happened—'

'Don't deny it, Sahi. I know what I saw.'

A couple of the dancers waiting to perform glare at us to be silent. Sahi grabs my hand and pulls me through the backstage door into the empty corridor.

'No, you don't,' she says when we're alone.

'You made him forget,' I insist, breaking away. 'You stood by and watched Imani kill Camil. Then you made Ejaz forget everything.'

'That's impossible.'

'Then explain to me what I witnessed.'

'A trial,' she spits, anger reddening her cheeks. 'A display of my power for the queen, just like the one you undertook in Nazeem.'

So she does know what was asked of me.

'Everything we do in the queen's presence is an audition,' she says. 'Last night was just one of many.'

A trial... At no other point in the loornas do the dancers showcase their magic for what it is: a weapon. I should have known this would be demanded of us.

I see again how my flames wrapped round Omar.

'That doesn't explain why Imani killed a man who did nothing but question what he'd heard,' I say. 'Or why Ejaz forgot who his friend was.'

'You've confused what you saw.' She tries to take my hand again, but I pull away, bumping into the wall behind me.

'No,' I say and even I'm rattled by how quickly I reacted. 'I haven't confused anything.'

Hurt wells in her eyes, her hand still outstretched. 'Aasira...' She breathes in deeply and I have to look away to stop my own tears when hers start to fall. 'It's not what you think.'

'Then explain to me what I saw.'

'I've told you: it was a trial. All of us have been given one since Queen Sana arrived. You would know that if you hadn't found every possible opportunity you could to avoid me.'

'That doesn't answer my question.'

I can see her fighting me internally from the way her shoulders stiffen.

'How did you make Ejaz forget?' I ask firmly.

'I didn't.'

I roll my eyes, frustration itching beneath my skin. 'Sahi.'

'I don't know what you want me to tell you.'

'The truth!' I exclaim. 'You're lying to me and I don't know why. What are you hiding?'

'Nothing, Aasira. You have to trust me.'

But I don't trust her. Not after what I saw last night or heard when Kaleb told her to watch me. She's my best friend yet I can't help but question all of it, right from the start. Were we ever really close or was it just that she always kept me close?

The backstage door swings open and an attendant appears. 'What are you doing here? You need to get ready for your solos,' she says and hurries us down the corridor to the dressing rooms.

Our silence is made up for by the bustling energy in the room as the rest of the dancers prepare for their solos, keeping warm with various stretches and quickly changing into their costumes.

Maya already has my dress draped over her arms and helps me change. She then applies a fresh layer of surma to my eyes and unpins my hair so it flows loose down my back, while the front is neatly plaited so as not to fall in my face while I dance. One by one, each elite dancer is called to the stage to perform and the dressing room empties out.

'You look stunning,' Maya says when I turn to the mirror and take in my full costume.

My skirt is layered with crimson and gold, and bleeds into a delicate ivory bodice that will glitter under the stage lights.

'Only because of your hard work. Thank you,' I say and hug her. 'I'm sure Queen Sana will want to employ you and your needlework expertise at the palace.'

Her eyes shine. 'We'll find out soon enough.'

'Dana!' an attendant calls through the door. 'Three more dances, then it's your solo.'

Dana smiles widely. 'Time to charm them with my serpents,' she says excitedly, her olive dress shimmering with an embroidered serpent that wraps round one of her sheer sleeves and down the bodice.

'Don't forget your routine,' Meera says, eyelids sparkling with a silver glitter.

Dana laughs. 'The same to you.'

I smile as she leaves, but I can feel it's half-hearted, my mind still racing after what just happened with Sahi.

'You two look more nervous than I would've expected,' Meera says when only me, her and Sahi are left in the dressing room, along with our seamstresses.

Sahi and I glance at each other, but neither of us speak.

'Or are you still seething after the argument you just had?' Meera adds while studying her dark nails. She smiles when we both stare at her and the heat in my cheeks rises. 'Don't tell me that the competition for Queen's Guard has finally come between your lovely little friendship,' she says sarcastically and I feel Sahi eye me awkwardly.

If Meera had heard my accusations, she'd say so. She's never been one to be coy.

'Well, I hate to burst your lead-soloist bubble,' she says directly to Sahi, 'but you two aren't the only ones in the running.'

Looking pleased with herself, Meera leaves before either of us can reply and relief washes over me that she didn't overhear our full conversation. But I'm still embarrassed that we might have been heard at all.

If only the role of Queen's Guard were the reason things have become so strained between Sahi and me. Now more than ever the position is beyond my reach, and besides, it's not a role I was hoping for. I've always known Queen Sana would never want me anywhere near her or the palace after the way my mother betrayed her. And, after seeing how I lost control of my magic the other morning, I can't even be sure she'll want me in her army.

'We should get you to the wings,' Maya says.

I smooth my skirt, stalling as I search for something to say to Sahi. But I don't have the words. I know she's holding something back from me and I only wish I had her ability so I could see what it is. Glancing over my shoulder, I take in the beautiful outfit she's wearing: midnight black velvet adorned with the silhouette of a crescent moon. She picks at her thumbnail while her hair is finished, and I can sense her avoiding my reflection in the mirror. Maya holds the door open and eventually I give in and leave.

Meera runs onto the stage for her solo just as we reach the wings. I watch as she elegantly leaps in time with the sitar. Her magic shimmers round her body, like a web catching flies in her dream-net. Our solos are an opportunity to display the subtle shimmer of our magic, but we're forbidden from using our abilities on the audience. I guess that's what the trials are for...

I peer through a gap in the curtain and see Mistress Zaina counting with the music. Kaleb sits to her left, a stern expression on his face as he watches the back of Queen Sana's head rather than the stage. I can't read her expression, but, as Meera reminded us, any one of the dancers could be chosen to audition at the palace for the Queen's Guard.

Before I know it, applause fills the theatre and Meera runs off the stage. 'Don't fall...' She brushes my shoulder and sniggers.

I don't rise to it. My focus right now has to be my dance. I have to put everything else to the back of my mind if I'm to perform well and show the queen I can be a faithful warrior of Amaar.

The lights dim and, with a deep breath, I take my place in the wings. The music branches out from below, tendrils of notes that ignite a spark inside me. Mistress Zaina's voice is in my head as she counts the beats with me and I wait for the fateful note of the flute before entering the stage. I resist the urge to look at the queen to see if she recognises the music my mother danced to when she performed her own solo at their graduation. I have to trust that Mistress's choice of music wasn't a mistake.

As the music grows and fills the theatre, my magic comes to the surface like I rehearsed with Mistress. It starts in my palms, a light touch of gold that whirls with each of my movements, then weaves like vines up my arms and round my body until I glow with a halo of golden light.

My dance expands and my skirt billows round me, the red and gold layers reminiscent of a fire that burns bright in the night. I'm lost in the melody, every part of me entwined with the notes and beauty of Amina's voice. I try to push it down but, as the music holds me in its grasp, everything from the past week comes to the surface.

The sandstorm... The dead villagers... Camil... Sahi...

My flames kindle along my skin, familiar and calm, unlike the way they wanted to burst from me in Nazeem. I hear Mistress. *'You are still the conductor in this relationship.'*

I slowly let go. More flames awaken along my arms and flicker a bright orange, but I don't let them spread as I turn, reining them in, close beneath the surface so they merely mingle with the gold shimmer that still emanates from my body. That same feeling, like my body is invigorated in a way beyond what I'm used to, engulfs me. Each note grows sharper and, as I turn, I make out each and every audience member, despite the darkness.

I don't want to let go of this feeling – every part of me in tune with what's around me and heightened in a way I've never experienced – but as my dance finishes the flames dissolve back into my body, no mark left but for the memory. I hold my last position as Mistress instructed and wait for the applause, but it doesn't come. There's only me and the stage spotlights as the sun beams through the window at the back of the theatre.

Self-conscious in the silence, I curtsy to Queen Sana, the rest of my audience and the musicians, then to the queen again. As I do, the clarity of my vision fades as the heat of my flames disappears further inside me. I curtsy again and look at the queen for an acknowledgement of what I just showed her; that I am in control of my power. Finally, applause chimes and I see Mistress Zaina stand, smiling broadly. I feel a little delirious as others join in and the weight of my past and future is lifted momentarily. With one last curtsy, I run swiftly into the wings and tears mist my eyes.

I may have danced to my mother's song, but that was my performance. It was me.

SIXTEEN

Today, on the third and final day of the loornas, I'm a member of the audience except for our final ensemble piece that we'll dance this evening, to close the ceremony. I flex my feet to release the tension in my calves as we watch the rest of the final-year students perform for the queen, their skills at the beating heart of Amaar's society.

My body is grateful for the respite after yesterday's performances, which were a show of endurance if nothing else. Once all the solos had been performed, we quickly changed into our matching kurtas to present our combat drills and archery skills, then finished the day with our second ensemble performance. Queen Sana gave nothing away as she watched, but she must have an idea by now of those she wants to audition for her guard and those who she'll send to defend the eastern border.

Sahi and I haven't spoken since our argument. We were seated next to each other at last night's meal and even though everyone else was too absorbed to notice the unfamiliar rigidness between us, I couldn't ignore it. I even hung back when we were entering the theatre this morning to make sure several girls would be seated between us.

This isn't how things are supposed to be, not when we're about to graduate. But I can't unsee what happened the other evening. Sahi's broken the trust between us. When I glance down the row, her focus is solely on the stage.

'This is the theatre,' Sahi said as we reached a set of large gold doors. With her back pressed against one of them, she put her whole weight behind it to open it.

Sunlight flooded the room. I followed her inside, head upturned to drink it all in. Row upon row of velvet chairs cascaded down towards the stage, where heavy, mahogany-coloured curtains were pulled back to reveal a desert scene. Instruments decorated the orchestra pit.

'It's the largest room here.' Sahi skipped over to the front row and leaned against one of the chairs.

I ran my fingers over the soft fabric as I joined her and could almost feel the memories within them, the many performances they'd witnessed.

'We don't use the theatre much, unless there are announcements or the older students are performing for their graduation. But sometimes we put on shows throughout the year and we younger students get a chance to dance on the stage too,' she said proudly.

After years of camping in the desert, I couldn't quite take it all in. The whole Leharanji looked like a palace, each corner more ornate than the last as Sahi whisked me round from studio to studio, then on to the common areas, where girls stared at us as we entered and whispered to each other. She introduced me to everyone, calling out their names in a list I knew I wouldn't remember and hoped I wasn't about to be tested on. After retracing our steps down the curved marble stairs, I was glad when Sahi led me out to the gardens. The air was warm yet fresh, fragranced by the roses and jasmine flowers that punctuated the greenery.

'Let me show you my favourite place.' Sahi took my hand and pulled me across the lawn in between groups of older students practising their skills. 'It's always quiet in here,' she said and pushed the iron gate to reveal the walled garden.

I could see why she liked it, with the birds hopping between the tree branches above and the hum of insects as they visited one flower after another. But it was the sunburst mosaic at its centre that caught my attention… I knew it already from my mother's stories.

'Sometimes, when we've had lots of classes and new routines to learn, I like to come out here to practise. I get less distracted than when I rehearse in the dormitory with the other girls watching. Some of them think I'm doing it to be the best.' Sahi rolled her eyes and crossed her arms. 'But I'm not. Really I do it because I don't want to forget anything.'

I nodded. My mother and I had practised my magic from dawn until dusk on several occasions, gently calling on my flames until they shuddered on the surface of my skin.

'You can join me if you like,' Sahi said tentatively.

'I would like that.'

She flashed me a toothy grin, pleased at my first words since arriving at the Leharanji with Kaleb that morning.

'There you are.' Kaleb beamed when he spotted us leaving the secluded garden. 'How is our newest recruit?'

I tried to smile back, in the hope that it might offer up enough of an answer.

Kaleb nodded as though he understood. 'It's been a long day and it's still only the afternoon,' he said and laughed softly to himself.

'Why don't you take Aasira to your dormitory for some rest, Sahi? Introductions to the mistresses can wait until later.'

Sahi nodded and curtsied. I followed suit, not quite sure if I was doing it right, but when I looked up Kaleb smiled again.

'We're very pleased to have you here at the sanctuary, Aasira.'

Tears bloom along my eyelashes. I miss Sahi. Even though she only sits a few places along from me, I miss her and the way we could tell each other anything. She never questioned me or my past. Never judged me for my mother's crimes. And in return I… I tried to be her friend when she pushed herself, almost to the edge, to perfect her skills. Just as she did for me.

Maybe I misunderstood what I saw between Sahi and Ejaz in the gardens, but I didn't misunderstand the murder I witnessed. And I can't forget how defensive Sahi was when I confronted her yesterday. I've known her too long, each flicker of emotion familiar to me as her features contorted against the truth and fed me a lie. I've never questioned her before now. Never even thought to, as from my first day here I knew I could trust her where I was wary of the others and their whispers. I admired her in the same way the other girls in our class did for her focus and determination.

But it was a different Sahi I saw the other night. One who has compromised the warrior I know she really is.

Applause brightens the stage and the same tears I held back earlier rise to the surface again. All of us elite dancers stand in a line, hand in hand, and bow to our queen and the audience. That was it. The last time we'll all dance together. Our final ensemble performance and the end to the loornas. I glance down the line and see the others laughing and crying as the applause wraps itself round us. Tomorrow we'll take our first steps into the futures we've trained so hard for and our group will be dispersed round the country.

Although we've prepared for this ceremony all year, the day still feels like it's come too soon. I've done everything I can to prove I'm not the person my lineage would suggest, but the decision is out of my hands. I know I am destined for the army. But what I can't know from the queen's expression is if she'll trust me in that role.

I fight the sadness that expands in my chest, suddenly overwhelmed by the emotions that flood the stage and me. Dana flings my right arm up into the air with a cheer, but my left is still firmly in Sahi's grip. She squeezes my hand and I'm momentarily reassured when I look at her. But as she purses her lips I understand the true meaning in her tears. Things have changed between us, our secrets no longer shared.

Kaleb walks onto the stage from the wings, a proud smile on his face as he brings the applause to a close and we file down the steps, taking a seat in the front row.

'Congratulations to all our elite students,' he says, commanding silence. 'You have shown great vigour in presenting your talents over the last three days and it has been a delight to see the work you have all put in to such a wonderful event.'

My mind tunes in and out as Kaleb continues to thank Queen Sana for gracing us with her presence. My palms begin to sting with all the applause as he goes on to praise the mistresses for their part in helping to nurture our magic during our eight years of training, and in particular Mistress Zaina and Sajid for their work during our final year. But it's like I'm watching from above, floating over the audience as the finality of it all hits me. Our time at the Leharanji has come to an end.

Curtain down.

The sun casts a lazy glow over the gardens before she sets behind the dunes in the west, the moon already up and poised to take her place. I spot Ejaz with Haniya near the fountain as I enter the walled garden, both locked in conversation. Ejaz isn't as animated as usual, his demeanour somehow muted, and there's a quizzical arch in his brow that wasn't there before. I could ask him what he remembers, even tell him what happened to Camil to trigger some sort of memory. But then I recall the way Camil was crushed by the force of Imani's power. Maybe it's better Ejaz doesn't remember. That he believes the story that's been concocted about Camil needing to return to his home village to care for his mother.

As I sit on the bench, I sift through my own memories, highlights that brighten my mind with moving images and colour as people and places emerge out of the black. But they're just that: highlights. When I try and remember my life before I came to the sanctuary, I realise just how fragmented my memories are compared to those from when I first joined.

I see my mother for the briefest second, her hair bouncing down her back as she dances. But, as quickly as my mind focuses on her, I lose her again before the rest of her features

can become defined. The stretches and dances she taught me…
they're in my muscle memory… What if the images I see of
us performing them together aren't even true? What if they're
just a figment of my imagination, conjured to complement the
routines I associate with her?

My heart races. Why can't I see her clearly? My mother.
The woman everyone calls an enemy and fears because of the
way her power consumed her. A power I don't even remember.

'Aasira.'

I jump at the voice behind me.

Kaleb.

The gate is still ajar and he pushes it open with his foot
before joining me. I can't read his expression. We've hardly
spoken over the last few days so I can only assume he's still
angry after what happened in Nazeem.

'I want to wish you well before tomorrow,' he says in that
tone I'm used to, light but with an air of authority. 'And to
apologise for what happened in Nazeem.'

I try to hide my surprise, but he notices and smiles as he
takes a seat beside me on the bench.

'I should have forewarned you of that traitor's relationship
with your mother. I see that now,' he explains. 'But I needed
you to see the truth of the lies we face, and the protestations
of innocence that follow. You saw for yourself what he had
done…'

I blink away the image of the bodies piled in the square, but
it's quickly replaced by Omar kneeling on the ground. 'He said
my mother wasn't a traitor,' I say quietly.

Kaleb sighs and when he shakes his head a strand of hair
frees itself and falls into his face. 'We all want to believe the

ones we care for are innocent. Sometimes it's easier to choose to look past a person's faults rather than admit their guilt.'

'You knew my mother,' I say, and the question that's sat on my lips ever since I first learned of her treachery tumbles from me. 'Was she really as awful as everyone would have me believe?'

Kaleb's mouth twitches. 'She cost our country peace,' he says firmly. 'And turned her back on us in favour of a king who would kill our people and overthrow our queen if our defences failed. I wish for your sake it wasn't the case, but that's a crime that cannot be forgiven.'

Countless times throughout my time at the sanctuary, I've been reminded of how my mother turned her back on Amaar and spread false accusations about our queen that are still believed today, but no one has ever explained why. Perhaps because the only person who can isn't here any more. I want to ask her why she gave up everything and turned on her people. Why she never told me any of this herself, but burdened me instead with her legacy.

'You have shown you're loyal to your country, Aasira,' Kaleb says gravely, filling the silence between us.

'But...'

'But if you're to prove yourself loyal to our queen, you must control the depth of your flames. What you manifested in Nazeem –' his fist tenses as he stands – 'such uncontrolled magic is what led your mother down the path she followed, and it's not one a person can easily be drawn back from.' His eyes brighten with a tinge of curiosity. 'Mistress Zaina tells me you've never exhibited that part of your magic in your rehearsals before. Where did it come from?'

I try to recall without seeing Omar burn within my flames, but the image is always there. 'I don't know.'

'You cannot risk displaying that sort of magic again. Not when you haven't been taught how to master it.'

'I won't.'

He nods once and hesitates at the gate. 'I will do what I can to advise Her Majesty, but ultimately the decision is Queen Sana's. She will give the final verdict on your future in the morning.' His words linger in the growing darkness when he leaves.

I've always known my future position is fragile, but it feels all the more so now. If I'm not recruited into the army, I have nowhere to go. No family. No village. The only place I have to call home is the sanctuary.

The air chills as the last tendrils of sunlight draw back over the sunburst mosaic, casting half of it in shadow. For the first time, I notice a distortion in the tiles where a small crack runs through them. I kneel and gently run my fingers along it and the sun's warmth recedes into the stone. The scar is so fine, but with time it will grow deeper, held together only by the earth below it. Like all us elites… Our roots are here at the sanctuary but, from tomorrow, each of us will branch out. I can only hope that in some way, we'll still be connected by what we are: dancers of the dawn.

SEVENTEEN

The theatre fizzes with anticipation as everyone takes their seats. Our performances are over and our futures decided. Nerves roll off the elites as we're guided to the front rows. Even though I'm resigned to my fate, I'm more anxious than I expected to be as I sit beside Sahi, the hairs on my arms on end as goosebumps prickle along my skin. I'm not ready to say goodbye, not like I thought I was.

Lost in my own thoughts, I'm a beat behind everyone when they stand for the queen's entrance. A flurry of curtsies follows as Queen Sana takes to the stage, Kaleb in tow, while Mistress Zaina and the head mistresses of the other factions stand stage left.

Queen Sana looks out at her audience and breathes in our silence. 'I am pleased I made the choice to come here in person,' she says with a smile. 'The loornas are a sacred ceremony and I would like to congratulate you all on your performances. Each and every one of you demonstrated the contribution you can and will make to our country. I am grateful to know so much talent has been fostered here. Talent that will help Amaar prosper.'

She goes on to announce the names of the students who will join her at the palace: Amina for her voice, Neesha with her violin, Maya for her sewing skills, Asha for the banquets she's produced during the queen's visit… The list continues. One by one, they walk up the steps to the stage where they shake Kaleb's hand and receive a new bell to add to their paayal from their head mistress. They then curtsy to the queen before standing in a line at the back of the stage.

I look down at my own paayal and remember receiving my first bell at the end of my first year, now the most tarnished, but still the most savoured.

'And now for the elite dancers,' Queen Sana says and my stomach flutters as she dismisses the students on the stage and they rejoin the audience.

Instinctively, I reach for Sahi's hand. Her head whips round in my direction, face full of shock, but she squeezes my hand back and smiles. An olive branch before we're cast adrift.

'It has been an honour to witness your skills and to see how your abilities will enhance our army. Having trained at the Leharanji myself,' she says with a smile to Mistress Zaina, 'I also know that while our talents are what make us unique, it is how we work as a collective that makes us formidable. You have demonstrated your connection with each other as an ensemble beautifully and I encourage you to take that asset with you when you fight for Amaar alongside your new comrades.'

A lump rises in my throat, my chest tight and tears threatening as the invisible string that's tied me to these dancers for the past eight years loosens further.

'It is with great pleasure that I shall announce who has graduated into Amaar's army.' Queen Sana unrolls the parchment Kaleb passes her. 'We begin with…Duaa Ali.'

Duaa hesitates, despite the applause that beckons her onto the stage. She nods slowly and I feel it, that sudden twinge of fear. We may have all trained for the honour of protecting our queen and country, but none of us know our fate once we're beyond these walls or what the fight with the enemy could entail. How many of us will survive…

Eventually, she takes her place on the stage and curtsies to Queen Sana. Sahi and I unclasp hands so we can clap for our sister as she leads the way for the rest of us dancers.

'Amara Yasin, Nasira Nahdi, Farah Mahmud, Zahra Karim…' Queen Sana continues reeling off names one by one and the dancers of the dawn are disbanded.

I wait to hear my name, the number of girls in our row quickly dwindling as they join the others onstage. My heartbeat races. I know I'm not one of the chosen few who will be asked to audition at the palace for the role of Queen's Guard so, if I'm not enlisted into the army, what does Queen Sana intend for me? Would she have me stay here, secluded in the desert?

'I congratulate you all,' Queen Sana says, looking up from the parchment in front of her. 'You have exhibited skills that will strengthen Amaar's ranks. From all of us, thank you.'

Another round of applause echoes round the theatre and I look down the line to see which of the elite dancers is still seated.

'And now for those who will audition for a role within my guard.' Queen Sana takes a second parchment from Kaleb, but it's obvious who her choice is as the girls still dot the front row. It's always been obvious, ever since the auditions were first announced.

There's a glint in her eye as she calls their names. 'Sahi Amin, Meera Jaziri, Dana Habib…'

My body flushes with my flames. I'm not trusted. My fate is sealed by my mother's past actions.

'And Aasira Bibi.'

I choke back a laugh. The others are already on their feet, Meera and Dana locked in an embrace as they walk onstage. Mistress Zaina beams as she bestows on them both their newest bell. But I don't move.

'Aasira.' Sahi's voice pierces the bubble I'm in. 'That's you.' She smiles, delighted tears in her eyes as she takes my arm in hers and hauls me up.

I'm in a daze as we take to the stage. I copy Sahi and shake Kaleb's hand, then collect my new bell. When I turn to Queen Sana, her eyes interrogate me just as I do her decision.

'Keep your friends close and your enemies closer,' Meera murmurs, reading my mind as I stand beside her.

For once, I believe she's right.

EIGHTEEN

Our lives at the Leharanji are packed into trunks by the attendants that same afternoon. I wake on our last morning here with the first ribbons of light on the horizon. Our trunks are lined up by the door with our new uniforms draped over each one: a white and gold kurta for those joining the army, and an ivory, gold and emerald kurta for Dana, Meera, Sahi and me as students of the Queen's Guard.

I dress quickly and slip silently out of the dormitory one final time. The sanctuary is still but for the guards, its breaths hushed before it comes alive and we say our final goodbyes. But I veer away from my usual route to the gardens, my body pulled towards the main studio instead. I glance through the doors of each studio as I walk down the corridor.

So many hours were spent in each one as we worked our way up through the year groups, more memories held within their walls than I realised until now. Studio three is where I first learned how to connect my magic to my dancing, and studio four is where I did my first triple turn after months of practice. But it's the main studio, a beacon at the end, where I felt most at home under Mistress Zaina's guidance. I glimpse her through the door, already preparing for her new elite dancers who will begin their classes with her tomorrow.

'Aasira,' she says when she sees me. 'Here for one last class?'

'Something like that.' I smile and join her, looking up at the domed glass roof and the mauve sky above. 'I'll miss it here,' I admit.

'You are always welcome back to visit.'

But the ex-students never return, except those in the Queen's Guard who accompanied her this year.

'Something troubles you,' Mistress says, noting my uneasy posture. 'You thought you were destined for the army.'

'Didn't everyone?' I shrug. 'I never considered I might be chosen to audition for a role in the Queen's Guard. I was so prepared to further my training in the army or even...' My thoughts race until they settle on one. 'I'm not sure I understand the reason behind Queen Sana's decision.'

'I wouldn't labour too long on that. Instead, concentrate on perfecting your ability through dance and showcasing the talents you have to those at the palace.'

'But the queen doesn't trust me. Why would she *want* me in her palace?' I ask. Meera's words ring in my head. *'Keep your friends close and your enemies closer...'*

'Do you trust *her?*' Mistress asks lightly. But it's the sort of question that got Camil killed.

'Of course,' I reply, though something knots inside me.

'Trust is earned, Aasira, and if anyone has reason to exercise caution it is our queen,' she says gravely. 'Queen Sana chose you because she saw something in your power that may be of use at the palace. If not, you are more than equipped for the army.'

Maybe I'm making too much of things. Second-guessing motives and letting other people's opinions fill my head.

'You and the queen are quite similar, you know,' Mistress continues. 'With your powers derived from nature. They're extremely rare. Perhaps the old stories are speaking to the queen again.'

'The old stories?'

'Oh, the Leharanji is full of them.' Her face lights up. 'The colours of the mosaics may have faded since I first trained here,' she says warmly, 'but they hold stories within them that will remain etched in these walls no matter whether we forget the old beliefs or not. They're a reminder of a time before any of us can imagine: before magic.'

Her fingers flicker lightly and the floor beneath her feet dances under the illusion of her power, bringing the patterns to life. 'Stories about how we came to have magic in the first place and its intended purpose.'

'What *was* its intended purpose?' I ask.

Mistress's illusion fades and the floor grows still again. 'To protect.'

'Isn't that what we're still doing?' I say, confused. 'Using our powers to protect our queen and country against invasion?'

'Indeed we are.' She smiles wistfully.

'Why are the old stories no longer shared?'

Mistress looks at me sombrely. 'As our powers faded, so did people's belief in the stories. The belief that our abilities are rooted in nature and that if we in turn offer nature protection, nature will continue to nurture those abilities.'

A wave of familiarity washes over me. 'Nature nurtured magic,' I whisper as I hear her voice in my head; how her laugh chimed in the breeze as we danced. 'My mother…' I say tentatively as Mistress's eyes narrow. 'What was her ability?'

Mistress looks at me curiously so I continue, filling the silence as I finally ask the question that's sparked through my mind since I was a child. 'I know her actions harmed our country, but who was she before that? When she was a student here? What was her ability that made her so powerful in our army before she betrayed us?'

'She never showed you?'

I don't know. I don't remember.

'Your mother had the ability to command the air: a zephyr,' she says slowly, features pinched.

A non-existent breeze shivers up my back as I picture the sand swirling round her as she would dance and spin over the dunes.

Amina's last morning song startles me as it echoes through the sanctuary, accompanied by the dawn chorus outside.

'You had better get ready,' Mistress says as my fellow students are summoned awake. 'It's time to say goodbye.'

We walk outside to where, so far, only Sajid, Tahir and members of the sanctuary guards wait in a group at the bottom of the steps.

'This is it,' Tahir says when I walk over to him.

I breathe in deeply and nod. 'This is it.'

'Whichever path lies ahead, as a Queen's Guard or as a soldier,' he says, voice suddenly hoarse, 'you are a fine warrior of Amaar, Aasira.'

My eyes prickle and I clear my throat in an attempt to speak, but all I can say is, 'Thank you.'

He places a hand on my shoulder, squeezing it gently.

When I turn to Sajid, who stands beside Tahir, he fixes his gaze elsewhere. 'Goodbye, Sajid.'

'Until we meet again,' he says, making his stance on Queen Sana's choice clear.

'I don't doubt we will.'

Students filter outside and I take my place on the main path alongside the elites. The dancers stand together, a look of determination on some faces while others are unable to hide their apprehension as they prepare to leave. Our goodbyes were all said last night, after the round of speeches from Queen Sana, Kaleb and Mistress Zaina. But Kaleb offers a final word to each graduate, shaking their hands as he walks down the line.

'Congratulations, again,' he says when he reaches Sahi, Dana, Meera and me. 'I look forward to seeing your performances for the role of Queen's Guard.'

'You're joining us at the palace?' Meera asks.

'I'll follow in a week, once the students here have settled into their new year groups. It will be good to spend a bit of time at the palace again and see how my old associates are getting on. I don't visit them nearly as much as I should,' he adds quietly, as though it were a thought he didn't intend for us to hear.

He smiles briefly then shakes their hands as he did the rest of the students. When he takes mine, there's a firmness in his grip and it's like he hits a pressure point as a sharp pain darts from my hand to my head. It throbs lightly as he releases his hold and smiles, clasping his hands behind him as he steps back.

'Look out for each other,' he says with a glance at Sahi. 'You have excelled in your training here, but much will be expected from you at the palace. Show them everything you've learned.'

Sahi gives nothing away, but both Dana and Meera nod, absorbing his words. I rub my temple and the throb eases as Kaleb re-joins Queen Sana on the steps.

'Attention!' Sajid commands the newest troops.

The new soldiers form two lines, uniforms gleaming in the golden light as they face Queen Sana, their right hands over their hearts. Tears well as I trace the faces in the front row of the dancers I've grown up with. Dana's hand clasps mine and I see then that she too fights back tears, as she looks out at the second row, at Haniya, who's being transferred to an army base along with nine other sanctuary guards.

'I hereby swear to uphold the light in service to our queen and will honour Amaar as a protector of our land,' the dancers begin, speaking in unison, and I mouth along with them the oath that we swore to when we joined the sanctuary. 'Only unleashing my magic in the face of the enemy and in the name of peace and unity. With every sunrise, until my final day, I pledge my life as a warrior and a dancer of the dawn.'

Sajid leads their parade through the gardens. We all bow our heads out of respect as Amaar's newest warriors march on down the path and through the gates, which close a final time behind them as they're released into the desert.

I watch them, my gaze lingering on the spot where the dust cloud hovered on the horizon not so long ago.

'I remember the day you arrived here as if it were yesterday, don't you?' Sahi says under her breath as Queen Sana bids farewell to Kaleb and the mistresses.

I do.

But the cracks in my memory and my life before I was brought here... The reason I didn't remember my mother's power until Mistress Zaina told me... Was it Sahi? Just like with Ejaz, has she cast my memories in shadow?

NINETEEN

The desert gives nothing away as we pass through her. She's calm and cunning all in one, yet I find solace in her familiar embrace. Still, there's the sense in her unchanging look that something could happen at any given moment, mirroring the way the palace guards keep a hand on their hilts at all times.

It's a three-day ride to the palace and we're already on our second day. It's just long enough to begin feeling used to riding a horse, but not so long for it to feel natural. Our journey is aided by Queen Sana's ability to manifest a constant supply of water and, though the queen might not admit it, my ability to keep the camp warm by lighting the fire with a flick of my hand when the cold sets in at night. And our spirits are lifted by Amina, who sings for us to pass the time.

I didn't sleep well last night. My first evening in the desert for eight years, I'd grown unused to its whisper and every ripple against the thick fabric of our tent shook me awake. The other students were silent and still, the last few weeks of training having finally caught up with them. But I sat up and listened for any sign that the wind might be something more.

That my mother might have been out there, even though I knew it couldn't be possible. There were numerous witnesses to her death, including Kaleb and Sajid. Her lies may haunt the desert, but the sandstorm wasn't of her making. It can't have been.

I must have drifted off eventually because the next thing I knew we were all being woken at dawn to continue our travels.

Now the sun is at its highest point and it doesn't matter how much water I consume, I can still feel the light-headedness set in. I readjust my dupatta, which has already been dampened by Queen Sana, but it only provides light relief from the harsh rays. I've grown so used to the undulating dunes in all directions, decorated with patterns like delicate lacework where grains have gathered, that I'm startled when spots of greenery interrupt the horizon and a village rises into view.

Imani and three of the palace guards break away from our party as we near. They gallop towards the village while Maryam and Fatima – the other members of the Queen's Guard – keep us on the invisible track we've followed. Even from this distance, there's an unusual stillness to the village. No people, no livestock in the paddocks. I see the bodies piled in the square in Nazeem again. Surely our defences aren't so easily broken that another village has been raided by Mezeeri soldiers? My magic tingles under the surface as Imani and the guards enter the village and are blocked from view by the cluster of huts.

'There's no one there,' Dana whispers as she rides up alongside me.

I strain to look back over my shoulder. Even if the villagers were in their homes and sheltering from the sun, there would still be signs of some activity. Dana's right: it's deserted. Yet it feels like there are eyes on us. We stay close and I see the shimmer that emanates from the serpent emblems on her palms. A sudden wind rolls over the dunes to our right, catching us all unawares as grains of sand fly up into our eyes. I shield my face with one hand and grip the reins with the other as my horse falters, eager to turn back.

The wind whistles again, fiercer this time, and our group splits as several horses buck and pull against their riders. Queen Sana regains control of her own horse and gestures for everyone to swerve back to the village, but the air simmers with menace. Just as we veer towards the nearest huts, Imani and the guards emerge, galloping in our direction, their shouts lost to the wind that hisses round us. Confused, our group fragments even more. Meera and Sahi pull in tight beside me and Dana. Their eyes change colour, anticipating company and ready to ambush our enemies' minds the moment they reveal themselves.

Silence.

The wind dies away and everything falls still. Until I hear her.

'Run!' Imani screams.

No one moves.

'Archers!' one of the other guards with her calls. 'Get to the queen—' He slumps forward over his horse, then onto the sand, a single arrow protruding from his neck.

Screams erupt and I jump from my horse's back, spinning quickly until my flames flare round me. As Imani reaches us, I push my flames out and towards the village to create a blazing wall in front of our group. The moment the arrows hit, they disintegrate into ash. The hail of arrows stops but, in their place, six men and women in gold and crimson armour sprint towards us.

I cast my flames round our group so we're protected from all sides, while Maryam circles back towards Queen Sana. Along with Heba and two palace guards, she creates a barricade round the queen, then leads her, the attendants and students without weaponised magic away from the fight. But not before she uses her magic to pluck one of the assailants from the sand and throw him behind a dune with her mind.

Dana's serpents slither through my curtain of flames towards our attackers. Imani swings back towards the action with Fatima and a palace guard on her heel, crushing a man with her magic from the inside out. As he falls, another five in gold and crimson emerge from the village.

'Meera!' I shout, willing her to disarm our assailants with her nightmares. But the magic has dissolved from her eyes and instead they're bloodshot with fear.

'Stay with Queen Sana!' I call to her. For once, she listens, galloping through the passage I carve with my flames to join the queen.

There's no time to dance to strengthen our magic like we've rehearsed. We're already on the back foot, even with our abilities.

'Swords!' I shout and the palace guards near me ready their blades. 'Go!' I release my flames and they run as the curtain falls away, leaving us exposed.

Dana summons more snakes from the sand, allowing time for my flames to cover my body. I form a golden orb of dust in each hand and shoot them towards the enemy. They hit the man and woman closest with such force, my dust burns through their armour like it's fresh kindling and they immediately retreat. The wind lashes again, stronger higher up the dunes than down in the village. More arrows sing towards us. Flames dance along my arms and the wind battles against them, but I focus my fire towards the barrage of arrows until none are left.

The crash of blades is overwhelming. I see Sahi locked in a fight with a man twice her size. Finally, she plunges her blade into his side where there's a gap in his armour, and pivots to face her next opponent. Imani grips a young woman with her magic and she rises above the sand, legs kicking out as her face pales from Imani's invisible grasp round her neck. Imani releases the girl and she drops heavily to the ground. Her breathing is laboured as a palace guard grabs her under the arms and drags her away.

I spin like I did when rehearsing in the studio, as fast as I can, until gold dust pours from me to create another shield. The sand ripples at my feet as Dana appears by my side again. Her hands sparkle with a green dust as she commands her own magic and creates more serpents than I've ever seen her conjure up before. They slither towards their prey, a writhing mass, and wrap themselves round the nearest assailant, strangling the last breath out of her before she can so much as reach for her sword.

The last three face me, expressions fierce. The woman is the first to break ranks, her sword raised. The fire in me burns.

I feel the resurgence of the white flames beneath my skin and the way their strength courses through me. She sees the challenge in my stance and turns back to her partners. But I can't let them escape. I leap to release my magic and white flames roar from my palms, tangling round the enemy. The trio scream as the fire rages over them and, like a chorus of dancers, they fall forward into the sand as one.

Aasira, the wind whispers before fading away.

I twirl towards the voice. Only Sahi stands behind me, her kurta splattered with someone else's blood, hands fumbling as she sheaths her blade. I scan the village and the dunes, waiting for more crimson and gold armour to glimmer on the horizon. But we're alone.

'Are you hurt?' Dana says to me and I shake my head.

'You?'

'No.' I follow her gaze towards the queen's party as they ride back towards us. 'I'll check on Meera,' she says.

'Collect your horses,' Imani orders me and Sahi. 'We need to get to the palace quickly. Some of our people are badly hurt.'

I look at the bodies scattered among the sand. Two of our guards lie motionless while another staggers between the bodies, moaning groggily, and Fatima clasps a bloody arm.

'Here,' Meera says, still riding her own horse as she guides mine towards me. There's an apology in her eyes. 'I was—'

'I know,' I say, saving her the embarrassment. 'So was I.'

Despite the sweat that trails down my forehead and back, a chill wraps round me. I'm uneasy as I take the reins, turning my horse away from the faces of the men and women we just killed.

'Are they all dead?' Heba asks as she and Queen Sana approach.

'Yes,' Imani replies. 'Except that one.' She nods towards the still-unconscious attacker she fought earlier, now under Maryam's charge. The young woman's weapons have been removed and her hands bound.

'Mezeeri soldiers?' Queen Sana asks, emerging from her barricade.

Heba breathes in deeply and no one speaks. More soldiers from Mezeer means more traitors within Amaar, helping them cross the border unnoticed.

'The villagers...?' Heba asks, looking at Imani.

'They were already dead,' she replies regretfully.

'So these troops did not intend to happen upon our queen,' Heba says quietly.

Queen Sana's brow creases as she looks at the corpses that now litter her desert. 'Sahi can soon discover the truth for us,' she says and glances at the prisoner. 'Regardless, further reinforcements must be sent to our borders.'

There are solemn nods all around the group.

'We will ride through the night. These sands are no longer safe,' Queen Sana says gravely. She then turns to Sahi, Dana, Meera and me. 'You protected the crown today. Thank you.'

Meera cowers while the rest of us curtsy. We may have our differences, but I don't blame her for freezing in the face of an attack.

'Bury the villagers,' Queen Sana tells the palace guards who aren't wounded. 'And your brothers and sisters,' she adds quietly. 'We will take their weapons home. They will be a memento for their loved ones and a reminder of their sacrifice to protect their country. It is the only solace we can offer.'

The guards nod and I see one of them shield his face to hide his glistening eyes as he kneels and touches the still chest of one of his comrades.

'And the Mezeeri soldiers?' another guard asks.

The queen considers the question. 'Leave them. Let their bodies be a warning to anyone else who passes through this desert intending to hurt our people.'

She looks towards the dunes in the east, in the direction the wind hailed from. Their silhouette is altered, the dunes' peaks smoother where the gusts grazed them. The wind died with the final three soldiers I killed, the air now still, leaving the sun's heat to claw at my skin once more. But it felt deliberate, the way the wind stirred only as we approached the village, then attempted to disorientate us before the attack. Queen Sana catches me staring at the dunes too and, though she speaks to the group, her gaze is on me.

'We must go. The storm may well return.'

TWENTY

Naru glitters in the distance as the desert is slowly eclipsed by greenery. Fields expand out to the east while Amaar's capital rises before us. An early-morning breeze ruffles my hair, carrying with it the heavy scent of salt and fish that drifts towards us from the harbour. After travelling all night through the darkness, I'm in awe of the Emerald Sea that sparkles on the horizon.

From here, I can see the city built into the cliffs, rows upon rows of colourful buildings unlike any I've seen before. But it's the palace that sits at the top, overlooking both city and sea, that keeps drawing my eye with its marble facade and jade minarets that reach high, as though trying to touch the topaz sky. A white cloud obscures one part of the cliff face directly beneath the palace, stretching down the length of it, and it takes me a moment to realise it's a waterfall.

'We're here,' Meera says, relief in her voice after yesterday's events. No one has said anything about the way she held back, too scared to conjure her ability, but the weight of what it could mean for her hangs heavy.

'It's beautiful,' Dana breathes. 'Haniya would love it.'

Sahi reaches over and puts a hand on Dana's shoulder. It's the first time she's mentioned Haniya since we left the sanctuary. I saw the longing in their eyes as they parted and their plans to miraculously stay together were shattered. But Dana isn't one to brood and her attention soon turns to what the food will be like at the palace.

'There'll be lots of fish, I imagine,' Amina says with a nod down to the small boats bobbing on the water.

The ten other students whom Queen Sana has selected finally look more relaxed as we leave the desert behind us and the threat of another ambush. Their schooling included little combat once it was realised their abilities weren't of use to the army and I now realise how lucky we dancers were to have had so much training in not only protecting our country but also ourselves.

The sea's melody swirls round us as waves rush up onto the beach on our left. I've never seen anything like it, the way they roll in then tumble away. A chorus of birds call to each other in notes different to those heard at the sanctuary and, as we approach the gilded gates, the bustle of life at the capital sings.

The gates swing open and Queen Sana takes the lead. Her skirt is the colour of twilight and glimmers as it trails down the back of her black horse, the beads catching in the light. Heba follows close behind along with the Queen's Guard, while we students bring up the rear with the palace guards and attendants. As we enter, a hush falls over Naru's citizens as they line the streets and bow their heads to the queen. When they see us, they don't hide their stares and children elbow their way through the crowd, curious about the new faces who accompany their queen.

The souk sprawls beyond the city gates and we're greeted by the powerful scent of incense, mingled with spices and herbs. Fruits in all shapes and colours are piled in handwoven baskets, and intricate tapestries are draped over long tables and the dusty ground. I've never seen so many people in one place and want to stay and explore, but Queen Sana keeps our procession moving. Faces emerge from the shadows of narrow alleyways as the souk gives way to small homes that are knitted close together.

As we wind our way up towards the palace, the houses grow sparser but more elegant with lush gardens that wrap round them. Those who greet us do so with faces free of the desert dust that swirls at the city's base, their clothes more elaborate and embellished with brightly coloured embroidery. The sounds of the souk below barely reach these heights. Instead, birdsong trickles down from the neem trees that border the palace walls, their branches overflowing with leaves, and I hear the distant rush of the waterfall that flows from the palace grounds into the sea below.

The ground levels out beneath us as we approach the palace gates, a welcome relief for the horses. The guards stationed there bow their heads then open the gates, and we ride down the stone path between rows of greenery and flowers that fill the air with their sweet scent. Fountains adorn the gardens, topped with marble statues laced with gold so that when the water splashes into the basin below it looks as though sunbeams decorate the surface.

I remember hearing about these fountains when I was younger and how the queen commissioned them when she took the throne. Each one is said to be designed in memory of her ancestors – the queens and kings that came before her – and holds subtle symbols along the smooth stone. Although I witnessed Queen Sana create water all of her own accord in Nazeem, I can see why she's chosen to stay in Naru during her reign. No matter where she is within the palace grounds, she has enough water at her fingertips to defend her city. And that's without calling on the sea.

The queen comes to a halt in front of us and we all follow her lead as she dismounts her horse. 'Welcome to my home,' she says and there's a lightness to her I haven't seen before. 'Come, you must rest before the festivities this evening.'

I try to drink it all in as we follow Queen Sana up the green marble steps and through the large mosaic archway into the palace. The entrance hall is light and airy with its glass-domed roof, much like the main studio at the sanctuary, and multiple corridors weave their way to the different wings. All of us are lost for words and I have to bite the inside of my cheek to stop myself from laughing in awe. I always thought the sanctuary was grand, but the palace makes it look like a child's doll's house.

Queen Sana waves over a group of young women who can't be much older than us. They all wear the same uniform: a white kurta delicately embroidered with emblems that replicate the waves of the sea below in gold thread.

'Each of you has been assigned an attendant and a guard who will look after you as you settle in,' the queen tells us. 'Please show our guests to their chambers,' she instructs the attendants. 'I will see you all this evening.'

We curtsy as she leaves in the opposite direction. The attendants then silently guide us up the grand staircase and down a long corridor.

'This room is yours,' one of the attendants says, ushering me forward. She opens the door to a room bathed in sunlight.

A large bed with an ornate wooden frame sits along one wall. On the opposite side of the room is an area piled high with cushions and a chaise longue.

'Please, make yourself comfortable,' she says. 'I'll draw a bath for you. You must be tired after your journey.'

I hover in the doorway. The room is the same size, if not bigger, than the dormitory I shared with the other elite dancers at the sanctuary. Everything is so crisp and clean, I don't want to dirty it with the desert dust embedded in my skin and clothes. I glance back at the others and see the same astonished looks reflected in their eyes.

Dana's room is opposite and I watch as she runs in and launches herself onto the bed, dissolving into a fit of laughter as she smothers herself in the sheets. I burst out laughing too, the tension of the past few weeks released momentarily. The attendant looks at me and smiles before disappearing behind a screen ornately decorated with hyacinths in full bloom. I'm not quite sure what to do with myself while I wait, so I walk over to where two slim, stained-glass doors open out to a veranda that overlooks the gardens and, beyond that, the Emerald Sea. I close my eyes and breathe in the salty air.

'Your bath won't be long,' the attendant says from behind me and I jump. 'Apologies, miss, I didn't mean to startle you.'

'You didn't,' I say, but my flushed cheeks betray me. 'Please, call me Aasira.'

Her smile broadens a little. 'If you wish, Aasira.'

'What's your name?' I ask as she passes me a glass of cool lemon water.

There's a hint of surprise in her eyes before she says, 'Amal.'

'Amal...' I repeat. 'It's lovely to meet you.'

TWENTY~ONE

T he girl staring back at me in the mirror doesn't look like a warrior. Dressed in a peach lehenga encrusted with pearls and jewels, delicately placed to depict sun and flame emblems, she looks like a royal. Her hair is pulled back into a soft low bun with a pearl tikka that runs down her middle parting and hangs over her forehead. To complete the outfit, she wears a gold necklace and large earrings that are probably more expensive than the dress.

Amal straightens my heavy necklace, then steps back. 'Is that comfortable?'

'Yes, thank you.'

'Then we'll go down.'

As if on cue, there's a soft knock at the door and, as Amal opens it a crack, I hear the excited chatter of the other girls congregating in the corridor.

'Come in,' Amal says and opens the door wide.

I expect to see Sahi or Dana, but instead a young palace guard enters, dressed in the traditional uniform of white and gold with an emerald wave on the chest. He takes two strides into the room then bows his head before speaking.

'May peace rise with every dawn.'

'And endure with every dusk,' I reply.

'This is Emir,' Amal tells me. 'The guard assigned to you during your training here.'

'It's a pleasure to meet you.' He bows his head again and his short ponytail bobs in agreement.

'And you,' I reply, although something gnaws at me. I'm used to having guards around, but not a constant chaperone. A shadow.

'Ready?' he asks.

'Yes.'

Amal dashes to my side and attends to a single stray hair. 'Now we're ready,' she says once it's neatly tucked back into place.

'After you.' Emir steps to the side to let us through. He can't be much older than me and yet the palace formalities are already ingrained in his every movement.

The other dancers sparkle in the sunlight that cascades through the open windows in the corridor, casting glittering lights along the walls. We're all dressed in lehengas, but that's where the similarity ends. Each lehenga is completely unique, representing the heart of our magic. Sahi's shimmers with pearlescent crystals down the bodice that arc like the moon; Dana wears pistachio green with gold accents round the neckline and waist; Meera's is a soft blue like the haze of a night sky, perfect for the nightshade.

'Does anyone else feel a little underdressed?' Dana says and we all laugh.

'Where are the others?' I ask, looking around.

'They've already gone down,' one of the guards says. 'And so must we.'

We're instructed to pair up and, out of habit, I stand next to Sahi at the front. It's like being back out in the desert again as our guards escort us down to the palace gardens. All four guards are young, no older than eighteen, but their expressions are stern and they're rigid in the way they move, clearly newly trained and eager to impress.

As she helped me get ready, Amal had told me a little about this evening's festivities to welcome us to the palace. They are to begin with a performance from the Leharanji's alumni who now reside here as members of the Queen's Guard. After that will come the feast. Amal's eyes lit up as she listed the many delicacies being prepared in the kitchens, too many for me to remember now as the aromas float through the palace and out into the gardens.

Groups of diplomats and courtiers are dispersed throughout the grounds, dressed in vibrant colours and dripping in gold jewellery. Most are locked in conversation until they see us newcomers approach. I feel their gaze on us, curious and cautious all at once, and even some of the guards who are stationed in every direction spare us a glance.

Kaleb had warned me that people might challenge my status once I left the sanctuary. I see the watchful glimmer in their eyes now as they try to figure out which of us is Lina's daughter, then the way they settle on me, on the flames that decorate my skirt. Did they know her? Or just think they did because of the stories?

I tune out the noise in my mind and concentrate on the undercurrent of the sea as it pounds against the cliffs below, a constant thrum. The buzz of insects rises from the shrubs and, as we walk down a gravel path through the gardens, it is clear magic has touched the trees and flowers. Their shoots shimmer with a mirage of colours in time with the breeze, which ruffles their leaves and petals. But it's not until I see the theatre that I'm stopped in my tracks and my breath skips.

Just as the city below is carved into the cliff, the theatre is carved out of the white rock too. A tiered seating area curves up and round in a semicircle, looking down on to the stage with the sea glistening beyond. The seats are a vibrant green and it is only as we get closer I realise that it's grass, adorned with brightly coloured cushions scattered along the rows.

'Look at that view,' Dana says as we're led to the row where the other students are already waiting. 'It's like you could dive straight off the wall and into the water.'

'Imagine performing on that stage.' Meera looks on wistfully and I smile at the thought. It would be incredible to perform in this setting, at the will of the elements.

Sahi is quiet as we take our seats. We haven't spoken properly since our argument, and while things don't feel as heated, they're not what they used to be either. How does she feel now we're all here, the chosen four, to audition for the role she was promised? With her every little movement and shift of expression, I find myself analysing her, searching for a deeper meaning. And yet the instinct is still there to look out for one another like when we were ambushed yesterday, despite the trust we've breached. Or perhaps it isn't instinct at all, but rather Mistress Zaina's voice in my head reminding me that strength comes from working together.

A hush falls over the theatre as large lanterns are lit round the stage and orange-zest flames flicker against the ruby sky.

Everyone stands when Queen Sana arrives, dropping into a curtsy or bow until she takes her seat on the raised platform at the back, Heba at her side. Silence falls when the palace musicians appear, signalling the start of the performance.

The music is stark, beginning with single beats of the dhol. Dancers materialise out of the gathering darkness, their movements low to the ground as they swirl round the stage. All thirty of the Queen's Guard perform, even Fatima whose arm has already been healed. I spot Imani and Maryam among some other dancers I recognise as ex-students of the sanctuary, along with older dancers I haven't seen before.

They're dressed identically, hair loose, each wearing a navy kurta with a long slit that runs down the front from the waistline, revealing slim trousers underneath as it flares with every turn and the silver beading catches the lantern-light. The haunting notes of a violin and sitar emerge, accompanied by a singer whose voice reaches notes beyond those I've ever heard before.

They're all perfectly in time with each other as they jump and spin, and I note how their dance style incorporates moves used in combat training. Some dancers split off and the music changes as more instruments are introduced and a new atmosphere descends over the theatre, livelier and more urgent. These women might serve their country as members of the Queen's Guard, but right now they're dancing simply to perform rather than to protect. The stories their bodies tell with each sweep of their arms make me want to rise to my feet and dance with them.

The sky is painted the colour of their costumes by the time the whole ensemble comes together again for their final dance.

I watch in awe as they fill the stage, all of them perfectly in place and moving as one. With every twirl, a spark of magic ignites until a cloud of shimmering dust forms round each dancer, their magic pouring from the symbols on their palms. They're so in control of both their bodies and their abilities, and yet they look so free as the dust spirals about them, a mirage of beautiful colours that bursts from their skin without inflicting harm.

As the dancers perform their final set of spins, they cast their hands to the sky where their magic mingles, the dust swirling into an iridescent circle with golden flames round its edge. The sun: a symbol of hope as the life-breath of our land.

The audience is silent when the performance ends, faces aglow as we stare up at the sun suspended above the stage. Slowly, it loses its form and a shower of dust falls like glittering stars over the stage. We're all on our feet then and our applause echoes round us, punctuated by the roar of the waves far below. The dancers form a line at the front of the stage and curtsy to Queen Sana, then their audience and orchestra. They curtsy three times before the applause settles and they disperse off the stage.

Everyone waits for Queen Sana to descend. She pauses when she reaches the side of the stage where the members of her guard who performed are huddled, congratulating them all individually. It isn't until they leave and the courtiers join them that our guards lead us back through the gardens to a long table set up on the lawn, lit by candlelight and decorated with cascading flowers.

Intricate layers of spice fragrance the air as we're ushered to our seats. I take in the many dishes filled with an array of vegetable and fish curries, more elaborate than anything we were served at the sanctuary. Large silver bowls filled with biryani and steaming saffron rice are interspersed between them, and I catch Dana eyeing the trays of roti, paratha and chapati.

We new arrivals are seated in the middle opposite Queen Sana herself. Once everyone is in their place, she gestures for us to begin. Attendants appear and pour our drinks, a sparkling pink liquid the flavour of rose. I'm hesitant to begin with, despite how delicious everything looks, but soon help myself to the dal tadka and okra closest to me. Amina and Neesha sit on my right and I'm grateful to listen in as they talk excitedly about how beautifully the musicians performed. But I feel both the queen and her advisor watching us keenly and feel self-conscious as I reach for a chapati.

'What did you think of the performance?' Queen Sana asks us.

'It was stunning, Your Majesty,' Dana replies, after quickly gulping down a mouthful of paneer.

The queen smiles, pleased. 'We only select the very best skills for the palace.'

'As their performance showed, your life as part of an ensemble does not end because you've left the Leharanji,' Heba tells us and the queen nods. 'There must be cohesion in our ranks, and none more so than between those who are sworn into the Queen's Guard. As for you –' she turns to Amina and Neesha – 'you should gain an insight into what you could achieve here while you learn from our country's finest musicians.'

'You have a busy time ahead of you.' Queen Sana addresses us dancers, drawing us back into her gaze while Heba continues to talk to Amina and Neesha. 'Mistress Soraya has put together a regime to test your abilities in isolation and as a group before your final performance in two weeks. I have already seen what you can all do – and witnessed you put it into practice yesterday,' she adds.

Meera shuffles uncomfortably in her seat, eyes cast downwards as a sheen illuminates her forehead.

'Sahi,' the queen says, 'your audition will begin tonight with our guest. It seems she is finally lucid.'

Sahi nods. Her work starts now then, on the prisoner.

With this evening's performance still reeling in my head, I'd almost forgotten that the reason we're here is to compete for a role within the Queen's Guard. These new auditions are like an encore to the loornas and I know I should feel proud of making it this far. But, as I look down the table and see the excitement that bubbles among the other students, a hole twists open in the pit of my stomach. While we sit here, enjoying enough food to feed several villages, our sisters prepare to join the fight that waits on the horizon. A fight I should be part of.

TWENTY~TWO

A hazy blur coats my vision as I wake. I'm disorientated at first, unsure where I am, until I realise the movement in my room is Amal as she quietly opens the curtains. Last night's festivities went on until the sky awoke and I can see from the slant of the shadows in my room that the sun now reigns over the palace.

'I've brought some breakfast for you.' Amal gestures to a silver platter piled with fruits and I reach for a slice of melon the colour of the desert. 'And your dance clothes are here.' I look over to where a long white skirt and short-sleeved top are laid over the chaise longue.

'How much time do I have?' My eyes are still heavy after so few hours of sleep.

'Emir will come for you shortly.'

I feel on edge, having missed the sunrise and the chance to stretch properly before class. Although we were still dancing at dawn, I suppose. Eventually, I relaxed into the festivities. The atmosphere was infectious as we were given the opportunity to shed our responsibilities, our duties, for an evening. All except Sahi, who was called away by the queen to interrogate the Mezeeri captive. I overheard some courtiers talking about the prisoner after the meal, and how she's being kept in a cell beneath the palace, deep within the cliffs.

Another slice of melon in my hand, I disappear behind the screen to splash my face with cool water. I instantly feel a little brighter, but as I glance in the mirror the dark circles under my eyes tell a different story. I splash my face another couple of times, then smooth my hair back into a low bun and quickly dress before Emir knocks for me.

Amal gives me an encouraging nod when there's a tap at the door. Emir steps aside as I join Sahi and Meera in the corridor, along with the guards appointed to them: Imran who's assigned to Meera, Ahmed to Dana, and Zayn to Sahi. They stuck very close to us last night and it quickly became apparent that we'll have little time away from them except for when in classes. The idea of it still makes me a little claustrophobic, unlike Meera, who was charmed by their conversation all night, enjoying the attention.

'We really must go,' Ahmed says, impatiently knocking for Dana a third time.

'She's coming!' her attendant calls from the other side.

'Finally.' Meera rolls her eyes, tapping her foot furiously on the floor when Dana emerges.

I fight a yawn and see Sahi do the same, her body tense and the muscles in her neck strained. She had even less sleep than the rest of us: I'm sure I heard her returning just as I was drifting off.

'I needed my beauty sleep,' Dana says playfully as though we're not about to experience a dance class that is likely to resemble an examination.

The guards walk briskly and there's little time to take in this new part of the palace as we near the studios. We round a corner and the beat of several tablas drifts towards us. The layered patterns thrum through the marble floor and up through my feet, the rhythms vibrating round us as we pass the studio in use. Inside, five members of the Queen's Guard rehearse, flipping through the air with grace, every muscle in their arms on show as they tumble across the room. From the way they combine dance and combat, it looks like a battle dance. When we were ambushed, Queen Sana said reinforcements would be needed along the front line, but I didn't expect that members of her guard would be chosen.

'Mistress Soraya will not appreciate you being late for your first class,' Zayn says and I realise all of us have stopped, mesmerised, as we peer through the crack in the door.

Reluctantly, we draw ourselves away until we reach a studio a few doors down. The guards immediately stand to attention as a slender woman steps out, her hazel eyes narrowed and grey hair scraped back off her face into a traditional bun.

'Precision and punctuality are paramount to my classes,' Mistress Soraya says, eyeing us acutely. 'If your aim is to survive during a battle, I suggest you learn the meaning of both.'

The drums still beat from the studio at the other end of the corridor, lending even more gravity to our new mistress's words. After a heavy pause, the silence thick between us, we all drop into a curtsy. Yet she doesn't smile at our show of respect, her gloved hands linked in front of her as though she's waiting for us to say or do something. Perhaps she is and no one has told us the protocol here.

'I am Mistress Soraya, the Head Dance Mistress at the palace,' she says eventually, but she hardly need introduce herself. Along with Mistress Zaina, Mistress Soraya is one of the most celebrated warriors of Amaar. I have to suppress a shudder as I hone in on her gloved hands again; hands capable of poisoning someone with a single touch. 'I already know who you are,' she continues. 'Your abilities will tell me anything else I need to know.'

Mistress Soraya flicks her hand and the guards bow their heads before marching back down the corridor. She turns, as swift as a chinkara, and we follow her into the studio. The four walls are lined with mirrors so there's no escaping our form as we dance. She indicates for us to stand at the barre at the back of the room, and I fall into my usual place between Sahi and Dana.

She observes us first from the front of the studio, then with more acute scrutiny as she walks over to analyse our posture. As she reaches me, I'm keenly aware of my position. Back straight, feet turned out, one hand on the barre while my other arm is outstretched and rounded at the elbow. I turn my head out towards an invisible audience, my chin up to lengthen my neck.

'At the Leharanji, you have been taught how to dance as a corps, as an army, but today I want to see you as soloists. While you train with me, you will dance like the rivals you are as you compete for the role of Queen's Guard. Understood?'

'Yes, Mistress,' we reply in unison.

'You will warm up, then begin.'

Three musicians enter and for a brief moment I'm back at the sanctuary in one of Mistress Zaina's classes. But I don't recognise them from my time there: they must be at least ten years older than us. They spare us only a glance as they sit in the corner where their instruments already wait: a tabla and flute. The other musician must be a singer. Once they have finished tuning up, Mistress counts the musicians in, then goes on to call out our moves. I work hard to listen and not let my muscle memory take over as she strings together movements in a different order to what we're used to.

'Your feet are sickling, Dana,' Mistress says over the music. 'One, two, three. Meera, you're behind the tempo. Find it.'

It goes on like this, with no breaks between exercises while Mistress Soraya calls out corrections and prods our legs, arms, cores and backs when she isn't satisfied.

'Chin up, but without the tension in your neck. Finish your lines,' she demands.

All of us are dripping with sweat when the barre exercises eventually end and Mistress beckons us to the front of the studio.

'I would now like to see each of you perform while manifesting your ability,' she says. 'Meera, you will go first. The rest of you can stretch at the side.'

Meera tries to hide her fatigue as she takes centre stage.

'So…you're the one who didn't fight to protect your queen,' Mistress Soraya says without even looking at Meera, which is just as well as her shoulders slump before she quickly corrects her stance. 'Have you not been trained in combat?'

'Yes, Mistress.'

'Then why did you not fight?'

Meera's eyes glisten under the accusation and my chest tightens for her. 'I…'

'Yes?' Mistress challenges her.

Meera looks down at her hands and runs a finger over the star on her left palm. 'I was scared,' she finally confesses. 'Everything happened so quickly and I couldn't feel my ability inside me. I couldn't use it to stop the people attacking us.'

'But you had your blade. Why not use that instead?'

Meera takes a deep breath. 'There is no excuse. I panicked in the face of danger.'

Her whole demeanour is deflated as she admits what we're all afraid of: that fear itself will grip us when we need our ability most. I haven't seen her like this since she first joined the sanctuary and tangled several of our classmates in her web of nightmares. She was practising while we slept and accidentally sent three of the girls into a trance only the healer could bring them back from. Kaleb was furious, until he realised the full potential of how her power could be used on our enemies.

'You are a nightshade,' Mistress Soraya says and Meera nods. 'You have the ability to send people into a nightmare-filled sleep... Perhaps whole armies, if you are taught how.'

Is that an indication of where Mistress thinks her ability is best placed: in the army?

'Show me,' she urges.

A familiar glint reawakens in Meera's eyes. 'Gladly.'

Mistress smiles for the first time as she opens the studio door and motions someone in. A guard enters with a young woman not much older than us, dressed in the attendants' uniform.

'Kali, please sit,' says Mistress Soraya as she pulls out a chair and places it directly opposite Meera.

Kali does so reluctantly. In the mirror's reflection, I see how bloodshot her eyes are as she watches the guard and stares at the door longingly as he leaves.

'This will teach you not to give in to gossip,' I hear Mistress say under her breath and a chill runs through me.

But Kali's features only harden. If Meera is being asked to use her magic on this girl, what will I be expected to do? And what gossip was she privy to that led to this punishment?

'Begin,' Mistress Soraya instructs.

Without music, Meera dances and her eyes instantly turn blue as her ability surfaces. She focuses her dance on Kali, who accepts her punishment without a sound as she waits for Meera's nightmare to grip her. Threads of shimmering midnight dust course from Meera's hands and encircle Kali, whose head suddenly falls forward as she's put into a deep sleep. Her body goes rigid while Meera's is fluid with her dance. I jump when Kali's head snaps up, eyes wide as she starts to shake against whatever nightmare Meera weaves through her mind.

It's not until Kali's mouth opens into a silent scream that Mistress Soraya intervenes.

'Enough,' she commands. 'You will not prove you're deserving of a position here by driving the girl into a delirium.'

The final wisps of dust retreat into Meera's palms and Kali reawakens, her breathing shallow. She recoils from Meera when she passes and all pity I felt for Meera earlier dissolves as she joins us in our stretching, a snide smile twisting her features.

Next, Mistress Soraya turns to Dana, ushering her forward. 'Dana… A serpent-whisperer.'

Kali visibly inhales at the words as Dana takes her place.

'More precisely, sand serpents. Tell me how you produce serpents from sand in a setting such as this one, without any sand in sight.'

Dana considers this a moment, worry creasing her brow. We always had the desert within reach at the sanctuary; it never occurred to me that there could be a barrier to Dana's ability.

'Well?' Mistress Soraya crosses her arms, one gloved finger tapping impatiently.

'I've always been in the desert when asked to perform my magic,' Dana replies. 'Like when I helped protect Her Majesty when we were ambushed,' she adds quickly.

But Mistress looks unimpressed. 'You may have shown your value then, but how valuable are you if you require sand at your feet to conjure your ability? The desert won't hear you up here. The most you can hope for is a trickle of grains from the beach.'

Dana doesn't need any more goading, her eyes already a bright green and palms turned skywards as she leaps and turns, calling to the sand at the base of the cliffs. She spins on the spot, her energy focused on an open window until, finally, in slithers a single sand serpent. It darts through the air until it lands on the studio floor, winding its way towards Kali. Terrified, the girl lifts her feet off the ground and onto the chair, almost toppling it backwards. But Dana isn't cruel. She commands the snake back to her like a pet, a smile on her face as sweat glistens on her forehead.

Mistress raises her eyebrows, a little impressed. 'Release your serpent and take a seat.' She turns to Sahi and me and looks us both up and down. 'Sahi,' she decides. 'Let us see what gossip our attendant thought was so important to share among her peers.'

Sahi brushes a loose strand of hair back from her face as she takes her place in the centre of the studio.

'I hear you had a busy evening with our prisoner.'

'Yes, Mistress.' She refrains from divulging any more and no doubt Mistress Soraya already knows everything she needs to.

'Begin,' Mistress says in an almost weary tone.

Sahi begins her dance slowly; her movements look tentative at first, or perhaps she's simply drained after last night's interrogation. When she commands her power, a glow emanates from the crescent-moon emblems on her palms and white dust weaves round Kali's head. Kali's eyes turn the same milky white as Sahi's.

Sahi stops dancing. 'Tell us of the gossip you heard.'

'A storm gathers in the east.' Kali's voice is deep as she's caught within Sahi's trance. 'Their army is coming.'

I shift out of the splits. We all know of the gathering threat on our eastern border. It's the very reason more palace guards are being sent to reinforce the front line. If that's believed to be gossip, the people here must lead a more sheltered life than even we did at the sanctuary.

Her irises cast white, Sahi looks at Mistress Soraya, who nods for her to continue. 'Our border is protected,' Sahi states, but I think of the ambush two days ago and the bodies of those killed in Nazeem. Mezeeri soldiers had found a way through somehow, although their route has surely now been discovered after Sahi interrogated the prisoner last night.

'Borders and Amaar's army do not hinder them.' Kali's voice cracks.

'This girl does not know what she speaks of,' Mistress Soraya interrupts. 'How dare she speak against the strength of her own country. I won't hear any more of it.' She signals for Sahi to end her interrogation.

Sahi holds on a little longer though, her forehead furrowed as she silently probes further.

'Enough!' Mistress Soraya claps her hands and the trance Kali was under lifts.

Sahi bows her head apologetically to Mistress before calmly walking back to where we stretch. But I recognise the look of puzzlement in her distant gaze. She saw something in Kali. Something she didn't share with us. But why would she go against our new mistress's orders? Has she just changed something in Kali's memories like she did with Ejaz? Like she might have done with me…? I swallow back the thought, not wanting to believe she would or could ever do that.

'Aasira.' Mistress startles me, waving me over, and I'm quick to my feet. 'Our flame-wielder. Although most know you here as the traitor's daughter.' Her words cut through me, sharpened with an admirable precision, just like the arch of her raised brow.

I don't grace the studio with a reaction. As I take my place, Kali whimpers and even the musicians flinch behind their instruments as they look me up and down. Kali's knees are pulled up to her chest and she starts whispering to herself.

When she finally falls silent and looks at me through her silent tears, all she sees is a threat.

'Do not flatter yourself,' Mistress scolds. 'Aasira's flames will not be wasted on you.'

They wouldn't have touched Kali even if Mistress had commanded it. I'm not Imani. My power is not one I'll use on our own people. At least, not on those who aren't traitors.

'Show me your flames without burning my studio to the ground,' Mistress orders.

I take myself back to my solo rehearsals with Mistress Zaina, recalling what she taught me about letting my magic flow, but also how to temper it so as not to lose control. I start to let my flames stir, feeling their comforting warmth as they branch through me and a gold hue appears along my veins. I spin to kindle them further and, as I whip my head round with each turn, I see the way the golden hue brightens until my whole body is cast in the sparkling glow of my dust. But I don't stop there. The gold suns on my palms burn bright as small flames erupt from them and lap up my arms and down my body. I stop spinning and let Mistress take in my magic, my flames reflected in her eyes.

Her lips twitch with the hint of a smile and she murmurs something to herself, before saying, 'I have seen enough.'

My flames melt into my body and part of me wonders if she might look more impressed had I conjured my white flames. But it's a risk I can't take until I understand how they manifest and how to control them.

'Warm-down,' Mistress says. She then dismisses the musicians and Kali, who sprints for the door.

Kali's dupatta slips from her shoulder as she runs, the light fabric catching on the sea breeze that floats through the open windows.

'We're certainly not at the sanctuary any more,' Dana says under her breath as she joins me at the barre, uncharacteristically subdued even though she displayed her ability despite Mistress's doubts.

'No,' I say and bend to catch Kali's dupatta as it drifts towards me. 'We're not.'

TWENTY~THREE

The afternoon wanes as we meander along the cobbled road that slopes down towards the souk. Laughter and music drift from the gardens of the large houses that sit on the palace's doorstep, as local residents entertain guests. Any thought of the conflict beyond the city walls seems a distant one. Here, the wealthy only ever have something to celebrate. As we pass by the gates of one mansion, I spot a young attendant watching us from the other side. At first, I can't read her expression, but when she puts her hand up to wave, I see the faint line of a floral mehndi design on her palm that mimics the symbols that decorate our hands. Magic may not run through her blood, but the fight to defend our country is still fierce in the glimmer of her eyes.

As the road grows narrower and busier, our party splits into smaller groups, despite our strict orders to stay together and with our guards. We dancers have been given the afternoon off to see more of Naru, along with the palace's newest apprentices, a rare opportunity we probably won't get again if the schedule Amal shared with me after class this morning is anything to go by. I hang back with Dana, Sahi, Amina and

Maya, while Meera and some of the others hurry ahead, giddy at being free of the confines of the palace. The air feels close the further down the cliff we venture and lanterns flicker like starlight to reveal the interlaced rows of stalls as a haze rolls in from the sea.

'How was this morning?' Maya asks us.

'Mistress Soraya isn't easily impressed – let's put it that way,' Dana says quietly, conscious of our chaperones, who are the queen's eyes and ears. 'There was a moment when I really believed I might not be able to conjure my sand serpents.'

'But then you did,' Sahi says encouragingly.

'And you'd already shown the strength of your ability in the desert,' adds Amina.

Dana beams at the memory.

Although she pretends not to hear us as she walks on ahead, I see Meera's shoulders tense momentarily at this further reminder of her poor performance when we were ambushed.

'Have you met your instructors yet?' I ask Maya and Amina.

Maya nods. 'Their skills are unparalleled. The level of detail in their designs... I've never seen anything like it.'

I smile at her enthusiasm.

'It's the same with the musicians,' Amina chimes in. 'Neesha and I listened to the orchestra rehearse this morning. Their ability is beyond anything we were ever taught at the sanctuary and I'm not sure I'll ever be up to their standard.'

'You're already brilliant,' Neesha says and puts an arm round Amina's shoulders. 'If you don't think you have a place among them, I certainly don't,' she jokes, but there's a tinge of real doubt there.

'That's not true,' Dana says, a sudden skip in her step. 'Soon, the whole city...no, the whole country will descend on the palace to hear you both play.'

The others laugh, but my mind wanders to our own class this morning and what Kali said when Sahi revealed her truth. *'Their army is coming. Borders and Amaar's army do not hinder them.'*

Mistress was quick to dismiss Kali's words as gossip, but we all know that the fight is already here. We saw it ourselves when the Mezeeri soldiers ambushed us on our journey and I still can't shake the image of the bodies piled up in the square in Nazeem. I try to drown the image by focusing on the sea where an ornate ship is anchored just beyond where the cliff juts out, ghostly beneath the thin veil of mist. Even from this distance, I can tell it's far larger than the two ships moored in the harbour to our right.

'*The Llahorien*,' Emir says, falling into step with me and following my eyeline. 'Or *Sea-Fey*, Queen Sana's most-prized naval ship.'

'Why isn't it in the harbour with the others?' Sahi asks.

'Because she's getting ready to leave,' he says, gaze flecked with awe. He then points to where smaller boats bob on the water, and a slew of men and women relieve them of their fresh catch. 'Before Amaar and Mezeer separated, this was one of the main ports where goods were brought in by ship, then transported to the old city where they were sold to the rest of the country.'

'You and your history,' Zayn mocks and Emir smiles, unfazed, before continuing.

'Silk, spices, cotton...the old city was at the heart of trade for centuries. It sits on what's now the border between Amaar and Mezeer and was nicknamed Quartz City, because of the way the stone would shimmer in certain light. It was a life source for so many, but when Larijaah was no more, the old city was abandoned.'

'I can visualise it,' Maya says quietly.

'Inspiration for your next design?' I say and her eyes light up as she runs over to the two other seamstress apprentices to share her plans.

A pang of jealousy stirs within me; that's how Sahi and I used to be.

Sahi listens intently, wearing a matching half-smile to Emir as he tells of *Sea-Fey*'s travels across the ocean to continents where, instead of deserts, the land is covered with ice. It's like she's completely mesmerised by him, her attentiveness bordering on Meera's behaviour with the guards last night.

That need to know if Sahi's played with my memories tugs at me again, as the crack that's opened gapes between us. I could ask her now while we're away from prying eyes and the others are distracted, but she'll likely deflect any questions as she did when I confronted her about Ejaz after performing our duet. And she's been so preoccupied with interrogating the prisoner that, despite what she might have done, I don't want to add to the pressure I can see already weighs on her shoulders.

The scent of the souk rises towards us, a heady mix of rose and spices and fish cooked fresh from the sea. A group of young children duck out from behind a low wall, giggling as they watch our party pass. I notice the guards at the front, Imran and Ahmed, shoo them away without a glance when they appear at their feet. But when Emir sees them he waves them over and puts a finger to his lips, whispering to them as he sneaks the eldest a copper coin. I smile despite myself as the smallest wraps his arms round Emir's legs before chasing after the others, who are already bartering with a stallholder for a handful of dates.

'It's busy,' Zayn says as the crowd thickens by the entrance to the souk. 'We should split up into smaller groups so we don't lose anyone.'

He rallies us dancers together while the others divide into two groups, one with Imran at the helm and the other with Ahmed, and instructions to meet back at the entrance at dusk. We veer off the main path that we followed when we arrived in Naru yesterday morning, instead threading through the alleys and deeper into the ancient marketplace. I can see why we were told to stay together now. Without the guards to follow, we'd soon be lost within the labyrinth.

Voices call out to us as we pass, shouting out figures as they try to sell us their goods. I want to stop and look at each stall and the handcrafted designs on display – collections of intricately painted pots, jewellery, rugs and clothes – but the guards keep us moving until we reach the food quarter. I don't know where to stop first; each stall is filled with an assortment of street food that washes over my senses in waves.

'Gulab jamun!' Dana exclaims excitedly when she spots the syrupy sweets, running straight for them.

Meera veers away too, towards a stall where biryani is cooked in large, deep pots.

'You'll want to try these,' Emir says and leads Sahi and me to a stall laden with samosas and pakoras.

'Emir.' The young vendor beams and reaches over the rickety table to embrace him. 'May peace rise with every dawn, brother.'

'And endure with every dusk. How are you, Hamza?'

'All the better to see you're still alive, brother. I was beginning to think you'd been sent out there.' He gestures over his shoulder, his tone suddenly serious as he says, 'Word is, more people are being called up to join the army. Is it true?'

'Our country's at war, Hamza. Has been for too long,' Zayn interrupts and pats Emir on the shoulder. 'You might want to consider signing up. The army could use a good cook like yourself.'

Hamza laughs at the comment. 'That life isn't for me,' he says as he pulls out some brown paper. 'One of each?'

'Make it two,' Emir replies then turns to Sahi and me, releasing himself from Zayn's grip. 'These are the best samosas in town.'

'In the country, brother!' Hamza laughs as he wraps several up for us. 'And for you?'

Zayn nods, handing over some coins.

'Careful,' Emir says as he passes a couple to me and Sahi then takes a bite of his. 'They're hot.'

I break off the top of my samosa and the pastry flakes effortlessly in my mouth, the filling a delicious blend of cumin and coriander that infuses the aloo and peas.

'It tastes of home,' Sahi says, self-consciously wiping a crumb from the side of her mouth.

'It's why I keep coming back for more.' Emir laughs, already on his second one. 'Try it with this.' He passes us a small bowl of imli chutney and I pour some on generously before taking another bite.

Now it tastes of home. The thought forms with such clarity, it stuns me. The flavour, the way the pastry melts and the sound as more samosas and pakoras sizzle and spit within huge pans...all of it takes me back to the desert. But, as I try to pull at the thread further, it disappears.

Things are so different here than at the sanctuary and palace. There are no abilities at play, the only magic being that of the vendors' skills as they share their recipes and traditions, which have been passed down from generation to generation. A thread that connects them to their past. To their roots. To home.

TWENTY~FOUR

I find my targets, one eye closed to pinch them into sharper focus. They're still, unaware of my presence as I crouch within the shrubbery. I shift slightly, the air thick with the scent of jasmine that clings to my hair and kurta. That, combined with the heat of the midday sun and my tired muscles after a dance class with Mistress this morning, makes my mind and body sway. But I regain focus and wipe from my forehead the sweat that threatens to obscure my view as it collects in my lashes. With steady breaths, I draw my right arm back, elbow level and arrow poised as I pull the bowstring into position.

'Now!'

One of the targets moves, rushing away from me across the lawn. I dart up, refocus, find the point in their chest and shoot. My arrow whispers through the air. Heart hammering, I watch as it lodges in the target, piercing the sandbag between the shoulder blades. The dummy falls to the ground as Maryam releases it from her grasp.

'Good,' Captain Nadim says. 'But that single arrow alone would not have killed your enemy. Aim a little further to the left and you would have found their heart.'

'Yes, sir.'

'Your form has improved already,' he adds as Maryam takes the bow from me, signalling the end of class. 'I'm pleased to see the Leharanji still respects archery as part of your training.'

I nod, but the style of sessions here is different to what we did with Tahir. He would have us practise on a stationary target at Sajid's command, who didn't trust us not to hit one of the other students or guards. It's like learning the skill all over again now as I have to follow the moving enemy, find their weak spot and strike at the perfect time.

My gaze is drawn to Maryam as she uses her magic to slot my bow back onto the rack with her mind. With a flick of her hand, she lifts the sandbag into the air and floats it over to where the rest of the kit is kept. This is our third full day of training based on the regime Mistress Soraya has put together for us. When Amal showed me my schedule, I was surprised to see that none of my classes are with Sahi, Dana and Meera. Instead, we rotate throughout the day between archery, blade combat, dance and a break to rehearse on our own.

Mistress Soraya clearly meant it when she said we will train like rivals while here in our bid for the position of Queen's Guard. Though I'm enjoying the training, it isn't a role I aim to win. Everything I learn now will only help me when I take my place in the army. The more I think about Queen Sana's decision to bring me here, the more I realise that I was selected so that those with any power in her court can scrutinise my skills and my ability. I'm here to earn their trust, to try to prove, as I always have done, that I'm not corruptible as my mother was, before they thrust me back into the desert to fight.

'Go and eat something before your next class. You'll need the energy,' Captain Nadim says, raising an eyebrow when Emir appears and takes shelter under the shade of a tree. 'I shall see you tomorrow.'

'Thank you.' I bow my head and quickly drain a glass of fresh lemon water.

On the other side of the lawn, members of the Queen's Guard run through their drills and I watch as Maryam jogs over to join them. About half the group are there and move in unison, their gold chainmail armour glinting in the sunlight. Maryam watches from the sidelines, beating her hands on her thighs to cheer them on. Gradually, others join her, including Imani, until only five members continue their drills: the same women we saw rehearsing on our way to class the other day.

Their movements are fluid, unimpeded by the armour that covers their bodies like a second skin. Maya was telling us about it over our meal last night: how it's created by a form of thread-magic, similar to her own, but by those who are particularly good at handling metals. I'm completely mesmerised when the dancers begin using their magic. One dancer morphs into a series of animals until she settles on a roaring leopard and races through the gardens, while another multiplies until she doubles the size of the group. In tandem, the other three dancers reveal their magic: blades formed from the air; speed that means an enemy won't see an attack; while the last disappears until she's invisible but for her shimmer.

'That was impressive,' Emir says, leaning against the trunk of an old oak.

'They're so talented,' I reply, watching as the five women say their goodbyes and prepare to leave for the border. Captain

Nadim ushers them round to the front gates, along with twenty members of the palace guard who've also been chosen to help reinforce the army. I should be joining them and taking up the position I've trained for all this time.

'I meant your archery skills,' Emir says kindly. He squints and puts a hand over his eyes as he emerges from beneath the tree's overhanging branches. 'Hungry?' he asks when I don't answer.

My stomach rumbles in time with our steps. 'Extremely.'

He passes me the small package in his right hand and I open it, the scent of thick, melted butter drifting towards me as I peel back the paper to reveal a steaming paratha.

'There isn't time to join the others for your afternoon meal, I'm afraid,' he says with a sheepish smile. 'Her Majesty would like to see you.'

'Now?' I'm suddenly not hungry, the pangs replaced with the flutter of nerves.

'The queen has asked to speak to all of you separately,' Emir says quietly, sensing my unease. He leans a little towards me in a way that borders on familiarity. 'She's eager to find out how you're all settling in and has already spoken to Sahi this morning.'

'Sahi told you that?' A twinge of annoyance ripples through me, but I don't know why.

'Zayn.' Sahi's guard.

I break off some of the paratha and it almost melts in my mouth. It's so soft, revealing delicate layers of aloo inside. But I only manage a couple of mouthfuls. Our footsteps echo on the tiles as we walk through the great halls and corridors, the guards stationed at every turn nodding to Emir as we pass.

When we finally reach a set of golden doors set within a gilded archway, the two guards stationed outside knock three times. A muffled voice replies from within. The doors open and I feel like I'm about to walk onto a stage for a performance I haven't rehearsed for.

Emir glances sideways at me and takes the half-eaten paratha, clasping it behind his back before walking into the queen's quarters. 'Aasira, Your Majesty,' he says with a bow.

I step forward and meet the queen's eyes briefly before curtsying. 'Your Majesty.'

Queen Sana dismisses Emir and he leaves with a final bow, the doors closing firmly behind him. An attendant hovers by the ornate desk, a beautiful deep green marble inlayed with a delicate mother-of-pearl pattern. Anticipating the queen's request, she pours two glasses of steaming spiced chai. Neither of us speaks until the attendant passes us each a glass.

'Thank you, Ria,' the queen says as her attendant ducks out of the room.

I feel suddenly small with only the two of us here and I'm struck by how unusual the room is. I expected to be taken to a large, imposing throne room, but instead this space feels intimate, despite its high ceiling where faded paintings of animals within the desert, forests and ocean play out. The wall too is covered in paintings, these ones gilded, and I imagine the painter casting their magic over this room years ago through every brushstroke. But it's the large tapestry that hangs behind the desk that captures my attention. The dark fabric is worn and damaged by the sunlight that streams in through the large window opposite, and I can't quite make out the pattern.

I catch the queen following my gaze and wonder if I should say something, though I don't want to break protocol that dictates the queen should be the first to speak.

'Thank you,' she says eventually.

I look round to see if Ria has returned, but we're alone.

'You showed great courage when the Mezeeri soldiers attacked.' A wave of rose oud rolls off the queen as she walks over to her desk, her jade lehenga swishing with each step. 'I wanted to thank you personally for your part in protecting me and my party.'

Her features soften slightly as she turns to me, her green eyes bright in the sunlight.

'I was performing my duty,' I say, voice quieter than expected. I cough lightly to clear my throat.

'Hmm.' She sips from her glass, then gently sets it down on her desk. 'You remind me of her.'

The shift in conversation startles me and yet it's the topic I've waited for the queen to broach ever since we first met in Nazeem.

'Your mother,' Queen Sana says as though my silence meant I didn't already know who she spoke of. 'Especially when you performed your solo to the same music she did when graduating from the Leharanji.'

I expect the queen to look annoyed, but there's the glimmer of something else in her eyes.

'We used to spend hours here staring at this tapestry as children. My father would always encourage us to go outside and play on the beach, but we loved nothing more than sitting right here —' she points to where the ornate rug is slightly worn — 'and trying to spot something new within the fabric.

Lina was sure the design had changed each time we looked at it. That the creatures transformed into something new entirely the moment we turned away.'

My chest tightens and a lump rises in my throat. 'I never knew that my mother spent time here as a child.'

Queen Sana's eyebrows momentarily arch like the peaks of dunes, but then she nods to herself. 'She practically grew up here,' she reveals. 'Your grandfather was an Amaari diplomat and travelled overseas for months at a time, so Lina and your grandmother lived in the palace grounds.'

Grandfather...grandmother... I've spent so long trying to rise out of the shadow of my mother's name, I've never really thought of the family who came before her or of the people I'm descended from.

'Your grandmother used to say that looking out on the Emerald Sea reminded her of her own home: Kaernow.' A smile plays on her lips and I feel one tug at mine too. 'She always spoke of how much she missed the rain, so would have me practise my skills for her. Mostly to cool down as she never quite got used to the heat and would burn easily if she stayed out in the sun too long.'

I look at my own arms, tanned from training outside, but they were slightly rosy even after our journey through the desert.

'She was fairer than you, but she had those same freckles,' Queen Sana says.

The lump in my throat catches as I trace the small dots along my arms. 'My grandmother wasn't from here...'

Queen Sana shakes her head. 'No, but Elowen grew to love Amaar and our customs.'

There's a fondness in her tone that warms me and I want to ask her to continue. When I was summoned here, I never thought this was the conversation we'd be having, especially after her coolness towards me at the sanctuary. But she's just painted my family with colour, a family I knew nothing about.

'Elowen.' My grandmother's name is strange on my tongue, but beautiful all the same. 'Is she still alive?'

'Both your grandparents passed away just before Lina graduated from the Leharanji. I'd asked her to join me here as a member of my mother's Queen's Guard, but she couldn't bring herself to.'

'So she joined the army...' I say quietly.

'Just before my own father passed away, he reminded me of the story of this tapestry. As children, he would tell us it was older than the palace itself, woven when Amaar and Mezeer were one country. A reminder of our roots, despite the separate paths our countries have taken.'

I join her, reaching my hand out towards the threadbare end, but hesitant to disturb it in case the fabric should crumble away at my touch. 'It looks like it was never quite finished.'

'It wasn't,' she says simply. 'The people who wove it were on opposite sides of the border when our countries parted ways. And so it hangs here, a reminder of what once was.'

My eyes trace the frayed edge, then work their way back over the tapestry to where a rust-coloured sun rises over a mountain range, a pale moon beside it. Olive green thread marks out the rows of trees at the base of the mountains, while glittering pearl-coloured thread depicts several rivers flowing towards an ocean cut off where the tapestry ends.

'*The sun and moon rose together, and through them the mountains and rivers and trees were born,*' I say, my mother's words flowing through me from somewhere deep within. '*As nature awoke, so did our abilities… Nature nurtured magic.*'

The hairs stand up on the back of my neck. I haven't heard my mother's voice in so long but, for a moment, it was like she was here. When I look at Queen Sana, recognition mingles in her expression too.

We're quiet for a moment as she opens the bottom drawer in her desk and takes out a small oblong box covered in red velvet. 'Before your mother left for the army, I gave her this.' Queen Sana passes me the box and I put down my chai. 'She loved the old stories my father shared with us growing up, so I had this made for her.'

I gently lift the lid to reveal a delicate necklace. Tears sting the backs of my eyes as I lift it out, the thin gold chain dangling over my hand as I rub my thumb over the sun pendant.

'I had the chain repaired,' she says, her voice thick as she too stares at the necklace.

I choke back a sob as my mother appears in my mind in a way I've never seen her before… She kneels in the sand, hands bound in front of her as the necklace I hold now is ripped from round her neck.

'I see her in you and the way you fought the other day, leading where others faltered,' Queen Sana continues. 'Your mother had that same heart. But in the end her loyalty was swayed and she betrayed everything she'd sworn to protect.'

Then there she is again. The woman everyone tells me she was: a traitor.

'Why?' I whisper to myself.

'For love.'

I struggle for words, brow furrowed as I try to understand what the queen means.

'She didn't tell you about your father?'

I think back and can almost feel a vein pulse at my right temple. 'Only that she met him while in the army,' I say, the memory vague but suddenly present.

'Your mother fell in love with the man she captured,' Queen Sana says sharply. 'A Mezeeri soldier who had wounded her in battle. She'd retaliated by wrapping him within one of her dust clouds, almost ripping the skin from his bones, and taking him prisoner. He was willing to give up information about his own army in exchange for his life, so he was kept alive in their camp. But your mother was the only person he would share that information with. She took that trust and turned it into meaning something else. Love.' The queen I met in Nazeem returns, her tone firm and features arranged in a practised expression to give little away.

'Only his love wasn't true. She knew relationships within the army are forbidden, let alone with the enemy. When hers was discovered, she lost control of her magic and killed her own soldiers in her sandstorm. She was stripped of the rank of general and fled before her trial, but not before the Mezeeri soldier coaxed her into setting him free. Before he ran, he enticed information from her: lies that fed King Faisal's narrative about why his land was dying while ours prospered.'

That Queen Sana had used her power to dry up the rivers in Mezeer...lies people still believe today. 'Lies she spoke in anger against you to distract from her own crimes,' I say.

I flinch as an invisible grip clasps my forearms. My mother flashes in my mind again, a sandstorm raging round her, screaming my name as I'm dragged away.

'When news of her betrayal reached me and I discovered that she'd fled, I learned what my mother had taught me above all else. That, as ruler of this country, I can trust no one,' Queen Sana says flatly. 'While at the same time I must protect everyone.'

Panic floods me as in my mind I'm consumed by a fresh image. I struggle against the hold on my arms. The sandstorm whips round me and I squeeze my eyes shut against the grains. When I open them again, a sword glints in the moonlight over my mother's frame. But when it comes down she's already gone.

My flames quiver inside me. I stare at the necklace again and the image of my mother knelt in the sand comes into sharper focus.

'Thank you.' I force out the words.

I pull back the clasp and drape the necklace round my neck. Queen Sana smiles, but I see the true meaning behind this gift. She may have given it to my mother, but she just told me herself: she can trust no one. Giving me my mother's necklace is all part of my test. A test of whether I'll follow her path and betray my queen and country. A test of my loyalty.

TWENTY~FIVE

I lie in bed, turning to the rhythm of the waves in a bid to get comfortable. But I'm restless, my mind alert. I touch the pendant I now wear: my mother's necklace. The moment I saw it I recognised the delicate sunburst, a replica of the mosaic in the walled garden at the sanctuary. My mother was never without it.

Until the day it was snatched from round her neck...

I see that same scene again, fresh and raw. The gust as it swirls and lashes at the sand around her. The gleaming sword...

I sit bolt upright, heart racing. Sweat beads along the back of my neck, sticking my loose hair to my skin. I don't know where the image came from, but the moment I laid eyes on the necklace, I saw it being pulled from round my mother's neck and falling to the sand. I try to rid my mind of the scene by counting through the steps for my solo in ten days. Slowly, my mother slips away, her features distorted until all that's left is her hazy silhouette, before she vanishes into the dunes.

How could I have known so little of my mother's past until today? Did my mother not tell me about her parents, or has

Sahi's influence stolen those memories from me? I was aware that my mother and the queen had been close during their training at the sanctuary, but not that my mother had grown up in the palace. Or that my grandmother was from another country overseas.

And the man my mother shared false information with… I try to imagine him, a Mezeeri soldier like those we crossed paths with in the desert. Was he my father? An enemy who somehow won my mother's heart. Maybe that's why Queen Sana told me everything she did…to remind me where I come from. The daughter of not just a traitor, but an enemy too.

My thoughts still whirring, I give up on sleep. I change into a black kurta and sneak out of my chamber, expecting to find a night guard on duty in the corridor. But it's empty. The halls are devoid of the bustle of the day as I make my way to the studios. The few guards in post doze on the spot, the solitude of a night shift a welcome rest.

The studios, too, are silent. I'm grateful to have the space to myself when I notice one of the doors is ajar. I peer inside and my chest flutters unexpectedly when I see who's rehearsing within. Emir. It's so unexpected and I feel like I'm watching a private moment no one was meant to see.

I've never seen a boy…a young man dance before. There's no thought behind each step, his body his guide as he turns then jumps into a split kick and falls, rolling out of the position. I recognise the emotions that emanate from him with each movement, that feeling of the music flowing through your body and taking you to a place that's safe. A place where you can be free.

I push the door open a little more when he leaps out of view. My flames itch to move, to hear the song he hears in his head and let it take over me. But I stay where I am, silent and captivated. This isn't a performance: he's dancing for himself. The music playing in his head must swell because his dance becomes more frantic in response, yet there's still an elegance to it as he effortlessly executes a triple turn, then jumps and spins at the same time. Without a sound, he crumples to the ground, his breathing heavy as he lies there and the imagined music ends.

I resist the urge to clap as he stands and wipes away the sweat on his forehead with a towel.

'Couldn't sleep either?' he asks, spotting my reflection in one of the steamy mirrors.

'You dance,' I say, caught out.

He pushes back the strands of hair that have fallen over his eyes. Worn loose, it hangs just below his ears in a soft wave. 'Not really.'

'You don't call that dancing?'

A laugh escapes him. 'Not after seeing your rehearsals.'

I blush and am grateful for the dimness of the room, which is lit only by a few lanterns along the far wall. 'Who taught you?'

His dark eyes glimmer and a smile tugs at his mouth. 'My mother,' he says fondly and throws his towel back into the corner of the studio.

'Was she a dancer at the Leharanji?'

'She went there when she was of age, but she didn't have an ability and returned to her village. My sister got to live out that dream for her though.'

'Would I know your sister?'

A distant look clouds his features. 'She… She was quite a bit older than me and graduated before your time…'

He falls silent and I don't press any further. 'The guards at the sanctuary never danced,' I say to change the subject. 'At least, not that I witnessed.'

He shrugs, his tone casual as he says, 'What's the use in boys learning to dance if it doesn't manifest an ability?' But there's a seriousness behind his words too; no doubt it's a statement someone has used to justify not offering to teach him.

'And yet here you are.' I gesture round the room. 'A studio all to yourself and a routine ready for the stage.'

'Here I am.' He smiles coyly and I can't help but laugh, my heady confusion momentarily lifted.

'I'll leave you to rehearse,' he says after a few moments, collecting his towel.

'No, stay,' I say a little too quickly and try to recover with, 'I'll use another studio.'

'Or *you* could stay,' he says as I turn to leave. 'We could dance together.'

My flames glimmer under the surface, soft in a way I haven't felt before 'Together?'

'A duet,' he offers tentatively.

'How, when we haven't been given any choreography?'

'We can improvise.'

But I've never improvised a duet and have certainly never danced with a young man.

'It was just a suggestion. We don't have to,' he says, sensing my uncertainty.

'It's just…how will we make it look like a cohesive performance if neither of us knows what the other is about to do next?'

'This isn't a performance.' He walks backwards into the middle of the studio, grinning as he holds his hand out for me. 'It's for fun.'

I picture Mistress Soraya hearing him say those words and glance at the door, which is still slightly ajar. But no one else is awake. No one will see. I join Emir in the centre of the studio, but can't quite bring myself to take his hand.

For a moment, we both stand awkwardly, each waiting for the other to move first.

'Should we begin?' he says.

I nod and he reaches his left arm out towards me. I follow him and reach out my right, our fingers almost brushing. It must be a trick of the moonlight, but as I sweep both arms over my head, sweat gleams on his hands and it almost looks like they glimmer in the mirror's reflection. His movements are slow at first and I wonder what music he hears in his head, if the first notes are like what I hear: a mix of strings and a voice that will later swell, joined by a tabla.

Emir turns and I take it as my chance to break from our mirror-dance. He hesitates, watching as I draw my left leg up, then extend it behind me. As I rise onto the ball of my right foot, Emir places one hand beneath mine and catches my glance in the mirror, where I nod to him. He gently rests his other hand at the base of my back, steadying me as I tilt my body forward.

It's like he can see the dance playing out in my mind as I straighten and his hands rest round my waist, ready for me

185

to turn on one leg. On my last turn, I finish facing him instead of the mirrors that are our audience. As I do a backbend, his hands remain round my waist to help me keep my balance.

Our eyes meet as I straighten up. I feel it then, the music in him and the way it grows.

We break away from each other and for a moment I stay where I am, unable to look away as Emir's movements expand and become grander. He leaps, legs in a perfect split. When his feet hit the ground, he trusts his body and effortlessly falls into a low spin, then flips with a lightness of touch back to standing. He's technical yet free. A classical dancer whose choreography goes beyond the traditional and has a style to it that was never taught at the sanctuary.

Aware of him watching me now, I leap before landing on one leg and sweeping into a deep lunge. He immediately copies and our styles entwine into something entirely new as our separate dances become one, a marriage of our two styles. Anticipating each other's movements, it no longer feels like we're improvising but are performing a duet. We spin away from each other round the room like two desert wanderers who've lost their way on a starlit night.

Our finale closes in as the music in our heads crescendoes. Emir stands in the opposite corner of the studio as I turn towards him, whipping my head round and always spotting towards him, until I jump. He doesn't falter and catches me. I'm weightless in his arms as he lifts me above his head, then onto his right shoulder, my golden dust shimmering as it weaves over my arms and Emir slowly turns.

His hands hover round my waist for a moment after he lowers me to the ground and slowly the shimmer withdraws, hiding beneath my skin again. But I feel exposed. We both catch our breath and I'm caught in the intensity of his gaze. He laughs a little self-consciously, perhaps feeling it too, the strange bridge between us.

'Thank you,' he says and retrieves his towel again, slinging it over one shoulder. 'For indulging me.'

The warmth I felt before glints again. 'It was fun. I only ever usually dance because I'm rehearsing for a performance or because at the end I have to…' I sigh, unsure why I'm telling him when I admit, 'Sometimes I think it would be nice to dance just because…I love dancing.'

He nods in understanding. 'I get that.'

'I know my duty though,' I add quickly.

And he doesn't question that I do. 'Maybe…' he begins, then looks away. 'If you ever need a respite from your duty, we could do it again sometime. You could teach me what you learned at the sanctuary.'

A silent laugh escapes me. 'You're already a great dancer. I don't think there's anything else I could teach you.'

He shrugs. 'I'll take the compliment. But there's always something new to learn.' When I don't respond, he drops into a low curtsy, mimicking the way we'd normally end a performance. My smile only widens as I curtsy too. 'Thank you, again. I really enjoyed that.'

'Me too.' *Thank you for distracting me.* But the words lodge in my throat as I feel the weight of the necklace that settles round it.

TWENTY~SIX

When Emir greets me outside my room the next morning, he wears a smile that leaves me light-headed. Dancing with him last night has revived an energy in me that I haven't felt in a while. It's different to the kind that ignites when I summon my magic, but feels familiar all the same. And it didn't just start when we were dancing together… It's crept up on me during the short time I've been here.

Even though we haven't known each other long, I've quickly grown used to his presence and this morning I woke up looking forward to seeing him. But I'm not here to start new friendships. I'm here to train and prove that, while I might be the 'traitor's daughter', I'm not an enemy in disguise. I can't help but smile though as I stand beside Emir. Being in his company almost reminds me of what it was like at the sanctuary, when Sahi and I never strayed far from each other. She comes out of her room, and there's a pang in my chest as I watch her greet the other students.

The palace apprentices chatter among themselves as we're led down to breakfast. But we four dancers are quiet. Perhaps they notice the glances in our direction too, the feeling of scrutiny as courtiers no doubt judge us behind the scenes in the lead up to our performances in just over a week.

An elderly woman stands near the entrance to the smallest of the banquet halls where we meet for breakfast and our evening meal. She's more conspicuous than the other courtiers, fixing us with her pale blue stare as she adjusts her hijab. Distracted as he talks to Imran, Zayn knocks into her as he enters the hall and, with the slightest of movements, a small folded piece of paper passes from her hand to his. He stops and apologises, brusquely tucking the note away in one swift action.

I glance around me to see if anyone else noticed, but the others are all either locked in conversation or already in the hall. As I sit down, I see she still watches us through the doors, her expression blank in a way that forces me to look away.

'Where did you get that?' Meera, sitting opposite me, points at my neck.

My hand flies to my mother's necklace.

Dana turns in her seat next to me to have a look, swatting my hand away as I try to tuck it under the neckline of my kurta. 'It's pretty.'

I notice Sahi trying to get a glimpse of it too from her seat next to Meera, who leans forward and rests her elbows on the table. 'Who gave it to you?'

'Was it one of the guards?' Dana teases when I don't respond, then whispers just loud enough for the other two to hear. 'Don't tell me: it was Emir. I saw that smile between the two of you earlier.'

'It wasn't from Emir,' I say a little too quickly and Dana chuckles to herself.

'It looks like very fine gold.' Meera raises her eyebrows. 'Did you steal it?'

'No, Meera.'

'That was a bit defensive.' She leans back in her chair as a group of attendants appear and pour us all a glass of lassi.

I'm grateful when the table falls silent as the food is brought out, and everyone helps themselves to the selection of fruits, eggs and roti. I'd started to hope they'd forgotten about the necklace when Dana prods me.

'You know you're going to have to tell us who gave it to you, right?'

I breathe in deeply. 'It was my mother's,' I say finally. 'Queen Sana gave it to me as some sort of test of my loyalty.'

'What makes you say that?' Sahi asks abruptly.

'Why else would she have given it to me?'

'It was a gift from the queen?' Meera says as though she completely missed everything else I said.

'Not really. It belonged to my mother so she thought I should have it.' But nerves trickle along my skin. I wish I'd given another answer. Or, better still, that I'd taken it off last night.

Dana's sudden silence makes me uneasy. She's usually the one to laugh things off, but her features are knitted together in a way that resembles Meera's. 'I think we all know who's favourite for Queen's Guard.'

'That's not what this is about.'

'Really?' she says in a tone that surprises me and even Meera looks taken aback. 'I thought the whole reason we're here is to compete for that role, and the fact you're receiving gifts –' she gestures towards my neck – 'from the person who will make the final decision is a reminder of that.'

Since when were you so desperate to become a Queen's Guard? I want to challenge, but I hold my tongue.

'And you're practically working as a guard already by trying to get information out of the prisoner,' Meera says to Sahi. 'I don't know why I'm even here,' she adds.

The conversation around us dissolves as several of the other girls look our way. I can't stomach the food in front of me and when I sip my lassi it leaves a sour taste in my mouth.

'This necklace isn't a gift,' I say quietly, eager to defuse the tension. 'It's a reminder of how my mother lost it before she was executed as a traitor to the crown.'

Neither Dana nor Meera look up, but I know they heard me. As did Sahi, who fidgets and picks at her thumbnail.

'You seem quiet.'

'Sorry.'

Emir slows so he falls into step with me while we walk to the studios. 'You don't need to apologise. Is everything all right?'

I sigh, slowing even more as we near the dance studio. 'Things are just a bit…tense with the other dancers.'

Emir's gaze strays awkwardly. 'I noticed a bit of friction over breakfast.'

I look at the floor, embarrassed to think even the guards overheard from their stations round the hall. 'This audition to become part of the Queen's Guard is getting to everyone in a way it never did when we were back at the sanctuary and we all thought the role was Sahi's.'

'Sometimes you don't realise how much you want something until it's offered to you and might be taken away. You've all had a taste of what life's like at the palace. No matter how honourable serving in the army is, it's a drastically different life to the one you could have here.'

Maybe that is what's motivating them, or at least Dana, who was always eager to become a soldier before now.

'Things will settle down,' Emir says as we reach Mistress Soraya's studio. 'Have a good class.'

He spins on the ball of his foot to turn back the way we came and smiles playfully. It has the intended effect as I smile back then wave.

I'm about to enter the studio when I hear Mistress Soraya talking to someone inside. I peer through the gap in the door and make out the back of a man's balding head. He paces in front of Mistress, his grey waistcoat and white shalwar kameez tailored perfectly to his lean frame.

'Everyone knows these auditions for the Queen's Guard are intended to distract people from the whispers,' he says, voice rising.

'Which are?' Mistress Soraya replies.

'That she's no longer fit to rule.'

A chill floods me. I feel suddenly exposed on hearing someone within the palace question the queen outright.

Mistress's expression hardens. 'Say that to the wrong person, Tariq, and it might be the last statement you make.'

'But you don't deny it.'

'Enough,' she replies sharply. 'The queen can choose the newest member of her guard if she wishes.'

Tariq steps aside as Mistress passes him and disappears out of my eyeline. 'But why this year? Prior to now, her courtiers have always chosen for her.'

'Because she cannot trust her courtiers,' Mistress says, disapproval evident in each syllable. 'As you are now proving to me.'

Tariq turns slightly and, as I see him in profile, I recognise him from his visits to the sanctuary for previous loornas. 'Yet she trusts the daughter of a traitor to walk these halls,' he seethes. 'I heard what happened in Nazeem: she produced white flames that left no trace. That sort of magic shouldn't be allowed here.'

'Perhaps this is something you should address with the queen herself, if you feel that threatened,' Mistress says, coming back into view.

'I'm not threat—' He falters under her glare then changes tack. 'We should all feel threatened. Innocent people are being killed by our enemy because we can't defend our border, or dying because their queen isn't strong enough to end the drought. She should be concentrating on healing our country before she doesn't have one to rule over any more. Not putting on some pageant.'

'You might profess to care for those beyond this city, but you haven't offered to help them. In fact, you seem quite content to continue living the lavish lifestyle the queen provides for you within the palace.'

Tariq shakes his head and turns for the door, before twisting back towards Mistress. 'Our country is suffering under her leadership. You can help bring an end to that.'

Mistress is silent as they stare at each other, almost goading him to say something else incriminating. 'Goodbye, Tariq,' she says at last.

I dart into the empty room opposite and crouch behind the door. His footsteps are short and sharp as his sandals clack along the marble tiles. I wait until I can't hear them any more before slowly emerging into the corridor.

Mistress stands in the doorway to her studio, arms crossed.

My heartbeat hammers. There's no hiding that I overheard everything. 'I—'

'You're late.'

I cower, too scared to follow as she walks back inside and removes her gloves. Hovering there, I wait for her to say something about her conversation with Tariq. To tell me I should never repeat what I heard or that I misunderstood. But she offers nothing, like it didn't happen.

'Are you going to continue to make me wait?' she says, voice steady and back turned to me. 'Or perhaps you think your solo is polished enough that you don't need any more rehearsals.'

My throat closes up and I don't answer as I enter, eyeing the corner where the musicians would normally set up.

'They're not required today. Here.' She holds out a short strip of black cloth, and when I don't take it she thrusts it into my hand.

I try not to recoil as our fingers touch and I see the steel-coloured symbols on her palms: two overlapping triangles.

She smirks. 'Not every touch of mine is poisonous. Surely you of all people know not to believe all the stories you hear?'

My brow furrows. Is she referring to what I just overheard between her and Tariq?

'I want to see how you perform when your senses are dulled. Put it on.' She gestures to the cloth in my hand. 'Over your eyes.'

I'm hesitant. I know everything we do at the palace is a test, but this feels different, like I'm being set up in some way. I've only ever seen Mistress with her gloves on. Why has she taken them off now? Would she use her magic on me?

'In the centre,' she orders, waving her hand. 'And dance your solo. You've already wasted enough of this class.'

Flames rising to the surface, I do as I'm told and slowly place the cloth over my eyes, tying it at the back of my head. I can still make out the sunlight, but can no longer see Mistress, and listen for any hint that she might be drawing near.

'Begin,' she says from somewhere on my right.

The opening bars of my solo play in my head, first the flute then the singer as she joins in. But, as I start dancing, I can't relax into each movement. I'm too aware of what I just overheard, of the obvious suspicions about my being here. What if Mistress Soraya shares those doubts and takes matters into her own hands?

My flames coil within me the more I dance. The routine is in my muscles after intense rehearsals, but I'm disorientated in a way I didn't expect and don't know if I'm still facing my front of stage. When I reach my spin sequence, it only becomes harder and I begin to feel dizzy as I'm unable to find one point to focus on with each turn.

'Hold your core,' Mistress says, sounding closer than I thought she was.

Panic grips me. The fire swells. Bright light flares through the cloth.

I rip it from my head and, for the first time, I see them. My flames billow round me. They burn bright, a fierce white like a jasmine flower in full bloom.

'Incredible,' Mistress says softly and reaches out as though to touch my blaze. 'It was as I thought… Your emotions must be heightened in order to unlock this part of your ability.'

'Heightened,' I echo. When I was in Nazeem, I was angry when I saw what had happened in the village I'd briefly called home. And confused when Omar protested his innocence while I was told to execute him for his crimes.

'It was the same with your mother.'

My flames dwindle. 'My mother?'

Mistress nods and looks me in the eye, her face grave. 'Your mother didn't just command air. She could become it.'

TWENTY~SEVEN

The image of my mother kneeling in the desert, a sword poised above her neck, plays over in my mind. Despite all my questions, Mistress Soraya wouldn't tell me any more about my mother's ability and dismissed me quickly, as if I'd done something wrong.

As soon as she told me my mother could become air, I knew it was true. But I can't place the memory, nor can I pretend any longer. I still don't want to believe Sahi might have taken my memories, but I saw what she did to Ejaz. She created some sort of block in his mind so he wouldn't remember Camil, and that's exactly what it's felt like for me. Other than tiny, hazy fragments, I remember so little of my life before the sanctuary. And now I need the truth; *her* truth. Last night I slipped a note beneath Sahi's door asking her to meet me on the beach at dawn, where we wouldn't be overheard.

A glimmer of pale light crests over the horizon and reflects off the calm water. I tread carefully down the deep stone steps cut into the cliff face, following the same path our guards showed us when they brought us here the other afternoon during a rare break. The cove it leads to is secluded, hemmed in on both sides by the cliffs the palace rests on. Emir explained the tides to us and how, as the day breaks, the sea pulls back to reveal the long stretch of sand that weaves eastwards past the city gates, until it merges with the desert.

The last step is the deepest so I crouch and push off with one hand, jumping over the small rock pool that sits beneath it. The sand is still wet and my footprints follow me to the shore as I walk between the large blackened rocks that are revealed when the tide is out. Sahi can't have arrived yet as there are no other footprints here. I take a deep breath. The last time I confronted her, she refused to open up and perhaps she fears that I have similar questions now and won't come. But I hope she will.

The waves are coaxed up the beach towards me, ruffling the sand as they drift in and out. I kneel and gather some sand in my hand, its texture and colour so different to that in the desert. Here it gleams white whereas in the desert it looks as though it's been infused with saffron and turmeric. I walk on a little further and shiver as the cool water rushes over my feet. It's a balm I've never felt before. Cold in a way that makes me catch my breath, but exhilarates me at the same time. I take another step, then another, until the sea rises over my ankles, my calves, my knees, soaking my kurta. I breathe in its fragrance, the saltiness rich and the seaweed slick as loose strands catch round my legs.

Large birds swoop down from the cliffs and dive towards the water, catching fish in their beaks with such efficiency, it's like a piece of perfectly timed choreography. The sea provides the song as the waves inhale and exhale, lapping at the base of the cliffs that glow the colour of apricots as the sun rises.

I close my eyes and dance, longing to emulate the feeling of dancing freely with Emir the other evening. With the sea as my partner, each movement relieves the tension in my body and clears my mind of the fog. It's like a veil is lifted and, suddenly, my memory of that night comes flooding back…

The lilt of a sitar drifted through Nazeem as dusk approached and sparks darted from the bonfire into the twilight. We'd only lived there a few weeks, but I felt as though I'd known the village my whole life. Even Ma was relaxed, a smile on her face as she chatted to Omar and one of the elders, Yara. They all laughed and Yara looked my way conspiratorially, beckoning me over with a flick of her knobbly walking stick.

'Did you help light this fire?' she asked me.

I scrunched up my nose, frustrated. 'No.'

She shrugged and patted my arm as if to say it didn't matter that I struggled to command my flames for more than a few seconds. 'You have plenty of time to learn. How about tomorrow we have a little practice?'

'I'd like that, thank you.'

Despite the news travelling through the villages of crops dying suddenly and continued droughts, there was a festival atmosphere in the air as the full moon shone over us and welcomed in a new season. Food was in short supply, but that evening we shared what we had, each household cooking a dish to be enjoyed by the whole village.

'I like it here,' I said as Ma squeezed me into her side.

'Me too.' She kissed me on the head, then took my hand and we followed Omar to where Iyad and Zora were gathered round the bonfire with the rest of the villagers, sitting on large rugs and cushions.

I sat between her and Omar, and they smiled at each other above me in a way I hadn't seen before. She had always worn a smile, even on the coldest, loneliest nights, but the constant moving had tired us both. I'd never understood why we didn't settle in one of the many villages or towns we'd passed before this one. Sometimes we stayed in an inn, if they had one, but only for one night before beginning our journey again. In time, I'd stopped asking. But something about Nazeem, whether it was the village itself or something else, made my mother stay.

Some of the villagers sang as they passed the food round and laughter rose under the stars. Stories were shared and prayers said, of hope for peace as word of conflict in the east reached us, and gratitude that we were safe for another night. All until a rogue flame flickered in the distance against the black sky. Another three flames came into focus as a group of riders on horseback appeared over the nearest dune. The singing and laughter stopped abruptly as the villagers dropped their plates and disappeared into their homes, including Omar.

He returned with a blade in his hand.

'What's happening?' I said to my mother who was on her feet now, alert. 'Ma?'

She crouched next to me and ran her fingers through my hair, her eyes glistening in the flames. 'You're going to stay with Omar and Yara, understand?'

'Why?' I said over the frantic shouts around us. 'Who are those people?'

Four figures approached, their silhouettes coming into sharper focus.

'I want you to stay out of sight, do you understand? No matter what happens, stay hidden.'

'Hidden,' I murmured. 'Why? What's going to happen?'

She pulled me into a hug and whispered into my hair. 'Nothing. I won't let anything happen to you.' She held me at arm's length and it was like I saw for the first time the warrior she once was. 'Look after her,' she told Yara as she walked away.

'Lina!' Yara called after her, her voice grave.

My mother turned but neither of them said anything else. Yara simply placed a palm over her heart and held it there. Ma nodded, repeating the gesture before she hurried towards the group who waited on the other side of the wall that surrounded the village.

'Help me up,' Yara said and I put my arm through hers as she leaned on me and her cane to stand.

'Where's Ma going?' I said, fighting back the tears.

But Yara didn't reply. Instead, she guided me into Omar's home. He followed us in and pulled down a tapestry that hung over the doorway. I darted to the hole in the wall that was the window, but Omar was at my side in an instant and pulled me out of view.

'Let me go.' I squirmed out of his grip.

'Stay down,' Omar whispered.

'Aasira,' Yara said from where she sat, 'listen to Omar. Now is not the time to disobey orders.'

'I don't understand!' I cried. 'What is Ma doing? Who are those people and why is everyone else hiding while she's still out there?'

I heard her name then in the silence and crept back to the window. Ma had now joined the group just outside the boundary wall and held her palms skywards, her muscles tense in the firelight as her magic cast a thin barrier of sand between herself and the visitors. Through the grains, I saw the three men and one woman dismount their horses.

'Hello, Lina,' one of the men said. While his companions wore Amaari armour, he was dressed in a white kurta that highlighted the threads of grey in his slicked-back hair.

'Kaleb,' Ma said.

My heart skipped a beat. I knew that name. The name of the man we had to hide from.

One of the men in armour edged forward and Ma built her sand-shield up even further. Kaleb put his hand out, indicating for his guards to stay back.

'Does she know you're here?' Ma asked and Kaleb cocked his head to one side.

'If what you'd really like to know is if she's asked us to bring you in alive, then no, she hasn't.'

'That wasn't what I asked.'

A crooked smile distorted Kaleb's features.

'My death would suit you nicely, wouldn't it? A way to silence your doubters while you decide which monarch and country you serve... Sorry, I mean which one best serves you.'

Kaleb's smile wavered. 'There's nowhere else for you to hide, Lina,' he said through gritted teeth. 'Give yourself up now and no one else has to suffer.'

'We both know that isn't true.'

Ma hesitated no longer. She threw her wall of sand in the direction of the intruders. They staggered back, crying out as it scratched their eyes and skin. Ma called on her magic again and sand filled the air within the whistling gust, but one of the guards was quick on her feet and thrust her sword towards Ma.

Tears streamed down my face. 'S-someone needs to help.'

'Bring her over here,' Yara said and Omar grabbed me round the waist. I kicked at his legs, but Yara's grip was even firmer as she hooked her shaking arm round me, holding me tight to her side.

But I couldn't do nothing. My whole body sparked with energy and my flames burst free with my scream. Yara fell back in her chair as I leaped from her arms and white-hot fire surged over my body. I was outside before Omar could stop me.

'Ma!' I screeched, running for her.

'Aasira! No!'

I sprinted beyond the boundary wall and charged at the man she called Kaleb, the one who was staring at me, transfixed.

'You have a daughter?' he said in disbelief. 'A flame-wielder...' A startled look crossed his face and he staggered away from me. 'Get her.'

His three guards faced me, blades held out in front of them. But they struggled within Ma's storm, the wind buffeting them with such force, they couldn't move towards me.

Fire raced across my skin, as bright as the moon above, and I saw their fear as my flames expanded chaotically around me, caught in my mother's whirlwind. But her magic dropped suddenly as she reached out for me. The guard closest to her tackled her. Ma pulled out the knife hidden at her ankle, beneath her trouser leg, and aimed it under the arm where his armour was weak. He recoiled as blade met flesh, but he didn't give in, pinning her to the ground then binding her hands. Two more guards rushed at me and my flames were quenched by my fear.

'Sajid, now!' Kaleb shouted and the largest of the guards grabbed me.

'Ma!' I struggled against Sajid, bruises already blooming beneath his fingertips.

'Let her go!'

Sand rained over us as, with Ma's rage, her storm grew again, trying to mask me within it. But Sajid refused to release me and cold steel met my left side.

'Take me,' Ma pleaded as the other two guards yanked her into a kneeling position. 'Leave my daughter out of your war, Kaleb,' she begged again.

He looked between us both. 'As you wish.'

The veil of grains around me fell to reveal a midnight sky. Ma knelt in the sand, hands bound in front of her and head bowed. Kaleb tore her *sunbeam necklace from her neck and in its place a blade swept down, gleaming in the moonlight.*

'No! Let go of me!' I shouted and dug my heels into the sand, desperate to get back to Ma. A sudden jolt stopped me. Searing heat pierced my side as I slipped from Sajid's grip.

'Aasira!' Ma's cry ripped through the pain and stars that dazzled before my eyes.

Sajid pulled me up and the pain only grew worse as I clutched his knife, which was now lodged in my side.

'What have you done?' Ma screeched.

The world was a blur behind my blinking eyes, but I saw the way her storm gathered with a final flourish.

Grains of sand rose up from the desert, crowding round her like a tornado. It spun on the spot, her form disappearing within it the thicker her veil became, until I could see nothing but the whirr of sand. And then it was gone and with it so was Ma.

In her place was nothing but a breeze tousling the mound of sand where she'd knelt. Then everything turned to black.

The sea swirls round my ankles, heart hammering in my chest as I struggle to stay upright. 'You weren't executed,' I whisper.

I watched my mother vanish that night within her storm. She didn't just command the air. She became it.

My breathing shudders. She might still be alive.

TWENTY~EIGHT

I stare out at the sea, which glitters red as dawn breaks within a cherry-stained sky. My head reels. Once the fragments started to slot together, my mind couldn't keep up as images flashed, one after the other, a constant stream as the gaps in my memory were filled in.

I feel footsteps behind me and turn round to see the white shimmering dust of Sahi's magic retreat into her palms.

'I'm sorry I took your memories from you.' Her tears mirror mine as her eyes fade back to amber. 'They were never mine to take, but they're back with you now, where they belong.'

'Why?' My voice breaks with the crash of the waves. 'When I saw what you did to Ejaz and realised just how broken my memories of my mother were, I couldn't bring myself to think you might have done that to me too. But you did.'

'I'm sorry.'

'I was there the night Kaleb came for her. I only started to remember when Queen Sana gave me this necklace,' I say, pulling it out from beneath the neckline of my kurta. 'She wasn't executed that night. She conjured a storm powerful enough that she vanished into the air.'

Sahi's body quivers as she breathes in deeply. She opens her mouth to speak, but her words are caught in her web, the truth not yet ready to escape her. So I tell her what I know, the gaps in my memory closing.

'My mother was a zephyr, but you already knew that. I have this memory of her dancing in the dunes, the sand whipping up at her feet, the one memory of her you left for me.' I wipe my tears with the back of my hand. 'I used to think the sand was kicking up the backs of her legs because of the way she danced so freely. But it was her ability manifesting around her. Just like the sandstorm near the sanctuary a few weeks ago.'

Sahi lets out a long breath and nods, confirming the truth.

'My mother's still alive…' I look up at the sky, hands clasped in front of my face. 'I should have realised it was her then, but of course I couldn't remember her power.' A laugh escapes me at the absurdity of my ignorance. 'I hadn't even thought to ask all those times people reminded me of her ability and how it corrupted her. I was so driven to prove I wasn't like her that I didn't stop to consider who she really was. Because of you. Because of the memories you took from me.' My voice rises, chest tight. 'The memories that told me who the real traitor was… Kaleb.'

Sahi sucks on her lower lip to stop it trembling as her tears flow again. 'There are no excuses for what I've done and I'm not asking for you to forgive me. But if you'll at least let me explain, it might help you understand…'

I shrug and she takes it as her cue.

'My ability to see the truth developed early. When representatives from the sanctuary visited our village each year, my mother would put me forward even though I was too young. But then, when I six years old, Kaleb came and, as soon as he heard of what I could do, he recruited me. He promised my parents that the mistresses could help nurture my skill into something that would one day help our country in our fight against Mezeer. It had been my mother's dream to become a warrior, but she had no powers of her own and, when she'd been at the sanctuary, only women with magic fought in the army. I was reluctant to leave, but then Kaleb offered my brother a position in the palace.'

Her voice wavers. 'My family had nothing. Our village was ravaged by drought like so many others. I couldn't take that opportunity for a better life away from him. And so we left, me for the sanctuary…'

'And Emir for the palace,' I finish for her. The familiar furrow in his brow and tilt of his half-smile…I'd seen them before in Sahi. Anger flushes within me at his blatant lie when he mentioned an older sister, and the way he implied something had happened to her. Unless…

'He doesn't remember who you are.'

Her chest heaves, the truth finally pouring from her. 'My first subject. Emir was as distraught as I was to leave home and that we were to be separated. I wanted to take the pain away. So, when I said goodbye to him, I altered his memory so he wouldn't remember me, his twin. Instead, he'd remember another sister, an older sister who'd died in the war.'

All the times I've caught her staring at him, listening intently…it's because she was with her brother for the first time in ten years.

'When Kaleb took me to the sanctuary, I was two years younger than the first years and never quite fitted in, so he became my tutor instead. It started so small. He would test my ability on the other dancers if they misbehaved and he thought they weren't being truthful. But then he grew bored with me and I wanted to prove I could be as valuable as the older girls.'

'So you told him you could do more than just see the truth.'

Sahi nods, more composed now. 'Almost a year after I'd joined the sanctuary, I told him about how I had altered Emir's memory. Kaleb didn't believe that was possible of course, so he had me test it on one of the first years. He was impressed. I was impressionable…' There's a hint of anger in her tone as she sits on one of the larger rocks, but I can't join her. It's like every nerve within me is filled with lightning.

She brushes her hair back from her face as the breeze ruffles through it, then continues. 'As new recruits joined the sanctuary, he asked me to alter their memories so they forgot their families and homes.'

I think of Meera and her story of how everyone in her village was executed by Mezeeri soldiers.

Sahi confirms my suspicion. 'But certain memories are too strong to forget, the bonds so deep that I had to make some of the girls believe they'd lost everything. And Kaleb had the perfect fuel for their anger, the perfect person to pin all their false grief on and feed their need for vengeance. Their need to fight.'

'My mother.'

'I was only a child myself and hadn't understood the scope of what he was doing. When you arrived at the sanctuary, he told me who your mother was and that in your memories I would see and hear her trying to protest her innocence, but that all of it was lies.'

'And you believed him?' But I flush hot. I couldn't see through his lies either. His betrayal.

'At first I did. But then the more I saw of your memories, the more I could see the truth in what your mother had told you. That it was an accident when she killed her own soldiers and she wasn't the one to feed lies to Mezeer about Queen Sana.'

I start laughing but it quickly turns to dry sobs. 'She wasn't a traitor... *isn't* a traitor. Yet you continued lying for Kaleb and manipulating the truth to cover up *his* treachery.' It all pieces together now, unfolding quicker than I can comprehend.

'I told Kaleb I wouldn't do it any more, but he threatened my family. What else could I do?'

I scoff, my flames reawakening, flickering to life beneath my skin.

'It's the truth,' she claims when I don't answer.

'Is it?' I fling back.

She stands and follows me into the shadow of the cliffs.

'You were never part of Kaleb's plan that night in Nazeem. He had no idea Lina had had a child in the time since he'd exposed her relationship with a Mezeeri soldier years before.'

'And used that information to set her up as the enemy,' I finish for her.

Sahi might not have used her magic on Kaleb to see his truth, but she saw the memories I have of my mother. And my mother always knew Kaleb was the one to fear.

'Queen Sana had given her orders when your mother escaped her trial: find Lina and bring her to justice. But Kaleb failed that night in front of a whole audience. The next morning, I was taken to Nazeem. There were guards there from the sanctuary to make sure no one could leave or speak about what had happened. I was told to alter the villagers' memories so they wouldn't remember that you or your mother were ever there.'

'But Omar did remember.' My voice hitches when I see him again and I have to stand in the water to douse the flames within me. 'He was stronger than your magic. And that's why Kaleb had me execute him, isn't it? Because Omar remembered everything.'

I see him again, kneeling in front of me just as my mother did before Kaleb. It was all choreographed. 'He wasn't a traitor helping Mezeeri soldiers into our country and he never colluded with my mother because she was never the enemy. He'd tried to protect me that night when Kaleb came for her...'

The darkness lifted as Sajid's grip on me loosened and I slumped to the ground, clutching the knife protruding from my side as someone launched themselves at him from behind. Ma had disappeared. I could feel myself slipping into sleep again, but desperately kept my eyes open so as not to be swallowed by the pain. Omar and Sajid grappled in the sand. Omar had the advantage, pinning Sajid to the ground where he pummelled his chest with one punch after another. Sajid managed to push him away then grabbed Omar in a chokehold, his arm squeezing tighter round Omar's neck until he was unconscious. Then he threw him to the ground beside me, leaving Omar for dead.

I touch my side and it's like I feel the knife pierce my skin all over again. It was Sajid who gave me this scar. But it was me, my flames, that took Omar from this land.

'I killed him. When I was taken out on that solo assignment... I killed Omar.'

'Aasira, I'm so sorry.'

I stagger away from Sahi as she reaches out for me. 'Don't.'

She recoils into the slanted shadows of the cliffs. 'I didn't mean for any of this to happen. I did what I thought I had to, to protect the people I love—'

'The only people you protected were yourself and Kaleb,' I spit.

And she doesn't try to deny it. 'You're right. I saw how he manipulated the truth and still I played his game, and helped him to do it. But I won't hide any longer.' She straightens her back as she walks towards me, but as the sunlight creeps over her it reveals the dark circles that haunt her eyes.

The sun's warmth goads me.

I'm a child again. Sahi stands opposite me in the walled garden all those years ago, dazzled by my flames when I asked, *'You're not scared?'*

Sahi's eyes flicker to where the flames spark in my palms. 'I'm not scared.'

TWENTY~NINE

My hands ball into fists at my side, suppressing the fire in me. I can't do it. Won't do it. Sahi may have aided Kaleb's lies, but I can see what she's lost too.

'Is that why you were so desperate for a role in the Queen's Guard? So you could be near Emir?'

'Yes,' she says simply. 'But I know all that is ruined now. I won't fight what comes next.'

'Which is?'

'The inevitable outcome of my confession.'

I can't hide my fear for what that would mean, and she smiles sadly.

'I could have ended all these lies a long time ago. When you arrived at the sanctuary and I saw your memories...I never should have twisted them the way I did.'

'No...'

A hush falls over us and my mind casts me back to that night.

'Get her back to the Leharanji!' Kaleb shouted.

Sajid scooped me up and onto the back of a horse, jumping on behind me.

'Ma...' I managed one final time. But she was gone.

Tears streamed down my face as I struggled to stay conscious all the way to the Leharanji. I'd conjured images of it in my mind from the stories Ma had told me about her time there as a girl. She'd called it corrupt, a school that had lost all essence of what it once was: a home of knowledge, of learning…a sanctuary. I was shivering in pain when we finally rode through the gates and down the path to the building's entrance.

'What happened?' A woman ran out dressed in a black kurta, hair wrapped in a tight bun.

'She has a daughter,' Sajid spat. He lifted me down from the horse and into the arms of a man who stood nearby.

'Has?' the woman asked as she hurried down the steps.

'Had,' Sajid corrected himself.

'She's bleeding,' the man holding me called out and I looked up to see him frown beneath his fluffy moustache. 'Is this your *knife?'*

I tried to turn my head in the direction he was looking, but every movement made me feel more nauseous from the pain.

'Get her to the healers. Quick, Tahir!' the woman demanded.

I must have blacked out because when I opened my eyes again I was lying on a bed and the woman in the black kurta was sitting beside me.

'You're awake,' she said kindly. 'Do you feel better?'

I nodded and was grateful that the pain in my side had gone. But the one in my chest still ached.

'The healers worked quickly to stop the bleeding, but you might have a scar.'

She was holding my hand and her gaze shifted. When I realised what she was looking at, I pulled away and clasped my hands together into a tight fist. Ma had said never to share my power with anyone I didn't already know.

'It's all right,' she said calmly and turned over her own hands, the symbols on her palms illuminated in the moonlight. I stared at the

designs and started to feel queasy as I honed in on the delicate circles. There were two, one inside the other, connected by lines that flowed between them to create a spiral.

'I'm an illusionist,' she said. 'I can distort what's around us to confuse people.'

My head began to spin and if I could have backed away, I would have.

'I knew your mother.' She smiled kindly, but I crossed my arms so there was no way she could see my sun symbols again. 'I used to teach her when she studied here. My name is Mistress Zaina.'

My shoulders relaxed slightly. I knew this woman, or at least knew of her. The one good person at the sanctuary, that's what Ma had called her.

'Can you tell me your name?'

I shook my head.

'Aasira,' Sajid said gruffly, appearing in the doorway.

My flames flickered beneath the surface. That wasn't his information to share. I knew I couldn't give myself away so I held my breath to stop my flames from showing themselves.

'She can conjure fire,' he added.

Mistress Zaina nodded slowly, as though she already knew. 'A flame-wielder.'

'Can you take me home?' I croaked. 'I want Ma.'

'Lina's dead—'

'Sajid!' Mistress Zaina stood quickly, blocking his way into the room.

'She isn't dead,' I said quietly. 'She disappeared into the air.'

Sajid's eyes narrowed. 'She doesn't know what she saw.'

But Mistress Zaina ignored him. 'Into the air?'

I nodded. 'Can you take me back to her?'

She shook her head and when she held out her hand again I took it. 'But your mother will find you.'

My dreams that night were of Ma's tornado whisking her away into the darkness. When I awoke again, the sun was up and a girl was sitting where Mistress had before.

'Hello,' she said. 'I'm Sahi.'

I tried to sit up, but there was a twinge in my side, reminding me of what had happened.

'Here.' Sahi leaped up when she saw me struggling and grabbed a terracotta-coloured cushion from the floor, placing it behind my back as I leaned forward. 'Is that more comfortable?'

I was too scared to answer, even though she seemed about my age. Instead, I looked around the small room; there were three more beds on my left and a faded tapestry along one wall.

'Most new students feel nervous when they first arrive,' she said. But I wasn't just nervous. The people here had tried to hurt me. And they'd made my mother vanish. 'I can help you feel better.'

'How?'

'I'll show you.'

I pulled away as her eyes glazed over, blanketed white, but there was nowhere for me to go. I started to feel light-headed as she took my hands, like I was floating above my body, and relaxed into the cushion to help stop the room from spinning so ferociously. Images flickered in my mind, moving pictures that rearranged themselves until I couldn't see them clearly any more. Ma…all colour drained from her as her face was plucked from my memory.

The weight of Sahi's hands on mine lifted as she asked, 'Who was your mother?'

I tried to see the woman she spoke of but couldn't. I felt her instead, her betrayal and the loss she had caused to both me and our country. Anger flushed through me. 'A traitor.'

THIRTY

'Aasira!'

I shudder out of the memory when I hear my name and look up to see Emir running down the steps within the cliff face.

'Sahi!'

She doesn't turn to him, her gaze fixed firmly on me as she discreetly shakes her head. Emir can't find out she's his sister. But if I keep her secret, I become part of the lies: the twisted truth.

'Zayn and I have been looking everywhere for you both.' Emir leaps down the last step onto the sand, speaking between breaths, sweat sticking loose strands of hair to his forehead. 'You missed breakfast and your first classes have already started.'

I look up at where the sun sits in the sky. I didn't realise we'd been down here that long.

'We lost track of time while rehearsing our solos,' Sahi says.

'Right,' Emir says, looking between us. 'Well, you need to come quickly. Mistress is waiting for you, Aasira. She's not impressed as apparently you were late for class yesterday as well, although I'm sure we arrived on time...'

'We did,' I murmur.

'And the queen's requested that you attend a meeting with the court, Sahi. It's about to begin.'

Sahi frowns. 'Do you know why court's been called?'

'Something to do with the prisoner, I believe. We really must go,' he says impatiently.

My thighs burn as we jog up the steep steps. I keep my eyes on Emir's feet in front of me, stepping where he does.

'Found them,' he says when we crest the cliff.

Zayn is waiting there. 'Finally. Everyone else has already gathered in the throne room,' he says directly to Sahi.

There's an edge in the air, a sense of anticipation, as we walk towards the western entrance of the palace. I can't help but notice how unusually quiet the gardens are but for the attendants and gardeners, who busy themselves with preparations for our performances next week by pruning the lawns and buffing the fountains. Perhaps it's because I'm still trying to take in Sahi's confession, and the memories that now swirl through my head, but it's like the energy has tilted. I get the sense Sahi feels it too as she fidgets with the hem of her kurta.

'You won't know because you missed him at breakfast,' Zayn begins, 'but Kaleb arrived last night. He asked after you when you didn't join us.'

'Kaleb?' Sahi and I say in unison.

'I thought he wasn't arriving for another three days,' Sahi says, and I hear the panic in her voice.

'Change of plans,' Zayn remarks and I recall the note that was passed to him. What was the message? Why has the court been assembled and why is Kaleb here earlier than arranged?

'The studios are this way,' Emir says when I continue following Sahi and Zayn in the hope of getting some answers. 'Aasira?'

Sahi looks back over her shoulder and nods slightly before they disappear round the corner.

'Is everything all right between you and Sahi?' he asks when I join him, holding the door open for me.

'We're fine,' I lie and offer a smile to convince him.

He sees through it but doesn't pry any further. 'I'll meet you here after class,' he says when we reach Mistress's studio.

But I don't go into my rehearsal, risking being in more trouble with Mistress. I wait until Emir turns down the next corridor before running back to the door we just came through, out into the garden and back round to the west wing.

Hushed voices drift through the hall as I creep towards the throne room. It's out of bounds to everyone but the queen and a select number of courtiers, a room I've only glimpsed in passing since arriving at the palace, but I know it has two entrances. I recognise the loudest of the voices as Kaleb's as I softly pad up the stairs just off the corridor where he and several others are gathered, greeting each other as they're ushered inside. I've seen several people come in and out of the throne room on my way to the studios, but only ever through the downstairs door. Not the one upstairs that I now gently push.

I peer round the door. There's no one up here. I release a slow breath as I slip inside and leave it slightly ajar behind me. I'm on the mezzanine level that wraps round the throne room below and, according to Emir, is only ever used for formal gatherings. I back into the shadows behind the dark wooden benches, away from the sunlight that streams through the glass roof above. I'm careful not to make a sound as I lean forward slightly to get a better look at the room below as the courtiers enter.

The walls glitter like jewels, covered in a labyrinthine design that adorns the floor then extends up the walls in shades of ruby and emerald. At the far end of the room, two pillars stand on either side of the large gilded throne and I can just make out the tree that decorates its back, with branches that fan out to resemble a network of meandering rivers and tributaries.

Quiet falls among the courtiers and they part to stand either side of the room and bow their heads. Queen Sana enters, her navy and silver lehenga sparkling as she walks the length of the room and up the red velvet steps to her throne. Heba is on the queen's right, while Imani, Maryam, Fatima and two other members of the Queen's Guard line up on her left. I look for Kaleb and Sahi and spot them together, towards the front of the room.

'Thank you for gathering,' the queen says and everyone bows once more.

'It has come to my attention that there are questions about the prisoner we hold, a Mezeeri soldier who was part of the ambush on me and my party on our return from the Leharanji.'

Agitation crackles in the room, the air thick with the heavy scent of musk.

'I refuse to stand here today and defend my decision not to execute the woman immediately after the attack in the desert.

I am sure you would all agree that if there is intelligence we can gain on Mezeer's plans, it should be obtained.'

There are nods, but I can't help noticing a group who stand completely still within the middle of the room, wearing looks of disapproval.

Tariq is among them and Sahi steps aside as he brushes past her to get to the front. 'And what information has she shared?' he asks. 'From what I've heard, the prisoner has been given a place to stay, is fed each day and shares nothing with us of how Mezeer keeps infiltrating our border and killing our people.'

'You make prison sound rather idyllic, Tariq,' says Queen Sana and I notice the hint of a smirk from Maryam, while Kaleb's expression is impassive. 'You're on the wrong side of the border if you believe torture is the way to obtain the answers you want.'

'I never said—'

'And gossip will not get you far in this court,' the queen adds firmly. 'You know very well my mother didn't stand for it, and neither do I.'

'Your Majesty.' Another man steps up, his greying beard trailing down to his chest. 'No one here is advising torture. We simply want to know that our families are safe. We've sent more soldiers to our border with Mezeer and yet their army have made it across undetected, their only trace the devastation they leave behind.'

Queen Sana and Heba exchange a glance.

'We will continue to send soldiers where they're needed, Abdul,' Heba says. 'Captain Nadim has already started putting together another new band of palace guards who will be stationed at the forts along the Imdaal river, and we're sending troops to patrol the mountains—'

'That's not enough,' the blue-eyed woman I saw outside the banquet hall cuts in. The one who passed a message to Zayn. 'For years, all we've done is sit back and wait for Mezeer to attack. It's time for us to fight back and send troops into *their* country, not wait until they reach the palace and raze it to the ground.'

'I will not be the one to start another war, Bushra.' Queen Sana raises her voice over the commotion that ensues.

'The war's already here!' someone yells.

Cheers clash with more shouts as everyone is desperate to make their voice heard.

'What about the truth-seeker?' Bushra calls out and the voices round her break off. 'Why haven't you been able to find out anything from the prisoner?' she half shouts at Sahi, who does her best to look calm. 'We should get her up here now, so we can all be witness to the truth and bring our enemy to justice. And the other one –' she flings up her hand and I know exactly who she's going to accuse – 'the flame-wielder. How are we to trust she isn't a traitor like her mother?'

My breathing grows shallow. I crouch further within the shadows, desperate not to be seen.

'I don't need to use my ability to tell you that Aasira is loyal to our queen and country,' Sahi says loudly.

'You will do as we demand, girl!'

'She will do as *I* command!' Queen Sana booms and a silence falls over the crowd. 'I will not listen to you accuse someone who protected us when we were ambushed. You're letting fear cloud your judgement and that is exactly what

King Faisal wants, for us to turn on each other and wage his country's war for him. Well, that is not who we are. We're a country that stands together, and we will continue to do so to protect our land and our people.'

Abdul steps forward again. 'You're right, Your Majesty. We are a country that stands together.' He hesitates, choosing his next words carefully. 'But, if I may, we have to understand how King Faisal's soldiers have been able to cross the border. The prisoner must be able to tell us this and what Mezeer plans next. Surely she can't hide that sort of information from the truth-seeker?'

Sahi moves to speak again, but is silenced as Kaleb finally offers his opinion. 'You assume the prisoner knows what Mezeer has planned.' His voice is measured and clear above the rattle of dissent from the other courtiers. 'But she's a soldier, not an army general. She is told where to go and to kill those who wear Amaari colours, not the logistics mapped out by Mezeeri commanders. Sahi cannot see the information you seek in the prisoner's mind because she's not privy to it.'

'Then why have we kept her alive?' Tariq exclaims and there's another roar of agreement.

A darkness creeps over the room, leaving only the flickering light of the lanterns as charcoal clouds mould together outside and block the mid-morning sun. I tremble against the wall. Queen Sana's palms are a dazzling iridescent blue as the shimmer of her ability plays over her hands and the first rainfall we've seen in months drowns out the clamour of voices.

'We will give our prisoner one last chance to tell us what she knows of Mezeer's plans,' Queen Sana instructs and the room falls quiet. 'And if she has nothing to share, come dawn in two days she will be executed.'

THIRTY~ONE

Dusk falls, signalling the change of the guards. I take my chance. I've had to feign a headache all afternoon after missing my rehearsal with Mistress, so it's been difficult to get Amal to leave my room. But as soon as she does, after checking on me for a final time, I change into my white kurta that looks most like the uniform the attendants wear, and cover my head with the matching dupatta in the same way some of the women do.

The prisoner will die at dawn in two days' time if she doesn't give up the information some members of the court want. They're losing faith in the queen and are unafraid to show it, their whispers rustling against the backdrop of her rainfall outside.

I haven't been able to escape the knot in my stomach ever since Queen Sana announced the prisoner's possible execution. Or the image of Imani's grin when it was declared, no doubt anticipating the role will fall to her. It's a thrill I've never experienced and a duty I will gladly leave in her hands. But if that turns out to be the prisoner's fate, I have to know something first: if my mother was there when we were ambushed, directing the winds in an attempt to distract us. And if she was, what does that mean?

My mind races with the memories I never should have lost. A lump rises in my throat and I touch the place where my mother's necklace rests beneath my clothes. She vanished that night in Nazeem and has been alive, somewhere, ever since. Why did she never come for me?

I keep my head down as I walk the corridors, blending in with the attendants who light the lanterns as the night guards take up their posts. The air is fresher than usual because of the rain and I'm reminded of Tariq's criticism of Queen Sana's powers, the magic she commands outside now a display of anything but weakness.

A shiver runs through me as I walk deeper into the palace, and the din of voices and footsteps grows ever more distant. The passage narrows and, even though I have to rely on the pale glow of the flame I ignite in my palm, I know I'm near as I saw Sahi come this way when she was summoned for another interrogation session after court this afternoon. Shadows tilt across the walls and floor and, as I creep through the wooden door at the end, the bright colours of the palace merge into black, mottled stone. I'm within the cliffs.

One hand still cradling the flame, the other grasps the frayed rope that lines the wall as I follow the steep steps down towards the prison. I tread lightly on the balls of my feet, careful to find the widest part of each step as the passage curves down, as though leading me into the depths of the sea itself.

I pause as I near the bottom and extinguish my flame, pressing my back into the dank wall as the voices of two guards drift towards me. The clang of metal bounces off the walls and ceiling, accompanied by the splash of water droplets that swell and pop when they meet the puddles that gather in the uneven ground. I walk carefully down the last few steps and peer round the wall that hides me from view. One of the guards approaches the prison cell, baton raised, and the ring of metal against metal echoes again as he strikes the thick bars.

'Wakey-wakey,' he taunts. 'Word is you only have two nights left to enjoy this fine residence. I wouldn't sleep through them if I were you.'

If the prisoner hears him, she makes no show of it, her head buried in her knees, which are pulled up to her chest. A plate of mouldy chapatis sits near the cell door. She no longer wears her armour and her tunic hangs loose over her shoulders, a ghost of the warrior she was when she ambushed us.

'I said wake up!' the guard shouts, spit flying from his mouth.

The briefest look of pity flits through the other guard's eyes. 'Leave her.'

'She's a criminal.'

'And will get what she deserves,' she replies in a bid to placate her partner. 'It'll be quite the display, I'm sure. But you heard Her Majesty earlier: she gave up nothing today and has one last chance to tell the truth tomorrow, so our job is to make sure she can.' She fetches the dirty glass that sits next to the plate of food, tips out the dregs of water and replenishes it. 'Here.' She pushes it back through the iron bars and the prisoner finally looks up. 'At least drink something.'

The prisoner nods but doesn't move.

'You ungrateful rat,' the other guard says furiously, but the woman holds him back.

My heartbeat tremors but the prisoner doesn't even flinch.

I have to get rid of the guards. Something scuttles in the shadows, giving me an idea. I reach for a handful of loose stones that have been shed from the walls and sit by my feet. Finding my target, I aim like I would in archery training, down the passage ahead of me where I can see more prison guards' armour stacked in the low light.

'What was that?' the larger guard asks, his gruff voice suddenly a higher pitch, when the first of my stones pings off a shield.

'Probably another rodent,' the other one replies.

I choose a larger stone and aim again, this time at a discoloured glass of water on a small table. It tips over, rolling off the table where it smashes on the flagstones.

'Who's there?'

I duck back against the wall. My foot hovers over the last step, palms hot and clammy, as the guards run down the passageway and I emerge into the flickering candlelight.

Queen Sana said the prisoner wouldn't be tortured, yet her hair is clotted with blood and bruises blemish her cheeks. Something resembling relief relaxes her features when she sees me and I realise she's only young beneath the desert dust that's hardened on her skin, likely a soldier fresh out of training.

She mutters to herself, but I don't hear what she says. I hesitate as, slowly, she crawls towards me. The chains that tether her to the furthest wall scrape against the stone as her lips quiver into a one-sided smile, revealing gaps in her teeth. She clenches the bars and pulls herself up to standing, but she's unsteady on her feet and her wrists and ankles drip with fresh blood where scabs peel beneath the iron that clenches them. I draw closer and the smell of her acrid breath brushes my face as she leans her head against the bars.

She continues to talk to herself until, finally, I hear her. 'L-Lina?'

My breath hitches and I'm suddenly cold.

'You came for me,' she whispers in almost perfect Amaari, though her accent is thick with a Mezeeri lilt. 'I knew you would.' She reaches out, but I pull away and her hand dangles there between us.

She thinks I'm my mother...

'We tried but they were too strong.' She clutches the iron bars with both hands again, head bowed. 'I'm sorry we didn't succeed.'

'Succeed in what?' I ask, but she doesn't hear me.

Shaking her head, she clamps her hands over her ears. 'I don't know,' she admits eventually and begins to cry. 'I don't remember.'

Sahi... What truth did she see in this girl that she needed to take?

There's movement in the darkness, along the same passage the guards left down earlier.

'I saw her,' she says suddenly, her eyes glistening and voice faraway as she looks round the cell then straight at me. 'I saw her in the desert and she's here now, in the palace.'

'Who?'

She nods to herself and a raspy laugh escapes her. 'The girl with the red sun in her blood...' she says, hope rekindling within her. 'The one you said would save our homeland from ruin.'

'*My little red sun…*' I jump at the voice in my head. 'What do you mean?'

The guards are close and their armour clanks with each step.

'Is that what my mother told you?' I ask urgently. 'Was she with you when you attacked us?'

But she just stares at me, confused, and I don't have much more time before the guards will see me.

'I can help you,' she says desperately as I turn away. 'I can help you find her and bring her to Sehar.'

'Who are you talking to?' the male guard shouts from the shadows.

Heart pounding, I sprint for the steps.

'Don't leave me here!' she calls after me. 'I don't want to die. Please!'

I run, but the steps slant downwards and I struggle to keep my balance, the rope burning my palms as I claw at it. Footsteps pound behind me, but I don't look back.

'Get back here!' he shouts.

When I reach the top, I heave the wooden door open and it creaks against my weight. The guard's faster than I expect, bursting through the door only a few beats behind me, and my chest burns as I pick up my pace. Other palace guards yell at me to stop as I emerge into one of the main corridors, but I can still hear him chasing me. My dupatta slips from round my head and, just as I glance over my shoulder to see if I can retrieve it, I collide with something. Someone.

'Aasira.'

Kaleb.

The guard skids to a halt behind me. Kaleb looks him up and down and I step away from them both, trying to conceal my fear.

'Can I help you?' Kaleb asks the guard, who rests his hands on his knees as he struggles to catch his breath.

'She… I have reason to believe she was in the prison, sir.'

'Is that so?' Kaleb says and his gaze flicks down to my neck, where the chain of my mother's necklace pokes out. 'Are you sure you haven't mistaken this student of the Queen's Guard for an attendant?' he asks, noticing the intention behind what I'm wearing.

'No one is permitted in the prison without a guard. And she was the one running from me,' he adds.

Kaleb smiles. 'I think I'd run too if you were after me.'

The guard looks confused, unsure if he's been insulted, but when Kaleb's smirk turns to a laugh he joins in.

'Maybe I was mistaken,' he says eventually.

'Maybe,' Kaleb repeats.

The guard eyes me again before giving in with a bow. 'Good evening,' he says and heads back towards the prison.

Neither Kaleb nor I speak, but I feel him watching me while I stare after the guard, making sure he leaves.

'Wandering the corridors after hours…' he tuts. 'You're not at the sanctuary any more, Aasira. But if it's a career in court that you want, then I'd say palace life suits you well.'

I suck in a breath. So he saw me earlier today, hiding in the throne room.

'As does the necklace,' he adds.

My breaths come hard and fast under his gaze, my heart beating loudly, but I don't break eye contact. I begin to see what he is now, beneath the cool exterior, and how he's been able to manipulate those closest to him.

'I hear you missed your rehearsal this morning,' he says, filling in the silence. 'I would encourage you not to do that. It isn't wise to abandon your duties, especially not at the palace.'

Did Mistress tell him, or was it one of the courtiers; one of his 'associates'?

'I'll see you in the morning.'

He leaves but I don't move, can't move, and it takes me a moment to compose myself. I walk as calmly as I can back to the dancers' quarters, aware of the guards who look in my direction. Any one of them could be privy to Kaleb's lies.

When I finally reach my room, a gloom coats it, casting everything in shadow as the grey clouds bruise violet outside. I'm light-headed, my breaths heavy as I gasp for fresh air. But it's turned humid and the air clings to me in a way I've never known. I clutch my head that's throbbing incessantly, like there's too much pressure building up inside it. I stagger to the veranda, unsteady, as though I'm floating and my feet can't find the ground.

'You'll save us one day, Aasira, my little red sun,' my mother said one night as she rocked me to sleep.

Rain lashed at our tent and I jumped as a purple thread flashed in the sky outside, followed by thunder that clapped overhead.

'You'll save us from the storm.'

THIRTY-TWO

My dreams restrain me, flooding me with images that twist and transform, one into the other.

I can't escape

all the deaths…

The faces

of those I've killed.

Omar, Hassan…so many more before that…

Wake up.

I gasp, my body cold with sweat and bound by the sheet that tangles round my legs. Bolting upright, I look around for Meera's silhouette. But it wasn't her nightshade ability that got into my head.

It was the truth. My truth.

For so long, my memories have been bound to someone else, tethered to Sahi's version of the truth: a version forged by Kaleb. But now the landscape of my past has shifted. Ever since Sahi released her hold on my memories, the fog has lifted, but they're disorganised and chaotic as they flit around in my mind.

I slip out of bed. It's still dark and night's warm embrace wraps round me as I walk out onto the veranda. The storm has passed, revealing the moon and a sky ready to awaken. There's movement in the gardens and I wonder if perhaps the preparations being made now aren't for our Queen's Guard auditions in a week, but for the impending execution. I can't even think about my solo any more. Whether I'm here or on the front line, I see now I'm part of the war, whatever the outcome may be. A war my mother tried to shelter me from.

My hands shimmer gold as I lay my palms flat on the veranda's marble balustrade and flames flicker along my skin. 'You never wanted me to train at the sanctuary and join the army you once led.'

My mother admired my flames, but wanted me to hide my magic. That's why she kept us on the move through the desert. We weren't running from her fate as a traitor. We were running from mine…as a soldier.

'Are you ready, Aasira?'

'I think so.'

'You only need call on the gold dust, remember? Hold on to your flames.'

I nodded and Ma smiled encouragingly as she pulled me up to standing. The sand was warm between my toes as I began to spin. My skirt flared out, the mirrored beads along its hem catching in the light as the sun's energy pulsed through my body and she cast her final rays over the desert, over us. I felt my magic before it showed itself, a gentle fizzing from deep within that slowly grew, until the gold shimmer crept from my palms and laced across my arms.

'That's it,' my mother said, laughing. 'Well done.'

'I'm getting dizzy.' I laughed too.

'That's because you forgot to focus your eyes on something,' she said, but I could hear the smile was still there, despite the reprimand. 'You can stop turning, but don't let your dust disappear, remember?'

'Yes.'

I did as Ma said, but teetered, my head still spinning as the gold dust I'd created fanned round me, sparkling in the sunlight. Ma did the same, twirling until she too shimmered a beautiful bronze, then came to a halt in front of me. But, unlike me, she'd allowed her magic to develop into a light breeze that encircled us like a shield and was warm, despite the cooling air. Her hands outstretched towards me, Ma blew softly on the dust within her palms. It danced over the swirled symbols decorating them, until each grain of her shimmer was swept up within her draught and floated round me. I watched in awe as my own golden shimmer peeled from my body, weaving in delicate strands until it too was caught in Ma's breeze and was indistinguishable from her own dust.

'What is that?' I asked as our dusts merged in front of us in one glimmering swirl and twisted into different shapes in the soft wind, the golden and bronze tones I was familiar with turning iridescent.

Ma's eyes glistened. 'It's us,' she said quietly. 'It's our magic working together.'

It looked so delicate and yet I wanted to reach out and touch it, to feel the energy that floated before us. 'It's beautiful.'

'Remember this, Aasira,' Ma whispered as she put her arms round me and we watched our magic dance over the dunes beneath the setting sun. 'Remember what your magic…what you…can do. You can create hope. You can create peace.'

'But you made that.'

'No.' She shook her head and the movement tickled as she nestled her chin on my shoulder. 'We did. We created it together.'

I'm out of my room and walking the palace corridors before I realise where I'm heading, ignoring Kaleb's earlier warning about roaming the palace at night. I don't need to have been shown where the library is to find it, my mother's voice a guide in my head as I retrace the steps she took as a child growing up here. The corridors are quiet, my only company the lanterns that decorate the walls as I head deeper into the heart of the palace.

The large doors aren't dissimilar from those leading to Queen Sana's quarters, set within an ornate emerald marble frame threaded with white. I push on one of them and it groans under my weight, as though it hasn't been opened in a while. The library is cast in a hazy blue and dust motes drift within the moon's glow, which filters through the clouds and the furthest window, gently caressing the shelves to my left.

A single flame ignites in my palm as I step over the threshold and absorb it all. The library is larger and grander than I thought it would be, unlike any room I've seen before. The shelves are crammed full with old texts that climb the walls and, when I look up, I see there are several levels with an ornate wooden mezzanine above, similar to the throne room.

My eyes scan the books and I breathe in the scent of parchment that radiates from them, unsure where to start as the memory of my mother's magic mingling with mine lingers in my mind. I pull one out from the nearest shelf, its cover a deep blue and its spine engrained with an inscription I don't understand, although I recognise the shape of the alphabet from wording etched into paintings at the sanctuary.

I set it down on a round table inlaid with a delicate silver pattern, and the spine cracks as I carefully open it to a page filled with illustrations of various flowers. There are scribbled comments in the margins of some of the pages, as though someone has noted what each of the plants are in their own hand alongside the text. But the writing is small, in some sort of shorthand, and I can't make out what's written. I gently close the book and pull out another then another, trying to decipher what they say, until a stack sits in front of me.

'There has to be something in here. You spoke about the library all the time...'

This is where my mother whiled away hours as a child. I remember now, remember how she would tell me about the vast alcoves and books buried within them, some filled with stories while others spoke of our country's history and geography. This is where the old stories that Queen Sana's father shared with her and the queen came to life for my mother. Where the first tendrils of belief in the myths so many have forgotten were sparked, before Mistress Zaina fuelled them further when she joined the sanctuary.

'Memories of the old stories are in everything around us: art, music, literature.'

Art. I've been looking in the wrong place. My mother didn't come in here to study the books. 'You came in here to study the ceiling...'

I crane my neck backwards, but can't quite make out the shapes, so enhance the flame in my palm until it glows brighter. It's just as she said it was. Delicate brushstrokes layer over each other, peeling in places, but still vibrant with little sun damage. The Hamaaj mountains rise in the north with rivers that meander down their surface, across the land and into the Emerald Sea in the south. I walk through the room, slowly illuminating new parts of the painting as I follow the coastline. The sparkling green-blue melts into a golden beach and the desert beyond, rivers crossing its length, while dots of green gather together into a forest that stretches to the base of the mountains.

Larijaah. The homeland. Undivided by the border that now scars its landscape to create the two countries we know today: Amaar and Mezeer.

I walk up one of the staircases that leads to the mezzanine to get a closer look and new details show themselves. Shadows I didn't see before cast by the painted moon that overlooks the forest on one side of the mountains, while the painted red sun rises on the other side, gazing over the desert and sea. Dawn and dusk together. It's not dissimilar from the tapestry in Queen Sana's office with its depiction of our country…or countries. A map of sorts. I focus on the area that stretches to where Mezeer is today and their desert meets the mountains, underneath which is some faded writing.

'Sehar.' The place the prisoner spoke of.

But there's more. It shocks me when I realise I understand it, the words familiar from when my mother used to write them in the sand.

'For in unity there is prosperity.'

Goosebumps shiver up my arms. My mother lived by those words. She even told me they're why she decided to abandon the war, because she didn't believe in it any more. And yet she abandoned me to the people who would shape me for war. To the people who no longer believe in our country's shared history the way she did. In our origins.

'For in unity there is prosperity, where nature will nurture the magic within that binds us.'

I remember now how she believed we had the potential to help save our country from the destruction it's seen over the last century. But if she believed that, why did she leave me? What stopped her from coming to the sanctuary for me? She must have known that's where I was. Unless...she really did have something to hide.

'I wondered when you'd find your way here.'

I jump at the queen's voice and the flame in my palm disappears as I wipe my damp cheeks. 'Your Majesty.' I curtsy to her silhouette in the doorway, then quickly make my way back down the staircase.

'I don't visit the library as often as I should these days,' she says as she looks up at the shelves. 'This was your mother's favourite room in the palace. When we were children, she would pore over the books, just as she did the old tapestry and the art on this ceiling.' Queen Sana gazes at the painting, while outside the first tendrils of pink thread the sky behind the broken clouds.

'Lina found comfort in reading about the different magical abilities and how they came to be. She thought if she knew their roots, it would help her better understand how to fight if she joined the army and was faced with them in combat.' Queen Sana smiles briefly. 'It was quite sensible really.'

I think of her in here, my mother's presence all around me as I look at the gilded stepladder she might have stood on to reach for a new book. The cushions piled high under the bay window where she might have sat and read.

'She loved to study and had the memory for it. It was like the page became engraved in her mind the way she remembered every word so perfectly.' The queen laughs fondly to herself. 'And her own stories… She would take one element of what she read about the old beliefs and weave them into something of her own. I'll never forget the one she told inspired by our abilities: "The Storm Sisters".'

I hear my mother now and warmth bubbles momentarily inside me as I remember the way she would weave stories to see us through the longest, coldest nights, including my favourite about the girl of water and the girl of air, and the storms they would create together with their magic. The same way we created a new version of our magic together.

'But she took the stories too far,' says Queen Sana and her smile fades as she walks towards me, stepping into the rosy glow that filters in from outside. 'Lina wanted to believe they had a deeper meaning, that *she* had a higher purpose and was somehow linked to the myth.' She looks up at the ceiling, her gaze on the painting.

'Nature nurtured magic,' I say and the queen wears the same look of recognition she did that day she summoned me to her quarters and gifted me my mother's necklace.

'That's what Lina believed.'

'And Mistress Zaina.'

The queen's eyebrows arch and a glimmer of regret creeps up the back of my neck.

'It's a story for children,' Queen Sana says sharply. '"Magic is born from nature, and the four elements were bestowed on those who would ensure balance, peace and unity in our country." It's a story your mother wanted to believe because

238

she longed to feel special and as if her magic was meant for more than war.'

'And what if it was?' I say hotly, forgetting myself. 'You told me yourself: "Elemental magic is of the rarest form."'

I expect the queen to be angry, but something resembling sympathy crosses her features instead. 'Elemental magic *is* rare, but it does not hold the power to unify what is already broken, like your mother and Mistress Zaina believed. No matter how much we might hope for calm on our shores, stories aren't the answer to achieving it. If elemental power has the ability to unify our land, why do your flames destroy everything in their path? Tell me where the peace is in that.'

I didn't ask to be made executioner, I want to say. But I'm stunned into silence. Stunned into the truth. There is no other role for me. My flames cause destruction... Death.

'And in the end, after all Lina's talk about peace and unity, she betrayed her country and fuelled the war against us.'

I shake my head, unable to make sense of everything. She'll never believe me if I say it was Kaleb. If she had any notion it could have been him, he wouldn't still be the leader at the sanctuary and a trusted member of her court today. And my mother wouldn't have fled.

New shadows fall across Queen Sana as she walks over to one of the windows and opens it, the sea singing below her. 'It wasn't just the stories your mother came in here to read though,' she says suddenly. 'She also liked to study the maps. That's where she really excelled. Apart from her power as a zephyr and her skill with a blade, it was her ability to lead soldiers on missions through the darkness of the desert, the map of our two countries like an impression on her mind, that enabled her to rise through the ranks in our army.'

Tears sting my eyes as I recall the way she would draw lines in the sand, plotting out the paths we would take.

'I imagine it was that skill, above any other, that helped her when she was on the run with you.' Queen Sana's tone darkens.

A chill runs through me, but I don't cave in under the weight of her scrutiny. The only sound is that of the wind that whistles over the waves.

'There are two sides in this war, Aasira. Don't do what your mother did and choose the wrong one.' She begins to leave, before turning to me when she reaches the door. 'Come dawn tomorrow, you will have your final opportunity to prove your loyalty and win yourself a place in my Queen's Guard.'

I inhale sharply and meet her gaze. 'You want me to execute the prisoner.'

'As befits your role, yes.'

I nod, not because I accept but because I now understand the system I'm a part of. The system that, despite whatever other decisions she made, my mother tried to protect me from. She knew the role that would be chosen for me: a role that I did not ask for. I was never a dancer or a warrior in Amaar's eyes. I've only ever been an executioner.

THIRTY-THREE

Dawn weighs heavy, the sky a dazzling expanse of burnt orange shot through with crimson.

I've struggled to concentrate all day, since Queen Sana told me my role in the prisoner's execution. Amal and I barely speak as she helps me get ready, fixing my hair into a low bun and finishing it with a small golden tikka that rests along my parting and falls over my forehead, before lining my eyes with surma. When she pulls out the lehenga I'm to wear, I briefly forget the occasion. It looks more like an outfit for a celebration than an execution. It was brought up late last night and completed only hours before by the queen's seamstresses, the shape inspired by the design they discussed in my fitting for our auditions. But it's hard to believe they created it so quickly with all the minute details stitched through the delicate skirt; details suggested by the queen.

In the library, Queen Sana told me magic isn't born from nature like my mother believed, but she can't truly believe that herself. Nature and the magic it creates are so clearly symbolised within my lehenga with its blue bodice and skirt, an homage to the queen's ability to wield water. Then there are the deep red and emerald panels, red for our sun and green for our country that she watches over, while tiny flowers and delicate swirling patterns are embroidered throughout for the earth and the air.

I can't understand why Queen Sana would have requested something so elaborate. I thought I'd be wearing something more traditional, like the simple ivory lehengas we would wear when on assignment at the sanctuary. But then this is a performance. A performance to remind those who question her that she is the ruler of Amaar.

Emir knocks, but I hesitate when Amal opens the door. It's so quiet in the corridor, the others having already left not long ago to take their places in the audience. The thought that people will watch makes my head spin. Emir waits in the doorway, his armour freshly polished and hair neatly pulled back into a ponytail. But he doesn't wear the smile I've grown used to. Instead, his brows are knitted together, as though he feels the shadow cast over the palace too.

'Ready?' he asks eventually.

I don't reply, concentrating instead on putting one foot in front of the other as we walk the halls and out to the gardens. As the outdoor theatre comes into view, I see Sahi in the front row, Dana and Meera on one side and Kaleb and Mistress Soraya on the other. Kaleb turns his head towards Mistress as she says something, but the dancers are silent and I can feel Sahi actively avoiding looking in my direction. Behind them sit the other students, then rows and rows of courtiers and guests invited from the city who talk among themselves. The nausea only rises in me.

A hush falls over the theatre as we near, followed by several gasps and murmurs. People point and I look behind me, but there's only Amal, and when I face the audience again I know that they're pointing at me. Unease quivers under my skin when Tariq stands up in the fourth row. He pushes his way past the people who sit along the same row. Bushra follows, along with three others, and we all watch as they descend the stone steps between the seating and hurry across the lawn.

This show was created for them. But then maybe they didn't know I would be the one performing the execution.

When we reach the side of the stage, Emir bows his head to me, then joins Captain Nadim and a group of palace guards stationed to the left of the audience, while Amal brushes at my lehenga as though there's something on it, before dropping into a curtsy. Then I'm on my own.

The gardens fall silent once more and everyone stands as Queen Sana arrives, dressed in a sparkling gold ensemble with a tiered skirt, her hair pulled back and lips blood-red beneath her surma-stroked eyes. Her Queen's Guard follow in pairs, Imani and a woman who was at the sanctuary before my time – Lyla – bringing up the rear, the prisoner within their grip. The young girl's head hangs low, her body frail beneath her black kurta and her hands tied behind her back. There are jeers from the audience as she's led onto the stage, but she doesn't look up.

I glance at the other dancers again and this time Sahi catches my eye. She should be standing here with me. They all should be. We perform as a quartet. But instead I must dance solo like I did in Nazeem. And, just like then, I feel something new rise within me. I breathe deeply to hold my white flames at bay. I can't let them escape. Not now.

The Queen's Guard sit down in the empty seats left for them in the front row, all but Imani and Lyla, who still hold on to the prisoner. I step back as they pass me, walking up the three steps to the stage without any acknowledgement. Queen Sana gestures for everyone to sit.

'I had hoped that when we next gathered here it would be for the auditions to become a member of my guard. A day of occasion that would honour the work of the Leharanji.' The queen's voice projects effortlessly to her audience as she steps further downstage, and Kaleb smiles at the mention of the sanctuary.

'But instead,' she continues, 'we are here to mete out justice. Justice for the crimes committed against the innocent people whose village crossed the path of a band of assailants, who then turned their weapons on me and my party. An assassination attempt orchestrated by those who would see our country fall into the hands of Mezeer's regime.'

Several audience members clap and mumble between themselves. The prisoner looks up then, registering those who applaud her death as the sun crowns over the cliffs.

'Aasira,' Queen Sana says. 'Please, join us onstage.'

I lift the hem of my lehenga to avoid tripping as, slowly, I join them. The stage is large with so few of us on it, swallowing me within its vastness. Waves collide with the cliffs below and I have the overwhelming urge to be wrapped up in them and swept away from what I must do.

Queen Sana steps aside, while Imani and Lyla pull the prisoner forward until she's centre stage. She doesn't resist as they roughly grab her by the shoulders and push her down into a kneeling position, facing the audience.

The sea's cooling breeze sighs like a collective breath as Heba makes her way onto the stage and awaits Queen Sana's signal before reading from the parchment she holds. Queen Sana nods to her advisor.

'Noor Farooq,' Heba reads with steady hands. 'You have been found guilty of the attempted assassination of Queen Sana of Amaar. You are hereby sentenced to death for your crime.'

Noor… She turns within the grip of the guards to lock eyes with me. Imani plants a firm hand on the top of her head, forcefully turning it so she faces her judges again.

'Aasira, step forward,' Heba tells me.

I take my place behind the prisoner.

Queen Sana gestures to Imani and Lyla, who turn Noor round to face me. I have to look at the ground. I can't meet her eyes again. The pair release their grip on the prisoner's arms, then bow their heads to the queen, before exiting the stage in perfect unison and taking their seats among the rest of the Queen's Guard. Both Queen Sana and Heba retreat upstage. It's time.

Terror grips me. A terror Noor doesn't mirror when I finally look up again. Shame creeps across my skin. If she can show strength, why can't I? The longer I draw it out, the more I prolong the torture for Noor.

'Aasira,' Heba says again as a restlessness grows among the audience.

I'm back in Nazeem, Omar crouched in front of me, white flames billowing… They're under the surface now as dread tenses my body. Killing Noor won't change anything either.

'I won't do it.'

Noor shudders and looks up to the sky, whispering under her breath.

'What did you say?' Queen Sana asks, a darkness shrouding her features in the same way clouds begin to crowd over the sea.

Imani shifts in her seat, hands twitching with an eagerness to step in.

'I won't do it,' I repeat. 'Noor isn't the one who should be on trial here.'

'You would disobey your queen?' Heba says.

'She's working with them too!' a man shouts from the audience.

'– spy –'

'– traitor –'

'– like her mother –'

I turn to Queen Sana. 'You know this will change nothing. Executing Noor isn't the answer to stopping this war.'

She glowers, anger pulsing in her hands as her eyes turn from green to blue. 'She is a criminal.'

'She isn't the only criminal here.'

I turn to where Sahi now stands, her eyes milky white and hands shimmering with her magic. Dana and Meera both watch her, startled, as she swivels and aims her gaze at Kaleb.

'No, you have both shown where your loyalty lies,' Queen Sana says.

I drown out the uproar around the theatre. I have to hear him. I have to hear his truth.

Kaleb stands as Sahi's magic swirls round his head. She holds firm, not backing away as he stands over her. But her hands become rigid and the tendrils of dust that flowed from them turn to wisps. Imran jolts towards her and I think he's going to help Sahi as she staggers back, but instead he tackles her to the ground.

A sudden gust of wind rushes through the gardens. I shield my eyes against the grains of sand whipped up from the beach. Confused screams and shouts echo throughout the audience. Queen Sana's storm rolls in with the waves until dawn is nothing but a ghost and large raindrops hammer down. Noor launches herself off the stage, but Imani is already there and pushes her to the ground. The wind only grows stronger, encircling the theatre. Queen Sana responds with a roar of thunder, as though the two storms speak to each other. It growls, punctuated like a drum with each lash of the wind that begins to howl.

Shouts turn to shrieks as the audience push their way through the stalls, clambering over one another as they run for the shelter of the palace.

'– Mezeer! –'

'What's happening?'

Queen Sana turns in the direction of the beach below, her voice so low I don't know if anyone else hears her when she says, 'Not what. Who.'

The bass grows louder and a series of horns blare to a rhythm I've never heard until now. The rhythm of war.

THIRTY~FOUR

The wind drops and the theatre falls silent but for the rain. My mother. She's here.

Anticipation leaks out across the gardens as people still run towards the palace. I'm like a statue poised in one of Queen Sana's fountains. Shouts mount again as Captain Nadim commands his guards and tries to restore order among the stragglers.

'Kaleb,' I hear Queen Sana say at the same time I see he's no longer with Dana and Meera. And Mistress Soraya... They must have gone when they couldn't be seen among the main throng.

My plan to expose him didn't work. Even with Sahi's magic, he managed to get away.

Queen Sana leaves the stage, Heba at her side. 'You.' She points at a palace guard then Noor, who's held down by Imani's knee on her back. 'Get her back down to the prison. Imani, take a group and search the palace for Kaleb. He knows the passages out of here. Bring him to me before he tries to make his escape.' Her expression is fierce as she looks in the direction of the beach, where the wind hailed from. 'He has a lot to explain.'

Imani doesn't hesitate, releasing her grip on Noor, who doesn't fight when the palace guard drags her up. A group of four falls in behind Imani and they all bow their heads to the queen, before jogging towards the palace.

'All of you,' Queen Sana says, gesturing to the rest of her guards, 'you're with me. That includes you, Dana and Meera.'

Bafflement creases their features, but neither objects as Queen Sana adds, 'And arrest them,' pointing at Sahi and me.

An older guard rushes to help Imran as Sahi struggles within his grip. My flames spark, but my view is suddenly blocked as Lyla jumps onto the stage. I pull back as her mauve eyes roam over me, her cropped hair revealing a scar that decorates her neck and creeps up beneath her hairline. She runs and I dart out of her way, my lehenga lighter than it looks because of the magic that created it. But she's quick, and as I sprint for the steps she barges into my side, pulling my arms behind my back and pushing me to the ground.

A horn clamours again from within the palace grounds.

Lyla's grip on my arm tightens as I try to stand. 'You're going nowhere,' she hisses in my ear.

'Get everyone to the south side!' Queen Sana orders Captain Nadim. 'Then send guards down into the city. I want everything locked down.'

'Your Majesty.' He nods sharply. 'And what of the intruders?'

'How many are there?'

'Five that we can see. They're approaching along the beach, Your Majesty. I'll gather the archers—'

'Gather them but don't let them be seen,' Queen Sana interrupts. 'You must wait for my signal. Lina has summoned my attention… I will deal with her.'

'Lina?' His gaze narrows on me.

'Captain,' Queen Sana says when he doesn't move. 'The city.'

'Yes, Your Majesty.' He falters for another moment, then snaps back into action.

I try to find Emir among the guards, but can't see him amid the frenzy of armour. Blood pulses in my ears.

The rain intensifies as Queen Sana hurries away, Heba and her guards in tow, and Dana and Meera close behind.

'Let's get you two to the prison as well, shall we?' says the older palace guard still standing over Sahi. His moustache is thick and curls over his lips as he smiles.

Lyla's nails burrow into my arms as she yanks me up, pulling me off the stage. Moustache signals for Imran to do the same and Sahi stumbles as he forces her up. It's eerily quiet, the theatre now empty but for the five of us, the rain and wind our only audience.

'Kaleb.' Sahi's eyes are wide as we're pulled away from the stage. 'I couldn't see his truth. I tried,' she says hurriedly. 'I promise I tried like we planned, but I couldn't see anything.'

'What do you mean?' But I saw it, the way her magic floundered when she tried to use it on him.

'Shut up!' Moustache shouts. 'Kaleb was right about you two. You're not to be trusted.'

A laugh bubbles in my throat that I have to suppress. 'Is that what he told you?' I should have seen it. I should have seen through him long before now and the way he would blame his treachery on us. 'And, when he was sowing these lies, did he also tell you we're the ones who are traitors?'

'Exactly,' Imran replies, fear etched in his voice as one hand grips Sahi's arm and the other reaches for the hilt of his blade. 'You knew Mezeer would attack today.'

'Is that true?'

I twist round in Lyla's grip, following the voice to where Emir stands behind us.

'No,' I say. 'We're not the ones behind this.' But I can see him trying to piece everything together; the way his trust breaks. My chest tightens, heartbeat hammering in time with the flames that throb beneath my skin as Lyla laughs.

'Why would anyone believe you, the traitor's daughter?' she sneers. 'You're exactly what everyone suspected the day you were found. And now you're poisoning those around you.' She looks from me to Sahi and I remember then how she cheered in court when some members argued I might be a spy like my mother.

Moustache and Imran follow her lead as she drops her grip, encircling Sahi and me as they draw their swords. Even Emir. Lyla leaps and, where a shimmering dust would usually form at the palms, strands of thick, dark smoke course over her hands. She moulds them into a single ball, as though fog in the dead of night has collected in her palms, before she extends her arms towards me and Sahi and releases her power. Dawn turns to dusk as the theatre is plunged into darkness. A shadow-spinner.

I can't see anything, the blackness darker than midnight. But I've been here before. In Mistress Soraya's studio with the cloth covering my eyes. I breathe in and out deeply and tune into the subtlest movements around me. Sahi…to my left, her breath shallow. Lyla…she doesn't move, her grip tight on her magic. Emir…he was in front of me. And Imran and Moustache…

The tension in me eases as my body shimmers gold. I duck beneath the first blade, spinning on the balls of my feet as my magic rises within me and I disorientate the guard with my sparks. They fly up and between us, glinting off the next blade that hurtles towards me. Moustache and Imran work together, relentless in their endeavour to find me in the gloom. Flames tingle in my palms and are met by screams as a wall of fire rushes up in front of me, temporarily blocking their path.

But there isn't time to pause. A sword swings at me again as Moustache dives round the wall of flames. He's lighter on his feet than I expect as he bounces back and forth, his blade extended. I dodge and jump over his swings while my flames curl across my hands, but they don't scare him. We dance like that until I extinguish my fire and throw up another round of sparks. He lurches back as they singe his moustache, sword clattering to the ground as he pats them away.

Footsteps retreat as Imran flees. The shadow doesn't lift from around us. Sahi, Lyla, Moustache and Emir… I can feel them, their energy. They're still here. Swords clang to my left as Moustache goes for Sahi instead. My flames reignite in time to see Lyla approach, her hands balled into fists in front of her face. She lunges towards me and jabs a punch at my head. She's taller and I swerve out of her reach, but she jabs again, first at my head with her other fist, then at my body, before spinning and grazing my thigh with a side kick.

I replicate the move, flying through the air as I kick out my right leg. But she catches my ankle with her forearm, knocking me off balance, and my left foot slips from under me. My breath hitches as I fall hard on to my back and my magic is smothered by the pain. We're still flooded by her darkness, but her own breaths are loud and I anticipate the blow before it hits, grabbing her round the ankle and pulling her down. The slam reverberates through the ground and I jump up, wincing against the ache that thuds in my lower back.

I hear Lyla scramble to her feet and put my arms up to protect my head. Unable to tell where she is, I punch a left hook, but hit air where I expect to make contact with her body. There's a shout on my left as she stumbles into something within her own midnight mist, and I dart round to face the direction the sound came from. Both of us falter as we seek each other out, then suddenly a white light pierces the black. I shield my eyes with my arms, peering between them to see where it comes from. Sahi… She spins on the spot and glows brighter than I've ever seen as her ability emanates from her whole being. I have to look away to resist her pull as she draws us into her trance. But it's not my mind she wants.

'Lyla,' Sahi says, her voice distant, despite standing only a few paces away.

Lyla grows still at the sound of her name.

Sahi walks towards her, illuminating the guard, who tries to cling on to her own power.

'We are not your enemy,' Sahi says calmly and I imagine her within Lyla's mind as she rethreads the truth. 'We're not the threat you must protect Queen Sana from.'

Lyla's eyes glow milky white under Sahi's influence and the shadows furl back towards her like a withering flower as Sahi silently continues to writhe through her mind. The darkness disperses to reveal Moustache running towards the cliff edge beyond the theatre, realising almost too late as he skids and comes to a stop.

And Emir... I don't move as he points his knife at my chest. His hands are steady while mine hover in front of me, palms down to show him I'm not a threat. I won't fight him.

Forehead creased, he debates his next move as Sahi's glow dissolves and Lyla stares at us all, dazed, as the final shreds of her darkness disappear.

'Emir,' Sahi says gently when she sees the blade.

'What did you just do to her?' The knife strays towards Sahi as he nods at Lyla.

Sahi doesn't flinch. 'I told her the truth...that we're not the enemy.'

'That's not what everyone is saying.' Emir's voice is calm, despite the weapon he's holding. 'How long have you been working for Mezeer?'

'We haven't been working with them,' Sahi says.

'But you were about to use your magic on Kaleb,' he says to her, then shifts the knife back to me. 'And you went against Queen Sana's orders.'

'Executing Noor would have achieved nothing,' I say.

He considers me for a moment, but then something flashes in his eyes, a defiance so unlike the easiness I've grown used to from him. 'The prisoner tried to assassinate the queen and your role is to *protect* the queen. Unless you really have been working with Mezeer this whole time like people suspect—'

'I haven't—'

'And you're going to help them assassinate Queen Sana.'

'No.' I step towards him, but he responds by doing the same and the knife almost touches my neck. 'I don't know how long Kaleb has been poisoning everyone here with his lies, but I promise you I'm not the threat.'

'She's telling the truth, Emir,' Sahi says from behind me and, for the briefest moment, something in him softens and I wonder if he recognises her.

'You really aren't working against the queen?' he asks me.

'No.'

'Then you'll come with me without putting up a fight...' But he already knows the answer from the way he leaves the question draped between us.

'No. I have to stop my mother and Queen Sana from killing each other in Kaleb's war,' I say without thinking.

His hard stare returns. 'Kaleb's?'

I nod and his gaze flickers between me and Sahi. I think he's going to put his knife away when, suddenly, he flips it within his hand. I pull back, eyes closed as I anticipate the pain.

When I open them again, Emir stands before me and is holding the blade flat between his fingers.

He nods at it and I take the knife from him, the handle still warm from his touch as he kneels and passes one of the other guard's abandoned swords to Sahi.

'We'll need every weapon we can get. Follow me...'

THIRTY~FIVE

'Aasira, are you sure this is a good idea?' Sahi says, grabbing my arm to slow me down as we run through the grounds after Emir. 'In Queen Sana's eyes, you're a traitor. If she catches you, it's only going to fuel her suspicions that you've been working with your mother.'

I stop suddenly, skidding along the wet grass, and almost pull Sahi down with me. 'I need to know why she left me, Sahi. And why she was working with a Mezeeri soldier when she always promised me she wasn't a spy for them. I need to know that she really is innocent.'

She nods slowly.

'You really believe Kaleb is the one who's been working with Mezeer?' Emir asks, uncertainty still etched in his brow.

'I know he is.' Of all the things my mother told me, I know one thing is for certain. We had to stay hidden: hidden from Kaleb.

'He's twisted the truth for so long,' Sahi says and tears well in her eyes, mingling with the rain that still falls. 'Aasira…'

'I know.'

Thunder rumbles overhead, accented by heavy armoured footsteps.

'We have to go,' Emir says as we glimpse a large group of palace guards. We duck out of sight as a band of archers position themselves along the wall overlooking the beach. Another batch of guards march in the opposite direction, out of the palace gates and down towards the city. 'This way.'

We run towards the west wing and I expect us to be heading for the entrance that leads to the throne room, but Emir stops when we reach a mosaicked alcove. He knocks on it in three places, then pushes against the wall to reveal a dark doorway. 'In here.'

'What is this place?' Sahi says as we follow him inside.

'The entrance to the tunnels. They run under the palace and all the way down to the city.'

'The passages Queen Sana mentioned...' I say and just catch Emir's nod before the world around us turns pitch-black as he slots the mosaic back into place. 'She said Kaleb knows of them—'

'Imani and the Queen's Guard are already after him,' Sahi reminds me.

'They could already be down here,' Emir says. 'They also lead to the beach so if Kaleb's heading that way, we'll find him.'

One hand alight, my pale orange flame reveals the jagged walls that close in around us, then open up suddenly to a series of passageways. Emir doesn't pause, some sort of internal compass guiding him unerringly down each tunnel until we reach a series of steps.

'Careful.' Emir's voice echoes.

I make the mistake of enhancing the flame in my palm and my head lurches with vertigo when I see how uneven and steep the steps are. I focus on Sahi's bun instead and place my right hand on the wall, the other still alight as, tentatively, I edge down each step.

Relief floods me when I hear the distant rush of water, and salty air greets us as we reach the bottom. We run towards a slice of light that beckons us like a crescent moon. The tunnel narrows in front of us and there's nothing we can do to avoid the black stone that scrapes against our arms as the walls close in. My back is still stiff from my fall but, as the ceiling bows above us, we have to crawl our way to the end. Emir strains as he wedges his hands into the slither of a gap and pushes at the boulder that seals us in.

'*Come on*,' he says through gritted teeth and slowly it gives. He breathes heavily, breaking for a second before he presses his feet against the large rock, using his legs to heave it out of place. The boulder slips away, crashing onto something hard below.

The world beyond is a blur as the waterfall that drapes over the cliffs from the palace gardens and into the sea shrouds us. It's so loud as the water rushes down, thick with white spray, that I can't hear Emir as he speaks. I try to lip-read as he looks out of the exit then turns back to us, and mimes with his hands to indicate the drop. He goes first, planting his hands on the tunnel's edge and jumping down. He disappears for a moment before his head pops up and he reaches a hand out for Sahi.

She shuffles forward and I follow close behind, copying what she did as I take Emir's hand and he helps me down. We're all soaked through within seconds. It's so exhilarating to be standing behind the waterfall, the natural power of it incredible as it crashes down from above. We carefully pick our way across the slick rocks until the curtain thins at one end and we emerge from its veil into the cove it shelters within. The tide is out and the water that streams from the waterfall carves a river in the sand leading down to the sea.

'It's so calm,' Emir comments.

The rain has stopped. Any hint of the storm has passed. In its place, the water glitters as the last tendrils of dawn melt into an azure sky. But I still feel her in a way I haven't for years; my mother is so close.

We skirt the base of the cliff as we run to the end of the cove where the cliff juts out. Now we have no choice but to dart into the uneven shadows it throws and hope we're out of view of the archers hidden along the palace walls. My heart races as, with my back against the rock, I make myself as small as possible and edge round the cliff and through the rock pools.

Emir flings his arm out suddenly to stop us as we leave the security of the cove behind and the beach expands in front of us. Sahi and I skid to a halt and that's when I see them: three silhouettes in the distance. Captain Nadim said there were five, but that there could be even more… Their attention is divided between the sea and the palace so, on Emir's command, we run through the long shadows and into a cave, careful not to splash loudly through the small pools that have formed.

Closer now, I search the three women's faces for my mother's.

My breath hitches. She's here, standing at the front of the trio. Sahi rests a hand on my shoulder just at the right moment, steadying me as the pain in my chest, the one that's been there for eight years, threatens to explode.

'That's her?' Emir asks.

I almost hadn't wanted to believe she could be here, but it's unmistakably her, despite how much she's changed. Her hair is shorter and hangs just below her shoulders. It's curlier than I remember and I touch the waves falling loose from my bun, but hers is threaded with strands of silver among the rich brown that matches my own. I can see why the prisoner mistook me for her with our shared eyes and nose, but my chin curves where hers is slightly longer and her smile has been replaced with a sternness I don't remember.

I don't recognise the women with her, both wearing the same armour embellished with gold and crimson details, so delicate it's likely crafted by specialist thread-weavers like our own soldiers' armour. The woman on my mother's right, who stands closest to us, looks older than her, white hair pulled back and eyes trained on the palace above. The woman on my mother's left might only be a few years older than me, her shaved head decorated with swirling black tattoos.

Drums and horns explode above us, reverberating off the rocks. I lean forward as far as I can within the shadows to see what's happening as my mother and the other two women all turn to face a larger cave, a little further along the beach.

Queen Sana rides out from the gaping cave mouth, her black horse unfazed as the sea bends to her magic and the low tide weaves back up the beach at her command. Seven members of her Queen's Guard ride close behind her and my heart lurches when I see Dana and Meera among them. We recoil into the darkness as Queen Sana passes us in Amaar's armour of white, emerald and gold, a jewelled headpiece dripping down her face like a cascade of golden vines.

I flinch when the sea rears and a wave crashes to the shore as Queen Sana pulls on the reins and her horse stops a pace away from where my mother stands. But my mother holds firm, unafraid of the queen's power or the sea that is still under her command and doesn't draw back as it should. The silence on the beach echoes as the women stare at each other.

'May peace rise with every dawn,' my mother says, her voice exactly as I remember it. She bows her head slightly.

'And endure with every dusk,' Queen Sana replies eventually.

'It's been too long.' When the queen doesn't grace her with a response, my mother scans the clifftop and says, 'I'm not here to fight, Sana. Though I can see you're prepared for such an eventuality.'

'Then why are you here?'

'You have something that belongs to me.'

My flames quiver. Does she mean me?

'Ah yes,' Queen Sana says. 'Is that where the other two members of your troop are? Retrieving our prisoner?' The way the queen says it, it's as though she's not concerned by the fact her supposed enemy may have broken into her palace.

My mother nods and it's like I'm sinking. Of course that's why she's here. She never came back for me before. Why would she now?

But then she looks at the women who flank Queen Sana and her gaze lingers on the youngest of her guards: Dana and Meera. 'Word is you have my daughter in your ranks.'

My breath catches.

A new menace crosses the queen's face as she smiles. 'Not any more.'

'Where is she?' My mother takes a step and Maryam reacts instantly, pulling forward on her horse.

Queen Sana puts up a hand to stop her guard from reacting any further.

'I told you, Sana. I'm not here to fight,' my mother says again. 'Where is my daughter?'

'Exactly where you wanted her. In the heart of Amaar, in the palace, where she could continue your work in trying to destroy our country.'

The air stirs with a slight breeze and, further down the beach, the tide changes direction.

'Is that what he would have you think?' My mother shakes her head, then adds, almost to herself, 'I see. When he could no longer use me as the scapegoat for his lies because I was supposed to be dead…at his hands, no less…he directed those lies on to my daughter.'

'Innocence never suited you, Lina,' the queen says and dark clouds stain the sky once again.

'You don't know, do you? You don't know what Kaleb is?'

Queen Sana laughs to herself. 'I know exactly what he is from the way he has stirred doubt in my court. He's a traitor, just as you are—'

'You can't still believe that of me?'

'How long were you working together before the night he supposedly killed you in Nazeem?' Queen Sana asks as though genuinely curious.

'You think I would ally myself with a man who would do anything to see our land crumble while all I've ever wanted is peace? You didn't see it, sitting here on your throne. You didn't see the devastation your war caused as it ripped families apart and with it the very fabric that makes up our country.'

'Is that why you killed your own soldiers? *My* soldiers!' Queen Sana shouts and her armour gleams as lightning flashes white over the sea and rain falls from the swollen clouds. 'Was spying for Mezeer and killing your own people all part of your righteous bid to save our country from ruin?'

Grains of sand stir at my mother's feet as her magic plays over her hands. 'That's not how it happened.'

'Then enlighten me,' Queen Sana challenges and the sea inches up the sand towards them.

'I would have seventeen years ago, had you given me the chance. But instead you ordered my execution.' Hurt creases my mother's face and her hands shimmer bronze as she contorts the air around her, whipping it into a frenzied breeze to push back the queen's oncoming tide.

My flames awaken, glimmering under the surface as my gold shimmer reveals itself.

'Aasira.' Sahi tries to pull me back, but I can't just stand here.

'Your Majesty,' one of the Queen's Guard calls out and points to something further down the beach.

'They have the prisoner,' Queen Sana says. 'Go!'

Two of the Queen's Guard swerve round my mother and towards the two figures who sprint out of a cave further along the beach. With Noor slung over one of the women's shoulders, they run in the direction of the city. But as quickly as they appeared, their forms dissolve until all that can be seen is the subtle shimmer of the woman who cloaks them with her magic.

Suddenly a whistle sings overhead as Queen Sana's orders are disregarded and flaming arrows arc over the beach, chasing down their invisible forms alongside the Queen's Guard.

'Serena!' my mother shouts. 'Now!'

The older woman extends her hands up towards the palace walls, directly above us. As her hands sway over each other, they begin to glow and it's like a blast hits us, almost throwing us back, as she casts out a pearlescent shield to block the oncoming arrows.

'And you said you weren't here to fight.' Rivulets thread from the queen's hands and up over her arms, like tentacles. She dismounts and her guards do the same, letting their horses ride free as they tighten their ranks.

But my mother holds firm and sand swirls round her, caught in the tornado she creates. Serena still blocks the arrows from above and the woman with the tattooed head crouches, placing one palm flat on the sand as she mouths something I don't hear.

I don't see who makes the first move.

Air and water clash. Sand swoops up between my mother and the queen, propelled by the wind my mother manifests. With nowhere to go, the water curves upwards, defying gravity as it rushes up the surface of my mother's air-shield before it arcs back down towards the queen, re-forming into neat rivulets that dance over her body.

Maryam turns her attention to Serena while Dana and Meera approach the tattooed girl.

'I have to stop them.' My magic stirs under my skin.

'Aasira, wait,' Sahi says. I'm ready to protest when she looks at Emir and he nods. 'We're with you.'

Flames rippling, I run out from the shelter of the cave with Sahi and Emir at my back, heading in the direction of my mother and the queen. I cast out my fire and it swirls over the sand like the mehndi that decorates my hands. They don't see it at first, not until my flames lace between them, cutting through the shield of wind and water they've created.

'Aasira...' My mother's voice is ushered on the breeze that loops towards me, then is lost beneath Queen's Sana's string of commands.

I feel her next move before I see it. The queen turns her attention to me and a plume of water hits me sidelong with such force, I crumple to the sand. I grip my ribs, where pain blooms as I cough up water. But Queen Sana hasn't finished with me. I don't have time to take a final breath as her power engulfs me completely.

THIRTY~SIX

Queen Sana wraps me within her wave and I'm powerless in its embrace. I tumble through the water as she drags me across the sand and towards the shoreline, gasping for air as she launches me into a sea that thrashes with her fury. Salt burns my throat. My chest screams. Waves roll above, holding me down. Arms pushing through the water, I try to swim, but I don't know how and it slips through my fingers. There's no way out.

Tiny white lights flare in front of me. Then I feel her. Feel her magic part the waves.

'Aasira…'

I'm choking, unable to take a breath.

'Aasira…'

A force pushes down on my chest, once, twice, and I retch, coughing up seawater and everything inside me.

My mother brushes my damp hair back from my face. 'Aasira, I'm here.'

I'm light-headed as my breaths come fast and slow all at once, unable to find their rhythm.

'It's all right, you're safe,' she whispers and kisses my forehead, cradling me like she did when I was a child. 'You're safe.' The way she keeps repeating the words, it's as though she doesn't believe them.

Neither do I.

'You're here,' I say as I find my voice again and my senses reawaken.

'I'm here. We're together again now.'

The sea swirls round us like a whirlpool as my mother manipulates the air, arcing it through the water to hold it at bay…just as she did to create her passage to me.

'My lehenga…' she says quietly as she touches my sodden skirt. She's completely dry but for the tears that dampen her cheeks. 'I thought I'd been thrown back in time for a moment and was seeing myself at my loornas.'

I look down at my outfit. It was never made for me or the execution… Is that why Tariq and the others left, because they recognised it as my mother's costume?

'This was yours?' I ask as I try to sit up.

'Careful.' She rests a hand on my back to steady me. 'You don't want to make yourself any sicker. You hit the water hard.'

I feel it in my chest and my muscles, my whole body aching from the force of Queen Sana's magic. The water is so clear as it swirls round us, drained of the emerald tones that give it its name, that I can see all the way through, like a pane of glass, to the beach where Sahi and Emir fight back to back against two members of the Queen's Guard. Queen Sana is the only one to watch us and a fear I haven't felt around her before rises in me. She would have killed me had my mother not been there. But then the queen's focus is pulled away.

'Naila can only keep Sana's attention for so long,' my mother says and I see the girl with the tattoos as she distracts the queen and Maryam with illusions that seem to make the beach tremor. I turn to watch Dana and Meera wrestle Serena as she casts her shield out even further to help the group escaping with the prisoner. 'I can carve us a path to the city and Serena is strong; she'll make sure she and Naila get out safely.'

My mother stands and reaches out a shimmering hand for me. 'Can you run?'

I can barely stand as she helps me up. 'Why? Where are you going?' Panic rises in me as I see her kneeling in the desert again, there one second then gone the next.

'I was coming for you so I could take you somewhere safe, away from all of this,' she says, her voice soft the way I remember it as she takes my face in her hands. 'Look at you.' She laughs to herself and her eyes well up again. 'All these years I thought... I thought I'd watched you die. But here you are, alive and more remarkable than I could have ever imagined.'

My vision blurs with tears, my voice thick as I say, 'You thought I was dead.' The scar on my side suddenly tingles. 'I thought you'd left me.'

'Never.' She rubs away my tears. 'If I'd known, I'd have found you sooner. But it wasn't until I heard the rumours of the girl made of fire that I realised you might still be alive.'

'You came to the sanctuary...'

'I had to know if it was true. I had to know it was really you.'

'And the village…'

Her smile disappears. 'A group of us tracked you, but we played it all wrong and you discovered us. The way you fought…you were so fierce.'

'The villagers…they were all dead. Was that you?'

A flicker of hurt crosses her face. 'No. They had already been killed before we reached them.' She sighs. 'The war between Amaar and Mezeer can't continue like this. With each life we take, we're taking from our country, draining it of the energy that gave our land life in the first place. Sana doesn't see it, but perhaps she doesn't need to. Perhaps we're strong enough, just the two of us—'

'Strong enough for what?'

'To heal what we've broken,' she says and there's a renewed vigour in her, emulated by the wind that whips round us and causes the sea to surge as she forges us a new path. 'It isn't far.'

'What isn't?'

'Sehar.'

The map painted on the palace library's ceiling flashes in my mind. 'Sehar? In Mezeer?'

Nausea clutches at me. She turns back when she realises I'm not following.

'Why are you going to Mezeer?' I ask.

'Because that's where it all began. And it's where it can end.'

'What can end? Are you working with them? With Mezeer?' I ask accusingly.

'No,' she says quickly and steps towards me, but I pull back. 'I have never worked with Mezeer, Aasira. Those were Kaleb's

269

lies. He wanted what I had: a close relationship with the queen and access to power. You can't believe anything he told you.'

'I don't believe him,' I admit. 'But you say you've never worked with Mezeer and yet that's where Noor's from,' I say, remembering her accent. 'And now you want me to travel there with you? To the country we're at war with. Where my father, one of their soldiers, was from.'

My mother takes a deep breath. 'Sana told you.'

'She told me a lot of things.'

She nods as though she already suspected it, then looks towards the beach, about to speak. But her words are lost. Her bronze shimmer fades.

'No…' The tunnel she created starts to cave in. 'Run!'

She grabs me by the wrist, her grip tight, and I ignore the ache in my ribs as we sprint through the water that closes in round us. She tries to hold it back, but her shimmer vanishes completely as we reach shallower waters and the tunnel that protected us splashes round us, leaving us exposed in the shallows.

My flames lurch within me when I see him.

Kaleb.

Imani and Lyla flank him. But he's no prisoner.

I summon my magic, but my flames don't hear me. It's like I'm wading through the water, dragged down by the seaweed that clings to my ankles. Even Queen Sana loses control of her magic and is stunned as the sea withdraws from her hold, followed by the rain and wind, which falter as the storm she and my mother created breaks overhead.

I'm heavy and light-headed at the same time, held down by an invisible weight yet weightless without my flames as they sputter over my skin, then fizzle out. I look at Sahi then the others as, just like with me, the shimmer that danced over their bodies dissolves beneath the sun that emerges from behind the clouds.

All but for one.

Kaleb's hands are a dazzling scarlet as he drains us all of our lifeblood. I know now what he is.

A silencer.

THIRTY~SEVEN

Kaleb lets out a long breath, luxuriating in our shock. 'It's so freeing to finally show one's true self, isn't it? And what better time than when we're all reunited,' he says, looking between the queen and my mother.

None of us speak and his laugh curls round us, but the notes fall flat against the sharp squawk of the gulls that fly overhead.

A crooked smile twitches at his lips. 'Come now, I may have silenced your magic, but surely I haven't silenced you completely.'

Both Dana and Meera flinch at his words as they finally see what he is. Sahi might have been under Kaleb's influence all these years, but from the way one hand twitches at her side, desperate for the magic that's been drained from her, I know she didn't foresee this. How could she? How could any of us? This is why she couldn't see his truth earlier.

I try to see everything I've missed over the years. I've been under his charm like the rest of his students, eager to listen and to please.

Anger floods me, but my flames don't follow, their song wiped from my body's memory. Instantly, I yearn for their rhythm and protection. Something he's taken from me.

'Kaleb,' the queen says eventually. Then her gaze shifts to the women at his side, Imani and Lyla, as they close in.

'Your Majesty. It would seem more than just your courtiers have shifted their loyalty,' Kaleb replies, his tone mocking. He looks at his hands, all of us mesmerised by the scarlet shimmer that decorates them. I search his palms for a symbol, but there's nothing there; nothing that could have revealed what he's been hiding. 'Who would have thought that we would ever see the day where a man could possess magic once more?'

The hairs along my arms stand on end and a ripple of unease threads through all of us as we anticipate his next move, struggling against the way he drains our energy. Even Emir looks uncomfortable, his jaw tense and his hand still round the hilt of his sword.

'Your father believed it would happen,' Kaleb tells Queen Sana. 'He believed magic could spread beyond the boundaries we'd set for ourselves and he was right—'

'Do not speak of my father,' Queen Sana says. 'Don't pretend he would have applauded you for your crimes—'

'Crimes?' Kaleb touches his chest as though genuinely taken aback. 'Is the possession of magic now a crime?'

'It is when it's used against your queen,' my mother answers and Kaleb's mask of innocence slips away.

'Oh, Lina, you always did want to believe the rules the rest of us abide by don't apply to you. I saw you two before, the way you fought like children.' He tuts, pointing between my mother

273

and Queen Sana, goading them, before stepping towards my mother and me. 'You're the most treasonous of us all.'

'Because I killed some of my soldiers and supposedly allied with Mezeer,' my mother says, her eyes locked on him.

'Finally, you admit to it,' he snarls.

'I admit to nothing. I am not the one who's been working with Mezeer—'

'But you killed your soldiers for them,' Kaleb says and his magic twists further, coiling round his wrists. 'Or at least, for *one* of them.' His gaze shifts to me and my skin prickles, desperate for my flames.

'It wasn't like that,' my mother rebukes. 'I never meant to—'

'Meant to kill them or get caught?'

'Enough!' Queen Sana shouts.

But Kaleb hasn't finished. 'You made it so easy that day, Lina. Everyone knew you weren't capable of commanding an army and you proved it all on your own.'

'Of course, the position "promised" to you.' My mother laughs. 'You never could stand it, could you? That I was chosen over you as our army's general.'

'Chosen by a childish queen,' says Kaleb scornfully.

'What is it you want, Kaleb?' Queen Sana asks and, from the way he smiles, it's as if that's the real question he's here to answer.

'You've waited all this time to reveal yourself,' the queen continues. 'Why? What are you after?'

'I want what we all do: to see our land prosper.'

'Is that so?' my mother says under her breath.

'Your influence is waning, Sana,' Kaleb says, ignoring her. 'I could have helped you all those years ago to strengthen your position as queen.'

'Ah yes. Your proposal…' Queen Sana says as though only just remembering. I blush as a glimmer of embarrassment flashes across Kaleb's face.

It's quickly replaced with an arched brow as he tries to recover. 'Your mother and father had wanted it.'

'So you always said.'

He nods, not hearing the amusement in her tone. 'But now look. The people are restless for something new.'

'Are they indeed?'

'You heard them in court the other day. They do not trust those you surround yourself with: traitors and spies.' He gestures to all of us, then clasps his hands together, and it's like his magic surges as the red shimmer intensifies and spreads across his body.

'But my court trust you, is that right?' Queen Sana says, her voice strained as she tries not to show she feels his power increase too.

'Many of them do, yes. They have had enough of being…' He looks away, searching for the word as though this isn't all rehearsed. 'Silenced.'

So have I.

'Aasira!' Emir slides his own sword towards me and I catch it as it spins over the damp sand.

The queen's guards unsheathe the blades hidden within their armour and Queen Sana raises the signal. Flaming arrows rain down over us again, clearing her a path as she pulls back towards the cliffs. Imani and Lyla, stripped of their magic too while Kaleb keeps his hold over us, gather round him and are joined by Fatima, who slinks out of the queen's ranks and shows her true allegiance. But my mother, Maryam and Meera are there in an instant, their swords clashing with those of Kaleb's guards, leaving us standing face to face.

Kaleb's lips twist into a smile as I approach and he spins his blade in his right hand, dusting off the skills he learned in the army.

'Let's see what you're left with when you don't have your flames, shall we?' he challenges.

We don't bother with Sajid's pleasantries. I block Kaleb's blade with my own as he sweeps down. Crouched, I put all my weight behind my sword, and our blades scrape along each other as I stand and force his sword down, metal grating against metal. It doesn't take him long to find his rhythm as he spins his sword in his fist again and curves it down, but I anticipate the move, arching back and away with all the flexibility the sanctuary's mistresses taught us. Our blades dance as we weave round each other to the beat of the orchestra of swords surrounding us.

My energy wanes as his magic strengthens, until I can't feel the hum of my magic at all. But I won't be overpowered by Kaleb. I grab the hilt of my sword with both hands and pour everything I can into my upwards swing. Kaleb steps back, but he isn't fast enough as I spin and lean into his attack, catching his left forearm with the side of my blade.

He winces, pulling back as blood oozes through the sleeve of his white kurta. His magic wavers round him and I take my chance, drawing on everything I have as our blades clash again and again and, slowly, his magic abandons him.

Suddenly I'm hidden by a veil of sand that rises between us. Ma shimmers bronze and my flames blossom within me too. They're tentative at first, like the first sparks on kindling, but then they remember and smoulder under the surface. Swords drop to the ground as the sky darkens again under the queen's influence and her waves hurry back up the shore. But as we regain our magic so too do Kaleb's guards.

A knife whistles past me and I dart out of its path, just missing an arrow that skims my shoulder. Fatima runs towards me and I shoot my flames along the sand. They soar towards her, leaping at her feet. She screams, but the sound is swallowed by the force of Maryam's power as she spins Fatima through the air and towards the cliffs, where Heba and more members of the Queen's Guard emerge from the same cave Queen Sana did earlier. I expect Maryam to turn her magic on me and reawaken my flames, but instead she nods before going after Imani.

The flurry of arrows stops as Serena's shield goes up once again and she blocks the path of the oncoming guards and the attack from above. But it's too late.

'Naila!' my mother shouts. I turn to see her run to the young girl as she falls to the ground, clutching her side where two arrows protrude. 'Serena, get her out of here!' my mother yells, then looks to where Queen Sana approaches with a fresh set of guards. 'Retreat, now!'

Serena's shield shrinks around her as she scoops Naila up into her arms, protecting the two of them as she runs down the beach towards the city like her comrades did with Noor earlier. Arrows bounce off the shimmering bubble that encircles them.

Meera and Maryam regroup as the new guards pick up pace behind the queen and Heba. The way they march, I can't tell if they're here for Kaleb or if I'm still a wanted traitor in their eyes. I look over to where Emir and Sahi's blades are locked with Lyla's and Kaleb's, all hint of his magic gone as he struggles against Emir's blows. Behind me, my mother tackles Imani to the ground with her magic.

I move to help when sand swells in front of me. At first I think it's my mother's doing, but it forms into long strands and, gradually, two sand serpents reveal themselves. I jump out of their way, but they follow, gliding towards me as new ones surface in their wake. My heart sinks as they gain momentum. I have no choice but to throw my magic towards them and my gold dust lights the sand until it's ablaze. But Dana's serpents are unharmed and I see the anger written in her face as she stands on the other side of my flames.

'Have you always known?' she asks as two new snakes form at her side while the others slink beneath the fire and wait for her command.

'Known what?'

I've never seen her so upset. Her expression contorts as she fights back her tears, until she isn't the Dana I recognise.

She shakes her head. 'That your mother was still alive… Have you been working with her this whole time?'

'No,' I say, quieter than I intend as tears prick behind my eyes.

'I thought we could trust each other!' Her voice breaks. 'I always stood up for you, and all along you played us…played *me*.'

'No, Dana, that's not true.'

But she doesn't believe me, the lie already embedded in her, along with the duty that's been drilled into us: to protect our queen and country. Dana's serpents rear up as she raises her arms and launches them at me. I spin to catch them with my flames, but they don't recoil like a real snake would, and one pounces, sinking its fangs into my calf, just above my ankle.

I lose all grip on my flames and the fire that separates us sinks into the damp sand. I claw at the snake, but it only clings tighter as its tail squeezes round my ankle and its venom burns through my skin. The agony is relentless and I can't hold back the scream that is wrenched from me. Still, Dana doesn't abandon her fury.

Another serpent writhes over the sand, but my flames are smothered by the pain. There's nothing I can do to stop it as the one round my leg clamps me to the spot. Bright pinpricks of white light flash in my eyes beyond the blurry haze of my tears. The new serpent flings itself at my other leg and the white lights dance before me, an ensemble who've abandoned all choreography. I brace myself for its bite. It doesn't come.

White light moulds into silver as a sword arches down and severs the serpent before it reaches me. Emir blocks each serpent as Dana's whispers fill my ears and more thrash towards us. He dives out of reach with the same lightness of foot as the night I watched him dance. I flinch when, finally, he slashes at the serpent's tail round my leg, but it only re-forms and digs its fangs in deeper. This is what Dana must have been rehearsing with Mistress Soraya, the warrior with poison in her veins.

Everything is plunged into darkness.

The sand serpent convulses, releasing its hold and I collapse into the sand. Lyla's magic consumes the light, turning everything to shadow until I can't see anything.

'Aasira!'

'Ma?'

Our calls for each other mingle with the shouts all along the beach as armour crashes into armour.

Someone collides into the back of me and my flames flare.

'It's me,' Emir says, and I just make him out in the gloom as he puts his hands up.

'He'll get away,' I say, panic rising. 'Ma!'

'Run, Aasira!' she shouts back.

But I can't. I can hardly stand.

'Sahi!' Emir shouts.

She doesn't answer.

He puts a hand under my right arm and the other on my back, helping me up. 'We have to get out of here.'

'How?' The darkness is everywhere.

I recoil as something ice-cold wraps round my feet. The sea. It rises round my legs until it's at my knees as Queen Sana floods the beach in her bid to trace Kaleb through the darkness.

'Sahi! Ma!'

Silence.

THIRTY~EIGHT

S lowly, the darkness peels away.

The sea glitters at my feet as the sun peers through the clouds and I have to cover my eyes as they readjust to the daylight. Queen Sana's magic crawls over the sand as she seeks Kaleb out. But, as the last tendrils of shadows disperse, they only reveal the beach.

He's gone. His guards too.

All except Imani. She's halfway down the beach and would be hidden within the cave's shadow if it weren't for her magic that shimmers round her. I see then who it's aimed at.

'Sahi!'

Imani's magic coils round Sahi's body, rooting her to the shoreline as she gasps for breath. My leg gives way under me as I run in the direction of the cave. The pain from the venom is unbearable as it shoots up through my calf, but I have to stop Imani. Flames surge in me, but they recoil at the sea's touch as I aim for her.

My mother's magic gets their first. The air bends at her will as she projects a howling gust towards Imani, sending her crashing into the cave wall. Imani's magic slips from the impact and she releases her grip on Sahi, who crashes into the shallow water. I spin round and reach her just as Emir does.

I kneel beside him and we turn Sahi over so her face isn't in the water. Blood trickles from her nose, her face and lips pale and hands cold within mine.

'Sahi? It's me. Wake up.'

She doesn't hear me, her body limp as she slumps in my arms.

'What do we do?' I ask Emir desperately.

'I...'

But his attention turns to the shouts behind us as Queen Sana gives orders to her guards. They start to run, some at us and some at my mother and Imani, who are still locked in battle.

'Take her,' I say quickly and Emir gently lifts Sahi off my lap. He rests her flat on the sand, one hand cupped beneath her neck where violet bruises bloom from Imani's magic.

'She's breathing,' he says, almost as if he doesn't believe it, and her eyelids flicker gently.

'Get her away from here,' I say as I struggle to stand.

I weave my hands over one another in the patterns I learned from Mistress Zaina, until my flames wrap round my body. The four women who approach hesitate, but they shimmer too, ready to attack. I don't give them a chance, casting a wall of fire between us that extends across the beach to block those pursuing my mother as well.

'No.' My magic diffuses when I turn and see her.

Imani flees into the darkness, leaving my mother who crouches on the ground in the mouth of the cave, her hands clutching her bleeding head. Sand rises, whipping round her as though caught in a current as she deflects the last of Imani's magic with her own. But it's like the night in Nazeem. The more sand that rises round my mother, the more it shields her from my view. But it isn't only that. I didn't imagine it then, just as I'm not imagining it now. The sandstorm she creates round herself intensifies until suddenly the grains disappear and she vanishes with them.

I look around me, expecting her to appear somewhere else along the beach, but she's gone.

My fire wall ebbs, but I have nothing else to give as the Queen's Guard close in. I'm alone. My mother is gone. Kaleb has fled. Sahi is injured. And Queen Sana would still take me prisoner, despite Kaleb's admissions. The way my energy wanes, it's like he's still here. But I won't let my magic be silenced again. I turn on the spot to muster what I can. The venom in my leg grips me though, willing me to fail until finally my skin shimmers gold. Emir fights his way through the guards, and I'm about to scream at him for leaving Sahi when I see Meera standing over her.

Meera's midnight dust dances over the guards closest to me, including Dana. She traps them within a trance, carving their dreams…their nightmares. When she locks eyes with me, they're swollen with tears as she crawls through the guards' minds and pushes them into unconsciousness.

Go, she mouths.

I stall.

There's no hesitation in her though. Before the other guards can retaliate, she flings her arms wide, then turns on the balls of her feet. Her shimmering dust floats from her palms and rolls over the beach, until it rains over Queen

Sana and the rest of her guards. They resist, some more than others, and Meera's hands tremble as she pulls them under. One by one, they succumb to her daze as she draws on a strength I've never seen in her before and holds them all within her power.

'Go,' she says again when she stops dancing. 'Find Kaleb.'

I shake my head as I look at where Sahi still lies in the sand. Meera looks between us both and, when her raven eyes find me again, she nods in understanding.

'Sahi will be all right,' she says as she works hard to keep everyone within her slumber.

A sob rises from deep within and catches in my throat.

'We need to go while we can,' Emir says. He starts to pull me away, but I pull back.

'We can't leave them.'

'We'll come back. But we have to find Kaleb,' he says urgently.

'Sahi…' How do I tell him that it's his sister we're leaving behind?

'She's breathing,' he says. 'And Queen Sana won't hurt her. She needs a truth-seeker in her midst now more than ever.'

I can't let Meera do this. When Queen Sana awakens and realises what she's done, she too will be branded a traitor…

'Don't fight me on this,' Meera says, reading my mind. 'Go!'

'Aasira.' Emir beckons.

Seeing Meera use her magic like this, I find the strength I need as I kneel and touch my palms flat to the sand, forcing my flames to rise above the pain until they flicker white and trail over the sand, wrapping round Queen Sana and her guards. It's the only chance I can give Meera to get away as her magic begins to waver.

She smiles but it doesn't hide her tears. I don't try to hide mine either.

'I think I know how Kaleb got away,' Emir says as he pulls me along as fast as I can run. 'There are tunnels leading in and out of the palace and to the city in all these caves. That must be how Lina's guards got to the prisoner. And how Imani esc—'

'It was this cave,' I say as I skirt the spot where my mother disappeared within her sandstorm.

Rock pools litter the cave entrance. I quickly lose sight of Emir in the darkness as he hurriedly searches out the tunnel Imani must have escaped through. And Kaleb...

'Here,' Emir says and I follow his voice.

I light the way as we duck inside and the tunnel opens up before us, leading us deep within the cliffs. 'You know how to get to the city via these tunnels?' I ask, trying to keep my rising panic at bay as the walls narrow in some parts, then widen in others. What if the whole cliff face came down over us?

'Emir?' I say when he doesn't respond.

'We'll find our way,' he replies from up ahead and I take comfort that he's here.

But in that same beat I wonder why he is. We shouldn't have left Sahi. *I* shouldn't have let him leave her. 'You take your role as chaperone very seriously, don't you?' I say, though it comes out harsher than I intended. 'Sorry, I just meant—'

'You're right, I do. This way.' He brushes my arm as a new passage opens on our right.

We're both silent for a while as he guides us through the tunnels. I listen for any hint of footsteps that aren't our own, but the only sound other than us is that of the water that drips down the stone walls.

'I used to come down here as a child,' Emir says as though sensing my unease. 'Me and some of the others had a game of who could get to the city fastest from the beach. It never made sense to me climbing that big hill if you wanted to be the first one back, so I learned my way round the tunnels. I got lost a few times –' he laughs to himself and it echoes round us – 'but who doesn't?'

'Are you lost now?'

'No.'

The nervous flutter in the pit of my stomach eases slightly. 'Do you think this is the way they went?'

'Queen Sana said Kaleb knows of the passages…'

'Then we could be close.'

'Maybe,' Emir says tentatively.

I nod to the darkness. 'What do we do if we don't find him?'

'The queen will have a party out looking for him by now.' Emir's right. There could be palace guards searching for Kaleb down here too. As though reading my thoughts, he picks up pace.

We can't get caught. But I can't hide and let Kaleb get away. Not after all the lies.

'Are there any tunnels that lead out of the city?'

'If there are, I haven't used them. And I don't think we should stray from the path I know. It's too easy to get lost down here.'

'Let's avoid that.'

Emir looks over his shoulder and there's the hint of a smile in my firelight, but then his expression turns serious. 'If there are tunnels leading out of the city and Kaleb knows them as well as Queen Sana believes, there's a chance he isn't in Naru at all any more.'

'Then we'll have to hope they don't exist and, if they do, that he doesn't know about them.'

'The city's locked down and there'll be palace guards on patrol,' he tries to reassure me.

'Who will know Queen Sana ordered my arrest.'

Emir stops and gazes upwards. 'How's your leg?' he asks as he stretches up, touching his palms to the roof of the tunnel.

'I can run,' I say, more assured than I feel, though the searing throb is now more a dull ache.

'Good.'

I extinguish the flame in my palm as he pushes on the stone above. Nothing happens at first, but then there's a crunch as stone grinds against stone and a piece comes loose. Gently and quietly, he lifts it out of place. Without speaking, he gestures for me to stand on his knee. His hands round my waist, he lifts me up and I grip the uneven rock to help heave myself up, then scan the street above ground. Confident that there's no one around, I hoist myself up, my lehenga snagging on the rock. I signal for Emir to follow and he pulls himself up in one swift movement, then replaces the flagstone that hides the tunnel beneath.

It's so quiet as we emerge in the heart of the souk. We run for cover and duck between two street carts filled with trinkets, where the sweet and musky scents of oud permeate the air around us. For a moment, I'm transported back to our visit here when we first arrived at the palace, but the memory is interrupted by the low din of armour.

Still crouched, we slowly make our way through a string of interwoven stalls until we reach a thin road with a narrow passageway on the opposite side. Emir goes first, checking both ways before dashing across and into the shadow of the alley.

I'm about to follow when footsteps echo to my left. I pull back and into the small gap between the stalls as the footsteps grow louder and faster. Whoever it is, they're running.

I can just make out the street and keep my eye on the spot in front of the alley, where Emir still hides. Someone yelps and my heart skips. The person running staggers into view, but I can only see their legs. I stoop down lower to get a better view and recognise the guard immediately as Ahmed. He cries out and slumps to his knees, mumbling to himself as shock blooms across his face. He jerks again, then drops forward, his head hitting the stone hard to reveal three arrows protruding from his back.

The archer approaches and slings a bow over one shoulder, but they have their back to me as they roll Ahmed over on to his side. Blood oozes from his forehead where he hit his head, his eyes wide open and staring at his killer. When I catch sight of his attacker's profile, ice crawls through me.

Zayn pinches Ahmed's cheeks and mumbles something I don't hear, before kicking him a final time in the chest. My heartbeat races as Zayn strolls back the way he came. I can just make out Emir within the gloom of the alley, staring at his friend lying motionless between us. It's like Emir startles awake when, suddenly, he waves his hand for me to join him. It's only a short distance, but if I time it wrong someone could see me. I inch out from my spot between the stalls and can almost hear Emir as he mouths for me to run. With a deep breath, I sprint across the road, dodging Ahmed's body.

'Kaleb,' I whisper, my breathing heavy when I reach Emir. 'He's managed to get into the heads of the palace guards too.'

He stares at the place where Ahmed lies, his hands gripping the hilt of his sword. 'I should've known about Zayn…'

'And I should have known about Kaleb.'

I jump when a stray dog barks from the direction we just fled from, sniffing its way between the stalls.

Emir puts a finger to his lips, then gestures for me to follow. We weave our way through the different quarters in the souk until we reach a set of cobbled streets I haven't seen before, with narrow houses either side. Their windows and doors are completely closed up, but I can still feel the eyes of the inhabitants on us as the clash of swords echoes somewhere on our left. We're about to veer right down another backstreet when a flash catches my eye. I step back and look down the path we just took.

'Aasira,' Emir whispers impatiently. 'Where are you going?'

'She's here…'

The pain in my leg dissolves as adrenaline kicks in and I race through the alleyways, anticipating her every turn, until the last passage opens up on to a large square. A leafless tree rises in its centre, like the one crafted into the mosaic at the sanctuary.

'Imani!' She spins round.

'What are you doing?' Emir tries to pull me back, but I can't let her get away. She must know where Kaleb is heading.

Imani stretches her neck to both sides, then cracks her knuckles, always one to make a show of things. 'Are you sure you want to do this?' she asks as though speaking to a child.

The familiar warmth of my power shimmers over me, turning me gold as both Sahi and my mother flash into my mind, wounded by her magic.

Imani smiles to herself as though someone's just told a vaguely amusing joke. 'I always thought you had potential,

Aasira. Like Sahi. But, like her, you don't have the ability to fulfil it.' She rolls back her shoulders as she stands beneath the overhanging tree branches. 'I wouldn't want to keep our audience waiting.' She winks at Emir.

Her eyes glaze as her black shimmer takes shape between her hands and she launches her power towards me. Flames spring from my palms, but Imani diverts her magic and something cracks behind me.

Emir screams out and clutches his right shoulder, his arm hanging awkwardly at his side.

'Emir...' I run to him, but he points behind me with his good hand, unable to form words.

Imani laughs as she spins another web of magic and throws it in our direction. I turn to catch it and her magic frays at the touch of my flames. She leaps, not giving up on her onslaught as she pummels my golden flames, crushing them the way she wishes to crush me.

But I won't be silenced any more.

I don't stop them as they rush to the surface, crackling along my skin. My white flames submerge me in their blaze. I flip through the air, everything in me aimed at Imani, until we could be dancing a duet as we weave our magic round each other. But she isn't scared of my flames as they fan out towards her feet with every turn. I aim higher. It's only then she cowers as I produce a continuous funnel of sparks that push her back towards the nearest building, before forming into pure white flames about her.

Her black shimmer recoils and her eyes fade back to brown, my flames reflected within them. She opens her mouth, but I don't let her speak. I jump from both feet, turning at the same time, and my flames twist round her, smothering her last words.

THIRTY~NINE

I can't look away. I need to be sure Imani's gone. That she can't
hurt us again. As with Omar, my white flames melt away,
disappearing into the ground along with any memory of Imani.

'Aasira.' Emir's voice is quiet as he joins me. He keeps a few
paces between us as my flames still linger, as though they're
unsure if they can withdraw just yet.

Horns rally in the distance and there's a new urgency to his
voice. 'We need to go.'

I killed her.

'Aasira?' he says again, more tentatively than before. His
hand is still clamped over his shoulder.

'Are you all right?' I ask, shaken.

'I'll be better when we're not in the open. Come on.'

My ankle throbs again as we run and the last of the
adrenaline washes away, leaving behind the reality of what
I just did. But I'm not the only one who's injured. Emir's body
is hunched towards the right as he tries to hold his shoulder in
place and he winces as we jog away from the horns that blare
throughout the city.

He leads us out of the square and down some older-looking alleyways where the buildings are boarded up at the windows and doors. The only sign of life is a stray cat that's curled up within an abandoned heap of crates and purrs as we pass.

We reach a dead end and I expect Emir to reveal another entrance to the tunnels, but instead he walks up the stone steps to the largest of the buildings, which rises up at the end of the alley. Its mosaiced walls have faded to a soft peach and tall pillars frame the angular archway and door, which Emir pushes against with his good shoulder.

'Here, let me,' I say as he grimaces.

I lean my weight into the old door and it gives, creaking on the hinges. We slip through the small opening before I push it firmly closed again.

'We can stay here until things quieten down,' Emir says. 'No one comes this way any more.'

My palms alight, I walk round the ground floor where beautiful emblems adorn the walls: the same emblems that embroider my lehenga.

'What is this place?' I ask and look up at the empty shelves that stretch round the walls.

Emir confirms my suspicion. 'It was a library.'

'Where are the texts?'

'They were removed a long time ago. This whole street used to be filled with goods and stories from across Amaar and Mezeer. But, as the war intensified and everything connected to Mezeer was destroyed, the people abandoned this street too. We'll be safe here for a while.'

'Safer than in the tunnels?'

He nods as he sits on the staircase.

'Your shoulder…' I say as I join him. 'Is it broken?'

'Dislocated, I think.'

I flinch at the thought of it. Then again when I see Imani wrapped in my white flames. Everything happened so quickly. 'I killed her… I killed her because I wanted to kill him.'

'No,' Emir says. 'You killed her because, if you hadn't, she would have killed you.'

Not if I hadn't gone after her. But I can't bring myself to say it. It's the first time I've killed someone of my own accord and not because I've been ordered to for our queen and country. And despite everything – the way Imani has worked with Kaleb and injured Sahi and my mother – bile still rises in my throat.

'All this time, Kaleb's been able to gather his own army at the sanctuary,' I say. 'There'll be more people on his side, biding their time until they show their true allegiance.'

Emir nods. 'And what about now? What do *we* do?'

The way he says 'we', the warmth in me bubbles again. *We go back for Sahi. We find Kaleb*, I think, but instead say, 'My mother asked me to go to Mezeer. To Sehar, on the border.'

'Is that where she's been all this time?'

'I don't know.' Shame prickles up my neck at the way I reacted to her offer. At the way I questioned her. 'She said it's the place where it all began and where it can end.'

Emir stares at something in the corner as he runs his left hand through his hair, pushing back the loose strands. 'Sehar…that's near the old city. It sits on what used to be the main thoroughfare for transporting goods from the sea to the mountains.'

'How do you know all this?' I ask, impressed yet again by his historical knowledge.

'Growing up, my parents had some old books at home that had been passed down. There wasn't much else to do in my village other than read.'

Talk of his family makes my shame burn even brighter. Would he have left the beach with me had he known Sahi was his sister?

'Is that your plan then? To go to Sehar?'

'I don't have a plan,' I admit. 'I don't know what's there or why my mother wanted to go. But I need answers and it's all I've got…'

'And Kaleb?'

I shrug. 'Where would you go if you were a rat being chased?'

'I wouldn't stay here.'

'Neither would I. I'd probably run to the king and spin more lies before word of my treachery could reach him.'

'It sounds like you're going to Mezeer.'

A shaky breath escapes me. 'You might be my chaperone but if I do choose to go there, you don't have to come with me.'

'I know,' he replies, level and steady. 'But I'd like to.'

I can't help but smile. The way he watches me, I have to look away and clasp my hands together to stop from fidgeting. 'I don't suppose the books you read growing up had much in them about the origins of magic?'

'No, they didn't,' he says and my heart sinks. 'But my mother used to tell my sister and me stories about it all the time.'

My eyes well up as I imagine him and Sahi with their parents, listening to these stories round a fire in their village. I have to tell him…when the time is right.

'Sehar's a long way to travel, especially with your leg the way it is. There's no knowing what the effects of Dana's venom are.'

'Unfortunately, I didn't pack a healer for this trek we're going on. I didn't pack anything actually.'

He goes to speak, but then stops himself, and suddenly he's the one who looks awkward.

'What is it?'

'I…I know it shouldn't be possible, and maybe if Kaleb hadn't shown his power today I wouldn't be telling you this, but you're injured and I might be able to help.'

'What are you saying?'

'No one else knows. I'm not sure what would happen if people found out…'

'Are you a healer?' I ask and try to catch a glimpse of his palms.

He notices and turns them up for me to see. There's nothing there, just like with Kaleb. But the glimmer I thought I saw when we were dancing together…was that his magic working then?

'Technically, I am. I'm just not a very well-rehearsed one, what with only girls having formal training with their magic.'

I start laughing despite everything that's happened. I feel awful when his face creases with embarrassment, but I can't stop. 'Are there any more surprises?'

He starts laughing then too. 'Seriously though. Your leg.'

'What about your shoulder?'

'I'll get to that.'

He ushers for me to stand and, as if in protest, my ankle gives way the moment I put pressure on it. 'When you say you're not very well-rehearsed, you mean…?'

'I've never used my magic on anyone but myself before. And the odd small animal.'

'And how has it gone on those occasions?'

'I've had no complaints.' He smiles and taps the spot next to him where I was just sitting.

I imagine what the mistresses would say if they saw me as I rest my foot on the step beside him.

'Here?' He gestures to where two red marks pulse beneath the skin and I nod.

His fingers are cool as they brush my ankle and rest over the wound. He closes his eyes, concentration scrunching his lids shut. Nothing happens, but I don't interrupt him. Then, slowly, a white shimmering dust dances over his hand and it's like I can feel the venom being pulled from my leg as the pain eases.

When I start laughing again, he opens his eyes and the shimmer vanishes. 'You are a healer,' I say, amazed.

'It worked?'

I nod, completely in awe as I test my weight on that leg. Where there was pain there's now just a faint hum. How many others could there be like him, with magic that hasn't yet been trained?

'Now your turn,' I tell him and point to his shoulder.

'That will have to wait a little longer. I'm not strong enough to heal both of us right now.'

'Emir…' I say, equal parts ashamed and grateful.

'And we can pop this back in place without magic anyway.'

I wince. 'You shouldn't have done that. But thank you.'

'My pleasure,' he says, smiling, and I sit alongside him again. 'Besides, we can't have the girl with the red sun in her blood injured.'

'Where did you hear that?'

'Everyone was talking about it. That's all the prisoner would say – that she'd found the girl with the red sun in her blood.'

Who would save our country from ruin…

The horns bellow in the distance and I'm reminded why I'm here. Why I'm in hiding and what I've had to leave behind. And where I'm going.

We'll come back. I just hope Sahi knows that.

'You'll come then,' I ask Emir. 'You'll come to Sehar?'

He smiles that one-sided smile. 'When do we leave?'

I glimpse the sun through a crack in the boarded-up windows, her rays casting shadows over the buildings across the alleyway.

'We leave as soon as we have the cover of darkness. At dusk.'

CAST OF CHARACTERS

AT THE SANCTUARY

Dancers of the Dawn

Aasira Bibi	a flame-wielder
Sahi Amin	a truth-seeker
Dana Habib	a serpent-whisperer
Meera Jaziri	a nightshade
Amara	a shapeshifter
Duaa	a shadow-spinner
Farah	an illusionist
Jamila	a shield
Jasmine	a mind-glider
Nasira	a shard-castor
Yasmin	a mimic
Zahra	a veil-conjuror

Kaleb	the leader at the sanctuary and advisor to the late queen
Sajid	leader of the sanctuary's guards and ex-soldier
Tahir	second to Sajid and an ex-soldier
Mistress Zaina	head dance mistress; an illusionist
Mistress Salma	dance mistress to the younger students
Amina	music student specialising as a singer
Nadia	music student specialising on the dhol
Neesha	music student specialising on the violin
Saara	music student specialising on the flute
Maya	seamstress student
Asha	student specialising in cuisine
Camil	sanctuary guard
Ejaz	sanctuary guard
Fasha	sanctuary guard
Haniya	sanctuary guard
Rahim	sanctuary guard
Arif	sanctuary attendant

AT THE PALACE

Queen Sana	the queen of Amaar; a water-weaver
Heba	Queen Sana's closest advisor
Mistress Soraya	head dance mistress; a poison-hand
Imani	a Queen's Guard; a corruptor
Maryam	a Queen's Guard; a mind-glider
Fatima	a Queen's Guard; a shard-castor
Lyla	a Queen's Guard; a shadow-spinner

Emir	palace guard and Aasira's chaperone
Zayn	palace guard and Sahi's chaperone
Ahmed	palace guard and Dana's chaperone
Imran	palace guard and Meera's chaperone
Captain Nadim	leader of the palace guards and ex-soldier
Abdul	a royal courtier
Bushra	a royal courtier
Tariq	a royal courtier
Ria	Queen Sana's attendant
Amal	Aasira's attendant at the palace
Kali	palace attendant
Hamza	street vendor in the souk
Noor	prisoner
Lina	Aasira's mother; a zephyr
Naila	a follower of Lina; an illusionist
Serena	a follower of Lina; a shield
King Faisal	the king of Mezeer
Hassan	a villager from Rahistha
Iyad	a villager from Nazeem
Omar	a villager from Nazeem
Yara	a villager from Nazeem
Zora	a villager from Nazeem

ACKNOWLEDGEMENTS

Aasira's been waiting in the wings to tell her story for a while and I have many people to thank who helped bring her to life, and who sprinkled their magic along the way.

My first thank you has to go to my parents. Mum and Dad, thank you for inspiring me to dream every day and for always encouraging me to be curious; for surrounding me with books and music, influencing my love of fantasy and taking me to my first ballet class (and many more!). You always have the right words and are the ultimate hype team. I couldn't appreciate your love and support more, and promise you can read the book now!

To my dearest sister, Iynaiyá. Who'd have thought that when I was making up your bedtime stories when we were little, I'd one day go on to write an actual book! You were my first reader/listener and I'm forever grateful that my love of storytelling started with you.

And to my family, especially Nanny Bibi and my nan and grandad, Shelia and Kevin, our roots are at the heart of this story. From the desert to the coast, the music and food, to

Aasira's surname, Bibi, there's a piece of all of us in the fabric of this world. Thank you for everything.

A big thank you to my husband Scott for being the best sounding board anyone could ask for. For always listening and bouncing ideas around, drawing maps and helping me find the right threads for my characters to follow. Thank you for believing in me when I didn't, for encouraging me through all the late-night writing sessions, and for reading every draft. I couldn't have written this book without your unwavering support.

To all my friends – the Ten who never doubted me when I said I wanted to write a book, especially Sami and Cathy who listened to all my earliest ideas, and my uni pals who were there when that dream started to take shape – thank you for being my biggest cheerleaders from the beginning.

This book wouldn't exist without my love of ballet and I owe a lot to the teachers I've had over the years: Ms Richards, Mrs Pascoe, Mrs Jones, Miss Strasberg, Mr Etheridge and Kim Jones. Some of my fondest memories from class, rehearsals and performing have crept onto the page when Aasira dances. Thank you for showing me what it means to be part of an ensemble and the magic of dance.

The first glimmers of this book were born in 2017 while I was studying for the MA in Writing for Young People at Bath Spa University. Thank you Lucy Christopher and C.J. Skuse, for giving me a place on the course, and to the rest of the tutors for sharing your wisdom and passion for children's literature: Julia Green, Janine Amos, Elen Caldecott, Jo Nadin and Steve Voake. You made us all believe we could one day be writers.

And you gave us a community I'm incredibly thankful for. To the Cinnamon Squad – Anika Hussain, Eve Griffiths, Fox Welsh, Kate den Rooijen, Lis Jardine and Stephanie Williamson – thank you for your constant motivation and inspiration. I'm so honoured we get to go on this writing journey together.

Thank you to my wonderful agent, Lauren Gardner, for believing in my dancing warriors before their story had even fully formed. From the moment I shared the idea with you, you saw its heart and I'm so grateful you took the plunge with me to discover Aasira's world. To everyone at Bell Lomax Moreton, thank you for championing my dancers from day one.

Finding a home at Rock the Boat has been a dream come true and I'm so thankful to everyone who's brought this story to life in a way I could never have imagined. A very special and huge thank you to my editor, Katie Jennings, for nurturing this book (and me!) through the whole process. Just as with Lauren, I knew from our first meeting that Aasira was in safe hands with you by her side. Thank you for trusting me through the edits as I took the characters on new journeys, and for helping me craft them into the story we have today.

And, of course, there's the brilliant team at Rock the Boat who've worked their magic and breathed a new life into this world. Thank you to all of you for your enthusiasm and care: Beth Marshall Brown, Ben Summers, Hayley Warnham, Matilda Warner, Mark Rusher, Lucy Cooper, Mary Hawkins, Julian Ball, Francesca Dawes, Paul Nash and Laura McFarlane. Thank you to my superstar copy-editor, Jane Tait, and proofreader, Claire Bell. Thank you also to Hamza Jahanzeb for the thoughtful authenticity read.

Micaela Alcaino, thank you for capturing Aasira and the essence of the book so beautifully. Every time I look at the cover I see the image that first sparked this story, of a girl dancing beneath a red sun. It's like you plucked Aasira from my mind and now she exists beyond the page through your stunning design!

Finally, dear reader, I'd like to thank you. I'm so grateful to you for picking up this book and for joining me and the dancers of the dawn on this adventure. This dream wouldn't be possible without you.

ZULEKHÁ A. AFZAL grew up in Cornwall, where the dramatic coastline inspired stories of other worlds and magic. She now lives in Bath where she studied English Literature with Creative Writing and completed the MA in Writing for Young People at Bath Spa University. When she isn't writing fantasy fiction or working as an assistant editor, you can find Zulekhá in a ballet class. *Dancers of the Dawn* is her first novel, and she is currently working on the second book in the series.

M000206722

HABITS
of the
HEART

365 Daily Exercises for
Living like Jesus

KATHERINE J. BUTLER

Tyndale House Publishers, Inc.
Carol Stream, Illinois

Visit Tyndale at www.tyndale.com.

TYNDALE and Tyndale's quill logo are registered trademarks of Tyndale House Publishers, Inc.

Habits of the Heart: 365 Daily Exercises for Living like Jesus

Designed by Ron Kaufmann

For information about special discounts for bulk purchases, please contact Tyndale House Publishers at csresponse@tyndale.com, or call 1-800-323-9400.

ISBN 978-1-4964-1806-7

Printed in China

23	22	21	20	19	18	17
7	6	5	4	3	2	1

CONTENTS

WEEK 8: *Seeking Humility*

Not seeing yourself as less, but rather seeing God as so much more—the one who is good, loving, and in ultimate control, and whose plans for you are far better than your own.

WEEK 9: *Becoming Teachable*

Being a lifelong learner, with the Lord as your teacher and guide.

WEEK 10: *Learning Discernment*

Learning to better recognize God's voice and becoming more sensitive to his direction in your life.

WEEK 11: *Choosing Joy*

Making a conscious decision to develop an attitude of appreciation, thanksgiving, and rejoicing—regardless of circumstances.

WEEK 12: *Practicing Conversational Prayer*

Bringing every thought and feeling to God in prayer.

WEEK 13: *Caring for Yourself*

Making time to care for your heart, mind, and body—all of which make up the soul.

WEEK 14: *Serving Others*

Intentionally recognizing the needs around you and then meeting them.

WEEK 15: *Welcoming Silence*

Creating quiet space in your noisy, chaotic days to hear from God more clearly.

WEEK 16: *Offering Worship*

Recognizing God's great work and gifts in your life and responding by giving him the praise and glory he deserves.

WEEK 17: *Living in Contentment*

Being at peace with how God made you, where he has placed you, what he has given you, and who you are in relation to him.

WEEK 18: *Practicing Generosity*

Giving freely and joyfully of your time, possessions, talents, and money.

WEEK 19: *Keeping an Eternal Perspective*

Living on earth with eternity in mind.

WEEK 20: *Being Steadfast*

Cultivating an enduring and patient trust in God's faithfulness.

WEEK 21: *Unplugging*

Detaching from routine distractions, especially technology, to be fully present with God and others.

WEEK 22: *Being Present*

Awakening to the world around you so you don't miss the gifts God has for you in the moment.

WEEK 23: *Listening*

Letting others know they are loved and valuable by paying full attention to what they say and showing them respect, care, and patience.

WEEK 24: *Practicing Thoughtfulness*

Being considerate and attentive to the feelings, needs, and situations of others.

WEEK 25: *Controlling Your Tongue*

Growing in awareness of what comes out of your mouth and then, with the power of the Holy Spirit, changing hurtful words into those that are gracious, grateful, encouraging, loving, truthful, and a blessing to others.

WEEK 26: *Praying for Others*

Coming before the Lord on behalf of another.

WEEK 27: *Developing a Heart of Compassion*

Opening your heart to the hurt around you and then doing something about it.

WEEK 28: *Being in Fellowship*

Exemplifying God's nature as you do life together with your brothers and sisters in the church.

WEEK 29: *Caring for Creation*

Seeing all of what God has made as "good" and then working to be a good steward over it.

WEEK 30: *Living Simply*

Letting go of things that clutter and complicate your life in order to keep your focus on Jesus.

WEEK 31: *Meditating on God's Word*

Deeply pondering God's Word and what it reveals about him.

WEEK 32: *Keeping Sabbath*

Setting aside one day a week to embrace rest so that you have space to worship and enjoy God.

WEEK 33: *Trusting in God*

Believing that God loves you, that he's absolutely good, and that he wants and is able to do good things in your life.

WEEK 34: *Witnessing*

Telling others about your experience of how you grew to know and love Jesus.

WEEK 35: *Making a Sacrifice*

Relinquishing something you think you need or that makes you feel secure in order to rely on God to provide what he knows you need.

WEEK 36: *Incorporating Prayer Postures*

Using your body in prayer to move your heart toward a place of humility, boldness, submission, gratitude, reverence, and worship.

WEEK 37: *Accepting Solitude*

Intentionally stepping away from normal human interaction in order to grow in your friendship with the Lord.

WEEK 38: *Hoping in God*

Choosing confident joy in the face of uncertainty as you trust God with your present and future.

WEEK 39: *Waiting Well*

Using your seasons of waiting to learn to walk with God in patience and hope and resisting the urge to rush ahead of his timing.

WEEK 40: *Using Imaginative Prayer*

Actively engaging your mind and heart in prayer by placing yourself in a scene in Scripture through the use of your imagination.

WEEK 41: *Keeping Secrets*

Keeping certain things between you and God.

WEEK 42: *Developing Hospitality*

Becoming a safe person and cultivating space for others to experience the welcoming presence of God.

WEEK 43: *Praying Scripture*

Reading the prayers in the Bible as your own.

WEEK 44: *Being Frugal*

Choosing to live below your means to be free from wants (and debts!) that would otherwise distract you from effectively knowing and serving God.

WEEK 45: *Resting*

Making time in your everyday life to intentionally restore your mind, body, and soul.

WEEK 46: *Guarding Your Heart*

Learning to be more alert to temptation and then guarding your heart from giving in to it.

WEEK 47: *Practicing Gratitude*

Staying connected to God by thanking him—no matter what life has in store for you today.

WEEK 48: *Letting Go*

Releasing your grip on things in this world that have come to replace your need for and trust in God.

WEEK 49: *Celebrating*

Opening up your heart to delight in, be thankful for, and fully enjoy God and the life he has offered you.

WEEK 50: *Memorizing Scripture*

Allowing God's Word to shape your mind and heart through repetition and reflection.

WEEK 51: *Reflecting on the Past Year*

Pausing to reflect on how God worked in and around you this past year.

WEEK 52: *Looking Forward to the New Year*

Pausing to reflect on how God might be leading you as you enter into the New Year.

INTRODUCTION

Do You Long for Lasting Change?

If you want to change your life, you have to do something different. Lasting change comes only from developing new habits. A "habit" is *a routine of behavior that a person repeats regularly and usually unconsciously.*

Many of us try to make physical exercise a daily habit. Or perhaps we want to become good at playing a musical instrument, so we get into the habit of practicing every day. If we want to graduate from college, we need the habit of regular study. *Developing a habit is really a way of training our bodies or minds to behave differently so often that it becomes routine.*

Many of us don't think about training our hearts, but the truth is, we train them every day. When we watch a TV show, we are training our hearts. When we focus on lies instead of truth, we are training our hearts. When we choose to pray instead of worry, we are training our hearts. The apostle Paul tells us that our whole lives are a training of some sort, whether we realize it or not: Everything we do is training our hearts either toward

God or away from him. When our hearts are conditioned to discern the Spirit of God and act upon what he wants, then we experience the greatest possible joy, peace, and satisfaction. It is essential that we develop the habit of "exercising" our hearts in the practice of godliness.

What shape is your heart in? Consider this book a training program to develop habits of the heart that will draw you into a deep and lasting relationship with God. This simple guide focuses on one essential aspect each week and provides daily exercises to make it become a habit. Each day begins with Scripture, followed by a question to prayerfully consider with the Lord or a spiritual exercise that calls you to put God's Word into action. The exercises are based entirely on Scripture and Jesus' life and teachings. Over the next year, you will be introduced to fifty-two spiritual disciplines that will connect you with God in new ways. The goal is to recognize the places where you currently live apart from God so that you can prayerfully invite him into all your daily moments. That is the beginning of real transformation.

A FEW GUIDELINES TO CONSIDER

Be open. What does it mean to "be open to God"? It means having a posture that is ready to receive. For example, if someone throws you a baseball, you need a posture to catch it. This requires not only having your hands out and open to receive the ball but also paying attention to the one who throws it. To keep yourself open to God, as you work through each devotion, ask him, "What do you want to teach me from this?" Some exercises may seem pointless and silly. Can listening to music, enjoying flavorful foods, driving in the slow lane, or using your imagination really be part of your spiritual transformation? Yes, they can! Anything that draws you toward God can be "devotional." Be open to the variety of ways God may teach you, trusting the Holy Spirit is in control.

Be patient. Spiritual exercises are not quick fixes to make you a "good" Christian. They are meant to *slowly* open and shape your heart to become more like Jesus. There is no right way to do these exercises. If, in a particular week, you feel you've failed to grow, that area may be one where growth is occurring more subtly. Just as your body is made up of many muscles, so it is with the soul. Feeling resistance is a sign a spiritual muscle needs to be strengthened. God may also use an exercise to show you something about yourself that you find difficult to accept. Remember, the only way he can transform your heart to be more like his is to first show you the places where you aren't like him. Learn to see this as a gift because God is showing you something that is keeping you from fully trusting and loving him.

Be expectant. God is active in the world and present in your everyday life. You have the very power of God inside you! As you go through this devotional, wake up each morning anticipating that the Holy Spirit is doing great work within your heart. The fact that you have picked up this book is evidence that God is already at work. Keep a journal to record your thoughts and prayers, frequently looking back and reflecting on your journey. May God bless you as he uses his Word to challenge and change you to be more like Jesus.

Jan
1

Look Again. Can You See Me Now?

If you look for me wholeheartedly, you will find me.

JEREMIAH 29:13

The Bible tells many stories of people who were in the very presence of God but were completely unaware of it. Jacob was camping overnight, for instance, when he realized he had missed God trying to communicate with him and exclaimed, "Surely the LORD is in this place, and I wasn't even aware of it!" (Genesis 28:16). Jesus' own disciples didn't recognize they were walking with him on the road to Emmaus (Luke 24:13-16).

What causes you to miss God's presence and activity in your day? Practicing God's presence is about awakening a constant attentiveness to God always being with you, working on your behalf. As you develop this awareness, worry, discouragement, and fear will lose their power over you.

This book intentionally begins with "Practicing God's Presence" because this sets the stage for the rest of the year. As you work through each devotion, remember God is with you in every moment. Don't miss what he is doing right in front of you!

I Am with You

The Lord your God is living among you. He is a mighty savior.
He will take delight in you with gladness. With his love, he will
calm all your fears. He will rejoice over you with joyful songs.

ZEPHANIAH 3:17

I am with you always.

MATTHEW 28:20

Because of Christ and our faith in him, we can now
come boldly and confidently into God's presence.

EPHESIANS 3:12

Set an alarm on your phone or place a note in your
home as a simple reminder that God is with you and
delights in you. When you see the reminder, pause for a few
moments and say to him, "Thank you for taking delight in
me, even though sometimes I have a difficult time accepting that. Help me to remember throughout this day that
you are by my side in each and every moment."

Jan 3

Open Your Eyes

I can never escape from your Spirit! I can never get away
from your presence! If I go up to heaven, you are there;
if I go down to the grave, you are there. If I ride the wings of
the morning, if I dwell by the farthest oceans, even there your
hand will guide me, and your strength will support me.

PSALM 139:7-10

How easy is it for God to get your attention throughout the day? In *Letters to Malcolm: Chiefly on Prayer*, C. S. Lewis wrote, "We may ignore, but we can nowhere evade, the presence of God. The world is crowded with Him. He walks everywhere *incognito*."[1]

Look for his presence all around you today in ways you hadn't thought about before (through the comfort of another person, a beautiful sunset, a song on the radio, or a Scripture that comes to mind).

Let Me Come with You

✦

This is my command—be strong and courageous!
Do not be afraid or discouraged. For the LORD
your God is with you wherever you go.

JOSHUA 1:9

I know the LORD is always with me. I will not
be shaken, for he is right beside me.

PSALM 16:8

Imagine God speaking these words directly to you:
"Do not be afraid . . . I am with you wherever you go."

How might this encourage you in the transitions you
currently face (such as moving to a new home, starting
a different job, experiencing a child's move out of the
house)?

Memorize one of the above Scriptures to remind
you that God is with you right now and will continue
to be with you every day for the rest of your life.

Jan
5

Let Go to Focus on Me

---✦---

The Lord said to her, "My dear Martha, you are worried
and upset over all these details! There is only one thing
worth being concerned about. Mary has discovered
it, and it will not be taken away from her."

LUKE 10:41-42

What details in your day distract you from being
present with Jesus?

Make a list of these disruptions and talk to the Lord
about each of them. Ask him to make his presence more
urgent to you than your distractions.

When you are done talking to God about your list,
place your Bible on top of the list to symbolize letting
those things go for today in order to focus on being
more present with him.

Remember Me

Commit yourselves wholeheartedly to these commands.
… Repeat them again and again.… Talk about them
when you are at home and when you are on the road,
when you are going to bed and when you are getting
up.… Write them on the doorposts of your house.

DEUTERONOMY 6:6-9

I know the LORD is always with me. I will not
be shaken, for he is right beside me.

PSALM 16:8

Every time you remember God's faithfulness, your
trust in his love and care for you grows stronger.
Today, carry something with you that can remind you
of God's constant presence.

For example, wear a special bracelet, place a token in
your pocket, or put your Bible in a visible spot in your
home or office. Whenever you see this item, thank God
for never leaving your side.

Jan 7

I Follow You with Blessing

✦

You go before me and follow me. You place
your hand of blessing on my head.

PSALM 139:5

God does not want you to go through this day alone.
As you think through the things you need to do,
close your eyes and picture God's hand on your head.

What blessing is he speaking over your day?

Write out that blessing and carry it with you throughout today as a tangible reminder to encourage you.

At the end of the day, come back to this page and
consider these questions:

✦ When did you feel close to God in the past week?
✦ What exercises helped you remember God's presence
  with you?
✦ How can you make practicing God's presence a habit?

Jan
8

Why the Hurry?

✦

He lets me rest in green meadows; he leads
me beside peaceful streams.

PSALM 23:2

In a culture that praises a hurried lifestyle, we are tempted to believe constant activity is fulfilling and important. But hurrying doesn't allow us to go deep, and thus it diminishes our ability to do things well.

God did not intend for us to race through the only life we have been given. If we did, we would miss those significant moments God wants us to enjoy or learn from.

The practice of *slowing down* is about resisting the need to always look toward the next thing. Slowing down replaces trust in our own speed and control with trust in God's timing and control.

As you begin to practice slowing down, you may experience anxiety, unease, or irritation. Pause and talk to the Lord about those feelings. Your heart and mind will need more than a week to *really* slow down, but this week will introduce you to the discipline of a life that is un-hurried, peaceful, and "in the moment."

Just Breathe

---- ✦ ----

How do you know what your life will be like tomorrow? Your life is like the morning fog—it's here a little while, then it's gone.

JAMES 4:14

Get into a comfortable position. Allow your body to relax, and notice where you hold your tension. Close your eyes and breathe in slowly, allowing your breath to fill your lungs completely.

As you inhale, thank God for the gift of life, and for his breath that gave life to all creation. When you breathe out slowly, imagine exhaling your stress, anxiety, and tension. Do this several more times. Finish by thanking God for the gift of his life-giving breath in your lungs.

Then think about how you can slow down today to be more present with God. For the rest of this week, commit to begin each day's devotion with this breathing exercise.

**Jan
10**

No Rush

---✦---

Be still, and know that I am God!

PSALM 46:10

Jesus said, "Come to me, all of you who are weary and carry heavy burdens, and I will give you rest. Take my yoke upon you. Let me teach you, because I am humble and gentle at heart, and you will find rest for your souls."

MATTHEW 11:28-29

To build your trust that God is in control, choose one activity to help you resist unnecessary hurry: walk slower, don't rush through a conversation, avoid multitasking, leave five minutes early, or let go of items on your to-do list.

Pray, "Lord, please make me aware today when I'm going too fast. Show me how to let go of my need to control my schedule. Help me to allow you to control my time instead. Teach me to resist hurry so that I can lean into you today."

Just a Moment

✦

LORD, remind me how brief my time on earth will be.
Remind me that my days are numbered—how fleeting
my life is. You have made my life no longer than the width
of my hand. My entire lifetime is just a moment to you;
at best, each of us is but a breath. We are merely moving
shadows, and all our busy rushing ends in nothing.

PSALM 39:4-6

Read the passage above again, but this time do it
slowly. What did you miss the first time? What does
this show you about how you read Scripture?

Now, *slowly* write down the Scripture and meditate on
the words. What might God be saying to you through his
Word?

Jan 12

Linger at the Table

Taste and see that the LORD is good. Oh, the
joys of those who take refuge in him!

PSALM 34:8

Someone once said, "There is a special bond of fellow-ship when people linger at the table around good food. Among Jesus followers, it becomes much like a Holy Communion." Consider these words and what they mean as you eat each meal today.

Set a note on your kitchen table (or wherever you eat) to remind you to chew your food slowly. Sit at the table if you usually eat on the couch or in front of the TV. Linger at the table longer than you normally would. Take time to smell, taste, and enjoy your food.

Allow this exercise to remind you how slowing down helps you better appreciate God's gifts in the moment.

Jan
13

Cherish the "Lasts"

Teach us to realize the brevity of life, so
that we may grow in wisdom.

PSALM 90:12

Think about the "lasts" that could happen today.
What if today were the last day of winter?
Or summer?

What if today were the last time your child crawled up
on your lap to snuggle?

What if today were the last time you heard the voice
of someone you love?

How does this change your perspective on life?

On today?

Make a list of three or four potential "lasts" that might
happen to you soon.

How does this make you want to slow down and cherish the things you just wrote about before they end?

Relaxed

Because so many people were coming and going that they did not even have a chance to eat, [Jesus] said to them, "Come with me by yourselves to a quiet place and get some rest."

MARK 6:31, NIV

Theologian Dallas Willard was asked to describe Jesus using one word. He chose *relaxed*.[2]

How might God be calling you to relax?

Perhaps by releasing control over a situation.

Or maybe by choosing not to stress over things that don't really matter.

Maybe by slowing down in order to connect with someone you typically would have missed due to your rushed lifestyle.

Whatever it is, write it down so you will remember.

✦ How did you do with slowing down this week?
✦ Which one exercise most helped you slow down and experience God in the moment?

Jan
15

Know You Are Loved

---◆---

Each day the LORD pours his unfailing love upon me.

PSALM 42:8

Do you believe, *really* believe, that God loves you? His love is not meant for you only to know about—it is meant for you to experience personally. Meditating on and receiving God's love is the foundation for how you live, make decisions, and relate to others. If you go through life with confidence that you are loved by God, you can remain secure and joyful—even when circumstances are against you.

As you meditate on and interact with the Scriptures about God's love for you, be honest with him about your feelings. You may experience numbness, apathy, or resistance. Don't try to force yourself to feel God's love this week. God might be making you aware of a resistance to receiving his love.

Remember, it takes a lifetime to really accept and experience God's one-of-a-kind love for you. This week will simply develop an awareness of *how* you experience God's love and will give you tools for opening yourself to more of his love in the future.

I Love You This Much

This is how God loved the world: He gave his one
and only Son, so that everyone who believes in
him will not perish but have eternal life.

JOHN 3:16

How easy is it for you to believe that God loves you personally?

"God loves each of us as if there were only one of us" is a quote often attributed to Augustine, one of the great church fathers.

This week, look for ways in which God might be showing his unique love for you.

Maybe it is through a sunset, an unexpected gift, or a moment where you feel his presence.

Set a reminder on your phone or on a notepad by your bedside to end each day this week by asking yourself, "Where did I notice God's love for me today?"

Jan 17

Another Word for Love

◆

The Lord is compassionate and merciful, slow to get angry and filled with unfailing love. He will not constantly accuse us, nor remain angry forever. He does not punish us for all our sins; he does not deal harshly with us, as we deserve. For his unfailing love toward those who fear him is as great as the height of the heavens above the earth.

PSALM 103:8-11

Read the above passage again, slowly.

What word or phrase stands out to you?

Make a mental note to come back to that word or phrase later today. This is a great approach for interacting with the Scriptures in a new way.

Ask God to reveal more this week about how this word or phrase relates to his unique love for you.

Jan
18

Hindrances

Can anything ever separate us from Christ's love? Does it
mean he no longer loves us if we have trouble or calamity,
or are persecuted, or hungry, or destitute, or in danger,
or threatened with death? . . . No, despite all these things,
overwhelming victory is ours through Christ, who loved us.

ROMANS 8:35-37

Sometimes it is hard to accept another person's love.
There are all kinds of reasons for this.

Perhaps you have been hurt and fear another rejection.

Or maybe it is difficult for you to believe that someone could actually love the real you. Sometimes it is even
more difficult to accept God's love.

What hinders you from receiving his love?

Tragedy? Shame? Doubt? Busyness? Indifference?

Think about these hindrances and talk to God about
each one.

Jan 19

Totally and Unconditionally

---✦---

I am convinced that nothing can ever separate us from
God's love. Neither death nor life, neither angels nor
demons, neither our fears for today nor our worries about
tomorrow—not even the powers of hell can separate us from
God's love . . . that is revealed in Christ Jesus our Lord.

ROMANS 8:38-39

Allow today's Scripture to sink in. How would your
life be different if you believed God loved you to-
tally and unconditionally?

Think of someone close to you—a spouse, child, parent, or friend. Unconditionally love that person today.

Refuse to harbor bad thoughts about them. Actively
encourage and bless them without expecting anything in
return, assume the best of them, and gift them with an
act of kindness.

You may not do this perfectly, but if you fail, thank
God that he *doesn't* fail in his unconditional love for you.

A Father's Love

---◆---

[Jesus said,] "Let the children come to me. Don't
stop them! For the Kingdom of God belongs
to those who are like these children."

LUKE 18:16

See how very much our Father loves us, for he calls
us his children, and that is what we are!

1 JOHN 3:1

Close your eyes and imagine yourself as a child.
Picture God as your father sitting in a chair and
inviting you to come sit on his lap and talk to him about
your day.

What emotions come up as you picture this scene?
Do you feel uncomfortable? Nervous? Afraid? Excited?
Comforted?

Share these feelings with the Lord in prayer. Ask him
to show you how these feelings impact your ability to
receive his love.

Accept the Gift

May you have the power to understand, as all God's people
should, how wide, how long, how high, and how deep his
love is. May you experience the love of Christ, though it is too
great to understand fully. Then you will be made complete
with all the fullness of life and power that comes from God.

EPHESIANS 3:18-19

What gifts has God given you that you feel unworthy to receive?

Salvation? Forgiveness? Mercy? Children? Abundant
resources? Special abilities or talents? How does it feel to
accept that God has given you these gifts just because he
loves you?

Over the past week, when did you experience God's
unique love for you?

How did those times affect the way you interacted
with others and how you thought about yourself as a
child fully loved by God?

Jan
22

Your Deepest Longing

+

God showed his great love for us by sending Christ
to die for us while we were still sinners.

ROMANS 5:8

Everyone longs for acceptance from others. But what do we do when
we feel rejected, lonely, or disappointed?

The longing for acceptance can be satisfied only when we know
beyond a shadow of a doubt that we are fully accepted by the one who
created us out of love.

God's love is not dependent on your behavior. He doesn't accept you
less when you sin, nor does your good behavior make him accept you
more. God accepts you and loves you just as you are.

The practices this week require honesty about where you search for
acceptance and how you receive God's acceptance. Let his promises of
love and approval sink into your heart so that you can bravely face difficult truths about yourself without feeling condemnation.

No Doubt about It

✦

Since we have been made right in God's sight by faith, we have peace with God because of what Jesus Christ our Lord has done for us. Because of our faith, Christ has brought us into this place of undeserved privilege where we now stand, and we confidently and joyfully look forward to sharing God's glory.

ROMANS 5:1-2

Take a moment to slowly read over and meditate on God's truth from Romans 8:1: "There is no condemnation for those who belong to Christ Jesus."

When you are finished, ask yourself, *In what ways does Satan currently tempt me to doubt that God accepts me unconditionally? That God sees me as worthy and valuable? That God has a special purpose for me?*

Jan 24

Fully Accepted

[You] . . . were once far away from God. You were his enemies, separated from him by your evil thoughts and actions. Yet now he has reconciled you to himself through the death of Christ in his physical body. As a result, he has brought you into his own presence, and you are holy and blameless as you stand before him without a single fault.

COLOSSIANS 1:21-22

What thoughts or actions, in the past or present, have hindered you from receiving God's full acceptance?

Have you looked elsewhere for acceptance?

Have you believed you were unworthy or unholy because of something you have done?

Have you listened to condemning thoughts?

Consider these hindrances and spend time talking to God about each one.

No Fault

✦

Even before he made the world, God loved us and chose
us in Christ to be holy and without fault in his eyes. God
decided in advance to adopt us into his own family by
bringing us to himself through Jesus Christ. This is what
he wanted to do, and it gave him great pleasure.

EPHESIANS 1:4-5

I magine God thinking about you.

What do you assume God feels about you right now?

Read the verse above and reflect on how your
thoughts are similar to or different from what the Bible
says God thinks of you.

Jan 26

Perfection Not Required

✦

Before the Passover celebration, Jesus knew that his
hour had come to leave this world and return to his
Father. He had loved his disciples during his ministry
on earth, and now he loved them to the very end.

JOHN 13:1

Jesus saw his disciples at their best—and their very worst.
They argued about who was the greatest, doubted
him even after witnessing his miracles, and betrayed him
in his time of greatest need. Yet he still loved them.

Read the passage again. Do you believe that God's
acceptance is dependent on your being at your best?

Talk to God about where you are not perfect.

Do you gossip?

Are you easily angered?

Do you struggle with fear or pride?

Whatever challenges you, thank God for his grace and
for loving you no less because of your struggles.

For Better or for Worse

God is so rich in mercy, and he loved us so much, that
even though we were dead because of our sins, he
gave us life when he raised Christ from the dead. (It is
only by God's grace that you have been saved!)

EPHESIANS 2:4-5

Think back to a time when you did something you
were not proud of.

Maybe you said something that hurt someone deeply,
lied to make yourself look good, or perhaps even committed a crime.

Now read the verses above one more time and inter-
nalize the truth that God loves you even in your worst
moments.

Tell God how this reality makes you feel.

How might this knowledge encourage you today
to respond to someone who may not deserve your
acceptance?

Jan
28

You Are Mine

◆

The one who formed you says, "Do not be afraid, for
I have ransomed you. I have called you by name; you
are mine. When you go through deep waters, I will be
with you. When you go through rivers of difficulty,
you will not drown. When you walk through the fire
of oppression . . . the flames will not consume you."

ISAIAH 43:1-2

Read the passage again and imagine God is speaking
directly to you. Then meditate on these statements
of God's love for you:

*I have rescued you. I have called you. You are mine.
I will be with you. You will not drown. You will not
be consumed by oppression.*

Which of these statements means the most to you?
Over the past week, when have you most felt accepted
by God? How might this impact your interactions with
yourself and others?

Jan
29

When God Comes to Mind

---+---

This is the way to have eternal life—to know you, the only
true God, and Jesus Christ, the one you sent to earth.

JOHN 17:3

What do you *really* think about God? What do you *absolutely know*
to be true about him? Your answers to these questions impact
everything you do. "What comes into our minds when we think about
God is the most important thing about us," wrote A. W. Tozer. [3]

Each day this week will focus on one of God's attributes. God's
"attributes" are simply who he really is and what he does. As you read
the reflection questions, be honest with yourself and God about any
inconsistencies between what you thought you knew about God and
what the Bible actually says about him.

Resist the urge to immediately "fix" your relationship with God in
those areas where you were wrong about him. Allow the Holy Spirit to do
the mending. Reread the Scriptures from the last two weeks if any feelings of condemnation or shame arise. The focus of this week is simply
knowing God better.

Ever Present

✦

"Am I a God who is only close at hand?" says the LORD.
"No, I am far away at the same time. Can anyone
hide from me in a secret place? Am I not everywhere
in all the heavens and earth?" says the LORD.

JEREMIAH 23:23-24

God is not restricted by space or time. His presence
fills every single atom and will continue to do so
throughout eternity.

With this truth in mind, we can walk through our
days with courage and confidence because our faithful
God has promised always to be with us.

Knowing this reality, ask yourself these questions:

*Do I believe that God is everywhere—especially that he
is always with me? When was the last time I truly experienced God's presence? How might today look different if
I absolutely believe God is with me?*

Forgiving

No matter how deep the stain of your sins, I can take it
out and make you as clean as freshly fallen snow.

ISAIAH 1:18, TLB

[You] were once far away from God....Yet now he has reconciled
you to himself through the death of Christ....As a result, he
has brought you into his own presence, and you are holy and
blameless as you stand before him without a single fault.

COLOSSIANS 1:21-22

God promises that when we ask, he forgives *all* our
sins and never thinks of them again.

Feelings of shame, self-condemnation, and dis-
grace have no place in those who have accepted God's
forgiveness.

Ask yourself, *Do I believe that God can forgive even
my worst sins? When have I experienced God's forgiveness? How might today look different if I fully accept God's
forgiveness?*

Faithful

The Lord your God is indeed God. He is the faithful God who keeps his covenant for a thousand generations and lavishes his unfailing love on those who love him and obey his commands.

DEUTERONOMY 7:9

God has given both his promise and his oath. These two things are unchangeable because it is impossible for God to lie. Therefore, we who have fled to him for refuge can have great confidence as we hold to the hope that lies before us.

HEBREWS 6:18

God cannot lie and therefore cannot break his promises. This means you never have to worry that God will change his mind about loving you unconditionally.

Knowing this truth, ask yourself, *Do I believe God is faithful to keep his promises? When have I experienced or witnessed God's faithfulness? How might today look different if I were confident in God's promises to be faithful to me?*

Feb
2

Good

Surely your goodness and unfailing love will pursue me all the days of my life, and I will live in the house of the Lᴏʀᴅ forever.

PSALM 23:6

How great is the goodness you have stored up for those who fear you ... blessing them before the watching world.

PSALM 31:19

Taste and see that the Lᴏʀᴅ is good. Oh, the joys of those who take refuge in him!

PSALM 34:8

Our God is inherently good. Not only is he the perfect example of goodness, but he also wants good things for your life. With that truth in mind, consider these questions: *Do I believe that God is absolutely good? When have I experienced God's goodness in my life? How might today look different if I believe that God, who is absolutely good, right now desires good things for me?*

Powerful

⁘

He counts the stars and calls them all by name.
How great is our Lord! His power is absolute!
His understanding is beyond comprehension!

PSALM 147:4-5

God is working in you, giving you the desire and the
power to do what pleases him.... The Spirit who lives
in you is greater than the spirit who lives in the world.

PHILIPPIANS 2:13; 1 JOHN 4:4

God spoke the universe into existence, and his great
power is displayed throughout his Word. This
means that we can pray boldy and with great expectations, because nothing is too hard for our God.

With this reality in mind, ask yourself, *Do I believe
God has ultimate power over everything? When have I
experienced or seen God's power in my life? How might
my prayers and attitude look different if I really believe
in God's great and unlimited power?*

Feb
4

Trustworthy

Trust in the LORD with all your heart; do not depend
on your own understanding. Seek his will in all you
do, and he will show you which path to take.

PROVERBS 3:5-6

"I know the plans I have for you," says the LORD. "They are plans
for good and not for disaster, to give you a future and a hope."

JEREMIAH 29:11

This week we have meditated on how God is present,
forgiving, faithful, good, and powerful. Knowing
these attributes, we can trust that he loves us and knows
what is best for us. He can be trusted with the details of
our days as well as the major plans for our future.

✦ Do you believe God has good plans for your life?
✦ When have you experienced God as trustworthy?
✦ How might today look different if you trust that God
has a great plan for you?

Feb 5

Getting to Know the Real You

Examine yourselves to see if your faith
is genuine. Test yourselves.

2 CORINTHIANS 13:5

Theologian John Calvin stated that true wisdom consists of two things: knowledge of God and knowledge of self.[4] If we know a lot about ourselves but not about God, we become self-absorbed. If we know a lot about God but not much about ourselves, we become proud. Knowing God and knowing ourselves are both vitally important.

This week's exercises will help you get to know yourself better. Growing in awareness of the self is called "self-examination," which involves voluntarily testing and examining your heart. It is about inviting the Holy Spirit to reveal what is true about you so that you can better understand where you are in relation to God and others. The goal of this week is not to bring shame upon yourself but to bring authenticity to your life with God and others.

This week focuses on truth and creating a desire to change, and next week will focus on confession, which is how you respond when you acknowledge your true self.

Feb
6

Open Heart Surgery

✦

Search me, O God, and know my heart; test me and know
my anxious thoughts. Point out anything in me that offends
you, and lead me along the path of everlasting life.

PSALM 139:23-24

Throw off your old sinful nature and your former way of
life, which is corrupted by lust and deception. Instead,
let the Spirit renew your thoughts and attitudes.

EPHESIANS 4:22-23

Picture God looking deeply into your heart and seeing
all the sins within it that have the power to damage
your relationship with him and others. Then picture him
lovingly bringing those things to the surface.

As you imagine this, does any sin immediately come
to mind? Before you can throw off your sin, you need to
know what it is. So end this time of prayer by thanking
God for helping you discover these truths about yourself.

Feb
7

What's in Your Heart?

Let us test and examine our ways. Let us turn back to the LORD.

LAMENTATIONS 3:40

> "You must love the LORD your God with all your
> heart, all your soul, all your mind, and all your
> strength."..."Love your neighbor as yourself." No
> other commandment is greater than these.

MARK 12:30-31

This week, consider the thoughts that enter your mind when you wake up in the morning and when you lie down at the end of the day.

Your first and last thoughts are good indicators of what is most important to you. They help reveal what you really care about—the true loves of your heart.

Over the course of the week, ask yourself whether those thoughts are focused more on your desires or on God's desires for you.

Honest Feedback

✦

The human heart is the most deceitful of all things, and
desperately wicked. Who really knows how bad it is?

JEREMIAH 17:9

This week, ask a close friend or family member to give
you honest feedback about your weaknesses. Here
are some questions to consider asking that person:

✦ Have I recently hurt your feelings in some way?
✦ Do you feel like I am present with you when we are
  together?
✦ Do you feel as though I genuinely care about your
  interests, dreams, or passions?
✦ Is there a blind spot in my life I need to become
  aware of?
✦ In what ways can I change my words and actions so
  I can love you better?

Without defending yourself, confess these short-
comings to your loved one and ask for forgiveness.

Feb 9

Why Do You Doubt?

❖

Oh, how great are God's riches and wisdom
and knowledge! How impossible it is for us
to understand his decisions and his ways!

ROMANS 11:33

Timothy Keller once stated, "Worry is not believing
God will get it right, and bitterness is believing God
got it wrong."[5]

Talk with God about the quote and Scripture verse
above.

Where do you feel anxiety or bitterness in your life?

How has that experience caused you to doubt that
God wants the best for you?

Choose one phrase you can say to yourself today that
will help you better trust in his infinite wisdom and
knowledge. For example, you may want to say something like "God wants good things for my life," "God's
decisions and ways are best," or "God's wisdom is far
greater than my own."

Is It Possible?

Moses raised his hand over the sea, and the LORD opened
up a path through the water with a strong east wind....
So the people of Israel walked through the middle of the
sea on dry ground, with walls of water on each side!

E X O D U S   1 4 : 2 1 - 2 2

Jesus looked at them intently and said, "Humanly speaking,
it is impossible. But with God everything is possible."

M A T T H E W   1 9 : 2 6

In what area of your life do you need the kind of help
that seems impossible? Maybe it's finding a job, forgiving another person, quitting an addiction, or grieving a
great loss.

Spend a moment right now talking to God about
why it is hard for you to have faith and trust him in this
particular area. Memorize one of the verses above to
remind you that God is all-powerful and able to do the
impossible.

Who Do You Want to Be?

It is the same with my word. I send it out, and it
always produces fruit. It will accomplish all I want
it to, and it will prosper everywhere I send it.

ISAIAH 55:11

The Holy Spirit produces this kind of fruit in our
lives: love, joy, peace, patience, kindness, goodness,
faithfulness, gentleness, and self-control.

GALATIANS 5:22-23

Think about the kind of person you want to be in ten
years. Write out which "fruit" you want to be known for.
What one step can you take today to begin to become
that person?

As you think back over the past week of working on
self-examination, what is one thing the Holy Spirit has
shown you about yourself that you didn't realize before,
positive or negative?

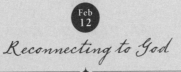

Feb
12

Reconnecting to God

---✦---

David said to God, "I have sinned greatly. . . . Please
forgive my guilt for doing this foolish thing."

1 CHRONICLES 21:8

It is human nature to hide and cover when we have done something
wrong. Adam and Eve hid in the bushes and covered themselves with
leaves after they sinned in the Garden of Eden. The guilt and shame of
their sin placed a relational barrier between God and them.

Do you let your sin come between you and God? If sin separates you
from God, confession is the bridge that reconnects you. It allows you
to go back to God so that you can receive his mercy and experience his
forgiveness. Confession is essential because it reminds you of your need
for Jesus and the Cross.

But this can happen only when you allow the Holy Spirit to bring the
darkest places of your heart into the light. As you practice confession
this week, remind yourself of God's unconditional love and acceptance
despite your sinful nature.

Sin Investigation

Tell me, what have I done wrong?
Show me my rebellion and my sin.

JOB 13:23

With the above verse in mind, ask yourself how often you say those words in prayer. If you were to be honest, how much importance do you place on confession?

Many people think they're pretty good, so they don't actively search the darkest corners of their hearts for sin. But when the roots of sin are left unchecked, they grow wild and untamed. Therefore it's actually healthy to root out anything in you that prevents you from having full and vibrant fellowship with God.

So pause right now and let the Holy Spirit point out something deep within you that you need to confess. Pray, "Lord, here I am. I present myself to you. I open my heart to you. Show me where I have sinned."

Feb 14

Hiding

✦

When I refused to confess my sin, my body wasted
away, and I groaned all day long.... Finally, I confessed
all my sins to you and stopped trying to hide my guilt.
I said to myself, "I will confess my rebellion to the
Lord." And you forgave me! All my guilt is gone.

PSALM 32:3, 5

Is there something you have been hiding from God and
others? What keeps you from confessing?

Fear?

Shame?

Apathy?

Denial?

Talk with God about it, remembering that he loves
you and wants to forgive you. Pray this: "Lord, I desire to
please you with every part of my day, although I know
my actions don't always show this. Show me where I hide
and cover my sin so that I can begin to allow you to love
me in those dark places."

Heart Check

If we claim we have no sin, we are only fooling
ourselves and not living in the truth. But if we confess
our sins to him, he is faithful and just to forgive us
our sins and to cleanse us from all wickedness.

1 John 1:8-9

Spend a few minutes thinking back over your interactions with others this week.

When did you hurt someone, either intentionally or unintentionally?

When did you manipulate someone with your words or actions?

Did you dismiss someone's feelings?

Did you neglect an apparent need?

Confess these things to God and accept his forgiveness. Pray, "Search me, O God, and know my heart. Show me why I chose to hurt this person. Open my heart to your truth, so I don't deceive myself."

Unsettled

Oh, what joy for those whose disobedience is forgiven, whose sin is put out of sight! Yes, what joy for those whose record the LORD has cleared of guilt, whose lives are lived in complete honesty!

PSALM 32:1-2

In *God's Outrageous Claims*, apologist Lee Strobel wrote, "Few things accelerate the peace process as much as humbly admitting our own wrongdoing and asking forgiveness."[6]

With this quote in mind, ask yourself, *Are there areas in my life where I don't have peace? Where I feel unsettled?* (Areas could include a relationship, home life, work decisions, or free-time choices.)

Ask God to point out any unconfessed sin you have in these areas. Pray, "Lord, I desire to live in complete honesty. I long to be free from my guilt. Please show me whatever is keeping me from experiencing joy, peace, and a full relationship with you and with others."

Filled Up

✦

True godliness with contentment is itself great wealth. After
all, we brought nothing with us when we came into the
world, and we can't take anything with us when we leave it.
So if we have enough food and clothing, let us be content.

1 TIMOTHY 6:6-8

Can you be content with what God has given you?
Think about one thing you often wish for but
don't really need and possibly may never achieve (such
as a new car, a remodeled kitchen, or thicker hair).

Spend a few minutes talking to God about the places
in your heart that are unsatisfied and ungrateful. Pray,
"Lord, I want to experience true contentment. I confess
my desire to always have more. May I be content in that
for today, I have enough."

Heart Health

✦

Guard your heart above all else, for it
determines the course of your life.

PROVERBS 4:23

___

What are you letting into your heart these days that will
likely lead to a rift in your relationship with God?

Are you watching a television show or movie that isn't
edifying? Listening to a radio talk show that uses crude
language? Looking at websites or magazines that glorify
looks, wealth, or sex? What is the first thing that comes
to mind?

Spend a few minutes talking to God about this.

Now reflect over the last two weeks and answer the
following questions: What have you learned about yourself (self-examination)? How has this discovery changed
your communication with God (confession)?

Ask God if there is a particular sin in your life that he
wants you to confess now to him and possibly to a close,
trusted friend. And then confess it.

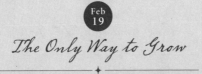

Feb
19

The Only Way to Grow

Anyone who becomes as humble as this little child
is the greatest in the Kingdom of Heaven.

MATTHEW 18:4

Pride, at its core, is the desire to live apart from God. Pride is convincing ourselves that, on any particular issue, we know better than he does. Practicing humility is essential because it helps us confront our pride long before we reach disaster. Humility begins with knowing who God is and who we are in comparison. It is not about seeing ourselves as less, but about seeing God as so much more—as the one who is perfect in goodness and all-loving toward his creation.

This perspective helps us trust that God's plans are far better than our own. We cannot force ourselves to be humble. However, we can ask the Holy Spirit to show us where we are controlled by pride (for example, in characteristics like stubbornness, distrust that God's Word is true, hypocrisy, or arrogance). In fact, almost every sinful action stems from pride, which is why it's so important to practice humility. Without humility, we become unteachable and miss out on learning from and growing with God.

Can You Let It Go?

✦

I know, Lord, that our lives are not our own. We are not able to
plan our own course. So correct me, Lord, but please be gentle.

JEREMIAH 10:23-24

In *The Great Divorce*, author and theologian C. S. Lewis
wrote, "There are only two kinds of people in the end:
those who say to God, 'Thy will be done,' and those to
whom God says, in the end, '*Thy* will be done.'"[7]

Which kind of person are you?

Do you willingly submit to God's will or feel reluctance
about his changes in your plans?

Think about your to-do list for today. In which area is
it difficult to say to God, "Thy will be done"?

With this in mind, read the verse above as a prayer.

Your Seat at the Table

◆

When you are invited to a wedding feast, don't sit in the seat of honor ... take the lowest place at the foot of the table. Then when your host sees you, he will come and say, "Friend, we have a better place for you!" Then you will be honored in front of all the other guests.

LUKE 14:8, 10

Spend a few moments thinking about what motivates your decision of where to sit at the table (either at home or on group outings).

Do you tend to sit near those with high status, or by those with whom you are most comfortable?

Do you choose the seat with the best view?

The next time you sit around a table with a group, ask the Lord to help you choose a humble seat.

Will You Ask?

Fools think their own way is right, but the wise listen to others.

PROVERBS 12:15

Get all the advice and instruction you can,
so you will be wise the rest of your life.

PROVERBS 19:20

In what area in your life would it be wise to get advice?
Maybe about a conflict in a relationship?

A financial decision?

A job change at work?

A dry time in your faith?

Help with a persistent temptation?

It takes humility to seek advice, especially in areas that are sensitive or those where people expect us to have the answers.

Think of a person who can help you with the advice you need. Exercise humility and ask him or her today.

O God, Have Mercy

Two men went to the Temple to pray. One was a Pharisee, and the other was a despised tax collector. The Pharisee . . . prayed this prayer: "I thank you, God, that I am not like other people— cheaters, sinners, adulterers." . . . But the tax collector . . . dared not even lift his eyes to heaven as he prayed. Instead, he beat his chest in sorrow, saying, "O God, be merciful to me, for I am a sinner." I tell you, this sinner, not the Pharisee, returned home justified before God. For those who exalt themselves will be humbled, and those who humble themselves will be exalted.

LUKE 18:10-14

Practice humility today by praying the words of the tax collector: "O God, be merciful to me, for I am a sinner." Repeat this prayer several times throughout the day.

What You're Proud Of

---◆---

This is what the LORD says: "Don't let the wise boast in their wisdom, or the powerful boast in their power, or the rich boast in their riches. But those who wish to boast should boast in this alone: that they truly know me and understand that I am the LORD who demonstrates unfailing love and who brings justice and righteousness to the earth, and that I delight in these things."

JEREMIAH 9:23-24

If you were to boast about anything that you've accomplished, what would it be?

Your appearance?

Your educational degrees?

Your children's achievements?

Your latest job promotion?

Your role in your church or community?

Be honest and vulnerable with God here. Take a few minutes to think about what this passage calls believers to boast in. When was the last time you "boasted" about God's love, justice, or righteousness?

The Greatness of a Humble Future

---◆---

"My thoughts are nothing like your thoughts," says
the LORD. "And my ways are far beyond anything
you could imagine. For just as the heavens are higher
than the earth, so my ways are higher than your ways
and my thoughts higher than your thoughts."

ISAIAH 55:8-9

Make a list of some things you are planning for your future—such as buying a home, having children, enjoying retirement, or seeking a career change.

Read over the verses above one more time with your plans in mind. Ask God what he thinks about your list.

If he shows you something to delete, are you humble enough to let it go?

If he shows you something to add to your list, can you accept it?

As you think back on this week focused on humility, what verse, question, or thought stood out to you?

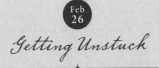

Getting Unstuck

Teach me your ways, O LORD, that I may
live according to your truth!

PSALM 86:11

The older we get, the more we tend to become stuck in our ways and
avoid the humbling feeling of learning something new. Scripture,
however, calls us to be lifelong learners, with the Lord as our primary
teacher and guide.

Practicing "teachability" means being open to new ways of doing
things, putting aside the need to appear intelligent or self-sufficient—
being okay with not knowing it all. Life is an adventure, and God always
has something new for us to learn. What if we woke up every day ready
to grow with God and absorb his wisdom? Isaiah 30:20 says that even in
days of pain and adversity, God wants to teach us. He longs for us to be
open to learning from him.

As you practice "teachability" this week, ask God to help you learn
how to live as an eager apprentice—ready to absorb something new
each day. Embrace the role of a student this week, remembering that
someday, "you will see your teacher with your own eyes" (Isaiah 30:20).

Open to Learn

❖

Wisdom will enter your heart, and
knowledge will fill you with joy.

PROVERBS 2:10

Intelligent people are always ready to learn.
Their ears are open for knowledge.

PROVERBS 18:15

This week, choose to learn something new in which
you have no previous experience or skill. For
example, try gardening, drawing, cooking, or identifying
the trees in your front yard.

Obviously you can't learn much in just a week, but
you can at least gain a broad overview. You don't have
to continue after this week unless you want to.

The point of this exercise is to begin disciplining
yourself to be teachable. Talk to the Lord about how
humbling it is to learn something you know nothing
about.

Feb 28

Self-Improvement

❖

Cry out for insight, and ask for understanding. Search for them
as you would for silver. . . . Then you will understand what it
means to fear the LORD. . . . Then you will understand what
is right, just, and fair, and you will find the right way to go.

PROVERBS 2:3-5, 9

Understand this, my dear brothers and sisters: You must all
be quick to listen, slow to speak, and slow to get angry.

JAMES 1:19

Ask someone today, "What can I do to be a better
_____?" (Fill in the blank: spouse, parent, boss,
sibling, friend, neighbor, coworker.)

Before you ask, though, take time to reread the
Scripture above to gain wisdom about how to approach
this conversation.

Listen

✦

They hated knowledge and chose not to fear the Lord. They rejected my advice and paid no attention when I corrected them. Therefore, they must eat the bitter fruit of living their own way.

PROVERBS 1:29-31

Fools think their own way is right, but the wise listen to others.

PROVERBS 12:15

How do you usually respond when someone corrects you or offers constructive criticism?

Do you become irritable and defensive, or open and willing to consider it?

The next time you are corrected, ask yourself if the constructive criticism might actually be from God, who has prompted a person to speak to you.

If you knew the correction was from God, would you be more open to learning from it?

Teach Me

✦

Fools have no interest in understanding; they
only want to air their own opinions.

PROVERBS 18:2

Wise people treasure knowledge, but the
babbling of a fool invites disaster.

PROVERBS 10:14

On a scale of one to ten (one being "very open" and
ten being "not open at all"), how would you rate
your openness to learning new ways of doing things?

This week, ask someone to teach you *their* way of
doing something. It may be as simple as cutting an
onion, making a bed, budgeting, or staying organized.

Do your best to set aside your own opinions and
knowledge in order to learn from someone else.

Who Can Teach Me?

+

I thought, "Those who are older should speak, for
wisdom comes with age." But there is a spirit within
people, the breath of the Almighty within them, that
makes them intelligent. Sometimes the elders are not
wise. Sometimes the aged do not understand justice.

JOB 32:7-9

A spiritual gift is given to each of us so we can help each other.
To one person the Spirit gives the ability to give wise advice.

1 CORINTHIANS 12:7-8

Picture yourself in ten, twenty, or thirty years.
Consider three character traits that you would like
to have then. Whom do you know with these traits who
could help you become that kind of person?

If no names come to mind, make it part of your daily
prayer to ask God to send people into your life who can
teach you these character traits.

Reflect and Learn

—◆—

Instruct the wise, and they will be even wiser. Teach
the righteous, and they will learn even more.

PROVERBS 9:9

Which practice in this devotional so far have you
felt you needed least? How about the most?

For the practice you chose as "least needed," consider
how this may reveal stubbornness to change.

For the one you chose as "most needed," thank the
Lord for helping you realize a need for change in your life.

As you reflect on the past week, make note of the
areas where you have grown in your desire to be more
teachable. Continue to focus on those.

Mar
5

In Tune, In Touch

Let those with discernment listen carefully.
The paths of the LORD are true and right, and
righteous people live by walking in them.

HOSEA 14:9

Discernment is about becoming more and more sensitive to God's voice and direction. God promises that he will guide and counsel you (Psalm 32:8), lead you to truth (John 16:13), and help you listen for his voice (John 10:27). However, this happens only when you live connected to him. Practically, this involves praying, reading Scripture, listening to God, opening yourself to his direction and to interruptions to your schedule, and recognizing how your desires and motives hinder your ability to hear him well. Discernment is being so in tune with God's voice that you recognize it when he speaks to you.

Some of this week's exercises will ask you to involve God in decisions that may seem silly or insignificant. Remember that God desires you to invite him into all your plans and decisions—both the big and the small. Learning to discern God's leading in small things will prepare you to better recognize his voice when the big decisions come along.

Can You Recognize My Voice?

My child, listen to what I say.... Tune your ears
to wisdom.... [A]sk for understanding....
[A]nd you will gain knowledge of God.

PROVERBS 2:1-3, 5

You must test them to see if the spirit they have comes from God.

1 JOHN 4:1

What tactics does Satan use to take your thoughts
and intentions from God? Does he tempt you
with a desire for more money or possessions? A deep
need for approval from others? An excessive focus on
your appearance?

As you practice discernment, ask God to help you
distinguish his voice from your own, from others', and
from Satan's. As you make decisions, get in the habit of
pausing to question which voice is speaking to you. You
can begin by asking yourself, *Is this decision leading me
toward or away from God?*

Lord, Where Should I Walk?

Your own ears will hear him. Right behind you a voice will say, "This is the way you should go," whether to the right or to the left.

ISAIAH 30:21

"The only answer to the question, How do we know whether this is from God? is *By experience*,"[8] says Dallas Willard in his book *Hearing God*.

Experience making decisions with God in a small way today. Go for a walk in your neighborhood or in a park.

As you walk, continually ask God, "Where would you like me to go? To the left or to the right?"

This may feel like guesswork, but trust that this is a small step to begin asking God questions and listening for his answers.

Notice the people or places that cross your path. God may invite you to make conversation with someone or simply sit alone in a beautiful place.

What Really Matters?

❖

I pray that your love will overflow more and more, and that you
will keep on growing in knowledge and understanding. For I
want you to understand what really matters, so that you may
live pure and blameless lives until the day of Christ's return.

PHILIPPIANS 1:9-10

Think over the items on your agenda today. Practice
being open to God's will as you ask him to help you
discern what really matters.

Then reflect on the following questions:

+ What really *needs* to get done today?
+ What on my schedule can I let go of today?
+ Is there something that is not on my agenda today
  that the Lord may be asking me to add?

Mar
9

Listen . . . and Speak

That night Paul had a vision: A man from Macedonia in
northern Greece was standing there, pleading with him,
"Come over to Macedonia and help us!" So we decided
to leave for Macedonia at once, having concluded that
God was calling us to preach the Good News there.

ACTS 16:9-10

Ask the Lord whom he might be leading you to
connect with today.

Is there an old friend or family member you haven't
spoken to in a long time who comes to mind?

Send that person a thoughtful text or a card, or call
and let them know the Lord put them on your heart.

Lead Me, Lord

The LORD says, "I will guide you along the best pathway
for your life. I will advise you and watch over you."

PSALM 32:8

You probably drive the same route regularly to get to
certain places. But when you get in your car today,
ask the Lord which route he would like you to take. Be
open to how God might lead you in a different way.

There is no wrong way to do this exercise. This is
about learning to ask and then listening to the voice of
the Lord so you can be more discerning as he leads you
in other ways.

Is It Time to Wait?

———————— ✦ ————————

Wait patiently for the LORD.... Yes, wait patiently for the LORD.

PSALM 27:14

Be still in the presence of the LORD, and
wait patiently for him to act.

PSALM 37:7

When we are tired, overworked, overwhelmed, or disconnected from God, it is wise to put off making big decisions until we are in a healthier place.

Think about a decision that you need to make.

Are you considering a job change?

How to spend your money?

Whether or not to have a difficult conversation?

Now reflect on your present circumstances and ask the Lord if this is the best time to make that decision.

As you end this week on discernment, look back through the last six days and ask the Lord if there is an exercise he would like you to repeat.

Mar
12

From Tears to Celebration

◆

Let all who take refuge in you rejoice; let them sing
joyful praises forever. Spread your protection over them,
that all who love your name may be filled with joy.

PSALM 5:11

Satan's mission is to kill, steal, and destroy everything good in your
life—especially your joy. So how can you remain joyful in a world
where there is so much to be sad about?

God's Word says that joy is good medicine for the heart and the
source of our strength, transforming our tearful moments into times of
celebration. Being joyful means choosing an attitude of appreciation,
thanksgiving, and rejoicing.

The exercises this week will help you learn to appreciate the gifts
God has given you, develop an attitude of thanksgiving, and rejoice with
God in response. Remember that it is impossible to force yourself to
feel joy. But you can ask the Lord to help you be aware of his gifts and
goodness in your life, which will help you develop an appreciative and
thankful heart—regardless of your circumstances.

First Thoughts for Your Day

This is the day the LORD has made.
We will rejoice and be glad in it.

PSALM 118:24

Write out this Scripture and place it next to your alarm clock or on the bathroom mirror so that it's the first thing you see every morning for the next week.

Read the verse to yourself three times each day, allowing it to impact your attitude and set your focus for the rest of the day.

Then ask the Lord to help you anticipate all he has in store for you and the things he will be doing around you in the coming hours.

Good Medicine

✦

A joyful heart is good medicine,
but a crushed spirit dries up the bones.

PROVERBS 17:22, ESV

As you look ahead to this day, what is the one part of it in which you will struggle most to be joyful?

Pause and ask God to open your heart and give you a joyful perspective about it; then read the above verse again.

Sometimes joy is a reaction to a happy circumstance. Other times, you must choose to be joyful even when it feels as though you have nothing to be joyful about.

How might God be calling you to choose joy today?

God Delights in You

The LORD delights in his people; he crowns the humble
with victory. Let the faithful rejoice that he honors
them. Let them sing for joy as they lie on their beds.

PSALM 149:4-5

Who in your life brings you the most joy?
Your spouse? Your child? A best friend?

If you, in your fallen and sinful condition, can rejoice
over this person, how much more does your perfect
heavenly Father rejoice over you?

Take a moment and let that sink in: The God of the
universe delights in you right now, regardless of what
you've done.

How would your attitude change if you really believed
God was cheering you on throughout this day?

Mar
16

Smile

◆

You will show me the way of life, granting me the joy of your
presence and the pleasures of living with you forever.

PSALM 16:11

Let all that I am praise the LORD; may I never
forget the good things he does for me.

PSALM 103:2

Think of your happiest memory. What is it about this
memory that made you feel so happy?

Reflect on that memory for a while and try to recapture the feeling of joy you had at that moment. Let yourself smile.

Now rejoice with God for the gift of that memory and
for his promise—what you've experienced in your happiest moment is just a taste of what you will eventually
experience every day for all eternity.

Mar
17

The Joy of Adversity

We know that God causes everything to work
together for the good of those who love God and
are called according to his purpose for them.

ROMANS 8:28

Dear brothers and sisters, when troubles of any kind come
your way, consider it an opportunity for great joy.

JAMES 1:2

What is one trial you are currently facing? How might God use this adversity as an opportunity for you to experience great joy? Is this experience making you trust him more? Is it humbling you? Is it causing you to be grateful for the good things in your life?

This is a hard exercise because it pushes against the direction your heart wants to go, the way of discouragement, sadness, and even bitterness. Pray that God will allow joy to push back so you can experience God's promise to bring good out of difficult circumstances.

Enjoy Today!

✦ ---

Go ahead. Eat your food with joy, and drink your wine
with a happy heart, for God approves of this!

ECCLESIASTES 9:7

How might the above verse encourage you to be
more intentional about enjoying today?

Perhaps by taking your time and not rushing? Eating
something special? Practicing gratitude? Going on a
spontaneous adventure?

Author Ann Voskamp wrote on her blog, "Joy isn't
about how much our lives have—but how much we
enjoy our lives."⁹

Where could you create space in your schedule to
enjoy life more today?

Over the past week, how has meditating on joy
impacted your perspective, attitude, and relationship
with God? Was there a moment or day when you were
thankful you chose to rejoice?

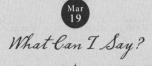

Mar
19

What Can I Say?

Pray in the Spirit at all times and on every occasion.
Stay alert and be persistent in your prayers.

EPHESIANS 6:18

Have you ever been in a situation with someone where you just couldn't think of anything to say? Have you ever experienced this in your relationship with God?

As in other relationships, almost every believer goes through seasons where talking to God feels stale, one-sided, unexciting, or even frustrating. Sometimes this is the result of unconfessed sin or because we are reluctant to get personal with God about our deepest needs and desires. Other times, God remains silent as a way to strengthen our faith. Whatever the case, the apostle John offers us some much-needed encouragement: "We are confident that he hears us" (1 John 5:4).

This week focuses on specific exercises to deepen and energize your conversations with God. Prayer is not just about telling him what your needs are—it's about engaging with the ever-present Christ in every moment. As you talk with God this week, keep in mind that you're forming and deepening the most important relationship you will ever have.

Why Do You Pray?

When you pray, don't be like the hypocrites who love to pray
publicly on street corners and in the synagogues where
everyone can see them. I tell you the truth, that is all the reward
they will ever get. But when you pray, go away by yourself,
shut the door behind you, and pray to your Father in private.
Then your Father, who sees everything, will reward you.

MATTHEW 6:5-6

What motivates you to pray?

Is it that you feel like you should?

You need something from God?

You want to know him more?

You desire to be a better person?

Don't be afraid to have an honest conversation with
God about why you pray. Ask him to reveal your real
motives for praying.

But first remind yourself that God accepts, delights in,
and unconditionally loves you.

Mar 21

Don't Stop Talking

Jesus told his disciples a story to show that they should always pray and never give up. "There was a judge . . . who neither feared God nor cared about people. A widow of that city came to him repeatedly, saying, 'Give me justice in this dispute with my enemy.' The judge ignored her for a while, but finally he said to himself, '. . . This woman is driving me crazy. I'm going to see that she gets justice, because she is wearing me out with her constant requests!'" Then [Jesus] said, "Learn a lesson from this unjust judge. Even he rendered a just decision in the end. So don't you think God will surely give justice to his chosen people who cry out to him day and night?"

LUKE 18:1-7

With this parable in mind, talk to God about a specific prayer request.

Talk about Anything

◆

Peter said to Jesus, "Explain to us ..."

MATTHEW 15:15

Don't worry about anything; instead, pray about everything.
Tell God what you need, and thank him for all he has done.

PHILIPPIANS 4:6

Learn to bring everything into your prayer life—even your distractions. Sit quietly in the presence of the Lord for a minute or so.

If distractions come to mind, talk to God about those. Remember, you are learning to talk with God, so talk to him about anything, even if it seems trivial or you are ashamed of what you are thinking.

If you feel free to share something with your closest friend, how much more freedom should you feel to share with God, your Creator, who loves you unconditionally?

What Are You Afraid Of?

◆

David asked God, "Should I go …?"

1 CHRONICLES 14:10

O LORD, you have examined my heart and
know everything about me.

PSALM 139:1

Whatever you ask in prayer, you will receive, if you have faith.

MATTHEW 21:22, ESV

Is there something you've wanted to ask God for, but you
felt as if you couldn't?

What keeps you from asking?

Do you feel like you don't deserve to ask or fear God
will reject your request?

Do you believe God doesn't care about your desires?

Talk to God about this and remind yourself that he
already knows every desire in your heart.

A Conversation with the Almighty

Pray like this: Our Father in heaven, may your name
be kept holy. May your Kingdom come soon. May your
will be done on earth, as it is in heaven. Give us today
the food we need, and forgive us our sins, as we have
forgiven those who sin against us. And don't let us yield
to temptation, but rescue us from the evil one.

MATTHEW 6:9-13

Read the above passage again slowly, but this time
pray it to God. Remember that you are enjoying
the privilege of conversing with the almighty God of
the universe.

What stands out as you pray through these words?

Talk with God about why this part of the passage
stands out from the rest.

As you engage in this exercise, picture yourself sitting
with God and conversing about his Word.

Comfortable Conversation

✦

If you need wisdom, ask our generous God, and he will

give it to you. He will not rebuke you for asking.

JAMES 1:5

What is a small decision you can talk about with God today?

Whether or not to run an errand?

Which friend to call this afternoon?

What to do with your evening?

This exercise is meant to help you get in the habit of talking with God about both the big and the small decisions throughout your day.

As you think back over this week, reflect on a moment when you felt a little more comfortable talking with God.

Which exercise helped the most?

How can you incorporate that into your daily routine?

Mar
26

Soul Starved

✦

Times of refreshment will come from the presence of the Lord.

ACTS 3:20

Most of us race through life trying to meet one demand after another. This kind of treadmill existence will inevitably wear us down and starve our souls. It is impossible to effectively serve from a depleted soul. Eventually, we will pass out.

Caring for yourself means carving out enough time to care for your own soul. This is not self-centeredness; caring for yourself creates space in your heart for God and others. Even Jesus had to get away from the crowds in order to experience rest and refreshment (see Mark 6:31).

This week's exercises aim to care for your heart, mind, and body—all of which make up the soul. Since God created each person uniquely, what restores your soul may be different from what someone else needs.

As you pay attention to the practices, people, and activities that most refresh you and connect you with God, you will learn to value yourself as God values you. Give yourself permission to set aside time with God this week for the sake of your soul.

Slow Down to Fill Up

Despite Jesus' instructions, the report of his power
spread even faster, and vast crowds came to hear him
preach and to be healed of their diseases. But Jesus
often withdrew to the wilderness for prayer.

LUKE 5:15-16

Schedule a time this week to get away from your every-day demands and do something with the Lord to help
restore your soul.

Take a long walk, read a book, enjoy a bubble bath, or
visit a coffee shop. Think of this time as just resting with
the Lord by inviting him to join you during this activity.

As you end your time, ask the Lord to reveal to you
what to let go of so you can have more times of soul care
with him.

Thirsty?

O God, you are my God; I earnestly search
for you. My soul thirsts for you.

PSALM 63:1

If someone asked you to describe what your soul looks
like, what would you say?

Is it thirsty or satisfied?

Chaotic or peaceful?

Confused or purposeful?

Fearful or confident?

Dark or light?

Weary or refreshed?

Empty or full of hope, love, and joy?

Take a moment to "check in" with God about the current state of your soul. Reflect on the word God brings
to mind. Keep that word in front of you this week to
remind you to care for your soul.

Soul Connections

◆

Don't you realize that your body is the temple of the Holy
Spirit, who lives in you and was given to you by God?
You do not belong to yourself, for God bought you with
a high price. So you must honor God with your body.

1 CORINTHIANS 6:19-20

Choose one way that you can better care for your
body today. Perhaps you could cut out your favorite
junk food, take the stairs, park at the far end of the lot
and walk, or get to bed earlier.

Research shows that the more you care for your body,
the more alert your mind is. And Scripture shows that
the more alert your mind is, the more you are aware of
God's work all around you.

Take a few moments to consider prayerfully how your
choice to care for your body will also care for your soul.

Mar 30

Mind Your Soul

✦

We are God's masterpiece. He has created us anew in Christ
Jesus, so we can do the good things he planned for us long ago.

EPHESIANS 2:10

Write these two sentences on a piece of paper:
(1) "I am God's masterpiece," and (2) "He has
planned good things for my life."

Place this paper where you will see it throughout the
day, such as on the mirror, your dashboard, the kitchen
counter, or the refrigerator.

As you do this, remind yourself that you are caring for
your mind and heart by focusing on truths from God's
Word.

What God Really Thinks of You

Thank you for making me so wonderfully complex!
Your workmanship is marvelous—how well I
know it.... How precious are your thoughts about
me, O God. They cannot be numbered!

PSALM 139:14, 17

What precious thoughts might God be thinking about you right now?

Are you funny? Creative? Good at details? A caring friend? Talented in a particular area?

Thank the Lord for creating you wonderfully unique and complex and ask him to help you value yourself the way he values you.

Send yourself an e-mail or text message with the words from the verse above: *How precious are your thoughts about me, O God.*

Read it several times today, thanking God that he loves you so much.

Deep Roots, Nourished Soul

◆

They are like trees planted along a riverbank, with roots
that reach deep into the water. Such trees are not bothered
by the heat or worried by long months of drought. Their
leaves stay green, and they never stop producing fruit.

JEREMIAH 17:8

Schedule a time today or tomorrow to buy a plant for
your home. As you care for this plant, allow it to be
a continual reminder of how important it is to also care
for yourself.

In the past week, which activities, people, or places
have refreshed your soul the most?

How might God be inviting you to make those experiences a part of your life's regular rhythm?

Why We Serve

Even the Son of Man came not to be served but to serve others and to give his life as a ransom for many.

MATTHEW 20:28

Servants know how to set aside some of their own needs, desires, and agendas to instead seek out and meet the needs of others. Practicing service begins by being intentional in recognizing the needs around you and then meeting them.

This is an important practice because when you serve others, you are actually doing exactly what Jesus would have done—blessing someone else by meeting a deep need in their life. When you serve others, you are helping them see Jesus.

The exercises this week encourage you to pay attention to opportunities to serve. You may miss some opportunities, and that is okay. Talk to God about this and receive his grace. Remember that serving can sometimes be difficult and often requires sacrifice. If serving is hard for you, ask the Holy Spirit to show you the places in your heart where you feel resistant. Trust that he will help you serve from your heart as you serve with your body.

Searching to Serve

✦

Jesus called them together and said, "You know that the rulers in this world lord it over their people, and officials flaunt their authority over those under them. But among you it will be different. Whoever wants to be a leader among you must be your servant, and whoever wants to be first among you must be the slave of everyone else."

MARK 10:42-44

Does serving others come naturally to you, or does it require intentionality and effort?

Ask the Lord to open your eyes and heart this week so you can see and act on opportunities to serve those around you.

Write the word *serve* on a sticky note and post it on your bathroom mirror to remind you to be on the look-out for a way to serve someone each day this week.

Six Ways to Serve Today

[Jesus said,] "I was hungry, and you fed me. I was thirsty, and you gave me a drink. I was a stranger, and you invited me into your home. I was naked, and you gave me clothing. I was sick, and you cared for me. I was in prison, and you visited me.... When you did it to one of the least of these ... you were doing it to me!"

MATTHEW 25:35-36, 40

Reflect on the six different ways to serve from the above Scripture:

✦ Feed someone.
✦ Give someone a drink.
✦ Invite a lonely person into your home.
✦ Give someone clothing.
✦ Care for someone sick.
✦ Visit someone who is shut in.

Choose one of these six ways to serve today and imagine you are serving Jesus. How does this affect your perspective on servanthood?

The Hardest Person to Serve

Love your enemies! Do good to them. Lend to them without expecting to be repaid. Then your reward from heaven will be very great, and you will truly be acting as children of the Most High, for he is kind to those who are unthankful and wicked.

LUKE 6:35

It's not hard to serve those we love, but sometimes God tests our hearts by asking us to serve outside our comfort zones.

How might God be calling you to serve a difficult person in a simple and unexpected way today?

Perhaps by giving a random gift, offering congratulations on a significant accomplishment, or sending a thoughtful text?

Unwrapping Your Gift

❖

God has given each of you a gift from his great variety
of spiritual gifts. Use them well to serve one another.

1 PETER 4:10

Look up the spiritual gifts mentioned in 1 Corinthians 12:7-10 and Romans 12:6-8. In addition, go online and find a resource that provides specific definitions of the spiritual gifts.

Which spiritual gifts do you think the Lord has given you? Pray about these gifts and ask God how he would like you to use your gifts to serve others.

What steps can you take this week toward serving in these ways?

The Sacrifice of Service

— ✦ —

We know what real love is because Jesus gave up his life for us. So we also ought to give up our lives for our brothers and sisters.... Dear children, let's not merely say that we love each other; let us show the truth by our actions.

1 JOHN 3:16, 18

Ask someone in your household or a close friend what you can do for them today, and then do it!

Reflect on where you recognize a resistance to serve. What is one way you can push through that resistance?

Perhaps by praying as you serve?

Imagining you are serving God?

Meditating on today's Scripture?

Remember, if you only served others when you felt like it, then you would probably never serve. Sometimes you must lead with your body and your heart will follow.

Grateful Service

✦

Be sure to fear the LORD and faithfully serve him. Think
of all the wonderful things he has done for you.

1 SAMUEL 12:24

Is there a person or people in your life whom you find
it difficult to happily serve?

Your church?

Your spouse?

A child with a bad attitude?

Your needy neighbor?

As you read the above verse again, think about some
of the wonderful things God has done for you. How
might this encourage you to serve with gratitude?

Think about what it has felt like to serve God by helping others this past week.

When did it seem most difficult to serve?

What exercises have best prepared your heart for
service?

Apr 9

Quieting the Noise

✦

> The LORD is in his holy Temple. Let all
> the earth be silent before him.
>
> HABAKKUK 2:20

We live in a world of noise, interruptions, and distractions where people, activities, and electronic devices are constantly vying for our attention. Because of this, many people experience silence as unfamiliar and uncomfortable.

So does silence really have a purpose? Is it even important in our relationship with God? Silence creates a space to hear from God more clearly. Practicing silence isn't only for the sake of "peace and quiet." Silence quiets the inner and outer voices in our days so that we can be alert and better listen to God.

This week, remind yourself that hearing God speak isn't the goal of silence. The goal is simply to show up and say, "God, I am listening if you have anything to say to me." And if God does decide to speak, then accept it as a gift! Lean into the discomfort of silence and learn to become more comfortable in the quiet. Each time you sit in silence with God, he is slowly teaching you to recognize his voice.

Rest in the Quiet

✦

This is what the Sovereign Lord, the Holy One of Israel, says: "Only in returning to me and resting in me will you be saved. In quietness and confidence is your strength."

ISAIAH 30:15

How do you usually experience silence?

Do you long for more of it?

Does it feel lonely?

Do you try to avoid it?

Ask the Lord to help you be open to his presence. Be patient with yourself as you practice silence this week.

Start by setting a timer on your phone or clock for one minute. After you press "start," do not look at the timer again until it rings.

If you haven't done this before, a minute will seem like a long time! Close your eyes and sit in God's presence, just content to be with him.

In Waiting, You Hear

---------- ✦ ----------

Let all that I am wait quietly before God, for my hope is in him.

PSALM 62:5

Drive without music or the radio today to practice being with God in silence. You may need to put a sticky note on your device to remind you not to turn it on.

As you drive, talk to God if something comes to mind, but focus more on being quiet and resetting your heart to be in tune with his, listening for what he has to say to you.

This exercise is about building a habit of creating and being comfortable with silent spaces during your normal routine.

Experience the Calm

— ✦ —

Soon a fierce storm came up. High waves were breaking
into the boat, and it began to fill with water. Jesus was
sleeping at the back of the boat with his head on a cushion.
The disciples woke him up, shouting, "Teacher, don't you
care that we're going to drown?" When Jesus woke up, he
rebuked the wind and said to the waves, "Silence! Be still!"
Suddenly the wind stopped, and there was a great calm.

MARK 4:37-39

Read the above passage again, but this time imagine
you are on the boat with Jesus:

Listen to the waves breaking against the boat.

Feel the cold water as the boat begins to fill.

Watch Jesus awake and rebuke the storm.

What is it like to see the waves disappear and the
water become still as glass?

Sit on the boat and breathe deeply. What do you feel?

Softly Spoken

After the wind there was an earthquake, but the LORD
was not in the earthquake. And after the earthquake
there was a fire, but the LORD was not in the fire. And
after the fire there was the sound of a gentle whisper.

1 KINGS 19:11-12

Practice being with the Lord in silence by breathing
deeply and slowly. Pay attention to the sounds
around you. What do you hear?

The quiet breathing of your napping children?

Sounds of nature?

The humming of appliances in your home?

Your heartbeat?

Thank God for the opportunity to hear those things
you could have missed if you hadn't been silent.

Talking Silence

The heart of the godly thinks carefully before speaking;
the mouth of the wicked overflows with evil words.

PROVERBS 15:28

In conversations with others today, practice incorporating more quiet into the conversation instead of speaking words just to fill the silence.

Be intentional about allowing space before commenting, giving advice, or asking questions.

Then set a reminder for the end of the day to check in with yourself about how you did. How can you improve in making space for silence in conversations tomorrow?

Perhaps you can count to three before speaking?

Quickly pray before responding?

Refrain from speaking during lags in the conversation?

Silent Prayer

✦

They were trying to trap him into saying something
they could use against him, but Jesus stooped down and
wrote in the dust with his finger. They kept demanding
an answer, so he stood up again and said, "All right, but
let the one who has never sinned throw the first stone!"

Then he stooped down again and wrote in the dust.

JOHN 8:6-8

This passage seems to suggest that Jesus remained
silent long enough for the religious leaders to keep
demanding an answer from him.

Pause for a moment to take a difficult situation to
God in prayer, and then spend some time in silence.

After you have been silent for a few minutes, ask God
if there is anything he would like to say to you about this.

How did silence help you notice the presence and
work of God this week?

Apr
16

Enjoy and Glorify

You are worthy, O Lord our God, to receive glory and
honor and power. For you created all things, and they
exist because you created what you pleased.

REVELATION 4:11

H ave you ever experienced incredible joy yet still felt like there was
something missing? Maybe it was a beautiful sunset, your child's
first belly laugh, or the wedding of a close friend.

C. S. Lewis wrote, "Fully to enjoy is to glorify."[10] Our joy in something
is made complete when we give praise and glory to the one who gave
it to us. This is worship. Dallas Willard expressed a similar sentiment:
"In worship we . . . express the greatness, beauty, and goodness of God
through thought and the use of words, rituals, and symbols."[11]

This week, release yourself from the expectation of having a divine
encounter with God. Perhaps he is teaching you to worship him for who
he is and not for an experience. Some exercises will help you be honest
about who or what you truly worship. Other exercises will involve reflecting on God's beauty in the world and his goodness in your life, and then
responding with praise to him.

Worship Is Thankfulness

Praise the LORD! I will thank the LORD with all my heart
as I meet with his godly people. How amazing are the deeds
of the LORD! All who delight in him should ponder them.

PSALM 111:1-2

Sing psalms and hymns and spiritual songs
to God with thankful hearts.

COLOSSIANS 3:16

Participate in worship at your church this week or
arrange a time for worship and singing at home with
your family, small group, or close friends.

Think deeply about the words you are singing.

What do these songs say about who God is?

How do they lead you toward gratitude for all he has
done?

Apr
18

Worship Is Beauty

◆

When I look at the night sky and see the work of your
fingers—the moon and the stars you set in place—
what are mere mortals that you should think about
them, human beings that you should care for them?

PSALM 8:3-5

The heavens proclaim the glory of God. The skies
display his craftsmanship. Day after day they continue
to speak; night after night they make him known.

PSALM 19:1-2

Go outside several times throughout the day and look
up at the sky (preferably at sunrise, at sunset, and
after dark).

Take in its vastness, variety of colors, and cloud for-
mations, and the moon and myriad of stars.

What do you feel as you stand below this display
of God's art? Allow this time to lead your heart to worship the creator of the heavens and the earth.

Worship Is Praising God with Words and Songs

I will sing to the LORD as long as I live.
I will praise my God to my last breath!

PSALM 104:33

The jailer put them into the inner dungeon and
clamped their feet in the stocks. Around midnight
Paul and Silas were praying and singing hymns to
God, and the other prisoners were listening.

ACTS 16:24-25

Paul and Silas worshiped in word and song even while
in prison. Choose to praise God in an unusual place
or situation this week—perhaps at the grocery store, at
the gym, or in the car.

Worship by praising God for who he is, or sing or
hum a favorite song about him. When you do this,
remind yourself that you are transforming a mundane
moment into a time of worship.

Worship Is Joy

Let the godly rejoice. Let them be glad in God's
presence. Let them be filled with joy.

PSALM 68:3

O LORD, I will honor and praise your name, for you are
my God. You do such wonderful things! You planned
them long ago, and now you have accomplished them.

ISAIAH 25:1

What gives you the most joy? Your family or friends?
A hobby? Your church or ministry?

Read the verses above once more with this person or
thing in mind. Then give praise and glory to the Lord
with thanks for giving you something that brings you
such joy.

Worship Is Remaining Faithful through Trials

---・---

Even though the fig trees have no blossoms, and there are no grapes on the vines; even though the olive crop fails, and the fields lie empty and barren; even though the flocks die in the fields, and the cattle barns are empty, yet I will rejoice in the LORD! I will be joyful in the God of my salvation!

HABAKKUK 3:17-18

We can rejoice, too, when we run into problems and trials, for we know that they help us develop endurance. And endurance develops strength of character, and character strengthens our confident hope of salvation.

ROMANS 5:3-4

Is your worship of God dependent upon his blessings in your life? How easy or difficult has it been for you to worship God through trials? Reflect on a previous trial. What things can you worship God for as you look back?

Worship Is Reflecting on God's Faithfulness

+

I love the LORD because he hears my voice and my prayer
for mercy. Because he bends down to listen, I will pray as
long as I have breath! Death wrapped its ropes around me;
the terrors of the grave overtook me. I saw only trouble and
sorrow. Then I called on the name of the LORD: "Please,
LORD, save me!" How kind the LORD is! How good he is!
So merciful, this God of ours! The LORD protects those of
childlike faith; I was facing death, and he saved me. Let my
soul be at rest again, for the LORD has been good to me.

PSALM 116:1-7

Using the psalm above as a model, write a psalm of
worship based on your life.

Who has God been to you?

What qualities do you love most about him?

What good things has he done?

Apr
23

Satisfied with Love

Satisfy us each morning with your unfailing love,
so we may sing for joy to the end of our lives.

PSALM 90:14

WEEK 17 // DAY 1

Contentment is one of life's most elusive qualities. Real contentment means being at peace with God and accepting how he has made you, where he has placed you, what he has given you, and who you are in relation to him. It is trusting he has a plan for you and will accomplish it.

You grow in contentment as you trust that God is in control and is working out his unique and wonderful plan for your life. The practice of contentment results in freedom, gratitude, and joy. When you are truly content, you are free from the need to strive, spend, and compete with others because you are full of gratitude that you have more than you deserve. Contentment protects you from jealousy, covetousness, and greed.

This week, be honest with God when you feel discontent. Allow him to use these exercises to change your heart to be at peace with who you are and who God is, and to accept that as enough for the moment.

No One Like You

✦

Peter asked Jesus, "What about him, Lord?" Jesus
replied, "If I want him to remain alive until I return,
what is that to you? As for you, follow me."

JOHN 21:21-22

Pay careful attention to your own work, for then
you will get the satisfaction of a job well done, and
you won't need to compare yourself to anyone else.
For we are each responsible for our own conduct.

GALATIANS 6:4-5

Where are you most tempted to compare yourself to
others? Your appearance, career, kids, or finances?
The size of your home or the number of your material
possessions?

Take a few moments to confess this to God and then
thank him for what you do have. For example, when you
find yourself wishing you looked as great as your friend,
thank God for specific features that are unique to you.

Advertisements as Reminders

Let them praise the LORD for his great love and for the
wonderful things he has done for them. For he satisfies
the thirsty and fills the hungry with good things.

PSALM 107:8-9

Everything else is worthless when compared with the
infinite value of knowing Christ Jesus my Lord.

PHILIPPIANS 3:8

When you see advertisements this week on television or billboards, online, or in your mail, use
them as reminders to thank God for what you do have
and for what he has given you.

This exercise will help you become habituated to
pray, "Lord, you are enough" when you see an ad that
communicates you are not enough until you have
something more.

Is It Enough?

*"What should we do?" asked some soldiers.
John replied, "Don't extort money or make false
accusations. And be content with your pay."*

LUKE 3:14

*Guard against every kind of greed. Life is not measured by
how much you own.... Look at the lilies and how they grow.
They don't work or make their clothing, yet Solomon in all
his glory was not dressed as beautifully as they are. And if
God cares so wonderfully for flowers that are here today and
thrown into the fire tomorrow, he will certainly care for you.*

LUKE 12:15, 27-28

How content are you with your income? There is
nothing wrong with wanting to earn more. The real
question is, Can you be content with what you have now?

Take a few moments to pray about your answer and
about how Jesus' words about money make you feel.

Relax and Receive

◆

Their voices rose in a great chorus of protest against Moses
and Aaron. "If only we had died in Egypt, or even here in the
wilderness!" they complained. "Why is the LORD taking us to
this country? . . . Wouldn't it be better for us to return to Egypt?"

NUMBERS 14:2-3

The Lord rescued the Israelites from slavery in
Egypt, yet they still complained and struggled with
discontent.

In what ways do you struggle to be content with where
God has placed you?

Maybe it feels difficult to accept your season in life.
Or perhaps you struggle to find contentment with your
geographical location or home.

Now read Jeremiah 29:11-14.

How can these verses encourage you to be content with
your current season or location in life, knowing that God
has good things in store for your future?

God Doesn't Make Mistakes

What are mere mortals that you should think about
them, human beings that you should care for them?
Yet you made them only a little lower than God
and crowned them with glory and honor.

PSALM 8:4-5

Nothing can ever separate us from God's love.

ROMANS 8:38

The enemy often tries to make us discontent with
who we are. Read the above verses again. With these
words in mind, remind yourself of how God sees you—
as a unique human he created, cares for, and loves deeply.
He crowns you with glory and honor.

Thankfulness grows your contentment, so take time
to thank God for how he made you and how much he
loves you. Write these words on a piece of paper: "Lord,
thank you for making me just the person you wanted me
to be." Carry it with you all day, reading it often.

The Key to Confidence

Don't love money; be satisfied with what you
have. For God has said, "I will never fail you. I will
never abandon you." So we can say with confidence,
"The LORD is my helper, so I will have no fear.
What can mere people do to me?"

HEBREWS 13:5-6

Think of something you are discontent with in your life
right now:

Your job or marriage?

Your appearance?

Feelings of inadequacy in a certain area?

Now read this verse again and imagine the Lord
speaking these words directly to you: "(Insert your
name), I will never fail you. I will never abandon you."

How do God's words to you make you feel?

Ask him to help you feel satisfied today with what you
have and confident in who you are so that you may experience a life of joy with him.

Apr
30

Keep Less, Give More

✦

You must each decide in your heart how much to give.
And don't give reluctantly or in response to pressure.
"For God loves a person who gives cheerfully."

2 CORINTHIANS 9:7

The world encourages us to make more and keep more. The Bible, however, focuses on how much we should give away. The way we spend our money reveals what we care most about.

Generosity doesn't just involve giving money to help others—it also concerns the giving of our time, talents, and possessions. We give because everything we have was given to us (see 1 Chronicles 29:14). Generosity is important because it teaches us to trust God with our resources and put others before ourselves. When we give, it helps us release our grip on the things we hold too tightly.

The exercises this week could be hard if God shows you a treasure in your heart that has taken priority over him. Talk to him about the areas where you find it hard to be generous. Ask him to unleash the gift of generosity in you so that you can receive the joy that comes from giving.

Random Act of Giving

---·---

The generous will prosper; those who refresh
others will themselves be refreshed.

PROVERBS 11:25

Remember the words of the Lord Jesus: "It is
more blessed to give than to receive."

ACTS 20:35

Look for an opportunity today to practice generosity
with your finances. Ask the Lord to help you obey his
promptings.

For instance, you may sense he wants you to pay for
the person behind you in the drive-through, offer to fill
up someone's tank at a gas station, or buy a meaningful
gift for someone.

Later on, take time to reflect on how you felt just after
your act of generosity.

Generous Hospitality

◆

[All the believers] met in homes for the Lord's Supper,
and shared their meals with great joy and generosity.

A C T S   2 : 4 6

Practice the generosity of hospitality like the believers in the book of Acts by inviting someone over this week for dinner or dessert.

Use this opportunity to share with them by cooking or buying a beautiful meal and enjoying warm fellowship together.

Go to your calendar right now, find an open evening, and e-mail or text someone an invitation.

The Paradox of Giving

God will generously provide all you need. Then
you will always have everything you need and
plenty left over to share with others.

2 CORINTHIANS 9:8

In *The Treasure Principle*, Randy Alcorn wrote, "The more you give, the more comes back to you, because God is the greatest giver in the universe, and He won't let you outgive Him. Go ahead and try. See what happens."[12]

Do you ever fear giving too much and coming up short for yourself?

Do you sometimes think that if you give more to others, you won't have enough?

Do you worry that God's resources will run out?

Can you trust God to provide what you need?

Take a chance today: Give to someone in need so generously that it hurts, and then watch what God does in return.

Valued Treasure

Jesus told him, "If you want to be perfect, go and sell all your possessions and give the money to the poor, and you will have treasure in heaven. Then come, follow me." But when the young man heard this, he went away sad, for he had many possessions.

MATTHEW 19:21-22

What is something you could give that would *really* be a sacrifice for you?

Perhaps a large financial gift, a possession you own that someone else admires, or your time during a busy week?

How can you begin the process of giving this gift today?

As you think about this huge act of generosity, tell the Lord how it feels to let this treasure go, and ask him to replace it with peace and joy.

Generous Measures

Give, and you will receive. Your gift will return to you in full—pressed down, shaken together to make room for more, running over, and poured into your lap. The amount you give will determine the amount you get back.

LUKE 6:38

How can you be generous with your time today?
Perhaps by letting someone go first in line at the grocery store or writing that belated thank-you note?

Lingering with a friend?

Helping an elderly parent or grandparent with shopping?

Letting go of something on your agenda to spend quality time with your child?

Ask God to help you trust that he will return your time in full measure.

God's Greatest Gift

✦

We praise God for the glorious grace he has poured
out on us who belong to his dear Son. He is so rich in
kindness and grace that he purchased our freedom
with the blood of his Son and forgave our sins.

EPHESIANS 1:6-7

Read the above verses again slowly; then think about
how generous God has been in forgiving you.

How might this encourage you to generously show
others mercy, grace, and forgiveness? Is there someone
specific who comes to mind to whom you can show mercy
and forgiveness, even though they don't deserve it?

In the past week, which exercise has been most difficult for you? Being generous with your money? Talents?
Time? Home? Possessions?

Spend a few minutes talking to God about this. Ask
him to challenge you to continue giving in this area so
you can keep growing in generosity.

Seeing What Others Don't

We don't look at the troubles we can see now; rather, we fix our gaze on things that cannot be seen. For the things we see now will soon be gone, but the things we cannot see will last forever.

2 CORINTHIANS 4:18

Humans suffer from shortsightedness. We focus on today's tasks and tomorrow's problems. But God offers a different perspective, urging us to make each day an investment in eternity. We are to think about heaven (Colossians 3:2), store up treasures in heaven (Matthew 6:20), and "live as citizens of heaven" (Philippians 1:27).

Developing an eternal perspective helps us view life differently by reminding us to invest in what will last forever. It gives us strength to persevere through trials because we know this life is not our final destination. The more focused we are on our eternal future with Jesus, the less attached we become to our own desires and plans and to the temporary attractions of this world.

This week, allow yourself to meditate on the beautiful future God has for you in eternity and notice how it affects your attitudes, choices, and relationships.

Who Would Have Dreamed?

No eye has seen, no ear has heard, and no mind has
imagined what God has prepared for those who love him.

1 CORINTHIANS 2:9

Write this verse down and put it in a visible place so
you can meditate upon it throughout the week.
Remember to read it slowly each day and reflect on
how its message can change how you think and what you
do. Allow your mind to imagine what God has waiting
for you.

Homesick for Heaven

Do not love this world nor the things it offers you, for
when you love the world, you do not have the love of the
Father in you. For the world offers only a craving for
physical pleasure, a craving for everything we see, and
pride in our achievements and possessions. These are not
from the Father, but are from this world. And this world is
fading away, along with everything that people crave. But
anyone who does what pleases God will live forever.

1 JOHN 2:15-17

What do you most long for? A new car? A different
job? A spouse or a child?

Have you considered that what you truly long for is
the person you were made for? We were made to be with
Jesus and live with him in heaven.

How might your present longing actually be a form of
homesickness for heaven?

Heavenly Bodies

✦

We know that when this earthly tent we live in is taken down
(that is, when we die and leave this earthly body), we will have
a house in heaven, an eternal body made for us by God himself
and not by human hands. We grow weary in our present bodies,
and we long to put on our heavenly bodies like new clothing.

2 CORINTHIANS 5:1-2

Take a few moments and tune in to your earthly body.
Are you physically weary?

Where are your aches and pains?

What traumas have taken a toll on your body?

Now imagine coming face-to-face with Jesus to
receive a new, heavenly body. What might it feel like
to "put on" that body like new clothing?

What part of your earthly body are you most eager
to leave behind?

What parts of your heavenly body are you most
excited to experience?

What If It Were Today?

Those who use the things of the world should
not become attached to them. For this world
as we know it will soon pass away.

1 C O R I N T H I A N S 7 : 3 1

How would you feel if you knew Jesus would be
coming back today? In complete honesty, is there
any part of leaving this world that would make you sad?

Perhaps not getting married?

Not being able to watch your children grow up?

Having your hard-earned career cut short?

Never traveling to a place you've always wanted to see?

This exercise is hard because your feelings may be
focused on family and friends.

Even so, ask God if you might be overattached to
certain aspects of your life. End your meditation time by
referring to 1 Corinthians 2:9.

May 12

No More

He will wipe every tear from their eyes, and
there will be no more death or sorrow or crying
or pain. All these things are gone forever.

REVELATION 21:4

Take a moment to think about what it would feel like to
never again experience death, sorrow, crying, or pain.

What would it be like to never again have to say goodbye to loved ones? To never have your heart broken or
experience a deep loss?

Consider how this future reality might give you perspective and encourage you in your present troubles.

Face-to-Face

When I saw him, I fell at his feet as if I were dead. But he laid
his right hand on me and said, "Don't be afraid! I am the First
and the Last. I am the living one. I died, but look—I am alive
forever and ever! And I hold the keys of death and the grave."

REVELATION 1:17-18

Think about your life with Jesus so far.

What have been your most cherished times together?

In what season did he feel most close?

In what season did he feel most far away?

When did you obey the hardest command he ever
gave you?

What was your most intimate time of prayer?

Now reflect on what it will be like to see Jesus with
your own eyes for the first time.

What are you both going to talk about when you are
face-to-face?

May
14

The Test

---◆---

My purpose in writing is to encourage you and assure
you that what you are experiencing is truly part of
God's grace for you. Stand firm in this grace.

1 PETER 5:12

One of the most challenging tests the Lord may give us is the opportunity to trust in his faithfulness during difficult times. We fail at these tests when we lose perspective about God's bigger plans for us.

That's why it is important to continually strengthen the spiritual muscle of steadfastness. Steadfastness means learning to endure patiently in faith, or having "courage stretched out." Because life is full of adversity, we will have many opportunities to practice this discipline. Although God sometimes delivers his people from difficult circumstances, he often calls us to courageous and enduring faithfulness in the midst of trials.

If you are in a difficult season, the Holy Spirit has orchestrated the timing of this week just for you. If you are in a season of joy and blessing, simply be uplifted by God this week so that when tough times do come, you will be better prepared to face them with courage.

God at Work in You

I am certain that God, who began the good work
within you, will continue his work until it is finally
finished on the day when Christ Jesus returns.

PHILIPPIANS 1:6

Write down the phrase *God will continue his good
work in me* on three sticky notes and put them in
three visible spots around your home—on the bathroom
mirror, on your bedside table, over the kitchen sink, etc.

Whenever you read them, remind yourself that God
is always at work in you, even if you feel powerless to
persevere.

When There Is No Way Out

✦

We think you ought to know ... about the trouble we
went through in the province of Asia. We were crushed
and overwhelmed beyond our ability to endure, and we
thought we would never live through it. In fact, we expected
to die. But as a result, we stopped relying on ourselves
and learned to rely only on God, who raises the dead.

2 C O R I N T H I A N S   1 : 8 - 9

Recall a problem in which you felt you had no way
out. How did God reveal himself during that time?
What is the biggest trial confronting you now?

To exercise your need to rely on God, kneel in prayer
and clench your fists.

Now slowly open your hands, palms up, as a symbol
of releasing your problem to God.

Ask him to help you wait patiently, and watch how he
will work in this situation.

The Upside of Doubt

When doubts filled my mind, your comfort
gave me renewed hope and cheer.

PSALM 94:19

I n what areas are you tempted to doubt God?
Perhaps you struggle to believe that he really cares
about you, that he wants the best for you, or that your
problems matter to him.

Take some time to really think about it. How do these
struggles impact your ability to persevere in your faith?

Doubt can actually be a blessing if it leads you to
honestly search for a better understanding of who God
is. Allow your doubts to lead you back to the Lord.

Each time you find yourself doubting God, use it as
a reminder to pray. Ask him to transform your thoughts
of doubt into thoughts of hope.

Strength to Keep Going

◆

With this news, strengthen those who have tired hands,
and encourage those who have weak knees.

ISAIAH 35:3

God, who encourages those who are discouraged,
encouraged us by the arrival of Titus.

2 CORINTHIANS 7:6

Whom has God put in your life to encourage you
and give you strength to keep going?

Call or text them right now and ask them to pray that
the Lord will replace any feelings of doubt or discouragement in your heart with hope and joy.

Be encouraged that you have trusted friends or family
members who are praying for you throughout this day.

A God-Sized Compliment

✦

I know all the things you do. I have seen your love, your
faith, your service, and your patient endurance. And I can
see your constant improvement in all these things.

REVELATION 2:19

I magine God speaking these words to you. What specific
things would he tell you he sees and is proud of?

Your work ethic?

Your care for your family or friends?

Your desire to grow closer to him?

How does it make you feel to be understood and
encouraged by the God of the universe?

Remember that as you strive to practice the discipline
of steadfastness, God sees you and is proud of you.

The Best Way to Grow

When your faith is tested, your endurance has a chance to grow. So let it grow, for when your endurance is fully developed, you will be perfect and complete, needing nothing.

JAMES 1:3-4

As difficult as it may be, spend a few moments thanking God for a trial in your life.

How did it help you grow?

What are some ways it made you rely more on him?

Did it end up turning your life in a different direction that was better than your original plan?

Ask God to use this time to strengthen you for future tests of faith.

And as you conclude these exercises in being steadfast in your faith, reflect on which exercise most encouraged you toward patient endurance and courageous trust in God.

May 21

Poor Connections

◆

Don't copy the behavior and customs of this world, but
let God transform you into a new person by changing
the way you think. Then you will learn to know God's
will for you, which is good and pleasing and perfect.

ROMANS 12:2

Jesus often withdrew from crowds and busyness to be with his Father.
If Jesus thought it essential to "unplug," how much more ought we
to do the same in an age of mass communication and technology?

We live with constant interruptions, and as a result, we have
become distracted, poor listeners, and unable to connect deeply with
others. Unplugging is detaching from routine distractions, especially
technology, to be fully present with God and others. Unplugging will take
effort and intentionality, but it is important for our spiritual growth and
relationship with God.

This week will focus primarily on helping you assess your use and
need of technology and how it impacts your relationships. You may feel
uncomfortable letting go of being "connected." When you are tempted
to reconnect too soon, focus instead on your connection with God.

The Weight of Technology

Let us strip off every weight that slows us down, especially the
sin that so easily trips us up. And let us run with endurance
the race God has set before us. We do this by keeping our eyes
on Jesus, the champion who initiates and perfects our faith.

HEBREWS 12:1-2

Read this verse again—slowly.

Now think about your use of technology.

How often does it slow you down spiritually?

Cause you to sin?

Take your focus off Jesus?

Ask the Lord how he would like you to be more intentional this week about unplugging.

For example, perhaps you could replace social media
with prayer or put all technology in another room when
you read your Bible.

Doing so may help you better keep your eyes on him.

May 23

Fixed Thoughts

--- ✦ ---

Fix your thoughts on what is true, and honorable, and
right, and pure, and lovely, and admirable. Think about
things that are excellent and worthy of praise.

PHILIPPIANS 4:8

How does social media impact your thought life?
This week, keep a journal of what your thoughts
are fixed on after spending time on social media.

Does it tempt you to sin by comparing and coveting?

Does it distract you from thinking about things that
are worthy of God's praise?

Every time you finish using social media, jot down
these thoughts.

Now set a reminder for the end of the week to talk to
the Lord about your observations.

What Is Truly Life-Giving?

Be careful how you live. Don't live like fools,
but like those who are wise. Make the most
of every opportunity in these evil days.

EPHESIANS 5:15-16

Schedule a time to go out in public this week just to observe how others use technology.

Go to a coffee shop, the park, or even the lobby after church. How many people are on their phones instead of talking to the person they are with?

Read the verses again with your own life in mind. After observing the use of technology in a public place, how do you think the Lord might be calling you to set aside your own devices in order to make the most of every opportunity?

May 25

Quiet Spaces

✦

I have calmed and quieted myself, like a weaned
child who no longer cries for its mother's milk.
Yes, like a weaned child is my soul within me.

PSALM 131:2

G o for a walk or run an errand today without your
phone. Use this time to calm and quiet your soul
without the temptation of looking at your phone.

As you walk, pray about what it feels like for you to
be without your phone during this time.

Is it freeing?

Do you feel insecure?

Are there any kinds of fears associated with not being
connected?

Face-to-Face

✦

Do to others as you would like them to do to you.

LUKE 6:31

How does it make you feel when someone gives you his or her undivided attention?

Choose one way to connect with another person "face-to-face" today:

✦ Invite someone for coffee without the interruptions of technology.
✦ Play a game with your family instead of watching TV.
✦ Send a handwritten letter, instead of an e-mail, to a friend.

As you do this, reflect on how it feels to connect more personally, and think about the negative impact technology may be having on your relationships.

Saying No to Technology Slavery

You say, "I am allowed to do anything"—but not everything
is good for you. And even though "I am allowed to do
anything," I must not become a slave to anything.

1 CORINTHIANS 6:12

Choose two hours today to unplug fully. Shut off your
phone, turn off the TV, and refrain from using the
computer.

Use some of this time to be with the Lord and reflect
on the above verse. What has this time revealed to you
about the way technology enslaves you?

As you reflect on the past seven days, consider
whether unplugging has revealed any ways in which you
have copied the behaviors of this world.

How might God be calling you to change the way you
think about technology?

Ask him to help you unplug more and more for the
sake of your thoughts, heart, relationships, and prayer
life.

May
28

Don't Miss Out

✦

Jacob awoke from his sleep and said, "Surely the LORD
is in this place, and I wasn't even aware of it!"

GENESIS 28:16

Too often we live our days on autopilot—being physically there but not really being *present*. In *Here and Now*, Henri Nouwen explains the power of being present by stating, "The real enemies of our life are the 'oughts' and the 'ifs.' They pull us backward into the unalterable past and forward into the unpredictable future. But real life takes place in the here and the now."[13]

Being present means waking up to the world around us so we don't miss God's gifts. This isn't meant to be practiced only in good times, but in difficult times too. God is always at work and has gifts for us that are just waiting to be unwrapped.

These gifts are harder to see in difficult seasons, and we won't find them by living in the past or looking to the future. So whether we are in a season of joy or sorrow, we can see every moment as an opportunity to discover and unwrap the wonderful gifts God has for us in the present.

Where Are You?

———————— ✦ ————————

The thief's purpose is to steal and kill and destroy. My
purpose is to give them a rich and satisfying life.

JOHN 10:10

————————————————————————

Don't allow Satan to steal moments from your day.
Set an alarm or a reminder on your phone, and
when it goes off, ask yourself these questions:

✦ *Am I being present with the people around me?*
✦ *Am I daydreaming instead of listening to someone?*
✦ *Am I wishing I were somewhere other than where I am?*

Make it a habit to ask God to help you be aware of the
rich and satisfying moments he brings before you every day.

Hidden Treasure

◆

I will give you treasures hidden in the darkness—secret
riches. I will do this so you may know that I am the LORD,
the God of Israel, the one who calls you by name.

ISAIAH 45:3

What hardship are you currently facing?
What treasures might God have hidden for
you during this dark season?

In difficult times it is especially hard to be present.
You may tend either to linger with regret over the past,
replaying the circumstances of your hardship, or to
dream about the future with a longing for better times.

Instead of wishing for the trial to be over, ask the Lord
to help you be cognizant of his presence during this difficult time.

What might he be doing in your life right now?
What gifts might he be offering you in the present?

Present at the Table

◆

I decided there is nothing better than to enjoy food and
drink and to find satisfaction in work. Then I realized
that these pleasures are from the hand of God. For
who can eat or enjoy anything apart from him?

ECCLESIASTES 2:24-25

How often do you multitask while you eat?
Do you check e-mails on your phone while
having lunch with someone, for instance, or watch TV
during dinner?

Practice being present today by taking time to smell
and taste your food. Chew slowly. Enjoy each flavor as it
hits your tongue.

How does this way of eating help you better enjoy
God's gift of food?

June
1

Soak It In

---------- ✦ ----------

Children born to a young man are like arrows in a warrior's
hands. How joyful is the man whose quiver is full of them!

PSALM 127:4-5

Think about the people you are going to see today,
and thank God for each person you interact with.

When you are with your family and friends (or even
those who are difficult to be around), take a moment to
soak in this privilege of being with each person God has
placed in your life.

You never know how long you will have someone, so
when you are with them, enjoy them!

Breathe In, Breathe Out

The Spirit of God has made me, and the
breath of the Almighty gives me life.

JOB 33:4

Close your eyes and spend the next few minutes focusing on your breathing.

Breathe deeply and slowly.

Pay attention to the sound of your heartbeat, the rising and falling of your chest, and the space of waiting in between each breath.

Simply receive this time as a gift and allow yourself to relax fully.

Now read this verse again as you thank God for making you and putting breath in your lungs at this very moment.

June
3

Sense the Moment

---------- ✦ ----------

Since everything God created is good, we should
not reject any of it but receive it with thanks.

1 TIMOTHY 4:4-5

Practice being present by allowing your five senses to
help you be in the moment.

What do you see, smell, taste, and hear?

What kinds of sensations do you feel against your skin?

Several times during the day, stop for a few moments
and ask these five questions.

Become more alive to God's world around you. Thank
him for the gift of your senses and reflect on the fact that
each moment is unique and special.

Now think back over the past several days you spent
practicing being more present.

When did you feel most present with God and others?

When were you most absent from God and others?

June
4

Can You Hear Him?

---- ✦ ----

Listen to me! For I have important things to tell you.

PROVERBS 8:6

God calls us to be "quick to listen, slow to speak, and slow to get angry" (James 1:19). Sadly, too often we are slow to listen, quick to speak, and quick to get angry. Listening is an art and one that is close to God's heart.

Since God always listens to us, we minister to others by listening to them. Listening is a form of love. We show others they are valuable when we listen with respect, care, and patience, and when we refrain from interrupting with our own thoughts and advice. We must set aside our schedules and distractions to be fully present and to hear every word that is being spoken. *Really* listening takes practice and will not be mastered in a week.

The exercises this week will reveal your current listening habits. God may use some of these exercises to show you how you could lovingly listen better—both to him and to others. Be encouraged that God is shaping your heart to love others well through the ministry of listening.

June 5

Come and Listen

---✦---

Come and listen to my counsel. I'll share my
heart with you and make you wise.

PROVERBS 1:23

My sheep listen to my voice; I know them, and they follow me.

JOHN 10:27

What does the voice of God sound like to you?
     Is it accepting or condemning?
   Demanding or gentle?
   Loud or silent?
   Ask God right now to help you hear his voice more
clearly this week as you practice listening.
   Make an effort to write down anything you hear God
tell you as you practice the discipline of listening.

Listen and Learn

If you listen to correction, you grow in understanding.

PROVERBS 15:32

You must all be quick to listen, slow to
speak, and slow to get angry.

JAMES 1:19

Ask a trusted, honest family member or close friend whether you have been a good listener to them in the past.

Do you give them space to talk?

Does your body language show you are engaged?

Do you ask questions that reflect you have heard and understood what they have been saying?

Sometimes good listening requires self-restraint, so welcome their feedback by listening without interrupting, getting defensive, or trying to explain yourself.

Listening to God's Word

Jesus replied, "But even more blessed are all who
hear the word of God and put it into practice."

LUKE 11:28

How often do you listen to God's Word when you
read it?

As you practice listening this week, read each day's
Scripture slowly, as if God is speaking it directly to you.

Take time to pause and listen after you have read his
Word. Pray, "God, what might you want to speak to me
through this verse?"

As you practice listening to God's Word, remind
yourself that if God is speaking to you, you won't want
to miss it!

June
8

Stop and Listen

◆

Don't look out only for your own interests,
but take an interest in others, too.

PHILIPPIANS 2:4

When you ask someone, "How are you?" do you actually stop to listen to his or her answer?

Or do you tend to rush right past them?

Are you so busy thinking about what you will say next that you don't even listen to what the other person is saying?

Practice listening to someone today by asking them, "How is your day going?" and then taking an interest in what they say, giving them your full attention.

Speak, O Lord

[Eli] said to Samuel, "Go and lie down again, and if someone calls again, say, 'Speak, LORD, your servant is listening.'" So Samuel went back to bed. And the LORD came and called as before, "Samuel! Samuel!" And Samuel replied, "Speak, your servant is listening."

1 SAMUEL 3:9-10

When was the last time you heard the Lord speak to you? Create space to hear God by setting a reminder on your bedside table to rest in the quiet with him before you fall asleep.

Simply pray, "Lord, what do you want to say to me about this past day? About tomorrow?" Lie in the quiet and reflect on anything (absolutely anything!) that comes to mind.

Ask yourself whether the words you hear might be from the Lord. Do they align with Scripture? Are they words spoken in love and grace? Do they point you toward God and his Kingdom?

Listening with Your Mouth

Spouting off before listening to the facts is both shameful
and foolish.... The tongue can bring death or life;
those who love to talk will reap the consequences.

PROVERBS 18:13, 21

Read the above passage again carefully and ask God
whether this is something you struggle with in
listening.

Do you tend to spout off before gaining the facts of
the whole story?

Do you love to talk more than listen?

Is it more difficult for you to listen to certain people
or in specific situations?

Ask forgiveness for ways you have failed to listen well
to others, and receive God's grace.

As you've practiced the art of listening these past few
days, what have you learned about the way you listen to
God and others?

June
11

The Best Example to Follow

How precious are your thoughts about me,
O God. They cannot be numbered!

PSALM 139:17

Live a life filled with love, following the example of Christ.

EPHESIANS 5:2

We can easily become wrapped up in our own lives and miss the needs around us. How do we change our focus to be more oriented toward the needs of others?

Practicing thoughtfulness helps us grow more considerate and attentive to the feelings and needs of those around us. Thoughtfulness, like listening, is a form of love. God's Word calls us to love others by looking for opportunities to do good for them.

The exercises this week aim to make thoughtfulness a regular way of relating to others in your life. Some will be as simple as offering a kind word, asking an insightful question, or giving someone the benefit of the doubt. Allow the Lord to lead you in big or small ways as you develop the habit of thoughtfulness over the next several days.

How Thoughtful Are You?

Let's not get tired of doing what is good. At just the right
time we will reap a harvest of blessing if we don't give up.
Therefore, whenever we have the opportunity, we should do
good to everyone—especially to those in the family of faith.

GALATIANS 6:9-10

Can you give an honest assessment of your thoughtfulness? On a scale from one to ten (one being "not
at all thoughtful," and ten being "extremely thoughtful"),
how would you rate yourself overall?

Does it come naturally for you to do good to others,
or do you need to work at it?

Do you often forget family members' and friends'
birthdays and milestones?

Ask God to open your eyes to see and your heart to
respond to opportunities for practicing thoughtfulness
toward others this week.

Thoughtful Questions

When Jesus saw him and knew he had been ill for a long
time, he asked him, "Would you like to get well?"

JOHN 5:6

Jesus often asked thoughtful questions that spoke to a
person's real needs.

Think of three people with whom you are close and
come up with a thoughtful question that speaks to each
one's real needs (for example, if someone has been going
through a stressful time, asking them if this week has
been any better).

Then be sure to ask each of them! If you have trouble
thinking of a question, think about what you would want
others to ask you.

Consider What's Best

I, too, try to please everyone in everything I do.
I don't just do what is best for me; I do what is
best for others so that many may be saved.

1 CORINTHIANS 10:33

Take a moment to ask the Lord if there is anything in
your life that might cause another person to sin or
stumble.

Have you been bragging about something you've
accomplished?

Complaining about something you don't have?

Grumbling about something you do have that someone else longs for?

Engaging in a habit that is a struggle for someone else?

You will know you have grown in thoughtfulness if
the next time you are with that person, you think about
them first before speaking or acting.

Your Love Language

◆

Love each other with genuine affection, and
take delight in honoring each other.

ROMANS 12:10

Author Gary Chapman is perhaps best known for his
wonderful book *The Five Love Languages*.

Choose someone close to you and consider which
of the five love languages fits them best: acts of service,
quality time, words of affirmation, physical touch, or
gifts. If you don't know what their love language is,
simply ask.

Prayerfully consider with the Lord how to honor this
person this week by loving them in the way they would
best receive it.

Thinking Better

◆

Always be humble and gentle. Be patient with each other,
making allowance for each other's faults because of your love.

EPHESIANS 4:2

Read this verse once more while thinking of someone who has recently offended you—whether they realized it or not. Today your exercise is to give them the benefit of the doubt.

For example, if another driver cut you off, could it be because they were late to something important?

Maybe they didn't see you?

Or maybe they just had a bad day?

This may be a hard exercise if someone has intentionally hurt you. Remember that most people who try to hurt others do it because they have been hurt themselves.

This exercise is not about excusing their behavior but rather about changing the way you see and think about them.

Do It

Don't be concerned for your own good but for the good of others.

1 CORINTHIANS 10:24

Whom do you know who is experiencing a trial or is in a difficult season?

Write down three things to encourage them this week. It could be something as involved as taking them a meal, or something as quick as sending an encouraging text. But do one of those three things today to keep practicing the act of thoughtfulness.

Think back over the past seven days of practicing thoughtfulness. How has it felt to engage in exercises that asked you to intentionally think of others? How might your sacrifices have pleased God over the past week? How might they have strengthened your relationships with others?

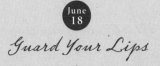

June
18

Guard Your Lips

Take control of what I say, O LORD, and guard my lips.

PSALM 141:3

Do you have a tendency to say things you later regret? Are there times you wish you'd just kept your mouth shut? Do you complain too much, gossip, use profanity, or criticize others?

If these things describe you, then you may have a problem controlling your tongue. Controlling your tongue is being aware of what comes out of your mouth and then, by the Holy Spirit's power, changing words that are destructive into those that are gracious, thankful, encouraging, loving, truthful, and a blessing to others. God emphasizes that even though the tongue is small, it holds incredible power. It can be used to praise God and bless others. But if not controlled, it can set one's whole life on fire (see James 3:5-6).

The exercises this week will ask you to reflect on what comes out of your mouth. Controlling the tongue is a practice that takes a lifetime to learn, and you will continually need God's help with it.

June 19

What Can You Say?

If you claim to be religious but don't control your tongue,
you are fooling yourself, and your religion is worthless.

JAMES 1:26

If you have a problem controlling your tongue, you are probably aware of it because you may have repeatedly hurt family and friends with your words.

What can you do to be more intentional about controlling your tongue? Think of one thing to practice today, such as *I will not speak if I am angry, I will ask a question before making a comment, I will start each conversation with a compliment,* or *I will count to three before I say anything.*

As you practice this exercise of changing your speech, ask the Lord to also change your heart to be more gracious to others.

Filing Your Complaints

Do everything without complaining and arguing, so that
no one can criticize you. Live clean, innocent lives
as children of God, shining like bright lights in a
world full of crooked and perverse people.

PHILIPPIANS 2:14-15

Be mindful of when you are tempted to complain today. If you catch yourself complaining, text the letter *C* to yourself or tally your complaints on a piece of paper.

At the end of the day, count how many times you have texted or written that letter. Ask for God's forgiveness and thank him that you are beginning to practice controlling your tongue.

Make a commitment that tomorrow, each time you want to complain, you will say something to express thankfulness in that situation, and remind yourself how words make a real difference in your attitude and relationships.

Truth Teller

◆

Some people make cutting remarks, but the words of
the wise bring healing. Truthful words stand the test of
time, but lies are soon exposed.... The LORD detests
lying lips, but he delights in those who tell the truth.

PROVERBS 12:18-19, 22

The truth is that we don't always like to tell the truth
because it exposes our motives, it can make us look
bad in front of others, and it forces us to be accountable.

In what situations are you most tempted to exaggerate, stretch the truth, or tell a little white lie? Commit
to telling the truth no matter what the potential consequences to you.

While the short-term consequences of consistent
truth telling might sometimes be painful, the long-term
outcome will be deep relationships with others because
they can always trust you. And remember that God will
honor your honesty.

June 22

Words of Encouragement

———— ✦ ————

Let us think of ways to motivate one another to acts of
love and good works. And let us not neglect our meeting
together, as some people do, but encourage one another,
especially now that the day of his return is drawing near.

HEBREWS 10:24-25

Ask God to bring to mind a person who would be
blessed by your words today.

Whom do you think of first?

What kinds of words would make them feel special,
loved, and encouraged in Christ?

Take a few minutes to write that person an encouraging note by hand, and mail it to them today.

The Weapon of Peace

✦

The LORD will fight for you, and you have only to be silent.

EXODUS 14:14, ESV

God blesses those who work for peace, for
they will be called the children of God.

MATTHEW 5:9

How often do you feel tempted to use words as a
weapon?

Ask the Lord if there is an area in your life where he
might be calling you to step back and be silent.

Or perhaps there is a situation in which you can work
to be a peacemaker with your words.

What comes to mind?

What can you do today to use your words to bring
peace to a person or situation?

Loose Language

✦

[Jesus said,] "I tell you this, you must give an account on
judgment day for every idle word you speak. The words
you say will either acquit you or condemn you."

MATTHEW 12:36-37

Don't use foul or abusive language. Let everything
you say be good and helpful, so that your words will
be an encouragement to those who hear them.

EPHESIANS 4:29

When was the last time you used profanity?
What caused you to do it?

An argument? Another driver? Stubbing your toe or
hitting your head on something?

Or has bad language slowly become a normal part of
your speech?

If so, confess this to the Lord. Now commit not to
use any profanity for the rest of the day. Keep practicing
until it is no longer part of your speech.

June
25

Lift Up Another

—— ✦ ——

Dear brothers and sisters, pray for us.

1 THESSALONIANS 5:25

Do you ever say you will pray for someone and then forget to do it? How often do you pray for believers around the world? For the leaders of your country? For your church?

God's Word urges us to pray for *all* people (see 1 Timothy 2:1). Praying for others means going before the Lord on their behalf. This requires humility because it causes us to set aside our own agendas in prayer to lift up someone else to our heavenly Father.

We may never know the outcome of our prayers in this lifetime, but God promises that our earnest prayers have great power and produce wonderful results (see James 5:16).

This week will stretch you to pray for others in your home, in your neighborhood, and across the globe. Some exercises will challenge you to pray for people you may not want to pray for. Ask God to give you a heart of compassion toward them. Trust that he will use your prayers to produce wonderful results you never thought possible.

Pray for Your Leaders

Pray for all people. Ask God to help them; intercede on
their behalf, and give thanks for them. Pray this way for
kings and all who are in authority so that we can live
peaceful and quiet lives marked by godliness and dignity.
This is good and pleases God our Savior, who wants
everyone to be saved and to understand the truth.

1 TIMOTHY 2:1-4

Spend some time today praying for those in authority
or those who have power over your country. Use the
above verse as a model for how to pray for them.

Pray for the Persecuted

✦

Bless those who persecute you. Don't curse
them; pray that God will bless them.

ROMANS 12:14

Stay alert and be persistent in your prayers
for all believers everywhere.

EPHESIANS 6:18

Go online and find sources that list the top countries
where Christians are being persecuted.

Ask God which country he would like you to pray for
over the next week. Write a note to remind yourself to
pray for this country every day.

Pray for those being persecuted within that country as
well as for those who are persecuting them.

Pray for a Place of Sacred Impact

[Solomon prayed,] "May you watch over this Temple night and
day, this place where you have said, 'My name will be there.'
May you always hear the prayers I make toward this place.
May you hear the humble and earnest requests from me and
your people Israel when we pray toward this place. Yes, hear
us from heaven where you live, and when you hear, forgive."

1 KINGS 8:29-30

Pray in the Spirit at all times and on every occasion.

EPHESIANS 6:18

Go on a prayer walk with the Lord. Walk slowly
through a place, such as your home, neighborhood,
or church, and intentionally pray for that place and the
people coming to and going from it.

Pray for Friends and Family

+

While Peter was in prison, the church
prayed very earnestly for him.

ACTS 12:5

We have not stopped praying for you since we first heard
about you. We ask God to give you complete knowledge of his
will and to give you spiritual wisdom and understanding.

COLOSSIANS 1:9

It is easy to tell people we will pray for them and then
neglect to do it.

Text or call someone today and ask how you can pray
for them this week. Then remember to do it!

Remind yourself to follow up with them later about
their prayer request, and ask them if they would like you
to continue to pray.

Pray for Your Enemy

❖

You have heard the law that says, "Love your neighbor"
and hate your enemy. But I say, love your enemies! Pray
for those who persecute you! In that way, you will be
acting as true children of your Father in heaven.

MATTHEW 5:43-45

Is there anyone whom you would consider your
"enemy" or who is very difficult to love?

Use the questions below to help you prepare to pray
for this person. Ask the Lord,

+ What do you want my prayer to be for this person?
+ Is there anything in me that is getting in the way of
  praying for this person?
+ Is there anything you want me to say or do on behalf
  of this person that would reflect your love for them?

Pray for God's Will in the World

--- ✦ ---

The Father who knows all hearts knows what
the Spirit is saying, for the Spirit pleads for us
believers in harmony with God's own will.

ROMANS 8:27

Look through a newspaper, watch the news, or search
online for important events happening around the
world today. Ask God whom he might be calling you to
pray for right now.

As you conclude your week of praying for others, look
back over the people you prayed for. Take a moment to
think about what it will be like to watch God answer
your prayers for friends and family.

Then imagine being in heaven one day, meeting
people whom you prayed for without knowing them
personally, and hearing how God answered your prayers
for them.

July
2

Step into It

---◆---

Be happy with those who are happy, and
weep with those who weep.

ROMANS 12:15

O ur world is full of people who desperately need to experience the
compassion of Jesus. Since Christ is always loving, tender, and
sympathetic toward us, how can we not be the same toward others?

Compassion means opening your heart to those hurting around you
and then doing something about it. It is both an emotion (feeling concern for someone) and an action (doing something to meet their need).
Compassion compels you to intentionally step into the pain of the world,
instead of trying to avoid it. You can't force yourself to feel compassion,
but it is possible to put your heart in the right posture to notice and
sympathize with the hurt all around you.

The exercises this week ask you to reflect on God's compassion
toward you and then to imagine yourself in the shoes of those in need.
Ask the Lord to change you into someone who notices the pain in the
eyes of others, who is sensitive to unspoken needs, and who is always
ready to serve.

Receiving God's Compassion

You must be compassionate, just as your Father is compassionate.

LUKE 6:36

Begin this week by reflecting on the ways God has shown compassion to you. How has he

+ cared for you during a desperate time (see Genesis 16:13)?
+ loved you even in your worst times of sin (see Romans 5:8)?
+ comforted you in the midst of your pain (see Psalm 34:18)?
+ healed your broken heart (see Psalm 147:3)?
+ given you a chance to start over (see Lamentations 3:22-23)?
+ met one of your deepest needs (see Philippians 4:19)?

How might this encourage you to show the same kind of compassion to others?

Comfort Others

All praise to God, the Father of our Lord Jesus Christ.
God is our merciful Father and the source of all comfort.
He comforts us in all our troubles so that we can
comfort others. When they are troubled, we will be able
to give them the same comfort God has given us.

2 CORINTHIANS 1:3-4

Today, practice compassion by comforting someone who needs it.

For example, if your friend is worried about losing her job, think about what she might be feeling.

Pressure? Fear? Anxiety?

Take time to listen, sympathize, and offer compassionate statements, such as "It sounds like you are feeling a lot of pressure," or "It seems like you're feeling a lot of fear right now."

Do not try to fix anything or dole out advice when you offer comfort; just be a compassionate listener.

Who Needs You Today?

---------- ✦ ----------

If someone has enough money to live well and sees a
brother or sister in need but shows no compassion—
how can God's love be in that person?

1 JOHN 3:17

Think of one immediate need around you today.
Perhaps a sick friend needs a meal, a lonely person
could use a friend, or a homeless person needs a blanket.

Imagine yourself in that situation. What might they
be feeling right now?

Ask God how you can act on meeting this need today
(or this week), and then make sure you follow through.

It's important to ask God before you act, because
there may be times when he will put into your mind just
the right way to serve the person in need.

Compassion to All

The LORD is good to everyone. He showers
compassion on all his creation.

PSALM 145:9

Do you believe some people deserve compassion
more than others?

How do you feel about showing compassion toward
those whom you see as lazy, rude, arrogant, vulgar, or
wealthy?

Read the above passage again and reflect on the
words *everyone* and *all*. Talk to the Lord about someone
who comes to mind who doesn't seem to deserve your
compassion.

How might God be asking you to show compassion
to this person today?

Perhaps it could be through an act of kindness, praying for the Lord to work in your own heart, or simply
putting yourself in their shoes.

Compassion in the Home

✦

Be kind to each other, tenderhearted, forgiving one
another, just as God through Christ has forgiven you.

EPHESIANS 4:32

Think of a family member who has been unkind,
critical, or offensive toward you. Practice compassion by putting yourself in their position and then thinking about these questions:

✦ How do you think it would feel to be this person?
✦ What hardships have they faced in life?
✦ How might their own unmet needs impact the way
  they interact with you?

Reflect on how God has shown you compassion.
Spend the next few minutes praying for this person.

Compassion toward Your Community

✦

A man with leprosy came and knelt in front of Jesus, begging
to be healed. "If you are willing, you can heal me and make
me clean," he said. Moved with compassion, Jesus reached
out and touched him. "I am willing," he said. "Be healed!"

MARK 1:40-41

How willing are you to reach out to the outcasts or
disenfranchised in your community—for example,
the sick, the homeless, the elderly, or the criminals?

How might God be calling you outside your comfort
zone to show compassion in one of these areas?

Perhaps by writing a letter to an inmate, taking flowers to a nursing home, serving food at a homeless shelter,
or donating to a food pantry?

If you are not able to do something today, schedule a
time in the upcoming weeks to serve with your family or
friends.

July 9

We Need Each Other

———————— ✦ ————————

When we get together, I want to encourage you in your
faith, but I also want to be encouraged by yours.

ROMANS 1:12

The discipline of fellowship helps you realize the importance of community in your walk of faith. You need others if you are to grow into
the kind of person God wants you to be.

The exercises this week encourage intentionality, authenticity, generosity, and love within the community where God has placed you. If you
already have a strong community, many of these exercises will be easy
for you. However, if you are still searching for a place of belonging, this
week might cause you to feel stretched and uncomfortable. Trust that
God will reward your efforts as you seek fellowship in your community.

Real community takes time and a lot of effort, but remember that
this week could be the beginning of some beautiful friendships. Doing
life with others is not always easy, but with the help of the Holy Spirit, it
is one of the best ways to grow and be transformed into Christlikeness.

My Community

We are many parts of one body, and we all belong to each other.

ROMANS 12:5

What role has community played in your life?
Take a few moments to pray over the community that the Lord has placed you in.

Does it feel nurturing or draining?

Do you feel a sense of belonging or isolation?

How does this community lead you closer or further away in your relationship with God?

Today, simply talk to God about what comes to mind as you consider these questions. Ask him to give you real openness toward fellowship this week.

United in Heart and Mind

❖

All the believers were united in heart and mind. And
they felt that what they owned was not their own,
so they shared everything they had. The apostles
testified powerfully to the resurrection of the Lord
Jesus, and God's great blessing was upon them all.

ACTS 4:32-33

Choose one way to model the community of Acts
within your own community this week.

Perhaps you could share your food, space, or time,
help a friend in need, or give away something of yours
that you know a friend needs or would like.

What can you do for someone in your community
today?

Build Others Up

Encourage each other and build each other
up, just as you are already doing.

1 THESSALONIANS 5:11

Being intentional to encourage others is an important
part of remaining in fellowship.

Whom in your family, workplace, or community can
you encourage and build up today?

Ask the Lord which friend he would like you to call,
text, or get together with.

Contact that person today to thank them for something they've done, tell them how much you appreciate
them, and encourage them in their faith.

Reach Out

All the believers devoted themselves to the apostles'
teaching, and to fellowship, and to sharing in meals
(including the Lord's Supper), and to prayer.

ACTS 2:42

Small groups can be great places to build community.
If you are not part of a small group, ask God if he
might be calling you to pursue getting involved in one.

Prayerfully consider a person, couple, or family with
whom you would like to connect.

Block out several times on your calendar that would
work to meet with them. Then contact them today to ask
if any of those times would work to get together.

Peacemaking

◆

If you are presenting a sacrifice at the altar in the Temple and
you suddenly remember that someone has something against
you, leave your sacrifice there at the altar. Go and be reconciled
to that person. Then come and offer your sacrifice to God.

MATTHEW 5:23-24

May God, who gives this patience and encouragement,
help you live in complete harmony with each other,
as is fitting for followers of Christ Jesus.

ROMANS 15:5

Is there someone in your community with whom you
are not in harmony? What steps can you take today to
work toward peace with this person?

Could you apologize for your part in a dispute? Ask
for forgiveness? Pray for this person? Work toward a
compromise of some sort?

Consider whether God may be asking you to take the
first step toward reconciliation.

Share Your Burdens

Share each other's burdens, and in this
way obey the law of Christ.

GALATIANS 6:2

Being vulnerable with others feels risky, but it is absolutely essential to building and deepening community.

Call or text a safe and trustworthy friend right now and ask them to pray for you.

Try to be more vulnerable than you are comfortable with, staying focused on your own struggles, temptations, and troubles instead of asking for prayers for your family members or friends.

What did it feel like to be encouraging, intentional, authentic, and generous toward your community this week?

Which of these practices might God be asking you to continue for the purpose of deepening your fellowship with others?

July
16

Be a Good Steward

In the beginning God created the heavens and the earth.

GENESIS 1:1

When you are attacking a town and the war drags
on . . . do not cut down the trees. Are the trees
your enemies, that you should attack them?

DEUTERONOMY 20:19

Caring for creation stands in opposition to today's consumerism and our own selfish desires to live an easy and convenient life. For Christians, caring for creation holds an added significance. It is an outgrowth of our faith, seeing all of God's creation as good and being wise stewards over it. Caring for creation challenges us to practice living within our God-given boundaries by not taking more than we need. It requires us to selflessly love our neighbors as well as future generations by making the earth a better place. It gives us the opportunity to care for something that was meant to glorify God and point people to him. What an amazing way to participate with God in his work! Ask God to open your heart this week to love and care for creation the way he does.

The World Then and Now

———— ✦ ————

God looked over all he had made, and he saw
that it was very good! And evening passed and
morning came, marking the sixth day.

GENESIS 1:31

I magine yourself in this passage, standing next to God
as he looks over his new creation.

What might God have felt toward the earth?

Did he marvel at its beauty?

Did he feel a sense of accomplishment at its amaz-
ingly complex design?

Did he feel joy as he listened to the sounds of trees
swaying in the breeze, bubbling brooks, croaking frogs,
and singing birds?

How do you think God feels when he sees the earth now?

With this picture in mind, ask God to open your heart
this week to care more deeply about creation.

Creation Keepers

◆

God said, "Let us make human beings in our image, to be
like us. They will reign over the fish in the sea, the birds
in the sky, the livestock, all the wild animals on the earth,
and the small animals that scurry along the ground."

GENESIS 1:26

What beliefs or habits inhibit you from being a
good steward over God's creation?
Is it too inconvenient?
Do you doubt your ability to make a difference?
Does it seem like no one else is doing it?

Think of one thing you can do today to be a better
steward of God's creation, such as picking up a piece
of litter along your street, turning off the water while
brushing your teeth, or recycling.

Plant and Watch

◆

The Lord God placed the man in the Garden
of Eden to tend and watch over it.

Genesis 2:15

After the flood, Noah began to cultivate the
ground, and he planted a vineyard.

Genesis 9:20

Abraham planted a tamarisk tree at Beersheba, and
there he worshiped the Lord, the Eternal God.

Genesis 21:33

This week, plant something either in your yard or in a
pot in your home.

Be intentional in caring for it to keep it alive.

What does it feel like to tend and watch over a part of
God's creation?

As you care for this plant, use it as a reminder that
God has also called you to care for his earth.

God's Care for Animals

--- ✦ ---

The LORD God formed from the ground all the wild
animals and all the birds of the sky. He brought them to the
man to see what he would call them, and the man chose
a name for each one. He gave names to all the livestock,
all the birds of the sky, and all the wild animals.

GENESIS 2:19-20

You care for people and animals alike, O LORD.

PSALM 36:6

Read the verses again and think about how God cares
for animals. Search online for a website that lists
endangered animals, and choose one animal to educate
yourself on.

Next, reflect on how God must feel to see his creations
ceasing to exist. Prayerfully consider how God might be
calling you to care for his animals—perhaps by donating
to an organization that helps endangered species or vol-
unteering at a local animal shelter.

Creation Renewal

---◆---

Against its will, all creation was subjected to God's
curse. But with eager hope, the creation looks
forward to the day when it will join God's children
in glorious freedom from death and decay.

ROMANS 8:20-21

Walk around your neighborhood or a park and take
a small bag so you can pick up any trash you see.
Remember that even if you pick up only one piece of
trash, your care of the earth pleases the Lord.

Notice the death and decay around you.

What does it feel like to play a small part in helping
restore and care for God's earth?

Shrinking Your Footprint

❖

The earth is the Lord's, and everything in it. The world
and all its people belong to him. For he laid the earth's
foundation on the seas and built it on the ocean depths.

PSALM 24:1-2

How often do you forget that everything on the earth belongs to God? Ask him if he would like you to do something from the following list as a way to decrease your environmental footprint:

+ Walk or bike once in a while instead of driving
+ Recycle
+ Compost
+ Conserve water by only running full dishwashers and washing machines
+ Turn off lights when you leave a room
+ Switch to more energy-efficient lightbulbs
+ Use jars or reusable containers instead of plastic bags
+ Buy local produce or start growing your own

July
23

Less Is More

Jesus prayed this prayer: "O Father, Lord of heaven
and earth, thank you for hiding these things from
those who think themselves wise and clever,
and for revealing them to the childlike."

MATTHEW 11:25

Success is often measured by how much we own and how busy our
schedules are. However, God calls his followers to a different way
of life—one that resists the "more is better" mentality and instead
focuses on our purpose for being on this earth. The practice of simplicity is about letting go of things that clutter and complicate your life in
order to keep your focus on the kind of life Jesus says is most fulfilling.
Simplicity is not about getting rid of all your things but rather about
experiencing freedom from being a slave to them.

This week will challenge you to practice simplicity in multiple areas:
your possessions, eating habits, speech, schedules, and relationships.
The areas that feel difficult to simplify are likely the areas to which you
have become too attached. Allow God to help you experience freedom
this week as you refocus on what really matters.

Treasuring Simplicity

◆

[Jesus said,] "Don't store up treasures here on earth,
where moths eat them and rust destroys them, and
where thieves break in and steal. Store your treasures
in heaven, where moths and rust cannot destroy, and
thieves do not break in and steal. Wherever your treasure
is, there the desires of your heart will also be."

MATTHEW 6:19-21

This week, if a person compliments you on something
you own or are wearing, give the item to him or her.

It could be a piece of jewelry or something small in
your home.

This is actually a common practice in many cultures.

What does it feel like to give away something you
treasure?

July
25

Eating Simply

✦

Not that I was ever in need, for I have learned how to
be content with whatever I have. I know how to live
on almost nothing or with everything. I have learned
the secret of living in every situation, whether it is
with a full stomach or empty, with plenty or little.

PHILIPPIANS 4:11-12

Simplify your eating for the rest of the week.
    For example, if you usually have two sides with
dinner, limit it to one.
    Or if you have meat every night, choose to eat it only
one night this week.
    Ask the Lord to show you how your eating habits have
become excessive or complicated.

Simple as That

—————————— ✦ ——————————

Just say a simple, "Yes, I will," or "No, I won't."
Anything beyond this is from the evil one.

MATTHEW 5:37

————————————————————

Read the above verse with your own life in mind.
How often do you say yes and later regret it?

To simplify your life and schedule this week, practice
saying no or asking, "Can I get back to you?"

When someone asks you to do something, take time
to pray about it before committing to an answer.

This week, your default answer should be no unless
God is clearly telling you otherwise.

Don't Overcomplicate It

One day an expert in religious law stood up to test Jesus by asking him this question: "Teacher, what should I do to inherit eternal life?" Jesus replied, "What does the law of Moses say? How do you read it?" The man answered, "'You must love the LORD your God with all your heart, all your soul, all your strength, and all your mind.' And, 'Love your neighbor as yourself.'" "Right!" Jesus told him. "Do this and you will live!"

LUKE 10:25-28

Think about the simplicity of Jesus' words.

In what ways have you complicated your relationship with God?

Do you try to work for God's favor?

Are your prayers full of excuses or unnecessary words?

Have certain rituals in your life become more like superstitions?

How might God be using these verses to guide you toward simplicity in your relationship with him?

Concern Yourself with One Thing

✦

The Lord said to her, "My dear Martha, you are worried
and upset over all these details! There is only one thing
worth being concerned about. Mary has discovered
it, and it will not be taken away from her."

LUKE 10:41-42

What details are making you fret today?
The clothes you are wearing?
Your messy home?
The amount of money in your bank account?
How might these things be distracting you from
focusing on what really matters?
What is the "little" thing you are most anxious about?
Write it on a piece of paper.
Then crumple the paper up and throw it in the gar-
bage as you ask God to free you from your anxiety over
this.

July
29

Living the Simple Life

---◆---

Beware! Guard against every kind of greed. Life
is not measured by how much you own.

LUKE 12:15

Take ten minutes today to simplify your possessions.
Go through your closet and give away three things
you don't often wear—clothing, shoes, belts, scarves.

Or find the things in your garage, closet, or storage area
that you keep "just in case," and give one of them away.

This exercise will be a good indicator of how attached
you are to your possessions. And it will help you become
familiar with your nearest Goodwill, Salvation Army, or
other collection center.

How did it feel to simplify your life over the past
several days?

Which reflections or exercises freed you up the most?

Ask the Lord how he might want you to continue
living simply.

July
30

Take Time to Think

---◆---

Study this Book of Instruction continually.
Meditate on it day and night.

JOSHUA 1:8

In our culture, the word *meditation* has become associated with
Eastern spirituality and mysticism. However, the concept of meditation is mentioned throughout the Bible. Joshua talks about meditating
on God's law day and night (see Joshua 1:8). David prayed that his
meditations would be pleasing to God (see Psalm 19:14). Meditation
is mentioned several times in the Psalms (see Psalm 63:6; 145:5). The
practice of meditation involves deeply pondering God's Word and what it
reveals about him.

How would your life be different if you strove daily to fill your mind
with thoughts about God and his Word? This week will encourage you
to think deeply about God's Word, his actions, and his presence in your
life. It may be difficult for you to stay focused. Meditation often involves
directing and redirecting your thoughts toward God. Take time to read
slowly through each Scripture verse. Do your best to let go of the thoughts
that preoccupy your mind so that you can better focus on being in God's
presence and soaking in his Word.

Meditate on God's Splendor

✦

I will meditate on your majestic, glorious
splendor and your wonderful miracles.

PSALM 145:5

Read this verse again slowly and think of a wonderful
miracle God has done in your life.

Spend some time reflecting on that experience.

What did you feel in that moment?

What did you learn about God's character?

If you have trouble thinking of a miracle, consider all
the ones you may take for granted—for example, think
about how your body heals after an injury, or how that
"close call" may have been God protecting you, or the
miracle of a new baby.

Meditate on God's Word

Let all that I am praise the LORD; may I never forget the
good things he does for me. He forgives all my sins and
heals all my diseases. He redeems me from death and
crowns me with love and tender mercies. He fills my life
with good things. My youth is renewed like the eagle's!

PSALM 103:2-5

Prayerfully and *slowly* read through the passage above
three times, using the steps below.

1. The first time you read it, choose one word or
   phrase that jumps out to you. What made it
   stand out?
2. During the second reading, ask yourself what you
   are feeling—either in general or about who God
   is—as you read this passage.
3. For the third reading, ask the Lord if there is
   anything he would like to say to you or teach
   you from this passage.

Meditate on God's Great Deeds

---◆---

He has given me a new song to sing, a hymn of praise
to our God. Many will see what he has done and be
amazed. They will put their trust in the LORD.

PSALM 40:3

I remember the days of old. I ponder all your great
works and think about what you have done.

PSALM 143:5

Meditate on three great works God has done in your life.
Take some time to really think about these and
write them down. Do you notice any themes in the way
he has worked with you?

Aug
3

Meditate on God's Presence

———————— ✦ ————————

Those who are dominated by the sinful nature think
about sinful things, but those who are controlled by the
Holy Spirit think about things that please the Spirit.

ROMANS 8:5

————————————————————

Set an alarm to go off three times today.

When you hear the alarm, take note of what you
are thinking at that moment.

Practice redirecting your thoughts to God and his
presence by simply talking to him about what is on your
mind right then.

Ask his Spirit to control your thoughts by reminding
you to give them over to God.

This exercise is about training your mind to focus
more on God than on things that are less important, or
things you know you shouldn't be thinking about.

Aug
4

Meditate on God's Unfailing Love

✦

O God, we meditate on your unfailing love
as we worship in your Temple.

PSALM 48:9

O my Strength, to you I sing praises, for you, O God,
are my refuge, the God who shows me unfailing love.

PSALM 59:17

You thrill me, LORD, with all you have done for me!
I sing for joy because of what you have done.

PSALM 92:4

Sing a hymn or worship song to God today (in the shower, in the car, or alone at home).

As you sing the words, meditate on what they say about who God is.

Take notice of how this kind of meditation impacts your attitude throughout the day.

Meditate in Prayer

❖

May the words of my mouth and the meditation of my heart
be pleasing to you, O LORD, my rock and my redeemer.

PSALM 19:14

Use the Jesus Prayer to help your mind focus exclusively on God and being in his presence. The Jesus Prayer reads, "Jesus Christ, Son of God, have mercy on me, a sinner."

This simple prayer is intended to help you refocus your heart back on God and is based on Luke 17:13, Luke 18:38, and Matthew 6:7-8.

When you pray this prayer, breathe in deeply as you say, "Jesus Christ, Son of God" and slowly exhale as you say, "Have mercy on me, a sinner."

Repeat this prayer several times and allow the words to sink into your heart.

How might this exercise help you focus on God in times of anger, anxiety, or fear?

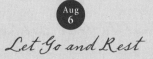

Aug
6

Let Go and Rest

✦

On the seventh day God had finished his work of creation,
so he rested from all his work. And God blessed the
seventh day and declared it holy, because it was the
day when he rested from all his work of creation.

GENESIS 2:2-3

For many, the Sabbath has become a day to catch up on chores or
prepare for the week ahead. But God wants you to focus on *rest*.
So why is it so important to take a day off from work?

You need a break from your normal routine in order to enjoy renewal
of body, mind, and spirit and to spend time with God and his people.

Keeping Sabbath calls you to set aside one day a week to embrace
rest so you have space to worship and enjoy God.

Practicing Sabbath calls you to let go of your busy life and to-do list
for twenty-four hours and to trust God with the things left undone.

Since the Sabbath is only one day, the other six days of this week
will involve reflection and preparation for the upcoming Sabbath.

WEEK 32 // DAY 1

What Is Your Sabbath?

◆

Remember to observe the Sabbath day by keeping it holy. You have six days each week for your ordinary work, but the seventh day is a Sabbath day of rest dedicated to the LORD your God.

EXODUS 20:8-10

How different does your Sabbath look from the other six days of the week?

What barriers make it difficult for you to keep the Sabbath?

Busyness?

Work?

Preparing for the upcoming week?

Other obligations?

Take a few moments to have a conversation with the Lord about this.

You are not trying to come to any conclusions right now; just talk to God about the Sabbath, why you struggle to keep it, why it is important to him, and anything else he brings to mind.

Start the Day with Rest

--- ✦ ---

Work six days only, and rest the seventh; this is to give your oxen
and donkeys a rest, as well as the people of your household.

EXODUS 23:12, TLB

Historically, Sabbath begins at sundown and continues until sundown of the following day.

Allow this biblical view of time to change the way you begin and end your days this week. As you fall into bed, view your sleep as the beginning of a new day.

What thoughts, attitudes, and prayers might God ask you to "start" each day with as you fall asleep?

Saying Yes to Rest

The Pharisees asked Jesus, "Does the law permit a person
to work by healing on the Sabbath?" (They were hoping he
would say yes, so they could bring charges against him.)
And he answered, "If you had a sheep that fell into a well on
the Sabbath, wouldn't you work to pull it out? Of course you
would. And how much more valuable is a person than a sheep!
Yes, the law permits a person to do good on the Sabbath."

MATTHEW 12:10-12

Write out a plan to keep the upcoming Sabbath holy
and set apart from the rest of the week.

What things do you think God would like you to say
yes to on that day—perhaps activities that help restore
and reset you?

Worship?

Extended time in God's Word?

Enjoying friends?

Aug
10

Saying No to Busyness

---- ✦ ----

Keep the Sabbath day holy. Don't pursue your own
interests on that day, but enjoy the Sabbath and
speak of it with delight as the LORD's holy day.

ISAIAH 58:13

Continue to write your plan for the upcoming
Sabbath.

What personal interests might God be asking you to
say no to on that day?

Perhaps activities that drain you, like work?

Running errands?

Preparing for the upcoming week?

Obligatory social events?

Resist the temptation to feel guilty for saying no by
reminding yourself that God desires this day to be set
apart for resting with him.

Worry-Free Sabbath

✦

I gave them my Sabbath days of rest as a sign between
them and me. It was to remind them that I am the
LORD, who had set them apart to be holy.

EZEKIEL 20:12

How can you rest from worry this Sabbath?
Make a list of things that promote stress
and anxiety in you, such as checking e-mail, budgeting, making to-do lists for the week, or having a tense
conversation.

When you find yourself tempted to engage in one of
these things, ask the Lord to help you relax instead.

How might refraining from worrisome activities help
you focus better on enjoying the Lord that day?

What Is God Doing on the Sabbath?

✦

Jesus said to them, "The Sabbath was made to meet the needs of people, and not people to meet the requirements of the Sabbath."

MARK 2:27

Scholar Eugene H. Peterson said, "If you don't take a Sabbath, something is wrong. You're doing too much, you're being too much in charge. You've got to quit, one day a week, and just watch what God is doing when you're not doing anything."[14]

Read the above verse again slowly with this quote in mind. Then ask the Lord what need of yours he desires to meet by giving you a Sabbath.

A need for rest?

Worship?

Surrender?

Comfort?

Healing?

End the week by thanking God that he cares enough to meet your needs through the Sabbath.

Aug 13

Choose to Trust

—◆—

You are God, O Sovereign LORD. Your words are truth, and
you have promised these good things to your servant.

2 SAMUEL 7:28

Do you tend to dwell on problems and give in to worry? Many of us
spend too much of our time fretting over things we cannot control.

Trusting God, however, means believing that he loves you, that
he's absolutely good, and that he wants to do good things in your life.
Growing your trust in God begins when you determine the places where
it is difficult to trust him and then choose to let them go into his care.

The exercises this week will help you wrestle with the areas where
trust is hard for you. They will encourage you to bring these areas before
God, cast your cares on him, and embrace trusting God one day at a time.

Trusting God is not only a moment-by-moment decision; it is a
lifelong process. Go to God as a little child and tell him your worries and
fears. Watch how he transforms your heart when you choose to believe
his promise that he has everything under control.

Needing to Trust

✦

Trust in the LORD with all your heart; do not depend
on your own understanding. Seek his will in all you
do, and he will show you which path to take.

PROVERBS 3:5-6

We learn to trust God when we put ourselves in
situations where we *need* to trust him.

What is something that you deeply desire to trust God
with?

The safety and care of your family?

Your finances?

Your job?

A difficult or stressful situation?

Prayerfully ask God how he might be urging you to
step out in faith and trust him today.

Do Not Be Afraid

✦

Be strong and courageous! Do not be afraid and do not
panic before them. For the LORD your God will personally
go ahead of you. He will neither fail you nor abandon you.

DEUTERONOMY 31:6

W hat event in the near future are you worried about?
What about that situation is stressing you out?

Take a few moments to imagine God already waiting
for you when you get there.

He has gone ahead of you.

Imagine him saying, "It's okay. I already know what is
ahead, and I will be there to help you."

How does this make you feel when you think about
getting to that situation?

Hand It Over to God

◆

Seek the Kingdom of God above all else, and live
righteously, and he will give you everything you need.
So don't worry about tomorrow, for tomorrow will bring
its own worries. Today's trouble is enough for today.

MATTHEW 6:33-34

Write down something that currently worries you.
Then read what you wrote.

With the above verse in mind, how do you think God
views this worry?

Tuck the paper in your Bible by today's verse as a way
to symbolize that you are giving that worry over to the
Lord for this day.

What Are You Afraid Of?

❖

You heard me when I cried, "Listen to my pleading! Hear my cry for help!" Yes, you came when I called; you told me, "Do not fear."

LAMENTATIONS 3:56-57

M ost worries result from being afraid of something that may or may not happen.

Fear does more to paralyze you than almost anything else:

It keeps you from joy.

It takes away your peace of mind.

It doesn't allow you to move ahead.

Read the verse again and think about the one thing you are most afraid of.

Listen to God speaking these words to you: *Do not fear. Do not fear.*

How do God's words impact your fears in this moment?

How can you carry these words with you throughout today?

Pour Out Your Heart

My victory and honor come from God alone. He is my refuge,
a rock where no enemy can reach me. O my people, trust in him
at all times. Pour out your heart to him, for God is our refuge.

PSALM 62:7-8

Pour out your heart to God about a situation that has consumed, or will consume, your thoughts.

Write on a piece of paper or type on your computer for several minutes without stopping and just see what comes out.

Don't try to filter your words; just write continuously.

Then read back your prayers, and end the time by asking God for guidance, peace, and perspective on this situation.

Empty Worry

◆

When I am afraid, I will put my trust in you.

PSALM 56:3

Nazi concentration camp survivor Corrie ten Boom stated, "Worry does not empty tomorrow of its sorrows; it empties today of its strength."[15]

Think about a worry that is currently on your mind. Engage your body in prayer by holding out your hands and making fists as you pray about this concern.

When you are done praying, open your hands to symbolize releasing control of this issue to God.

As you finish this week of practicing trust in God, think about the areas where have you made progress.

What aspect has been most difficult for you?

The Greatest Story

---◆---

Jesus called out to them, "Come, follow me, and
I will show you how to fish for people!"

MARK 1:17

Some of Jesus' last words on earth were about witnessing. He said
to his disciples, "You will be my witnesses, telling people about
me everywhere—in Jerusalem, throughout Judea, in Samaria, and to
the ends of the earth" (Acts 1:8).

To "witness" simply means to tell others about something you have
experienced. Your story of how you met and grew to love Jesus is the
greatest story you can ever tell.

Most of the exercises this week will encourage you to grow as a witness through prayer, preparation, and practice.

Remember that this week is not about leading others to Christ—
although that is always a desired outcome! The two main goals of these
exercises are for you to better articulate your own story and to grow in
courage to tell it.

What's Your Story?

✦

If someone asks about your hope as a
believer, always be ready to explain it.

1 PETER 3:15

We must be familiar with our own stories in order
to be ready to explain them to others.

Write down a few sentences about why you have
placed your hope in Jesus.

Don't worry about the wording or the order in which
everything happened—just write from your heart.

After you've finished, ask yourself whether this was
easy or difficult.

If it was especially difficult, then keep working
on your story over the next several days until you
feel assured that you could confidently share it with
someone else.

What Holds You Back?

One night the Lord spoke to Paul in a vision and told him,
"Don't be afraid! Speak out! Don't be silent! For I am with you."

ACTS 18:9-10

What hinders you from telling others about how you met Jesus and why you follow him?

Is it fear of rejection?

Lack of confidence?

Feeling like your story isn't good enough?

Take a few moments to talk to God about this.

Choose one specific word to pray for this week: "Lord, as I practice witnessing this week, help me to be _____ (brave, unafraid, confident, etc.)."

WEEK 34 // DAYS 2 & 3

Aug 23

Never Be Ashamed

✦

God has not given us a spirit of fear and timidity, but of
power, love, and self-discipline. So never be ashamed to tell
others about our Lord. . . . With the strength God gives you,
be ready to suffer with me for the sake of the Good News.

2 TIMOTHY 1:7-8

Think of someone whom you desperately want to
know Jesus. Put their name somewhere you will see
it frequently to remind you to pray for them.

How can you intentionally create an opportunity to
share the life and love of Jesus with them?

Perhaps by doing something kind for them, telling
them you are praying for them, or speaking truth into
their life?

Sing of His Faithfulness

I will sing of the LORD's unfailing love forever!
Young and old will hear of your faithfulness.

PSALM 89:1

Read the verse again. Then reflect on something that God has done in your life recently and write a few sentences to post on social media.

For example, what could you thank God for?

What has he brought you through?

How has he answered your prayers over the past year?

What have you recently learned about who God is?

If you don't use social media, find a way to work your reflections into a conversation today.

Growing in Boldness

❖

[Jesus said,] "I tell you the truth, everyone who
acknowledges me publicly here on earth, the Son of Man
will also acknowledge in the presence of God's angels."

LUKE 12:8

The members of the council were amazed when they saw the
boldness of Peter and John, for they could see that they were
ordinary men with no special training in the Scriptures. They
also recognized them as men who had been with Jesus.

ACTS 4:13

Grow in boldness by mentioning in a conversation
with an unbelieving friend or acquaintance that you
follow Jesus.

This may not be an easy thing to do, but ask the Lord
to make you confident as you step out in faith.

Write out these verses above and put them somewhere visible to remind you to be bold with those in
your life who don't know Jesus.

Witness with Your Life

❖

Be careful to live properly among your unbelieving
neighbors. Then even if they accuse you of doing wrong,
they will see your honorable behavior, and they will
give honor to God when he judges the world.

1 PETER 2:12

Over the past week, what have you learned about
your own story with Jesus?

How have you grown in courage to share your story
with others?

End this week by asking the Lord to empower you to
fulfill his great commission by continuing to tell others
about him through your words and actions.

Aug
27

Letting Go for Something Greater

---+---

Everyone who has given up houses or brothers or sisters or
father or mother or children or property, for my sake, will receive
a hundred times as much in return and will inherit eternal life.

MATTHEW 19:29

Sacrifice is not just giving things up; rather, it is a kind of substitution. You give up one thing to obtain something of greater value.
You relinquish something you think you need or that makes you feel
secure and instead rely on God to provide what he knows you need.

Sometimes God will ask you to give up material possessions, attitudes, comfort, time, desires, or habits so you can better experience
them in the context of his plans and presence.

Over the next several days, you will reflect on the sacrifices the Lord
may be asking you to make in order to experience the better gifts he
wants to give you in return.

It will be hard if you look only at the sacrifice involved. Remind
yourself of the flip side of sacrifice and trust that God has something
even greater in store for you as you learn to let go.

The Cost of Sacrifice

✦

While Jesus was in the Temple, he watched the rich people dropping their gifts in the collection box. Then a poor widow came by and dropped in two small coins. "I tell you the truth," Jesus said, "this poor widow has given more than all the rest of them. For they have given a tiny part of their surplus, but she, poor as she is, has given everything she has."

LUKE 21:1-4

True sacrifice costs something.

Take a moment to pray over what the Lord may be asking you to sacrificially give away this week.

It may not be money or material possessions.

It may be time that you had planned to enjoy working on a hobby.

It may be a habit.

How might this stretch you to rely on God?

Aug
29

A Sacrifice of Praise

Let us offer through Jesus a continual sacrifice of praise
to God, proclaiming our allegiance to his name.

HEBREWS 13:15

Sometimes a continual sacrifice of praise requires us
to give up attitudes that hinder or distract us from
thanking God.

What would it mean for you to offer "a continual
sacrifice of praise to God" today?

What feelings or attitudes might God be asking you
to give up so that you can better praise him?

Anger?

Resentment?

Bitterness?

Self-pity?

Vow to let go of those attitudes for today. If you find
yourself engaging in them, use it as a reminder to praise
God instead.

The Sacrifice to Make after Sin

◆

The sacrifice you desire is a broken spirit. You will
not reject a broken and repentant heart, O God.

P SALM 51:17

King David wrote this psalm after he committed
adultery with Bathsheba and arranged for her husband's murder. David is saying that the only sacrifice
one can offer to God after sinning is a broken, repentant
spirit. You sacrifice your pride, and in return God gives
you his mercy and forgiveness, which leads to a restored
relationship with him. Your sacrifice is always less than
what God gives in return.

Are you able to sacrifice your pride, rationalizations,
and excuses, or do you try to make other "sacrifices" to
appease him? For example, do you read your Bible after
you explode with anger, or give to the church after spending money on something that doesn't honor God? These
activities may help us refocus our hearts, but we must
never use them to simply assuage any guilt we may feel.

Aug
31

A Sacrifice of Thanks

✦

Let us come to him with thanksgiving. Let us
sing psalms of praise to him. For the LORD is
a great God, a great King above all gods.

PSALM 95:2-3

I will offer you a sacrifice of thanksgiving
and call on the name of the LORD.

PSALM 116:17

Sometimes thanking God for our trials feels like a
sacrifice.

Perhaps that is because it is hard to let go of feelings
of anger, resentment, or entitlement that have become
a comfortable habit.

For what difficult situation can you offer a sacrifice
of thanksgiving to God?

If it feels too difficult to thank God for your trials
right now, try instead to thank him simply for who he is.

Sacrifice for God's Word

I plead with you to give your bodies to God because
of all he has done for you. Let them be a living and
holy sacrifice—the kind he will find acceptable.

ROMANS 12:1

While you are reading this devotional, you are sacrificing a certain amount of time in order to engage with it. You are disciplining your body and mind to give up something else in order to do this.

Sacrifice five more minutes of your time right now by opening your Bible to Psalm 28 and enjoying the Lord and his Word.

Offering Moments to God

❖

As for me, my life has already been poured
out as an offering to God.

2 TIMOTHY 4:6

Practice offering your life to God today by sacrificing
the need for immediate gratification.

As you go through the day, be aware of when you
want to satisfy an impulse, such as a craving for choco-
late, the urge to turn on the TV, or a desire to check your
social media. Then spend a minute to sacrifice that desire
or impulse to the Lord.

See if he has something better in mind for you, or
just enjoy an extra minute in his presence. Expect him to
speak to your heart.

As you conclude these days of practicing sacrifice,
when has God graciously allowed you to experience
blessing from sacrifice this past week?

Sep
3

Lead with the Body

Pray like this . . .

MATTHEW 6:9

When prayer becomes stale or feels like we are just "going through the motions," it can be helpful to do something different.

One way to do this is to use our bodies during prayer. Different postures help us physically express the attitudes of our hearts to God.

The postures in the exercises over the next week will use your body to move your heart toward a place of humility, boldness, submission, gratitude, reverence, and worship.

Communication with God does not require a certain physical position, and God won't be more likely to answer your prayers because you are on your knees rather than sitting. But remember that the body and heart are very much connected. Often when you lead with the body, the heart will follow.

This week's exercises may feel unnatural for you. Lean into the discomfort and be honest with God about what you feel as you engage in these exercises. Ask God to open the posture of your heart as you use your body in prayer.

Face Down

✦

Moses and Aaron turned away from the people and
went to the entrance of the Tabernacle, where they
fell face down on the ground. Then the glorious
presence of the LORD appeared to them.

NUMBERS 20:6

Lying down before the Lord with our faces toward the
ground puts our hearts in a posture of humility.

Begin today prostrate before God, confessing your
tendency toward sin and recognizing the depth of your
need for his mercy, forgiveness, and provision.

Realize your inadequacy and your inability to live this
day apart from him.

If there is a certain crisis in your life, acknowledge
that God is the only one who can deliver you.

Stand Up

Solomon stood before the altar of the Lord in
front of the entire community of Israel. He lifted
his hands toward heaven, and he prayed.

1 Kings 8:22-23

Standing before a king means that you have been legally justified to be in his presence.

When you stand in prayer, it reflects confidence in your place of undeserved privilege before God because of Christ (see Romans 5:2).

Stand boldly before God in prayer today.

Thank him that you can stand before him clothed in righteousness because of what Christ has done.

End the prayer by telling him what you are confidently and joyfully looking forward to in eternity with him.

Sit Down

King David went in and sat before the LORD and prayed.

2 SAMUEL 7:18

In Scripture, sitting signifies having a permanent relationship with God and enjoying his presence.

When you sit before God, you acknowledge your place of belonging in his family. Christ has saved you a seat next to him in heaven at the banquet table because you have been adopted by God (see Ephesians 2:6).

Sit with God in prayer today.

Thank him for adopting you as his own and giving you a place of permanent belonging.

Continue on in prayer, imagining what it will feel like to sit with Jesus at his table in heaven.

Kneel before Him

When Solomon finished making these prayers and petitions to
the LORD, he stood up in front of the altar of the LORD, where
he had been kneeling with his hands raised toward heaven.

1 KINGS 8:54

King Solomon knelt before God and prayed for the
Temple and the entire congregation of Israel.

When you ask God for help, kneeling before him puts
your heart in an attitude of submission.

Kneeling signifies that no matter how he chooses to
answer your prayers, you can trust that it is the best thing
for you.

Kneel before the Lord today and begin your prayer by
acknowledging that he is Lord of all the earth.

Present your requests to him and end your prayer by
asking that his will be done.

Look Up

They rolled the stone aside. Then Jesus looked up to
heaven and said, "Father, thank you for hearing me."

JOHN 11:41

The Bible mentions several times that Jesus looked up
to heaven and prayed.

When you look someone in the face, it shows that you
have an intimate relationship with them. You trust that
person enough to be honest and open with them.

Lift your face to God in prayer today.

Acknowledge that he is your trusted helper, friend,
and confidant.

Tell him about something on your heart that you
would say only to a very close friend.

Raise Your Hands

Lift your hands toward the sanctuary, and praise
the LORD. May the LORD, who made heaven
and earth, bless you from Jerusalem.

PSALM 134:2-3

Raising your hands in prayer symbolizes seeking
God's mercy and blessing.

When you raise your hands, you reflect a readiness
to receive all God has for you today, and you remember
all his provisions in the past.

Raise your hands to God in prayer.

Thank him specifically for how he blessed you
yesterday, and humbly ask him to help you see his
blessings today.

Sep
10

Step Away and Take a Pause

The LORD is my shepherd; I have all that I need. He lets
me rest in green meadows; he leads me beside peaceful
streams. He renews my strength. He guides me.

PSALM 23:1-3

We live, in fact, in a world starved for solitude, silence, and privacy, and therefore starved for meditation and true friendship," wrote C. S. Lewis.[16]

Solitude involves intentionally stepping away from normal human interaction in order to grow in friendship with the Lord. We do not enter solitude to *do* things for God; we enter solitude to simply *be* with God. Solitude helps us pause regularly from work, endless activity, and overwhelming obligations to focus on God. Many of us avoid and even fear being alone—perhaps because without our distractions and defenses, we are left to face ourselves in the light of God's truth.

As you practice solitude this week, you may experience feelings of confusion, distraction, irrational fear, emptiness, or even condemnation. If this happens, acknowledge these feelings before God and remember his promise to always be with you.

Just Be with Me

❖

Before daybreak the next morning, Jesus got up
and went out to an isolated place to pray.

MARK 1:35

What small spaces of alone time are already incorporated into your day—time spent showering? Driving? Exercising? Mowing the lawn? Cooking?

Choose one of those times to dedicate to being alone with God. Before you do this, turn off any additional noise that may compete for your attention.

Don't try to make anything happen; simply use the time and space to focus on being in God's presence and to talk to him about whatever comes to mind.

Step Back to Draw Close

✦

Immediately after this, Jesus insisted that his disciples get
back into the boat and head across the lake to Bethsaida,
while he sent the people home. After telling everyone
good-bye, he went up into the hills by himself to pray.

MARK 6:45-46

Read the verses and think about what it might have
been like for Jesus to send away his disciples in
order to be alone.

Which relationships are difficult to step back from in
order to spend time alone with God?

In the next few minutes of solitude, acknowledge this
tension in prayer and then offer that person or those
people to the Lord, trusting they are in his care.

A Walk with God

❖

When the cool evening breezes were blowing, the man and his wife heard the LORD God walking about in the garden. So they hid from the LORD God among the trees. Then the LORD God called to the man, "Where are you?" He replied, "I heard you walking in the garden, so I hid. I was afraid because I was naked."

GENESIS 3:8-10

Adam and Eve recognized the sound of God walking in the garden. Perhaps the evening was their special time to walk and talk together.

Schedule a time to take a walk alone with the Lord today—even if the walk is only five minutes.

Picture him being beside you.

Resist the urge to fill the time with any sounds or words, and just enjoy being in God's company.

The Role of Solitude in Decisions

One day soon afterward Jesus went up on a mountain to pray,
and he prayed to God all night. At daybreak he called together
all of his disciples and chose twelve of them to be apostles.

LUKE 6:12-13

Jesus made one of the most important decisions of his
ministry—choosing his disciples—after he spent time
alone praying to God.

What big decision or transition is coming up in your life?

Is it a financial decision?

Deciding whether or not to continue a ministry?

A difficult choice involving your children?

Schedule a time on your calendar right now to spend
an extended amount of time with God before you need
to finalize this upcoming decision.

Sitting in Silence with God

◆

The LORD is good to those who depend on him,
to those who search for him. So it is good to wait
quietly for salvation from the LORD.... Let them sit
alone in silence beneath the LORD's demands.

LAMENTATIONS 3:25-26, 28

What do you usually do when you spend time alone
with God?

Do you pray? Read your Bible? Journal?

As good as these activities are, sometimes they can
distract you from simply being with God.

Let go of "doing" and "producing" in your time with
God today. Don't try to make something happen—just
be yourself with the one who created you.

Sit in silence with God for at least five minutes.

Begin by praying, "Lord, I just want to be with you."
If distracting thoughts come to mind, jot them down to
deal with another time.

Your Special Place with God

———— ✦ ————

Accompanied by the disciples, Jesus left the upstairs
room and went as usual to the Mount of Olives.

LUKE 22:39

The Mount of Olives was a sacred space that Jesus
shared with God the Father.

Where are the special places of companionship between just you and God?

If you haven't had such a place, think of somewhere
you'd like to declare as your private space with him.

Perhaps you could choose a favorite room in your
home, a beautiful spot in nature, or the corner of a coffee
shop. (If you are having difficulty deciding on a location,
think about where you have felt closest to God in the past.)

Make it a habit to go to your special place regularly to
spend time with the Lord.

The Anchor of the Soul

✦

O Lord, you alone are my hope.

PSALM 71:5

There is a universal expectation for good in this life—even in the midst of adversity. The need or desire to trust that things will get better is what the concept of *hope* is all about.

When you long for life to get better, where do you place your hope—in your own abilities, good fortune, or help from others? Or does your hope come from trusting God? Only when you trust God with your future can true hope begin to grow, because he created you with a great future in mind.

This week you will practice hoping in God, not just experiencing hope itself. This will require addressing where your current hope lies and choosing instead to hope in God. Hope in God gives you confident joy in the face of uncertainty because it anchors your soul and future to him (see Hebrews 6:19).

Begin this week by being honest with God about your hopes. Many of these exercises involve meditating on God's wonderful promises in his Word and allowing these truths to grow your hope in him alone.

What Do You Hope For?

---- ✦ ----

Lord, where do I put my hope? My only hope is in you.

PSALM 39:7

How would you finish this statement: "I am hoping for ..."?

Are you hoping for a new job?

A new relationship?

A life change?

How would your happiness be affected if what you hoped for didn't happen?

Ask God what it would be like to let go of this hope.

How would this open you to your need for him?

Sep
19

Hope from God's Word

---   ✦   ---

Such things were written in the Scriptures long ago to teach
us. And the Scriptures give us hope and encouragement
as we wait patiently for God's promises to be fulfilled.

ROMANS 15:4

Read the introduction to this week one more time.
Then choose a Scripture that encourages you to
place your hope in God.

Write it down and post it somewhere visible this
week. (Suggestions: Romans 8:28; Lamentations 3:22-23;
2 Corinthians 5:17; Jeremiah 29:11.)

In Whom Is Your Confidence?

--- ✦ ---

Don't put your confidence in powerful people; there
is no help for you there. When they breathe their last,
they return to the earth, and all their plans die with
them. But joyful are those who have the God of Israel as
their helper, whose hope is in the LORD their God.

PSALM 146:3-5

Are there certain people you have come to rely on
more than God?

What qualities do they possess that make you trust them?

Do you have trouble believing that God possesses
those same trustworthy characteristics? Why?

Remember that God loves you and desires an authentic relationship with you, so take time to talk honestly
with him about what keeps you from fully trusting him.

Looking Back for Future Hope

---✦---

Now all glory to God, who is able, through his mighty power
at work within us, to accomplish infinitely more than we
might ask or think. Glory to him in the church and in Christ
Jesus through all generations forever and ever! Amen.

EPHESIANS 3:20-21

Write down a hope you have for the future.
    Now think back to a time when God did something that exceeded anything you could have ever hoped for.
    Write a prayer underneath your future hope, asking God to help you place your hope in him rather than in your own plans.
    This could be the start of a prayer journal to encourage you in difficult times.

Where Hope Is Most Needed

Let us hold tightly without wavering to the hope we
affirm, for God can be trusted to keep his promise.

HEBREWS 10:23

Read through God's promises listed below and ask
yourself which of them you need to hold most
tightly to today.

+ God's promise to be with you (see Deuteronomy 31:6)
  God's promise to always love you (see Romans 8:38)
+ God's promise to always be ready to help in times of
  distress (see Psalm 46:1)
+ God's promise to fulfill good plans for your life (see
  Jeremiah 29:11)
+ God's promise to secure your eternal salvation
  (see 1 John 4:9-10)

Once you have chosen a verse, read it aloud several
times until it really sinks in. Think of a situation that is
heavy on your heart. With this in mind, ask God to help
you hold tightly to the promise you just read.

Expect Great Things

✦

I am trusting you, O LORD, saying, "You are my God!"
My future is in your hands.... How great is the goodness
you have stored up for those who fear you.

PSALM 31:14-15, 19

R ead the verses again with your own future in mind.
Remind yourself not simply to desire good things
for your future, but to *expect* great things for your
future—because that's what God has promised you.

As you end this week of practicing "hope in God,"
thank him for having your future in his hands and for
the great things he has in store for you.

Sep
24

Wait and Watch

———— ✦ ————

As for me, I look to the LORD for help. I wait confidently
for God to save me, and my God will certainly hear me.

MICAH 7:7

————————————————

We are all waiting for something—a different job, a restored
relationship (or a new one), physical healing, a loved one to come
home, or things just to get better.

Each of us has prayers that remain unanswered. Seasons of waiting
can seem like a waste of time, but what if waiting is actually a gift?

The practice of "waiting well" is making the most of the time at
hand. The only way to grow into a person who "waits well" is through
experience—in other words, through a lot of waiting!

The next week focuses on learning from our seasons of waiting to be
more hopeful in God's plan for us, to be persistent in prayer, to be more
confident and courageous as we wait, and to resist the urge to rush
ahead of God's timing.

No matter how difficult or pointless waiting feels, trust that God will
use your waiting as a gift of time, not a waste of it.

Growing Your Hope

❖

Let all that I am wait quietly before God, for my hope
is in him. He alone is my rock and my salvation,
my fortress where I will not be shaken.

PSALM 62:5-6

Choose one thing you are currently waiting on the
Lord for. Think back to last week's practice of hope
and reflect on where you put your hope as you wait.

Do you place your hope in believing it will all work out?

In anticipation that God will answer your prayer in
the way you would like him to?

Or in confidence that God is already at work carrying
out the plan he knows is best for you?

What would it look like to hope only in God as
you wait, knowing that he is preparing you for what
lies ahead?

Growing Your Service

◆

Be still before the LORD and wait patiently for
him; do not fret when people succeed in their ways,
when they carry out their wicked schemes.

PSALM 37:7, NIV

Hymn writer P. Doddridge wrote, "Blest are the
humble souls, that wait with sweet submission to
his will; harmonious all their passions move, and in the
midst of storms are still."[17]

As you wait for God to do his work in situations you
can't control, don't be idle.

Serve him where you are, doing the little things right.

Ask God how he might want you to use your times of
waiting. Does he want you to be still?

To rejoice?

To read his Word?

To pray?

To serve someone else?

Growing Your Patience

✦

> Better to be patient than powerful; better to
> have self-control than to conquer a city.
>
> **PROVERBS 16:32**

Practice patience by intentionally putting yourself in a place where you need to wait a little longer.

For example, choose the longest checkout line at the store, drive in the slow lane, or make a recipe that takes longer to cook.

While you are waiting, reflect about what is going on inside your heart.

Are you anxious? Tense? Angry?

Use the time to talk to the Lord about what it feels like for you to wait.

Growing Your Perspective

---◆---

[God said,] "I will send terror ahead of you to drive out the
Hivites, Canaanites, and Hittites. But I will not drive them
out in a single year, because the land would become desolate
and the wild animals would multiply and threaten you.
I will drive them out a little at a time until your population
has increased enough to take possession of the land."

EXODUS 23:28-30

God's decision to slowly drive out the Hivites,
Canaanites, and Hittites was actually for the
Israelites' good so he could protect them and ultimately
provide more abundantly for them.

Was there ever a time when God didn't fully answer
your prayer right away?

As you look back, what blessings came during that
time of waiting?

What are you waiting for now?

How might your wait yield far better results than if
you got what you asked for now?

Growing Your Soul

✦

She called Mary aside from the mourners and told her,
"The Teacher is here and wants to see you." So Mary
immediately went to him.... When Mary arrived and
saw Jesus, she fell at his feet and said, "Lord, if only you
had been here, my brother would not have died."

JOHN 11:28-29, 32

Read this passage again. Imagine you are Mary and it
is your own brother who has died.

You have been waiting for Jesus to help your brother,
and now Jesus has finally arrived four days after his
death.

When Jesus asks to speak with you, what do you want
to say to him?

How does your response reveal how your heart
handles seasons of waiting?

Growing Your Confidence

I am confident I will see the Lᴏʀᴅ's goodness while I am
here in the land of the living. Wait patiently for the Lᴏʀᴅ.
Be brave and courageous. Yes, wait patiently for the Lᴏʀᴅ.

Pꜱᴀʟᴍ 27:13-14

Rejoice in our confident hope. Be patient
in trouble, and keep on praying.

Rᴏᴍᴀɴꜱ 12:12

Make a list of things you have waited for that God
eventually provided.

Now make another list of things you are currently
waiting on God for.

How do answered prayers from the past encourage
you to wait with patience and confidence in the present?

Oct 1

Enter into God's Story

Then Jesus told this story . . .

LUKE 13:6

Sometimes it is easy to fall into a routine of praying the same way until you "check out" and don't even realize what you are praying or to whom you are talking. How can you revitalize your prayer life?

Your imagination can be a powerful tool to help you engage with God in a new way. Imaginative prayer is an active way of praying that engages your mind and heart as you imagine yourself in a scene from Scripture. In his book *Prayer*, Richard Foster writes, "We begin to enter the story and make it our own. We move from detached observation to active participation."[18]

This week you will practice entering into Scripture with Jesus as you watch the story evolve. The instructions are the same for each day: Read the passage once, and then read it again—this time imagining yourself in the story.

Remember that your imagination is a gift from God. Ask the Holy Spirit to use this gift to deepen your relationship with Jesus as you experience him through his Word.

Blind Bartimaeus

✦

Bartimaeus . . . began to shout, "Jesus, Son of David, have mercy on me!" "Be quiet!" many of the people yelled at him. But he only shouted louder, "Son of David, have mercy on me!" When Jesus heard him, he stopped and said, "Tell him to come here." So they called the blind man. "Cheer up," they said. "Come on, he's calling you!" Bartimaeus threw aside his coat, jumped up, and came to Jesus. "What do you want me to do for you?" Jesus asked.

MARK 10:47-51

I magine yourself in the scene.

✦ Who are you? A main character or a bystander?

✦ Engage your senses. What do you see, smell, hear, taste, and feel?

✦ What emotions rise up as you imagine yourself in this scene?

✦ What do you want to say to Jesus in response to his question? Make this your prayer for today.

The Woman Who Couldn't Stop Bleeding

A woman who had suffered for twelve years with constant
bleeding came up behind him. She touched the fringe
of his robe, for she thought, "If I can just touch his robe,
I will be healed." Jesus turned around, and when he saw
her he said, "Daughter, be encouraged! Your faith has made
you well." And the woman was healed at that moment.

MATTHEW 9:20-22

Imagine yourself in the scene.

+ Who are you? A main character or a bystander?
+ Engage your senses. What do you see, smell, hear,
  taste, and feel?
+ What emotions rise up as you imagine yourself in this
  scene?
+ What do you want to say to Jesus? Make this your
  prayer for today.

The Sick Man by the Pool

---✦---

Inside the city, near the Sheep Gate, was the pool of Bethesda.
... One of the men lying there had been sick for thirty-eight
years. [Jesus] ... asked him, "Would you like to get well?" "I can't,
sir," the sick man said, "for I have no one to put me into
the pool when the water bubbles up. Someone else always
gets there ahead of me." Jesus told him, "Stand up, pick up
your mat, and walk!" Instantly, the man was healed!

JOHN 5:2, 5-9

Imagine yourself in the scene.

+ Who are you? A main character or a bystander?
+ Engage your senses. What do you see, smell, hear,
  taste, and feel?
+ What emotions rise up as you imagine yourself in this
  scene?
+ What do you want to say to Jesus? Make this your
  prayer for today.

Jesus Quiets a Storm

✦

Jesus got into the boat and started across the lake with his disciples. Suddenly, a fierce storm struck the lake, with waves breaking into the boat. But Jesus was sleeping. The disciples went and woke him up, shouting, "Lord, save us! We're going to drown!" Jesus responded, "Why are you afraid? You have so little faith!" Then he got up and rebuked the wind and waves, and suddenly there was a great calm. The disciples were amazed. "Who is this man?" they asked. "Even the winds and waves obey him!"

MATTHEW 8:23-27

I magine yourself in the scene.

✦ Who are you? A main character or a bystander?
✦ Engage your senses. What do you see, smell, hear, taste, and feel?
✦ What emotions rise up as you imagine yourself in this scene?
✦ What do you want to say to Jesus? Make this your prayer for today.

Jesus Dies on the Cross

Jesus shouted, "Father, I entrust my spirit into your hands!"
And with those words he breathed his last. When the
Roman officer overseeing the execution saw what had
happened, he worshiped God and said, "Surely this man
was innocent." And when all the crowd that came to see the
crucifixion saw what had happened, they went home in deep
sorrow. But Jesus' friends, including the women who had
followed him from Galilee, stood at a distance watching.

LUKE 23:46-49

Imagine yourself in the scene.

+ Who are you? A main character or a bystander?
+ Engage your senses. What do you see, smell, hear,
  taste, and feel?
+ What emotions rise up as you imagine yourself in this
  scene?
+ What do you want to say to Jesus? Make this your
  prayer for today.

Jesus Appears to His Disciples

---✦---

The two from Emmaus told their story of how Jesus had appeared to them. . . . And just as they were telling about it, Jesus himself was suddenly standing there among them. "Peace be with you," he said. But the whole group was startled and frightened, thinking they were seeing a ghost! "Why are you frightened?" he asked. "Why are your hearts filled with doubt?"

LUKE 24:35-38

I magine yourself in the scene.

✦ Who are you? A main character or a bystander?
✦ Engage your senses. What do you see, smell, hear, taste, and feel?
✦ What emotions rise up as you imagine yourself in this scene?
✦ What do you want to say to Jesus? Make this your prayer for today.

How have the last several days of practicing imaginative prayer changed your perspective on praying?

Oct
8

Can You Keep a Secret?

*When you pray, go away by yourself, shut the door
behind you, and pray to your Father in private. Then
your Father, who sees everything, will reward you.*

MATTHEW 6:6

Have you ever done something really kind for someone else and then wanted to slip it into a conversation with others? The practice of "secrecy" is keeping certain things just between you and God. Secrets are usually seen as bad, and sometimes they are. There are many places in Scripture, however, where the ability to keep a secret is an important character trait. Jesus asked those he healed to keep their interactions with him a secret. He spoke of the importance of keeping some prayers and good deeds secret in order to keep one's motives pure.

This week, you will practice secrecy in three different ways: first, by abstaining from telling others about your good deeds in order to deny yourself attention from them; second, by intentionally keeping the secrets of others in order to strengthen your trustworthiness; and third, by developing secrets with the Lord as a way to deepen your relationship with him.

Give Anonymously

❖

When you give to someone in need, don't let your left hand
know what your right hand is doing. Give your gifts in private,
and your Father, who sees everything, will reward you.

MATTHEW 6:3-4

Give to someone anonymously today.
For instance, pay for the person behind you at
the drive-through, leave an encouraging note on a wind-
shield, drop off a small gift on someone's desk or doorstep, or donate to a charity without telling anyone.

How does it feel to give gifts in secret?

Read the verse above again and ask yourself this question: "Is God's reward enough for me?"

Giving Motives

When you give to someone in need, don't do as the hypocrites
do—blowing trumpets in the synagogues and streets to
call attention to their acts of charity! I tell you the truth,
they have received all the reward they will ever get.

MATTHEW 6:2

Spend a few minutes with God reflecting on these questions:

+ Do you give so others can see how "spiritual" you are?
+ Do you mention your gifts or volunteer work in
  conversation to receive praise?
+ When you give, are you more focused on what others
  think about your gifts than on simply pleasing God?
+ Do you feel hurt, rejected, or disappointed when
  someone does not respond the way you want over a
  gift you have given them?

If you answered yes to any of these questions, what
can you do today to begin to change your attitude?

Prayer Motives

✦

When you pray, don't be like the hypocrites who
love to pray publicly on street corners and in the
synagogues where everyone can see them. I tell you
the truth, that is all the reward they will ever get.

MATTHEW 6:5

Spend a few minutes reflecting with God on the following questions:

✦ Do you pray or mention prayer in conversation so
people can see how "spiritual" you are?

✦ When you pray with others, are you more focused on
what they think or on simply pleasing God?

✦ Do you try to sound more intelligent, religious, or
passionate when you pray publicly than when you
pray alone?

As you did yesterday, if you answered yes to any of
these questions, what can you intentionally do today to
begin to change your attitude?

Instantly the leprosy disappeared, and the man was healed.
Then Jesus sent him on his way with a stern warning: "Don't
tell anyone about this. Instead, go to the priest and let him
examine you. Take along the offering required in the law
of Moses for those who have been healed of leprosy. This
will be a public testimony that you have been cleansed."

MARK 1:42-44

W hat secrets exist just between you and God?

Do you have a secret place you share together?

A favorite memory that only you and God know about?

A meaningful time of confession where you felt his
grace and forgiveness?

Spend some time reflecting on how these secret moments impact your intimacy with God.

What secret can you share with God today that you
have told no one else?

Oct
13

A Trustworthy Confidence

---- ✦ ----

A gossip goes around telling secrets, but those
who are trustworthy can keep a confidence.

PROVERBS 11:13

When arguing with your neighbor, don't betray another
person's secret. Others may accuse you of gossip, and
you will never regain your good reputation.

PROVERBS 25:9-10

Make a commitment before the Lord that you will
keep the secrets others have entrusted to you.

Ask him to prompt your conscience when you are
tempted to share secrets.

Pray right now for strength to control your tongue so
you can be a trustworthy confidant.

Bragging Rights

---✦---

Don't be selfish; don't try to impress others. Be humble,
thinking of others as better than yourselves.

PHILIPPIANS 2:3

What situations or people most tempt you to brag
about your actions, achievements, or talents?

What is your motive for doing this?

Is it to feel like you measure up?

To gain approval?

To feel better about yourself?

Take a few moments to confess this to God.

End these exercises on secrecy by telling God about a
need you have. Don't tell anyone else about it.

Write down this secret need so that when God decides
to meet it, you will know it was because of him and not
someone else.

Open Your Home and Your Heart

Don't forget to show hospitality to strangers, for some who
have done this have entertained angels without realizing it!

HEBREWS 13:2

Many people avoid hospitality because they feel that their homes or
cooking skills are inadequate. Some may find it difficult to share
their time, space, and resources. Jesus didn't have a home, yet he was
constantly welcoming people into his presence.

We are called to do likewise with the resources we have—to graciously receive others into our homes, feed them, and make them feel
welcome. Hospitality is about becoming a safe person and cultivating
a safe space in which others can experience the welcoming presence of
God. It is a way to obey and serve God, because God calls us to love and
serve others as though we are serving him.

This week, set aside your own expectations and insecurities in order
to practice hospitality. Don't just open your home to entertain others—
embrace them fully by giving them your presence and sharing your life
with them. Remember that it is your presence, not your presentation,
that makes others feel welcome.

Put Out the Welcome Mat

❖

Cheerfully share your home with those
who need a meal or a place to stay.

1 PETER 4:9

How can you "cheerfully" practice hospitality this week?
Can you cook dinner for someone without
complaining?

Open your home without fretting over the mess?

Graciously allow others into your space?

Thank God for your friends and your home as you
prepare for their arrival?

Ask God whom he would like you to invite over.

Call, text, or e-mail that person today to set up a time
to have them over for a meal, a cup of coffee, or dessert.

Prayer Preparation

As soon as they arrived, they prayed for these new believers.

A C T S   8 : 1 5

The people of the island were very kind to us. It was cold
and rainy, so they built a fire on the shore to welcome us.

A C T S   2 8 : 2

There are many things we can do to welcome others into our homes. But one thing we often forget to do as we prepare for others is to pray.

Get in the practice of praying for others before they arrive at your home.

Think through the week ahead and pray for those who may come through your doors, such as family members, neighbors, out-of-town visitors, or people doing work on your home.

Write down their names and spend a few moments praying that each person who enters your home will feel peace and the welcoming presence of Jesus through you.

Oct
18

A Place in Your Father's House

[Jesus said,] "Don't let your hearts be troubled. Trust in
God, and trust also in me. There is more than enough
room in my Father's home. If this were not so, would I have
told you that I am going to prepare a place for you?"

JOHN 14:1-2

Hospitality is close to God's heart—so much so that he
has promised to prepare a room especially for you.

Close your eyes and imagine walking into the room
Jesus has prepared just for you in his heavenly home.

How do you picture it?

What details has God included that he knew you
would like?

What kind of host is God?

As you consider how God prepares for you, what
special thing can you prepare to let your guests know you
were looking forward to hosting them?

Feeling Welcomed

May the Lord show special kindness to Onesiphorus and
all his family because he often visited and encouraged me.
He was never ashamed of me because I was in chains.

2 TIMOTHY 1:16

Author Jen Wilkin describes the difference between
entertaining and hospitality by stating, "Entertaining
seeks to *impress*. Hospitality seeks to *bless*."[19]

How often do you try to impress others rather than
bless them?

Ask a few close friends how they felt in your presence
the first time they were invited into your home.

Did they feel welcomed and safe?

Did you try to get to know them by asking thoughtful
questions?

Did you give them your full attention when you were
together?

Be open and receptive to their answers. Set aside any
defensiveness; simply listen and be open.

Golden Rule Hospitality

❖

Do to others whatever you would like them to do to you. This
is the essence of all that is taught in the law and the prophets.

MATTHEW 7:12

When have you been blessed by the hospitality of another? Think about what specifically blessed you.

Was it the food and drink? An atmosphere of warmth? A listening ear? Good conversation and thoughtful questions? Your host's undivided attention?

How can you follow the Golden Rule and serve others as you would like to be served?

Write out a short mission statement for you and your family of how you would like to treat those who come into your home.

For example, your statement could be "It is the goal of our family to create a safe and nurturing space for our guests by feeding them good food, asking them good questions, and being good listeners."

Routine Welcome

✦

When God's people are in need, be ready to help
them. Always be eager to practice hospitality.

ROMANS 12:13

What are some ways you can welcome someone into
your everyday routine?

Perhaps you could invite someone to join you on errands
or as you pick up your kids from school. Or you could offer
to help someone cook a meal or get ready for an event.

As you come to the end of this week of practicing hospitality, in what specific area have you felt most convicted?

Ask God for the commitment and perseverance to
continue your spiritual exercises in that area.

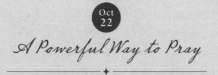

Oct
22

A Powerful Way to Pray

✦

Revive me by your word.

PSALM 119:25

Does your prayer life feel dry? Is it overly focused on your own agenda and needs? Do you find it difficult to find the words to pray?

Praying Scripture is a powerful practice that uses the Bible as fresh language for prayer. When you don't even know how to begin to pray, the book of Psalms is a great place to start.

This week, begin each morning by taking a few moments to be silent before the Lord and then reading the day's psalm out loud as a prayer. As you pray the honest, heartfelt prayer of someone who lived thousands of years ago, think about how the words relate to your life.

The reflection questions after each psalm can help you continue the conversation with God. If your prayers still feel dry, short, or too simple, that's okay!

Trust God to listen and to honor even the messiest and most imperfect prayers. Allow yourself to simply rest in God's presence, confident that he knows and cares about everything on your heart.

WEEK 43 // DAY 1

Show Me Where to Walk

I lift my hands to you in prayer. I thirst for you as parched land thirsts for rain. Come quickly, LORD, and answer me, for my depression deepens. Don't turn away from me, or I will die. Let me hear of your unfailing love each morning, for I am trusting you. Show me where to walk, for I give myself to you. Rescue me from my enemies, LORD; I run to you to hide me. Teach me to do your will, for you are my God. May your gracious Spirit lead me forward on a firm footing.

PSALM 143:6-10

As you pray through this psalm, choose a word or phrase that most resonates with your heart.

Spend a few minutes talking to God about what in your life caused you to choose this word.

Finish by praying through this Scripture one more time.

Create in Me a Clean Heart

———————— ✦ ————————

Have mercy on me, O God, because of your unfailing love.
Because of your great compassion, blot out the stain of my sins.
Wash me clean from my guilt. Purify me from my sin.... For I
was born a sinner—yes, from the moment my mother conceived
me. But you desire honesty from the womb, teaching me wisdom
even there. Purify me from my sins, and I will be clean; wash me,
and I will be whiter than snow. Oh, give me back my joy again;
you have broken me—now let me rejoice.... Create in me a
clean heart, O God. Renew a loyal spirit within me.... Restore to
me the joy of your salvation, and make me willing to obey you.

PSALM 51:1-2, 5-8, 10, 12

W hat do you need to confess to God? Continue in
prayer, using these verses as a guide.

You Are My Safe Refuge

✦

O God, listen to my cry! Hear my prayer! From the ends of the
earth, I cry to you for help when my heart is overwhelmed. Lead
me to the towering rock of safety, for you are my safe refuge, a
fortress where my enemies cannot reach me. Let me live forever
in your sanctuary, safe beneath the shelter of your wings!

PSALM 61:1-4

Talk to God about what is overwhelming you. Then
read this passage again with your burdens in mind.
End this time by thanking God for being "a towering
rock of safety" and a "safe refuge."

Hear Me As I Pray

---- ✦ ----

O Lord, hear me as I pray; pay attention to my groaning.
Listen to my cry for help, my King and my God, for I pray to no
one but you. Listen to my voice in the morning, Lord. Each
morning I bring my requests to you and wait expectantly....
Lead me in the right path, O Lord.... Make your way plain
for me to follow.... [L]et all who take refuge in you rejoice; let
them sing joyful praises forever. Spread your protection over
them, that all who love your name may be filled with joy.

PSALM 5:1-3, 8, 11

Continue in prayer by bringing specific requests to
God and asking him to help you wait expectantly
for his answers and his timing.

Your Hope Is in God

✦

"LORD, remind me how brief my time on earth will be.
Remind me that my days are numbered—how fleeting my
life is. You have made my life no longer than the width of
my hand. My entire lifetime is just a moment to you; at best,
each of us is but a breath."... And so, Lord, where do I put my
hope? My only hope is in you.... Hear my prayer, O LORD!
Listen to my cries for help! Don't ignore my tears. For I am
your guest—a traveler passing through.... I cry out to God
Most High, to God who will fulfill his purpose for me.

PSALM 39:4-5, 7, 12; PSALM 57:2

Talk with God about the brevity of life and how you
desire this knowledge to impact what you do and say
every day.

Rejoice in the Lord

❖

Let all that I am praise the LORD. O LORD my God, how
great you are! You are robed with honor and majesty.…
O LORD, what a variety of things you have made! In wisdom
you have made them all. The earth is full of your creatures.
…When you give them your breath, life is created, and
you renew the face of the earth.… I will sing to the LORD
as long as I live. I will praise my God to my last breath!

PSALM 104:1, 24, 30, 33

Thank God for his beautiful and amazing creation,
for your life, and for the lives of your loved ones.
Praise him, marveling at the fact that the God of
the universe chose to create you and wants to have a
relationship with you.

Oct
29

Freedom from Indulgence

No one can serve two masters. For you will hate one and
love the other; you will be devoted to one and despise the
other. You cannot serve God and be enslaved to money.

LUKE 16:13

Almost everyone has heard the phrase "Money is power." Whether
we live in wealth or poverty, money has the power to replace God
as master of our lives.

Frugality means choosing to spend less money on our own pleasure,
prestige, and comfort. It is living below our means to be free from wants
(and debts!) that would otherwise distract us from effectively knowing and
serving God. Frugality is similar to sacrifice and simplicity, yet it is more
about recognizing the surplus in our lives and choosing to stop indulging.

This week will encourage you to reflect on your spending habits,
standard of living, and finances, and it will reveal the desires of your
heart. The goal is to help you experience freedom from indulgence so
you can develop the habit of being more focused on loving others and
walking closely with God.

WEEK 44 // DAY 1

Heart Test

—◆—

Fools spend whatever they get.

PROVERBS 21:20

Think about your spending habits.

Do you tend to live above or below your means?

Ask God to help you examine your spending habits this week and what they reveal about the desires of your heart.

What is one practical way you can choose to refrain from using your money today to satisfy a desire?

Could you eat at home instead of eating out?

Not buy something in a store that you probably would have bought if you hadn't read this today?

Do something yourself instead of paying someone else to do it?

Oct
31

Pride Test

✦

Teach those who are rich in this world not to be proud and not
to trust in their money, which is so unreliable. Their trust should
be in God, who richly gives us all we need for our enjoyment.

1 TIMOTHY 6:17

Shop in places below your usual "standard" this week.
Instead of going to the usual brand-name depart-
ment stores, go to a thrift store or secondhand shop.

Buy food at a less expensive store instead of a high-
end grocery store.

How easy or difficult is this for you?

Ask the Lord to show you any pride in your heart
as you shop, and then confess that to him.

Confusing Needs and Wants

—————— ✦ ——————

Guard against every kind of greed. Life is not
measured by how much you own.

L U K E 12:15

—————————————————

What things do you desire?

A new car? A new pair of shoes? A new couch?
A new phone?

Write out a list, and next to each item, indicate
whether it is a true need or simply a want.

Next, read the above verse again.

What thoughts and feelings come up as you look at
your want/need list?

Take a few moments to talk to God about your list.

Nov
2

Enslaved to Debt

✦

Just as the rich rule the poor, so the
borrower is servant to the lender.

PROVERBS 22:7

Owe nothing to anyone—except for your
obligation to love one another.

ROMANS 13:8

What role does debt play in your life?

"Nothing is a good deal unless you can afford
it," states Randy Alcorn in *Managing God's Money*.[20]

If you are in a great amount of debt, make an appointment today to get help from a financial advisor, or see if
your church or community offers financial classes.

Ask the Lord if there is anything he might want you
to give up now so you can more quickly pay back what
you owe.

Entitlement

+

Those who love money will never have enough. How
meaningless to think that wealth brings true happiness!

ECCLESIASTES 5:10

Reflect honestly before the Lord about any things you
feel entitled to.

What do you believe you should not have to give up?

A nice home?

A well-earned vacation?

Eating out at a nice restaurant once a week?

The latest smart phone?

Cable television?

What has influenced how you view these things?

Confess to God any feelings of entitlement and ask
yourself if he might be leading you to downsize or elimi-
nate some of your "entitlements."

A Matter of the Heart

What do you benefit if you gain the whole world but lose your own soul? Is anything worth more than your soul?

MARK 8:36-37

Those who belong to Christ Jesus have nailed the passions and desires of their sinful nature to his cross and crucified them there.

GALATIANS 5:24

Frugality is one of the most difficult disciplines to practice because it gets to the heart of what most keeps us from God—pride.

How might God be asking you to continue the practice of frugality?

Over the past week, how easy or difficult has it been for you to be frugal? In what areas have you struggled—a desire for pleasure or comfort, pride in thinking of how others might view you, a belief that you can spend your money any way you want, or conviction over debt?

Nov
5

Rhythms of Rest

[Jesus said,] "Are you tired? Worn out? Burned out on religion?
Come to me. Get away with me and you'll recover your life. I'll
show you how to take a real rest. Walk with me and work with
me—watch how I do it. Learn the unforced rhythms of grace."

MATTHEW 11:28-30, MSG

In this fast-paced world, rest seems so attractive yet so elusive.
However, Jesus doesn't suggest that you rest; he commands it. The
practice of rest involves making time to intentionally restore your mind
and body for the sake of your soul. Whereas Sabbath rest focuses on
setting apart one day each week for rest and worship, this practice
focuses on integrating regular rhythms of rest into your day.

These exercises are designed to create intentional moments of rest
each day, helping you become more aware of activities, people, and places
that restore you, as well as those that drain you. It may feel difficult to
allow yourself to truly accept God's invitation to rest. Accepting that your
mind, body, and soul need rest means accepting your limitations. Use your
limitations as reminders to rest, restore, and reflect on your need for God.

WEEK 45 // DAY 1

Sit for a Bit

◆

You chart the path ahead of me and tell me where to
stop and rest. Every moment you know where I am.

PSALM 139:3, TLB

Read the verse again, pausing to reflect on each sentence.
What would it feel like to have God tell you to
stop and rest?

Can you accept that he actually wants you to do this?

Does rest feel like a gift to enjoy or an imposition in
your day?

Do you feel guilty for resting?

Sit right where you are for another five minutes and
try to do nothing but relax your body, quiet your heart
before God, and be open to whatever he might want to
say to you.

Restrain Yourself and Rest

There is a special rest still waiting for the people of God.
For all who have entered into God's rest have rested from
their labors, just as God did after creating the world.

HEBREWS 4:9-10

In *24/6: A Prescription for a Healthier, Happier Life*,
Matthew Sleeth states, "Rest shows us *who* God is. He
has restraint. Restraint is refraining from doing everything that one has the power to do. We must never mistake God's restraint for weakness. The opposite is true.
God shows restraint; therefore, restraint is holy."[21]

Think about three areas where you can practice restraint today so you can embrace rest.

For example, you could (1) say no to a social engage-
ment, (2) skip an unnecessary errand, and (3) choose
not to take work home.

At the end of the day, talk to God about how it felt to
refrain from those activities and to rest.

A Restful Friend

Jesus said, "Let's go off by ourselves to a quiet place and rest awhile." He said this because there were so many people coming and going that Jesus and his apostles didn't even have time to eat. So they left by boat for a quiet place, where they could be alone.

MARK 6:31-32

Is there anyone you know who has the ability to help you slow down and rest?

If so, call or text them today to schedule a time to do something restful and restorative this week.

For example, you could take a walk, play cards, or go out to dinner together.

If you don't know such a person, ask God to send this kind of friend into your life.

A Restful Moment

It is useless for you to work so hard from early
morning until late at night, anxiously working for
food to eat; for God gives rest to his loved ones.

PSALM 127:2

Set an alarm on your phone to go off at a random time
today. When it does, allow yourself freedom to stop
"doing" and just "be" with God—even if only for a minute.

Close your eyes, breathe deeply, clear your mind of all
the tasks you need to do, and simply thank God for this
brief moment of rest.

Accept God's Gift of Rest

The LORD is my shepherd; I have all that I need. He
lets me rest in green meadows; he leads me beside
peaceful streams. He renews my strength. He guides
me along right paths, bringing honor to his name.

PSALM 23:1-3

Sheep are by nature anxious animals.
Unless their shepherd makes them rest, they will
continue to roam until the point of exhaustion.

Read the above verse again, and think about how God
might be inviting you to rest your body today.

It could be through something as small as going for a
slow walk, enjoying a bubble bath, eating a healthy dinner, or going to bed early.

Embrace this time of rest as a gift from God.

Bring Rest into Your Day

✦

The Lord replied, "I will personally go with you, Moses,
and I will give you rest—everything will be fine for you."

E X O D U S   3 3 : 1 4

Take a moment to think about the people and activities that fill the day ahead.

Next, read the verse again, but replace Moses' name with your own, as if God were speaking these words directly to you.

End this time by taking a few deep breaths.

Imagine breathing in God's presence and exhaling your anxiety and fears for the day ahead.

As you end your week of "rest" exercises, think back to which ones really helped you rest.

Ask God how he might like you to integrate them into your life's regular rhythm over the next several weeks.

Nov
12

Heart Problems

I fear that somehow your pure and undivided
devotion to Christ will be corrupted, just as Eve was
deceived by the cunning ways of the serpent.

2 CORINTHIANS 11:3

Which sins most tempt you? Are you aware of when you are most vulnerable to Satan's attacks? Wherever you are most susceptible to temptation is where you will discover a "heart problem." In the Bible, the heart is considered the center of thought and feeling. God cautions us to guard the heart above all else, because it determines the course of our lives (see Proverbs 4:23). Therefore, one of the most important things we can do is to watch over it closely. The practice of "guarding your heart," also called "watchfulness," is being alert to Satan's temptations.

These exercises will help you grow in self-awareness, which is essential if you are to withstand being blindsided by the enemy. Self-awareness alone is not enough to produce watchfulness. You need to ask for help from the Holy Spirit and godly friends. Ask the Lord to help you be proactive in your battle for those places in your heart most vulnerable to the enemy's attacks.

WEEK 46 // DAY 1

First and Last Thoughts

---- ✦ ----

"Why are you sleeping?" he asked them. "Get up and
pray, so that you will not give in to temptation."

LUKE 22:46

Over the next week, write down what thoughts enter your
mind when you first wake up and as you go to sleep.

Are these thoughts mostly centered on yourself and
your agenda?

Do you think much about God and how you can
align your heart with his?

Put a note by your bed right now, reminding you to
make your last thoughts today about God and to guard
your heart throughout the day tomorrow.

Now refer back to February 7 to see your thoughts on
this same exercise.

How have your thoughts or desires changed over the
past year? Do you notice any new sin tendencies?

Knowing Your Weak Spots

We are familiar with his evil schemes.

2 CORINTHIANS 2:11

In *Journey with Jesus*, spiritual director Larry Warner asserts that an evil spirit sent by Satan is a "brilliant military commander, who will attack you again and again at two points: your personal weakness and places of internal complacency."[22]

Do you know where you are most vulnerable to temptation? Are you familiar with how Satan likes to tempt you in these areas?

If not, take note of where your mind often tends to drift. Since Satan knows your weak spots, make every effort to know them as well so you can defend yourself against his attacks.

Today, ask God and a trusted friend where your weak spots are. Be willing to be open to what you hear. Then whenever you find yourself tempted in those areas, pray instead, asking God to rule over your mind and heart.

Words That Defeat Temptation

✦

Jesus was led by the Spirit into the wilderness to be tempted
there by the devil. For forty days and forty nights he fasted
and became very hungry. During that time the devil came
and said to him, "If you are the Son of God, tell these
stones to become loaves of bread." But Jesus told him, "No!
The Scriptures say, 'People do not live by bread alone, but
by every word that comes from the mouth of God.'"

MATTHEW 4:1-4

Based on Jesus' responses to Satan's temptations, schol-
ars believe that during his time in the wilderness, Jesus
had been meditating on the book of Deuteronomy.

After learning more about your own sin tendencies,
choose one Scripture to write out and place it where you
will frequently see it.

This will help your mind stay focused on God's Word
during times of temptation.

To Whom Are You Listening?

"You won't die!" the serpent replied to the woman. "God knows that your eyes will be opened as soon as you eat it, and you will be like God, knowing both good and evil." The woman was convinced. She saw that the tree was beautiful and its fruit looked delicious, and she wanted the wisdom it would give her. So she took some of the fruit and ate it.

GENESIS 3:4-6

God's voice is always loving, kind, and patient. Satan's voice is contradictory to God's—demeaning, accusatory, and demanding.

Take a moment to be still before the Lord.

Now think about the kinds of thoughts that occupy your mind throughout the day.

Are they God's words, yours, or the enemy's?

Emotional Attacks

Guard your heart above all else, for it
determines the course of your life.

PROVERBS 4:23

Preacher Charles Stanley once stated, "Disappointment
is inevitable. But to become discouraged, there's
a choice I make. God would never discourage me. He
would always point me to himself to trust him. Therefore,
my discouragement is from Satan. As you go through the
emotions that we have, hostility is not from God, bitterness, unforgiveness, all of these are attacks from Satan."[23]

How might Satan be attacking you through your
emotions?

Are you experiencing discouragement? Hostility?
Bitterness? Unforgiveness? Self-loathing?

Confess these things to God to break their power over
your heart.

Be Careful . . .

If you think you are standing strong, be careful not to fall.
The temptations in your life are no different from what
others experience. And God is faithful. He will not allow the
temptation to be more than you can stand. When you are
tempted, he will show you a way out so that you can endure.

1 CORINTHIANS 10:12-13

What sin do you feel you have conquered or have
moved beyond?

Prayerfully read the verses again.

What comes to mind as you read them?

How might this sin come back to catch you unaware?

End today by praying the Jesus Prayer: "Jesus Christ,
Son of God, have mercy on me, a sinner."

(For a reminder of the Jesus Prayer, refer back to
August 5.)

Nov
19

Give Thanks

---◆---

I will offer you a sacrifice of thanksgiving
and call on the name of the LORD.

PSALM 116:17

Give thanks to the LORD, for he is good!
His faithful love endures forever.

1 CHRONICLES 16:34

There have probably been days, months, or even years when you've had more than your fair share of suffering. But being thankful can actually help you in difficult times by changing the way you look at life. Complaining connects you to your unhappiness—gratitude connects you to the source of real joy. Expressing gratitude to God is actually a form of worship. Similarly, you honor others when you thank them, respecting them for who they are and what they have done. There may be times when it feels hard to find something to be thankful for. Ask God to open your heart to his blessings in your life—those right in front of you and those that have not yet unfolded. This attitude of gratitude will allow you to see life as a gift to enjoy instead of a burden to bear.

Daily Gifts

✦

This is the day the LORD has made.
We will rejoice and be glad in it.

PSALM 118:24

Set an alert on your phone for every day this week to
remind you to ask yourself, "What can I thank God
for today?"

When the alarm goes off, take a moment to thank
God for whatever gifts come to mind—another day of
life, family, a roof over your head, a smile someone gave
you, an encouraging word you heard, or owning a Bible
without fear of being persecuted.

The more you look for those things, the more you'll
discover that you have many things to be grateful for.

Surprised by Gratitude

✦

Always be joyful. Never stop praying. Be thankful
in all circumstances, for this is God's will
for you who belong to Christ Jesus.

1 THESSALONIANS 5:16-18

In retrospect, what is something you could have been
thankful for at the time it was happening, but you weren't?

For example, you might now be thankful God worked
out good through a bad experience, or you might be thankful you went through a difficult time because it caused you
to learn a lot.

Does this realization surprise you?

What is something you are not thankful for right now?

Might this be something for which you will be thankful when you look back months or years from now?

Thank God for the work he is currently doing, which
you will someday recognize and appreciate.

Your Work in Progress

Be strong and immovable. Always work
enthusiastically for the Lord, for you know that
nothing you do for the Lord is ever useless.

1 CORINTHIANS 15:58

Whether you work in or outside the home, how can
you thank God for the work in your day?

Are you thankful for your coworkers?

Your boss?

Your commute?

Your paycheck?

Being able to stay home with your children?

Being physically able to do household chores?

Thank God for these things and ask him to give you
strength to work enthusiastically for him today.

Gratitude for Answered Prayers

---- ✦ ----

Keep on asking, and you will receive what you ask for.
Keep on seeking, and you will find. Keep on knocking,
and the door will be opened to you. For everyone
who asks, receives. Everyone who seeks, finds. And
to everyone who knocks, the door will be opened.

MATTHEW 7:7-8

All too often, we pray and pray and then forget to
thank God when he answers us!

Has God recently answered a persistent prayer of yours?

Take a moment to remember how you received what
you asked for, and then thank him for it!

Gratitude Set to Music

--- ✦ ---

Be filled with the Holy Spirit, singing psalms and hymns
and spiritual songs among yourselves, and making music
to the Lord in your hearts. And give thanks for everything
to God the Father in the name of our Lord Jesus Christ.

EPHESIANS 5:18-20

Make music to the Lord in your heart today by
giving him thanks.

Choose a hymn or spiritual song to sing or play
throughout your day (in your car, in the shower, as you
do dishes, as you go for a run, etc.).

Listen to the words as you worship, and allow them to
lead your heart to praise God for who he is and what he
has done for you.

Beautiful Gratitude

❖

O LORD, what a variety of things you have made! In
wisdom you have made them all. The earth is full of
your creatures. Here is the ocean, vast and wide, teeming
with life of every kind, both large and small.

PSALM 104:24-25

Poet Ralph Waldo Emerson stated, "Never lose an
opportunity for seeing anything that is beautiful;
for beauty is God's handwriting—a wayside sacrament.
Welcome it in every fair face, in every fair sky, in every
fair flower, and thank God for it as a cup of blessing."[24]

Look for something beautiful and take a picture of it
to remind you to thank God for blessing your life with
beauty today.

How have these exercises in thankfulness impacted
the way you think, feel, and live?

Have you noticed any improvement in your attitude
as you practiced gratitude?

Nov
26

Let Go to Save Your Life

If you cling to your life, you will lose it, and
if you let your life go, you will save it.

LUKE 17:33

At first glance, Jesus' words seem like a paradox. But they make
sense when you think about letting something go before grasping
something else.

The practice of "letting go" is releasing your grip on anything that
has taken God's place in your life. Not only does it help build trust in
God, but it eventually results in true freedom.

You are free when you no longer need anyone or anything besides
God for your fulfillment, satisfaction, or identity. This is what Jesus
meant when he said, "The truth will set you free" (John 8:32).

The exercises this week will help you recognize and confess the
attachments that make you a slave to this world so you can rebuild
your trust in God alone.

Give yourself grace this week, remembering that the hard choice
to "let go" is one you will need to make over and over again.

The Paradox of Control

✦

Those who love their life in this world will lose it. Those who care nothing for their life in this world will keep it for eternity.

JOHN 12:25

Where is it difficult for you to let go? Ask a close friend or family member for their opinion.

Do you feel a need to control the day's activities?

Do you try to control everything about your future?

How about your desires for your family?

Do you need to let go of anger or bitterness that you have held on to for a long time?

Ask God to show you how to begin letting go of this thing over the next week so you can be free from its control over you.

Out of Your Hands

Give all your worries and cares to God, for he cares about you.

1 PETER 5:7

Practice the following prayer of "letting go."

Begin by opening your hands with your palms facing up. With your hands still out, tell God the things that are hard for you to trust him with today.

A relationship?

A work situation?

All the things you need to get done?

When you are finished praying, flip your hands over to symbolize "letting go" of these issues into God's care.

If those worries come up again throughout the day, remind yourself that you already let go of them and placed them in God's care.

Can You Give It Up?

"I've obeyed all these commandments," the young man
replied. "What else must I do?" Jesus told him, "If you want
to be perfect, go and sell all your possessions and give the
money to the poor, and you will have treasure in heaven.
Then come, follow me." But when the young man heard
this, he went away sad, for he had many possessions. Then
Jesus said to his disciples, "I tell you the truth, it is very
hard for a rich person to enter the Kingdom of Heaven."

MATTHEW 19:20-23

Practice "letting go" this week by giving away something you are attached to.

Perhaps it is a possession, your time, or your space.

Take a few moments to pray silently and ask the Lord
to bring something to mind.

How can you begin the process of letting it go?

Out with the Old

---- ✦ ----

My old self has been crucified with Christ. It is
no longer I who live, but Christ lives in me. So I live
in this earthly body by trusting in the Son of God,
who loved me and gave himself for me.

GALATIANS 2:20

What parts of your "old self" might God be calling
you to let go of?

Anger?

Sin habits?

An attachment to image?

A need to be the best?

Confess these things to God and ask him to help you
let go of them so you can center your identity on the
truth that you are loved by him.

The Loss of Letting Go

---◆---

When Mary arrived and saw Jesus, she fell at his feet and said, "Lord, if only you had been here, my brother would not have died." When Jesus saw her weeping and saw the other people wailing with her, a deep anger welled up within him, and he was deeply troubled. "Where have you put him?" he asked them. They told him, "Lord, come and see." Then Jesus wept. The people who were standing nearby said, "See how much he loved him!"

JOHN 11:32-36

Letting go can feel like a loss.

Read the above passage again and think about Jesus weeping with those he loves.

What have you recently let go of that grieves you?

How does Jesus weep with you in this loss?

The Greatest Love

After breakfast Jesus asked Simon Peter, "Simon
son of John, do you love me more than these?"

JOHN 21:15

Imagine Jesus asking you this same question: "(Insert
your name), do you love me more than these?"

Whenever you have trouble letting go of something,
this is an indicator that you love it more than Jesus.

Over the past several days, what has been hardest for you
to let go of?

What loves have replaced your love for Jesus?

Confess this to the Lord, asking him to change your
heart so that he is your first love.

Dec 3

Reasons to Celebrate

✦

Enter his gates with thanksgiving; go into his courts with praise. Give thanks to him and praise his name. For the LORD is good. His unfailing love continues forever, and his faithfulness continues to each generation.

PSALM 100:4-5

We celebrate anniversaries, birthdays, victories, promotions, milestones, marriages, and new babies. We also celebrate occasions such as the Lord's Supper and baptism. The ultimate reason to celebrate is that God has rescued us from the consequences of sin and shown us the wonders of eternity. Celebration is a powerful tool to take our focus off our troubles and put it on God's blessings, and ultimately on God himself. Those who love him truly have the most to celebrate!

The exercises this week will awaken you to things worth celebrating. Some may seem insignificant, but think of them as small steps to incorporate a spirit of celebration into daily life. These enjoyable experiences are a tiny taste of the joyous celebrations you will experience in eternity. Feel the freedom to laugh with God and others, delight in the ordinary, and live with a spirit of thankfulness that God wants you to celebrate!

Celebrate Routine Accomplishments

The master said, "Well done, my good and faithful servant. You
have been faithful in handling this small amount, so now I will
give you many more responsibilities. Let's celebrate together!"

MATTHEW 25:23

Celebration gives you the opportunity to savor the
joy of work, creates a spirit of gratitude, and renews
your energy for the work still to be done.

To open your heart to the practice of celebration,
think of one thing that you routinely accomplish every
day but have never thought to celebrate—putting a good
meal on the table, going to work every day, paying your
bills, or tucking the kids into bed.

Celebrate one of these daily accomplishments by
doing something you enjoy.

For example, go out with your spouse or a friend for
dinner or maybe just relax by the fire with a good book.

The Ultimate Celebration

◆

After this I saw a vast crowd, too great to count, from every nation and tribe and people and language, standing in front of the throne and before the Lamb. They were clothed in white robes and held palm branches in their hands. And they were shouting with a great roar, "Salvation comes from our God who sits on the throne and from the Lamb!" And all the angels were standing around the throne and around the elders and the four living beings. And they fell before the throne with their faces to the ground and worshiped God.

REVELATION 7:9-11

Read the passage again, but this time imagine yourself in this ultimate celebration scene.

What feelings come up as you look around you?

As you see God on his throne?

What can you do today to celebrate that this will one day be a reality?

A Person to Celebrate

"Kill the calf we have been fattening. We must celebrate with a feast, for this son of mine was dead and has now returned to life. He was lost, but now he is found." So the party began.

LUKE 15:23-24

Ask God to put on your mind a person who would benefit if you celebrated them this week.

Take them to lunch, buy them a small gift, or write them a letter simply to say that they are valuable to God and to you and are therefore worth celebrating.

A New Way to Celebrate

✦

David danced before the LORD with all his
might, wearing a priestly garment.

2 SAMUEL 6:14

We can serve God, not in the old way of obeying the letter
of the law, but in the new way of living in the Spirit.

ROMANS 7:6

Celebrate God in a new way this week.
For example, you may want to dance to worship
music, attend a worship service that isn't necessarily your
style, or praise God out in nature.

What is it like for you to engage in a different type of
celebration than what you are used to?

From Trouble to Celebration

For the despondent, every day brings trouble;
for the happy heart, life is a continual feast.

PROVERBS 15:15

Rather than focusing today on your present troubles, choose something small to celebrate instead—such as having your needs met, seeing a change in the weather, or enjoying a free night with family.

Celebrate this in a way that sets it apart from everyday life.

For example, have friends over for dinner, go out for ice cream, or buy something small to remind you to celebrate the little things more often.

Celebrating You

--- ✦ ---

The LORD your God is living among you. He is a mighty savior.
He will take delight in you with gladness. With his love, he will
calm all your fears. He will rejoice over you with joyful songs.

ZEPHANIAH 3:17

What do you think God is celebrating about you?
Perhaps that you trusted him through a hard
season, enjoyed a particular moment more, responded to
a difficult situation with grace, loved someone well, were
faithful to read his Word?

How has this past week encouraged you to celebrate
the victories and blessings in your life with God?

Dec 10

Hide His Words in Your Heart

---✦---

I have hidden your word in my heart, that
I might not sin against you.

PSALM 119:11

Increased access to information through the Internet is making memorization a lost art. However, the Bible states that something important happens in your heart when you meditate and memorize God's Word. The Lord wants you to store up his Word in your heart (Psalm 119:11), apply your heart to learning his Word (Proverbs 3:1-2), and commit yourself wholeheartedly to living by his Word (Deuteronomy 11:18). When you practice memorization through repetition and reflection, it shapes your mind and heart into a closer reflection of God's image and character.

The exercises this week will focus on memorizing just one verse, an Old Testament prophecy of the coming Messiah. Each day has a small section of the verse to think deeply about and commit to memory. If memorizing is difficult for you, give yourself grace. It may take you longer than a week to memorize a verse, and that is okay. What you commit to memory will always be with you, regardless of whether or not Wi-Fi is available.

A Child Is Born to Us

--- ✦ ---

A child is born to us, a son is given to us. The government
will rest on his shoulders. And he will be called: Wonderful
Counselor, Mighty God, Everlasting Father, Prince of Peace.

ISAIAH 9:6, EMPHASIS ADDED

Read the whole verse once.
Now read it again, but this time read it slowly.
Memorize the italicized words of this verse.
Picture Jesus coming into the world as a small, help-
less child.
Try to repeat these words throughout the day to
solidify them in your memory.

A Son Is Given to Us

A child is born to us, *a son is given to us.* The government will rest on his shoulders. And he will be called: Wonderful Counselor, Mighty God, Everlasting Father, Prince of Peace.

ISAIAH 9:6, EMPHASIS ADDED

Write the entire verse and post it in a place where you can read it often—such as on your bathroom mirror, at the kitchen sink, or on your bedside table.

Repeat the section you memorized yesterday and then memorize the italicized words for today.

Reflect on what it must have felt like for God to give us his Son.

The Government Will Rest on His Shoulders

A child is born to us, a son is given to us. *The government will rest on his shoulders.* And he will be called: Wonderful Counselor, Mighty God, Everlasting Father, Prince of Peace.

ISAIAH 9:6, EMPHASIS ADDED

Repeat several times what you have memorized so far. Next, slowly read the italicized section for today.

Imagine the government being led by someone who is absolutely wise, loving, and caring, who treats all people equally, and who rules with perfect justice.

It's hard to wrap our minds around what it would be like to live in a country with a leader who could do those wonderful things.

Rejoice and thank God that someday this will be a reality for the whole world.

Wonderful Counselor

A child is born to us, a son is given to us. The government
will rest on his shoulders. *And he will be called: Wonderful
Counselor*, Mighty God, Everlasting Father, Prince of Peace.

ISAIAH 9:6, EMPHASIS ADDED

Repeat several times what you have memorized so far.
Then read the italicized section for today and
reflect on the words *Wonderful Counselor*.

How often do you seek Jesus out as your counselor for
wisdom, advice, and discernment?

How have you experienced him as a Wonderful
Counselor?

Take a moment to reflect on this as you memorize
today's section of the verse.

Mighty God

A child is born to us, a son is given to us. The government
will rest on his shoulders. And he will be called: Wonderful
Counselor, *Mighty God*, Everlasting Father, Prince of Peace.

Isaiah 9:6, emphasis added

Repeat what you have memorized so far and memorize the next italicized section for today.

Often we think of Jesus only as gentle and kind. But
he will return as a mighty warrior to defeat evil forever.

Think about times when Jesus has proven himself to
be mighty in your life.

How do you need him to be mighty right now?

Everlasting Father, Prince of Peace

---✦---

A child is born to us, a son is given to us. The government
will rest on his shoulders. And he will be called: Wonderful
Counselor, Mighty God, *Everlasting Father, Prince of Peace.*

ISAIAH 9:6, EMPHASIS ADDED

Repeat the verse several times *slowly*. Allow its truth
to sink in as you recite these words.

Now read and memorize the final italicized section.
Reflect on Jesus being an Everlasting Father and think
about living under a perfect ruler for eternity.

Reflect on Jesus as the Prince of Peace and imagine
living in a place where there will be no wars or conflict
with others.

End the time by reciting from memory the entire
passage of Isaiah 9:6.

How has memorizing this verse prepared your heart
to celebrate Jesus in a fresh way?

Dec
17

Pause and Reflect

---◆---

Keep putting into practice all you learned and received
from me—everything you heard from me and saw me
doing. Then the God of peace will be with you.

PHILIPPIANS 4:9

In a world that pressures you to keep moving, reflection helps you
pause and remember how God has worked in and around you.

The end of the year is the perfect time to reflect with the Lord on
what has happened and what you learned. Think about the victories and
hardships of this past year and be attentive to how God might use them
to guide and direct you into the New Year.

Because it is difficult to deeply reflect over an entire year and a new
year in just seven days, this practice is stretched into two weeks. The
first week focuses on looking back at what God has done in your life over
the past year. The second week focuses on how God might be leading
you as you enter into a new year.

May God bless you and give you peace as you continue to put into
practice all you have learned.

Reflecting on Your Growth

--- ✦ ---

I remember the days of old. I ponder all your great
works and think about what you have done.

PSALM 143:5

As you have walked with God through the spiritual
practices in this devotional, was there one practice
in particular that helped you grow the most?

Write down some examples of when you noticed
growth. Be as specific as you can.

End today by thanking God for his work in your life.

Throwing Off the Old, Putting On the New

✦

Throw off your old sinful nature and your former way of life,
which is corrupted by lust and deception. Instead, let the
Spirit renew your thoughts and attitudes. Put on your new
nature, created to be like God—truly righteous and holy.

EPHESIANS 4:22-24

What was one of the hardest truths God showed
you about yourself over the past year?

Was there a specific practice that challenged you the most?

Take five or ten minutes to think about this and come
up with one possible reason for why this was the area in
which you needed to be challenged.

Life-Giving Words

Such things were written in the Scriptures long ago to teach
us. And the Scriptures give us hope and encouragement
as we wait patiently for God's promises to be fulfilled.

ROMANS 15:4

What is the best word of advice or encouragement
from Scripture you received this past year?

Write this verse or phrase down and put it in a visible
spot this week to help you reflect on how God is faithful
to encourage us through his Word.

Divine Appointment

❖

You Philippians were the only ones who gave me financial help when I first brought you the Good News and then traveled on from Macedonia. No other church did this. Even when I was in Thessalonica you sent help more than once.... At the moment I have all I need—and more! I am generously supplied with the gifts you sent me with Epaphroditus. They are a sweet-smelling sacrifice that is acceptable and pleasing to God.

PHILIPPIANS 4:15-16, 18

Whom did God put into your life at just the right moment this past year?
Thank God for how he provides for you.

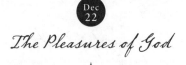

The Pleasures of God

—————————— ✦ ——————————

You will show me the way of life, granting me the joy of your
presence and the pleasures of living with you forever.

PSALM 16:11

—————————————————————————

I will sing to the LORD because he is good to me.

PSALM 13:6

—————————————————————————

What is one of the happiest moments you shared
with the Lord over the past year?
Take a moment to reflect on that special time with him.
What did this experience teach you about who God is?

Choose Not to Be Afraid

✦

The LORD is my light and my salvation—
so why should I be afraid?

PSALM 27:1

The LORD is for me, so I will have no fear.
What can mere people do to me?

PSALM 118:6

Fear paralyzes; courage releases you to move forward.
The Bible speaks of the courage to stand firm
against evil, to remain strong in your faith, to resist
temptation, to do the right thing, to confidently hope
that God will work good in your life.

Where did you grow most in courage this past year?

Dec 24

The Greatest Gift

❖

Praise the Lord . . . because he has visited and redeemed his people. He has sent us a mighty Savior.

LUKE 1:68-69

There is a great difference between Adam's sin and God's gracious gift. For the sin of this one man, Adam, brought death to many. But even greater is God's wonderful grace and his gift of forgiveness to many through this other man, Jesus Christ.

ROMANS 5:15

Whatever is good and perfect is a gift coming down to us from God our Father, who created all the lights in the heavens.

JAMES 1:17

This week, we'll look ahead to next year, holding on to what we've learned and practiced while considering how we can keep those habits alive and strong. In order to do that, first think about this important question: What was the greatest gift God gave you this past year?

Carry It Forward

◆

My child, never forget the things I have taught you. Store
my commands in your heart. If you do this, you will
live many years, and your life will be satisfying.

PROVERBS 3:1-2

I am certain that God, who began the good work
within you, will continue his work until it is finally
finished on the day when Christ Jesus returns.

PHILIPPIANS 1:6

What is one new thing you learned this year that
you look forward to carrying into the next year?

Who Is Doing Your Planning for Next Year?

---◆---

Look here, you who say, "Today or tomorrow we are going to a certain town and will stay there a year. We will do business there and make a profit." How do you know what your life will be like tomorrow? ... What you ought to say is, "If the Lord wants us to, we will live and do this or that." Otherwise you are boasting about your own pretentious plans, and all such boasting is evil.

JAMES 4:13-16

What plans have you already made for the new year? Write your three biggest goals.

Now draw three blank lines below those goals.

Pull out this paper at the end of next year to see if you can fill in those lines with plans God had for you that you hadn't foreseen.

Always Learning

◆

I know the LORD is always with me. I will not
be shaken, for he is right beside me.

PSALM 16:8

God has made everything beautiful for its own time. He has
planted eternity in the human heart, but even so, people cannot
see the whole scope of God's work from beginning to end.

ECCLESIASTES 3:11

I will lead blind Israel down a new path, guiding them
along an unfamiliar way. I will brighten the darkness
before them and smooth out the road ahead of them. Yes,
I will indeed do these things; I will not forsake them.

ISAIAH 42:16

What hard experience from this past year are you
still learning to trust God with? What do you think
he is trying to teach you through it? In what ways can you
use the practices you've learned to help you trust God?

Don't Sweat the Details

❖

Her sister, Mary, sat at the Lord's feet, listening to what he taught. But Martha was distracted by the big dinner she was preparing.... "Lord, doesn't it seem unfair to you that my sister just sits here while I do all the work? Tell her to come and help me." But the Lord said to her, "My dear Martha, you are worried and upset over all these details!"

LUKE 10:39-41

What details and distractions keep you from being present with others and with God?

As you head into the new year, consider one way to let your expectations go regarding how your home or appearance "should" be.

For example, don't pick up your child's toys until the end of the day.

Ask God to remind you that loving others well is more about your presence than about your presentation.

Dec 29

Prayer for the New Year

✦

Your Father already knows your needs. Seek the Kingdom of God above all else, and he will give you everything you need. So don't be afraid, little flock. For it gives your Father great happiness to give you the Kingdom.

LUKE 12:30-32

Write down a prayer for the new year.

It can be about anything—a prayer for someone close to you, a prayer for growth, or a prayer for the healing of a relationship.

Keep this prayer and reread it on the first of each month to see how God continues to work in this situation.

To Do or Not to Do

For everything there is a season, a time
for every activity under heaven.

ECCLESIASTES 3:1

Take a few moments to write down your primary
commitments from this past year.

Be specific. For example, don't just say "church" but
list all the different ways you were involved there.

Pray through each one and ask the Lord if there is
anything he is asking you to let go of or add to your list
for the next year.

Spend time quietly listening for his voice.

From This Day Forward

---◆---

Remember the things I have done in the past. For I alone
am God! I am God, and there is none like me. Only I can
tell you the future before it even happens. Everything
I plan will come to pass, for I do whatever I wish.

ISAIAH 46:9-10

Keep putting into practice all you learned and received
from me—everything you heard from me and saw me
doing. Then the God of peace will be with you.

PHILIPPIANS 4:9

What things are you already anticipating or anxious
about for this next year?

Offer these things to the Lord as you read the
Scriptures again. Ask him to help you be present with
him in each of these moments.

Then look back over all the spiritual practices you
worked through. Ask God which one or two practices
he would like you to continue working on.

ADDITIONAL RESOURCES

The additional books listed below will help you continue your growth as you develop the spiritual practices you've learned.

May God give you the strength and motivation to continue exercising your spiritual muscles this next year. May you develop more habits of the heart that will help you grow in your faith and keep you walking close to him.

Spiritual Disciplines Handbook: Practices That Transform Us by Adele Calhoun
Celebration of Discipline by Richard Foster
Practicing Basic Spiritual Disciplines by Charles Stanley
The Spirit of the Disciplines by Dallas Willard
Renovation of the Heart by Dallas Willard

Acknowledgments

Thank you to the most wonderful, insightful, and caring professors and mentors—John Coe, Betsy Barber, and Judy Tenelshof. So much of this book is based off the things you taught me!

Thank you, Larry Warner and Jackie Sevier, for being my spiritual directors and continually pointing me back to Christ.

Thank you, Ron and Becki Beers, for countless hours of editing and, most importantly, for raising me to know and love the Lord.

And my biggest thanks goes to my husband, Stetson. Thank you for the countless hours you sat with me to brainstorm, process, and pray for this devotional. Thank you for the early mornings you took our girls so that I could write. Thank you for loving me and cheering me on until the very end.

ABOUT THE AUTHOR

Katherine Butler was first introduced to spiritual formation as an undergraduate at Biola University.

There she attended a special program for a small number of students and faculty, where they lived together at a retreat house for several weeks, studying the topic of spiritual formation and practicing spiritual disciplines within community.

It was during that time that Katy felt her heart awakened to know God deeply and to feel loved and known by him in return. This experience led her to pursue a master's degree in spiritual formation and soul care from Talbot Seminary in Southern California, where she also became a certified spiritual director.

Katy is passionate about walking with others as they learn more about who God has created them to be. She believes God works with each of his children in ways that are special and unique to them.

Her desire is to help others open themselves to a greater awareness of God's deep and faithful love for them and his presence in their everyday lives.

Katy lives in Illinois with her husband and two beautiful little girls.

NOTES

1. C. S. Lewis, *Letters to Malcolm: Chiefly on Prayer*, quoted in *The Quotable Lewis*, eds. Wayne Martindale and Jerry Root (Carol Stream, IL: Tyndale, 2012), 255.
2. Bill Gaultiere, "Dallas Willard's One Word for Jesus," *Soul Shepherding*, June 11, 2008, http://www.soulshepherding.org/2008/06/dallas-willards-one-word-for-jesus/.
3. A. W. Tozer, *The Knowledge of the Holy* (San Francisco: HarperOne, 1961), 1.
4. John Calvin, *Institutes of the Christian Religion*, trans. Henry Beveridge (Peabody, MA: Hendrickson Publishers, 2008), 4.
5. Tim Keller, Twitter, October 11, 2013, https://twitter.com/dailykeller/status/388624900111335424?lang=en.
6. Lee Strobel, *God's Outrageous Claims* (Grand Rapids, MI: Zondervan, 1998), 23.
7. C. S. Lewis, *The Great Divorce* (San Francisco: HarperOne, 2015), 75.
8. Dallas Willard, *Hearing God* (Downers Grove, IL: IVP, 2012), 218.

9. Ann Voskamp, "When Your Plans Don't Turn Out at All—What Turns Out to Be the Actual Case," *Ann Voskamp* (blog), July 6, 2015, http://annvoskamp.com/2015/07/when-your-plans-dont-turn-out-at-all-what-turns-out-to-be-the-actual-case/.

10. C. S. Lewis, *Reflections on the Psalms* (New York: Harcourt, Brace & Co., 1958), 97.

11. Dallas Willard, *The Spirit of the Disciplines* (San Francisco: HarperSanFrancisco, 1988), 177.

12. Randy Alcorn, *The Treasure Principle* (Colorado Springs: Multnomah, 2001), 71.

13. Henri Nouwen, *Here and Now* (New York: Crossroad Publishing, 1994), 18.

14. Joshua Lujan Loveless, "Eugene Peterson on Being a Real Pastor," *Relevant*, June 7, 2011, http://www.relevantmagazine.com/next/blog/6-main-slideshow/1262-eugene-peterson-on-being-a-real-pastor.

15. Corrie ten Boom, quoted in Max Lucado, *Life to the Full* (Nashville: Thomas Nelson, 2005), 48.

16. C. S. Lewis, *The Weight of Glory* (San Francisco, HarperOne, 1949), 160.

17. P. Doddridge, *The Works of the Rev. P. Doddridge, D. D.*, vol. 3 (Leeds: Edward Baines, 1803), 485.

18. Richard Foster, *Prayer* (San Francisco: HarperSanFrancisco, 1992), 147.

19. Jen Wilkin, "Choose Hospitality," Proverbs 31 Ministries, January 19, 2016, http://proverbs31.org/devotions/devo/choose-hospitality/.

20. Randy Alcorn, *Managing God's Money* (Carol Stream, IL: Tyndale, 2011), 173.

21. Matthew Sleeth, *24/6: A Prescription for a Healthier, Happier Life* (Carol Stream, IL: Tyndale, 2012), 33.

22. Larry Warner, *Journey with Jesus* (Downers Grove, IL: IVP, 2010), 115.

23. "Charles Stanley: Satan 'Always Attacks the Mind,'" beliefnet, accessed January 4, 2017, http://www.beliefnet.com/faiths/christianity/2004/10/charles-stanley-satan-always-attacks-the-mind.aspx#rmdxLyUCShY8QgV7.99.

24. Ralph Waldo Emerson, quoted in Helen Granat, *Wisdom Through the Ages* (Poulsbo, WA: Miklen Press, 1998), 21.